TAMESIDE LIBRARIES
3 8016 0145
KU-690-022

WITHDRAWN
TAMESIDE LIBRA
Tameside

'I believe that you have something to tell me.'

'There's no easy way to say this, Captain Hawke.' Georgiana looked up at him suddenly, her eyes wide and clear, her voice elegant and polite. 'The fact of the matter is that I'm not who I appear to be.'

'I'd gathered that much. And you're now about to do me the honour of revealing your true identity.' His tone was dry but there was an encouraging gentleness in his eyes and Georgiana knew that Nathaniel Hawke was a fair man.

'Yes. I am Miss Georgiana Raithwaite, recently of your acquaintance at Farleigh Hall.'

'You cannot be Miss Raithwaite. You're a…' A horrible sinking sensation was starting within Nathaniel's stomach, for beneath the grubby urchin face he could see what had previously eluded him—the fine features of the young woman he had pulled from the River Borne. 'Dear God!' Nathaniel could not suppress the exclamation.

'Yes, quite. How ironic that my present trouble has arisen from my refusal to bathe when that is one of the things I've longed so ardently to do these two weeks past.' She smiled then, a smile that lit up her face.

Nathaniel stared, and stared some more. Inadvertently his eyes dropped lower, as if he would see what lay beneath the torn blue jacket.

AUTHOR NOTE

I had often heard maritime folklore tales of women joining the navy disguised as men, but was surprised to learn that several of these stories are based in truth. It intrigued me to think that any woman could escape detection living within the confines of a ship with an all-male crew, and under the harsh and demanding conditions of the Georgian navy.

At that time Britannia did indeed rule the waves, and Napoleon was well founded in saying, 'Wherever you find a fathom of water, there you will find the British.' Britain's command of the sea was largely due to discipline and a number of charismatic captains within her navy. It was a time of honour, when good men strove to do what they believed to be right, an era when captains, such as Nelson, inspired true loyalty and affection in their crews and became the great heroes we still remember today. 2005 sees the 200th anniversary of Nelson's victory against the French fleet under Villeneuve at Trafalgar.

All these factors combined to inspire a story about Nathaniel Hawke, a naval captain who advanced his career in spite of his father, and Georgiana Raithwaite, a courageous but headstrong young woman who inadvertently finds herself as his ship's boy. Thrown together within the intimate confines of the ship, Nathaniel and Georgiana unite to hide her secret. But can they fight the attraction escalating between them? This is their love story, and takes them from the rolling Hampshire countryside, across the high seas to the Rock of Gibraltar and back again, during the dark winter months of 1804.

The Captain's Lady is my first book, and I found the whole subject of the Georgian navy completely fascinating.

THE CAPTAIN'S LADY

Margaret McPhee

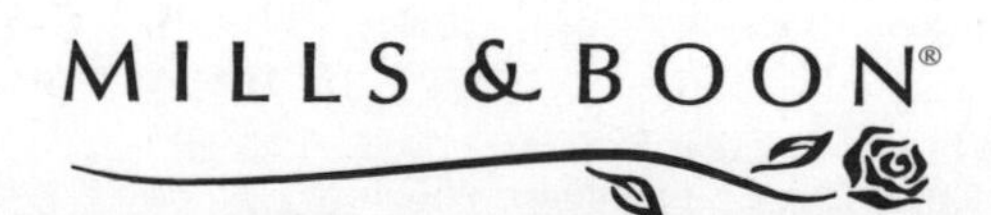

First published in Great Britain 2005
Harlequin Mills & Boon Limited,
Eton House, 18-24 Paradise Road, Richmond, Surrey TW9 1SR

ISBN 0 263 18822 1

Set in Times Roman 12 on 13¼ pt.
08-1005-85628

Printed and bound in Great Britain
by Antony Rowe Ltd, Chippenham, Wiltshire

Margaret McPhee loves to use her imagination—an essential requirement for a trained scientist. However, when she realised that her imagination was inspired more by the historical romances she loves to read rather than her experiments, she decided to put the ideas down on paper. She has since left her scientific life behind, retaining only the romance—her husband, whom she met in a laboratory. In summer, Margaret enjoys cycling along the coastline overlooking the Firth of Clyde in Scotland where she lives. In winter, tea, cakes and a good book suffice.

The Captain's Lady is Margaret McPhee's début novel for Mills & Boon® Historical Romance™

Chapter One

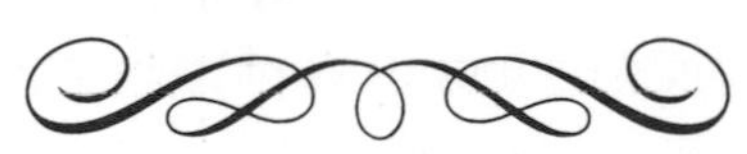

November 1804

'Mr Praxton, you're mistaken in your assumption!' Georgiana Raithwaite staggered back from the hard thin lips pressed to hers. Her hand scrubbed at her bruised mouth as she attempted to escape.

'Come now, Miss Raithwaite, don't play coy with me. We both know the truth of your feelings on the matter.' Walter Praxton grasped Georgiana's wrist, the bones of his fingers biting into her. Relentlessly he dragged her closer until she was pressed fully against his frame.

'No! Let me go! I haven't encouraged your interest.' The dark green wool of his finely tailored coat scraped against her cheek, releasing a rush of cologne. 'We've been gone for an age and our party will be here at any moment.' She struggled harder. 'Leave me be!'

He sniggered, a harsh and petty sound against the rush of the nearby river, and his ruthless mouth touched the locks of her unbound hair. Her bonnet lay crushed amidst the hawthorn bushes where he had thrown it just moments before. 'Indeed, they will, my dear. Let them come upon our lovers' tryst.' His handsome face cracked with a smile that did not touch the coldness in his ice-blue eyes.

'How dare you! My papa won't believe your lies!' Georgiana wrenched her face away from his. 'Release me or I swear I'll scream.'

Even as she sucked the breath in to fulfil her threat, his left hand snaked around the slim column of her throat, crushing with a slow even pressure that ensured her silence.

He stared into her eyes, eyes that were wide and round with fear and loathing, and whispered softly against her ear, 'I won't brook such disobedience when we're married.'

The sound of voices murmured in the distance. 'Not long now, my dear. To be caught in such a compromising situation… You're fortunate indeed that I'm a gentleman and can be relied upon to do the honourable thing.' His mouth contorted into a sweet smile.

It was then that Georgiana understood the exact nature of the trap closing around her. Walter Praxton meant to have her for his wife, despite all of her refusals. It did not matter that he had callously engineered the situation for his own ends. Once Mama, Papa, the Battersby-Browns and Mrs Hoskin had witnessed her in this dishevelled state, with Mr Praxton's mouth upon hers and his odious hand kneading at her breast, nothing would save her. Her papa had worked hard to achieve a standing in society and nothing, but nothing, would be allowed to sully that, even her claims of assault. And Mr Praxton was so very suitable, the wealthy young owner of several paper mills in the area, respectable, influential. No wonder her family were irritated and incredulous that she saw fit to decline the gentleman's addresses. But to be forced to wed against her will, and to such a man… Georgiana felt the sensation starting in her toes. It crept slowly up her legs. Once it reached her head she knew that she would pass into the black realms of oblivion…leaving Mr Praxton's plan to successful fruition.

'Don't fight me, Georgiana.' Mr Praxton's voice scratched against her ear.

She knew she had but one chance, one hope of escaping this vile man and a life at his mercy. And she must take it now, if at all.

Her knee raised in a violent jerk, landing precisely in Mr Praxton's closely situated groin.

'Damnation!' Walter Praxton's body convulsed and he bent double, releasing his hold on Georgiana to clutch at the front of his breeches. 'Hell and damnation, you'll pay for that, you little bitch!' His cheeks paled and a scowl twisted his features.

Georgiana did not delay. Immediately his grip had released, she pivoted and ran.

His voice rasped thick, tinged with malice and pain. 'There's nowhere to run to. Unless you can walk on water, that is.' He leaned heavily upon his thighs and managed to straighten a little.

Georgiana looked beyond to the fast-flowing river, swollen from the heavy November rains. He was right. Dear Lord help her, but he was right. The small clearing was surrounded on three sides by dense shrubs. The gap through which Mr Praxton had coerced her was now firmly blocked by his enraged form. Her heart beat fast and furious as her skirts wrapped themselves around her fleeing legs.

'I fear that you've made a very grave error, my dear, and one for which I'll exact full payment, unless you make yourself amenable to me, Miss Raithwaite.'

In that moment Georgiana made her choice. There could be no other. Before her courage—or foolery, as her papa would term it—deserted her, she leapt from the grass banking straight into the river.

Walter Praxton's mouth gaped with incredulity. Even the strongest swimmer would be hard pushed to survive such conditions. 'Stupid girl, you're going to drown yourself!' The realisation of just what he stood to lose loomed large in his greedy mind, not to mention Edward Raithwaite's reaction when he discovered that his stepdaughter had drowned whilst in Mr Praxton's care. 'Bloody hell!' he swore through clenched teeth, and scrambled about to find a branch to hook Miss Raithwaite back to safety.

The plan was not proceeding quite as Mr Praxton had envisaged.

A scream shrilled behind him. Mrs Raithwaite collapsed into a crumpled heap and Mrs Battersby-Brown appeared to be in the throes of hysteria, not helped by Mrs Hoskin's high-pitched screaming.

'Good God, man! What the…? Georgiana?' Mr Raithwaite looked at Mr Praxton, confusion clear upon his face.

Walter Praxton turned to the older man. 'Against my advice Miss Raithwaite insisted on examining the river at close quarters. Such a wilful girl! Sir, quickly pass me that large stick, and I'll fish her out.' Mr Praxton's fingers raked his perfect golden locks with ill-concealed agitation.

Georgiana's body submerged beneath the river, its freezing waters rushing to infiltrate the snug warmth of her clothing. Already it clung like a dead weight. Ice-cold water swirled all around, dragging at her skirts, conspiring to pull her beneath its bubbling surface to the dark unknown depths below. Her lungs constricted and would not function save but to gasp for air when there was nothing but water. She tried to scream, but could find no voice. Cold terror prickled at her scalp and her head ached where the freezing water beat her down. Her arms flailed, wildly seeking something, anything, on which to anchor, even as she sank lower. And, just as the darkness closed in upon her so that she could but look up to the lightness of the sky so very far above her head, her hand found purchase. Her fingers closed upon it, clinging for dear life to that saviour. With her heart pumping fit to burst, she pulled herself up and broke the surface, coughing while gasping in air that had never tasted so sweet. She embraced the clump of reeds, unmindful of its sharp-edged leaves lacerating the palms of her hands. Still the river fought to keep her, tugging mercilessly at her grip on that one small patch of vegetation.

'Catch hold of the end, Miss Raithwaite, and I'll pull you to safety.'

Fortunately, or as it now transpired, unfortunately, she was some way beyond the reach of Mr Praxton or, indeed, her stepfather. Through the soaking hair plastered across her eyes she saw Walter Praxton extend the branch towards her. Heard his cruel voice turned velvet with concern. Time stopped still. The river roared in silence, battering her body into numbness. Mama lay motionless upon the ground, and Mrs Battersby-Brown's and Mrs Hoskin's mouths moved in the shape of screams. But for that single instant Georgiana knew nothing, felt nothing, except the terrible certainty that by her own rash actions she had just played right into her unwanted suitor's hands. How well he feigned the hero. And how well her papa would reward him for saving her life. Walter Praxton knew it too. She could see it in his narrow calculating focus.

'Miss Raithwaite, Georgiana!' His honeyed voice pulled her back to consciousness. 'The stick…'

For all that she despised the man and his cruelties, she had not the courage, nor the folly, to sacrifice herself to the river. Death was more fearsome than Walter Praxton. Even as she reached to grasp the stick she saw the glimmer of a smile flicker across his lips, and all the while those cold pale eyes held hers, filled with the promise of what was to come.

Slowly, painfully, he dragged her closer, inching her towards the safety of the bank and the danger of what stood with such concern upon it. 'Nearly there. Just a little more. Hold tight, my dear.' Never once did she shift her gaze, fixed so markedly upon her rescuer.

'Do as Mr Praxton bids. You're almost within reach.' Papa's voice was relief edged with irritation. But then again, did he not always say she was a vexation to his soul, an inconsiderate stepdaughter with a selfish unruly streak?

'Georgiana!' The tips of Mr Praxton's long fingers reached to hers.

She was his. Caught. Landed with all the skill of an expert angler delivering a fine fat trout.

'Mr Praxton.' Her hand stretched towards him. Reaching for her captor. Her eyes closed in anticipation of the feel of his clammy skin. She heard a scream, felt the force of the rushing water pull her with a raging ferocity, saw Walter Praxton recede with the distant bank.

The woman was still yelling. 'Do something, Edward! Dear God, somebody help us!' Her mother's white face twisted with terror.

'Mama!' The word croaked from Georgiana's water-filled mouth as the river swept her downstream with an urgent insistence, ripping her away from the safety of her family and the threat of Mr Praxton. Mercifully Georgiana Raithwaite knew nothing more as the turbulent water claimed her as its own, within the scenic setting of Hurstborne Park.

'I dare say that you're right, Freddie, I should spend more time at Collingborne. Especially now, with all that's happened.'

Nathaniel Hawke's grey gelding trotted contentedly next to the smaller bay.

Lord Frederick eyed his brother speculatively. 'Then you'll stay?' The question was pointless. He already knew the answer.

'I cannot, even if I wanted to. The *Pallas* sails in two weeks' time under orders from the Admiralty. There's nothing I can do to change that.' The reins tightened beneath his fingers, but his face did not betray any hint of the emotion that struggled within. 'Both you and Henry will be there to attend our father, and my presence is sure only to...aggravate the situation.'

'Perhaps you're right.' Lord Frederick sighed. 'But you'll have to confront him over this blasted nonsense at some point—he's threatening to disinherit you from all that he can.'

Nathaniel smiled grimly at the words. 'Have no fear for me, Freddie. I'm more than capable of making a success of my life without the Earl of Porchester's help. And now we should talk of more important matters.'

'More important matters?'

'Indeed. Just how do you mean to explain your *friendship* with Lady Sarah to Mirabelle! That lady will eat you for breakfast, little brother.' Nathaniel raised an eyebrow in wry amusement, and revealed his teeth in a broad grin, ready to hear the tale.

Freddie laughed, then suddenly stopped. 'Nathaniel, what's wrong?'

All traces of humour left his brother's face as he stared in the direction of the river.

'Nathaniel?'

Dark eyes opened wide in shock. 'There's someone in the river!'

The younger man's brow furrowed. 'But the water's too high and too cold for swimming.'

'I doubt that swimming is quite what he had in mind. Quickly, Freddie, there's no time to lose, the fellow will soon be drowned, if he isn't already dead.' Nathaniel spurred the gelding to a gallop and shouted, 'Head towards Holeham's Hook, wait for me on the bridge.'

'But where are you going?' Freddie's words flitted weakly into the wind. Worry growled in his gut. He hoped that Nathaniel wasn't about to do something foolhardy. But wasn't his brother's life a string of foolhardy ventures, with scant regard for the danger in which he seemed permanently embroiled?

Nathaniel's jaw set firm as he directed the gelding to the swollen river. Now that he had drawn closer, he could see that the boy had lost consciousness and was being dragged within the grip of the sweeping current. The slight body tossed and tumbled down the central line of the river beyond all hope of reach. Even as he weighed the situation, Nathaniel knew what he must do. Not once did he flinch from his purpose. He bellowed the words at Freddie's blurred image, 'I'll meet you at the bridge. Be ready to haul us out!' Urging the horse on, he raced alongside the river for some distance.

Just short of the muddied bank he leapt from his horse, snaring the reins over a bush as he ran. First his boots were discarded. Then his superfine coat. Just as the boy swept past Nathaniel plunged into the fast-flowing water. Icy shock bit deep and he schooled himself not to gasp. 'Hell's teeth!' The curse escaped him, but there was no one to hear him over the river's roar. With immense strength of will he forced his legs to kick and swam like he had never swum before in the direction of the poor battered body. The writhing water, pounding in his ears, stinging his eyes, transported him to his quarry.

He felt the slim arm before his saw it, and his fingers closed firm. *Not far to Holeham's Hook. Hold on. Kick hard. Steer towards the right-hand side.* The thoughts came with deliberate logic even as fatigue and pain assailed his body. *The lad's heavy, so heavy. Arms growing numb.* Determination focused as he fought. *Hold fast. Keep his head up. Nearly there.* Through the blinding water he saw the bridge coming up fast and braced himself. He turned his body to absorb the worst of the impact and grunted as it hit hard. His right hand shot up and grasped the sodden wood, striving for anchorage, pulling for safety. But the river would not relinquish her prize so readily, raging against his legs and the limp body he gripped so keenly. Slowly his fingers moved against the post, a minuscule motion, barely noted, but a portent of what was to come. 'No!' he cried out as his palm slid against the wood. And just as it seemed that the river had won, something warm and strong grabbed his wrist. Freddie.

After he had dragged them both out, she lay on the muddied grass beneath Nathaniel. Not a lad at all, but a young woman, her face deathly pale, her sodden clothes revealing a slim but shapely form, long dark hair splayed in the mud around her head. Working with a speed that belied his growing exhaustion, Nathaniel pressed his fingers to the side of the girl's throat and touched his cheek to her mouth. 'Her heart's weak, but she's alive.' He looked up to meet Freddie's concerned gaze. 'She isn't breathing. Help me lift her up.' Once she was cradled in his arms, Nathaniel let her head and chest drop back low towards the ground. 'Slap her hard on the back,' he instructed his brother.

Freddie looked dubious.

'Just do it, man!'

Freddie shrugged and did as he was told.

Water spilled from the girl's mouth as she coughed and spluttered.

'Thank God!' Nathaniel hoisted the slim body back up into his arms and looked down into the girl's face.

A pair of grey-blue eyes stared up into his, and in them he saw the mirror of his own surprise, before the fear closed in.

'Don't be afraid, miss. You're quite safe.' Water dripped in rivulets down his face, splashing on to her cheeks.

She tried to speak, her words but a hoarse croak.

Nathaniel's arms tightened around her. 'Your throat will be sore for a few days yet, but there should be no lasting damage. Don't speak until you're able.'

Her blue-tinged lips tightened and she nodded.

He stared down at her for a moment longer, then sprang into action. 'Freddie, take the girl up on your horse and transport her to Mirabelle. Whoever she is, we cannot leave her here, and the sooner she's dried and warmed, the better. Wrap your coat around her for the journey.'

His brother nodded, clambered on to his horse and reached down for the woman.

'I'll be right behind you.' And so saying, a shivering Nathaniel Hawke set off across the grass in his wet-stockinged feet to retrieve his boots, his coat and his trusty steed.

It was just as his toes squelched down inside the highly polished leather that he heard the shout.

'Excuse me, sir. You over there!'

Nathaniel looked up to see a robust grey-haired gentleman waving from the opposite bank. Two well-dressed men hovered at his side.

'Young man!' Mr Raithwaite shouted louder still.

'How may I help you, sir?' Nathaniel stood tall and, oblivious to his sodden state, executed a small bow in the man's direction.

Edward Raithwaite peered through the spectacles perched on the end of his nose. 'Your appearance suggests that you have just suffered an encounter with the river.'

Nathaniel resisted the reply poised so readily upon his tongue. Rather, he pushed his weary shoulders back and affected to be polite. 'That is indeed the case, sir. Have you an interest in the matter?'

'Yes, sir,' the corpulent man replied. 'I've lost my daughter. Silly chit walked too close to the river.' He glanced towards the young man behind him with blatant irritation. 'Mr Praxton here tried to help, but unfortunately the water took her before he could pull her out.'

Nathaniel's gaze sharpened with interest.

The young man pushed forward. 'Mr Raithwaite's daughter fell into the river about a mile upstream. Considering your appearance, we wondered if you might have tried to assist the young lady.' He gripped the older man's arm. 'Her father is most distressed.' Belatedly adding, 'This is Mr Edward Raithwaite of Andover.'

'I'm pleased to make your acquaintance, sir, and can put your mind at ease. I pulled a girl from the river not fifteen minutes ago.'

Nathaniel shrugged into his coat. 'Suffering from cold and shock, but no worse hurts that I could see.'

Mr Raithwaite's elderly head sagged and he pressed his hand to his brow. 'Thank the Lord!'

The handsome man spoke again. 'We must be sure that it is Miss Raithwaite. Was she dark-haired and slender, wearing a yellow walking dress?'

Something in the tone grated against Nathaniel's ear. 'I believe the lady matched your description.' He eyed the man with disdain and turned to address his further comments to Mr Raithwaite. 'My brother has taken Miss Raithwaite to Farleigh Hall. It's situated nearby and she'll be well tended.' He climbed upon his horse and looked directly over at the small group of gentlemen. 'You're welcome to attend your daughter there, sir.'

Mr Raithwaite nodded and mumbled a reply. 'Got to see to the ladies first, then I'll come over.'

'You sent her to Viscount Farleigh's residence?' The voice was curt and heavy with suspicion.

Even Mr Raithwaite turned to look at the man by his side.

'Indeed.' Nathaniel raised an enquiring eyebrow.

'Why?'

Mr Raithwaite cleared his throat and touched a restraining hand to the golden-haired man's arm. 'Mr Praxton, don't worry so. This gentleman means to help us and I believe his actions to be nothing but honourable.' Turning to Nathaniel, he said by way of explanation, 'Mr Praxton has a great fondness for my daughter and is concerned for her.' Then, as if catching himself, 'Please forgive my manners. These are my friends, Mr Walter Praxton and Mr Julian Battersby-Brown.'

Nathaniel acknowledged the introduction with a quick nod of his head. 'Nathaniel Hawke, sir.' He looked directly at Mr Praxton. 'Viscount Farleigh is my brother.'

'*Lord* Hawke!' Mr Battersby-Brown uttered with reverence.

'Please excuse me, gentlemen. I've an inclination to change my clothing.' And with that he made off into the distance with some considerable speed.

* * *

Georgiana awoke to find herself tucked firmly into a vast four-poster bed. A fire leapt in the hearth and the room was quiet save for the crackles and spits that emitted from its warm golden flames. She remembered her arrival at the house with the fine young gentleman, but thereafter nothing. She wrinkled her brow in concentrated effort, but there was nothing except a haziness to recall. Sitting up, she became aware of the luxurious nightgown draped against her skin and that her hair was now dry, but tumbled around her shoulders. Just as her toes contacted the floor the door positioned in the far corner of the room swung open. In waltzed a petite lady wearing a fashionable dress of blue muslin.

'Miss Raithwaite, you're awake. Are you feeling better?' Without waiting for an answer, the woman wafted towards her in a cloud of fragrant lavender. Her lively cornflower-blue eyes dropped to where the tips of Georgiana's toes touched upon the carpet. 'My dearest girl, what can you be thinking of? You must not attempt to get up just now. Doctor Boyd has said that you're to rest, and rest you shall. You've suffered a shock and it's likely to take you some time to recover.' The lady chattered on.

Georgiana looked on in mild confusion.

'Now, pop your feet back beneath those bedcovers and rest against the pillows. I'll instruct Mrs Tomelty to bring you a little broth.' She pressed a hand to her mouth in sudden consternation. 'Oh, but whatever am I thinking of? You've not the faintest idea of who I am.'

'I—' Georgiana opened her mouth to speak.

'No, my dear. It's quite inexcusable of me. I'm Mirabelle Farleigh, wife to the brother of Nathaniel and Frederick, the two gentlemen who rescued you from your most unfortunate incident.' She smiled sweetly at Georgiana and helped to rearrange the covers upon the great bed. 'My husband is Henry, Viscount Farleigh.'

'I must thank you, ma'am, for your kindness and for taking me into your home.' Georgiana's voice was husky.

Lady Farleigh's golden ringlets bounced as she shook her head.

'Think nothing of it, dear Miss Raithwaite. You're very welcome.' Her small pink mouth crinkled into a smile again.

'You already know my name, ma'am?' Georgiana's brow lifted in surprise.

'But of course, Nathaniel has told us all. And let's dispense with all this "ma'am-ing", please call me Mirabelle.'

Georgiana smiled at the small woman before her. 'Thank you…Mirabelle, and, of course, you must call me Georgiana. But how did you come to know my name? Has my papa—?'

'Forgive me, my dear.' Lady Farleigh interrupted. 'I'm ahead of myself as usual. Let me retell the story in full just as Nathaniel did.'

'That would be very kind. Thank you, Mirabelle.' Georgiana's eyebrow twitched slightly, but she made no further comment as she leaned back against the pillows and prepared to listen.

Mirabelle settled herself into a chair close by the bed. 'I had just visited baby Richard in the nursery when—'

A brisk knock rapped and not one, but two, gentlemen entered the bedroom.

Georgiana pulled the bedcovers higher to meet her chin and eyed them with suspicion.

Lady Farleigh gave a squeak of delight. 'Nathaniel, Freddie! You've come to check upon poor Miss Raithwaite! What impeccable timing you have. I was just about to explain all about Nathaniel's meeting with Mr Raithwaite, but now that you're here I'll leave all that to you. Miss Raithwaite is positively agog to know how we came to discover her name.'

An uncharitable thought popped into Georgiana's mind. Would Lord Nathaniel, whichever of the two men he happened to be, be able to squeeze a word in edgeways in the presence of the effusive Mirabelle? And then she had the grace to blush at her quite appalling lapse.

Nathaniel Hawke looked at the subtle play of emotions flitting so clearly across Miss Raithwaite's surprisingly fine features. Curiosity followed suspicion, guilt trailed humour. Mirabelle's chatter allowed him to study the girl with her pale skin and expressive eyes. Her long ebony-coloured hair splashed its dark luxury against the stark white of the nightgown, sweeping down to hang as two heavy curtains. Nathaniel experienced an urge to tangle his fingers in it. She was young, and a lady to boot. Two very good reasons why he should resist the compelling physical attraction he felt towards her.

Mirabelle had paused in her introductions and was pushing him forward with pride. 'Nathaniel really is quite the hero despite his protestations.'

The grey-blue eyes glanced up to meet his…and stopped.

'Miss Raithwaite, I'm glad to see that you're somewhat recovered from your ordeal.' He held her gaze, and smiled.

Georgiana's mouth suddenly felt dry, and the room hot. Indeed, her cheeks burned uncommonly warm. 'Sir,' she managed to croak at the man standing before her. She owed him her life, of that she was certain. It was his strong arms that had pulled her from the river, his courage that had saved her from a watery grave. Those same dark eyes that had held such concern on the riverbank were now regarding her with amusement. The hair that had hung in sodden strands now sprang in mahogany-coloured curls around his rugged face. She should have proclaimed her gratitude from the very rooftops. But Miss Raithwaite, who had been raised to behave with the utmost decorum, suddenly found that it had deserted her, along with every other rational thought. For Lord Nathaniel Hawke was having a most peculiar effect upon her sensibilities. And she was certain that she did not care at all for such a situation.

The wicked smile crooked upon his face deepened as if he sensed the riot of emotion that roared within her. Dear Lord, surely he could do no such thing? The mere thought heightened the intensity of the two rosy patches glowing upon her otherwise pale cheeks. She cleared her raw throat and struggled to regain some measure of composure. 'I'm very grateful to you.' She glanced towards Lord Frederick standing further back. 'I wouldn't be here if it were not for you.'

Freddie smiled and stepped closer. 'It was Nathaniel who went into the water to save you. My part was relatively minor in the whole affair.' He looked towards his brother.

'And where would both Miss Raithwaite and I be without your presence on the bridge?' Nathaniel demanded. 'I won't take the credit for your part in the rescue.' Turning once more to the girl, he offered an explanation. 'Freddie pulled us from the water. Indeed, we both owe him our lives.'

Freddie's face coloured in pleasure and he mumbled, 'Nonsense.'

It seemed that Nathaniel was determined to share the glory.

'Thank you both.' Miss Raithwaite smiled shyly.

Freddie's cheeks grew redder.

So his brother had noticed Miss Raithwaite's attributes. The girl was undeniably fetching, but as the daughter of the owner of several coaching inns, she was strictly off limits to both of them. Neither marriageable material nor otherwise. He had best have a word with Freddie.

'Miss Raithwaite,' he continued, 'before leaving Hurstborne Park I had the good fortune to meet your father and his companions. Naturally they were concerned about you, and I reassured them of your safety. Your family know that you're here and will call as soon as possible.'

'Oh,' Georgiana Raithwaite said in a small voice. The memory of Mr Praxton's outrageous actions appeared with clarity. Having survived the river, she now felt that her biggest ordeal was yet to come. Just for a moment a look of horror and desperation flitted across her face before she masked it once more with polite indifference. 'Thank you, my lord, you're most kind.' She settled her wounded hands together in a demure gesture. Only Nathaniel noticed just how white her knuckles shone.

Nathaniel Hawke swirled the brandy around the finely engraved balloon glass. 'Our Miss Raithwaite didn't seem to regard being reunited with her family as entirely favourable. Did you see the expression upon her face when I mentioned her father?'

'Mmm.' Freddie regarded him quizzically as he lounged back in the winged chair. 'You think there's more to the matter than meets the eye?'

'Perhaps. We shall discover soon enough.'

Gravel crunched from the drive and a carriage emptying its passengers sounded through the library window.

'Mr Raithwaite,' Freddie said distractedly. 'Georgiana's a fine-looking girl, don't you think?'

Nathaniel's face became somewhat grim. 'Don't get drawn down that line, little brother. There's no dalliance to be had there. Miss Raithwaite is a coaching-inn owner's daughter, albeit a wealthy one. Our father would most heartily disapprove, and you don't want to risk becoming as black a sheep as me.' He twitched an eyebrow, and offered an imitation of the Earl of Porchester's voice, 'Think of the scandal, dear boy, the scandal.'

Laughing, the brothers departed the library and went to meet Mr Edward Raithwaite.

Georgiana's back scarcely felt the soft plumpness of the pillows supporting it. Nor did she notice the cosy warmth of the finely-stitched quilt covering the length of her body. Mirabelle had lent her a dressing gown and sent her own maid to dress her hair so that she might feel more comfortable with receiving visitors. But none of the small woman's kindness could obliterate the uneasy feeling in the pit of Georgiana's stomach. She stretched a smile upon her mouth and turned to face her stepfather.

'Georgiana, thank goodness you're safe and well. Your poor mother is distraught with worry. She's taken the headache and been forced to bed,' Mr Raithwaite chided his stepdaughter, but his relief was plain for all to see.

'Poor Mama, I didn't mean to worry her.'

'Quite so, quite so.' He nodded. 'I dread to think what would have happened without the quick actions of the two gentlemen. We would have lost you for sure.'

'I'm sorry to have caused such distress, Papa, but—'

'And how did you come to fall into the river? Do you know no better than a child?'

Georgiana lowered her eyes. 'I…' She paused. 'There…'

Mr Praxton stepped forward, looking immaculate in his green coat. 'I'm sure Georgiana has had ample time to consider her folly in strolling so close to the river's edge. She's given herself a nasty fright as well as the rest of us, and is not likely to repeat the same mistake again.' He touched a hand to Edward Raithwaite's sleeve. 'Mr Raithwaite, I beg of you, don't be too hard on the girl.'

'You're too damned soft with her, Praxton,' the old man growled, then spoke to his daughter once more. 'Do you hear how Mr Praxton pleads your excuses? And what have you to say in your defence?'

Walter Praxton threw a long-suffering smile at Lady Farleigh. The indulgent suitor to perfection.

It did not escape Georgiana's notice. Neither did Lady Farleigh's subtle knowing nod.

Her body tensed in anger. Walter Praxton was a conniving knave. And it seemed he had hoodwinked them all. Well, if he thought her fool enough to stay silent over the precise cause of her winter plunge, he had another think coming. 'Papa, I have no excuses, only reasons. As they are of a delicate nature, I would prefer to discuss them with you in private.'

Mr Raithwaite looked at her knowingly. 'Mr Praxton has already spoken to me of the matter, and, much as I cannot pretend that I'm happy with your behaviour—' he stroked his chin '—I understand that young women are somewhat excitable in response to such declarations.'

'Exactly what has Mr Praxton revealed?' Georgiana's grey-blue eyes glittered dangerously, her temper soaring by the minute.

'Georgiana!' He glanced apologetically at Lady Farleigh. 'Have a care with your manners. Now is clearly not the time to discuss the matter.' His countenance was turning ruddier by the minute.

'Oh, please do excuse me, Mr Raithwaite, Mr Praxton, Georgiana,' Lady Farleigh said. 'I've just recalled a pressing matter downstairs.' Mirabelle fluttered out of the bedroom and straight to the library to apprise her relatives of the news that the delectable

Miss Raithwaite had indulged in scandalous behaviour with Mr Praxton. And who could blame her with such a thoroughly handsome beau?

Georgiana looked from her father to Mr Praxton and back again. 'Lady Farleigh has left us. Surely we can speak of *the matter* now.' Her teeth gripped firmly together.

'You're trying my patience, girl. When will you learn to leave things be? Is it not enough that you've…that you behaved in such a way? Your mother would be shocked to hear of it. Mr Praxton and I have decided that Mrs Raithwaite should not learn of your actions prior to this afternoon's incident. We informed her only of the betrothal.' Mr Raithwaite nodded sagely.

She could feel the steady pulse beating at her neck, pumping the anger throughout her body. 'I don't know what untruths Mr Praxton has told you but be assured, Papa, that I've done nothing dishonourable. I'm neither compromised nor ruined, and marriage to Mr Praxton is not necessary. You may tell the truth to Mama.'

'Enough!' Mr Raithwaite said. 'I'll hear no more. Mr Praxton has confessed the truth of those stolen kisses. As a gentleman, he felt it his implicit duty to do so.' His cheeks bulged a puce discoloration. 'He will make you a good husband, Georgiana.'

Walter Praxton was fairly glowing with angelic piety. 'I'm afraid Miss Raithwaite has stolen my heart, sir.' He sighed and glanced down at the rug.

Mr Raithwaite looked at him strangely. 'Then you had best take more care of her. She is not yet your wife, Mr Praxton.'

Their eyes locked for a few silent moments before the younger man inclined his head in subtle compliance.

The elderly hand moved to stroke the grizzled beard. 'That said, I believe the wedding should be convened with some haste.'

The blood beat strongly in Georgiana's ears. How could her stepfather take the word of an acquaintance over hers? Did he truly judge her character so lightly? 'Papa,' she tried again.

Edward Raithwaite turned a steely eye upon his stepdaughter. 'Say no more, Georgiana. It's clear that your experience this afternoon has adversely affected your mind. I trust that a good night's rest will return you to your senses. I'll have the carriage sent round to collect you tomorrow.'

'Adieu, Miss Raithwaite, until tomorrow.' Mr Praxton bowed.

Together the two gentlemen turned and left the room.

An irate Georgiana stared at the door that closed so firmly behind them. Her jaw clenched with determination and her fingers stole to worry at the lobe of her ear. If Papa thought the affair settled, he was to be grossly disappointed.

It was some time later that Georgiana heard the discreet knock at the door and found Nathaniel Hawke entering the bedroom for the second time that day. *The Italian* fell limply from her fingers, pages fanning open to lose the sentence she had been forcing herself to concentrate upon just moments before. She glanced up to find him walking purposefully towards her with a large tray in his hands. The elderly and rather rotund Mrs Tomelty hobbled in his wake. Setting the tray down upon the table positioned beside the bed, he gestured towards the cook. 'Mrs Tomelty has made you some of her famous broth. If you would care to try a little, I can personally vouch for its healing properties.'

Georgiana's gaze flicked from the strong tanned fingers that curled around the handles of the tray to the dark warmth of his eyes. Lord Nathaniel had brought her the broth, in person! Unwittingly a crinkle of suspicion crept across the bridge of her nose. She wetted her suddenly dry lips and looked at the cook.

'That he can, miss,' beamed Mrs Tomelty. 'Could never get enough of my broth, could Lord Nathaniel. Always had to have a bowl full to the brim every time he fell out of a tree or come off his horse. Never known a little 'un like him for getting himself into mischief. Why, I remember the time him and Lord Henry were swimming, bare as the day they were born, in the—'

'Thank you, Mrs Tomelty,' said Nathaniel rather forcefully.

A smile tugged at the corners of Georgiana's mouth. Suddenly the tall, athletic gentleman standing only a few feet from where she lay in bed didn't seem quite so intimidating.

Mrs Tomelty moved forward to pat Georgiana's hand. 'Now, duck, you eat that up, and it'll do you the world of good. I'll be just over there in that chair by the fireplace so that there won't be no problems 'bout Lord Nathaniel bein' in a young lady's bedroom.' The elderly servant remained blissfully unaware of the ghost of a grimace that flitted across Nathaniel's face. She hobbled the distance to the fireplace, eased herself into the rose brocade chair, and made herself comfortable.

'Please forgive my intrusion, Miss Raithwaite. I know that I should not be here, but I wished to speak to you...alone...to reassure myself that you are well.' There was a slight uneasiness about him, as if he wanted to say something, but didn't know quite how to go about saying it.

Georgiana's suspicion should have escalated, but it didn't. Instead, it fizzled away to be replaced with an intrinsic trust. *Has your experience with Mr Praxton taught you nothing of gentlemen?* the little voice inside her head insisted. But something outside of logic and common sense assured her that the man standing before her now was nothing like Walter Praxton. Mr Praxton revolted her, but Lord Nathaniel... A shiver tingled up her spine and she deliberately turned her mind from that vein of thought. 'I am very well, thank you, my lord,' she managed with a politeness of which Mama would have been proud.

He was looking at her as if he knew the words that tripped from her tongue for the lie that they were.

The pause stretched.

Georgiana felt the first hint of a flush touch her cheeks. Lord, but he couldn't possibly know the truth. She must stop acting like a ninny-hammer and pull herself together.

'I wanted to ask you about your accident. Were you alone with Mr Praxton when it happened?'

The gentle hint of colour in Georgiana's face ignited with all the subtlety of a beacon. Her heart set up a thudding reverberation in her chest. She swallowed once, and then again. 'Yes.' Her fingers moved to gather hold of Mrs Radcliffe's book lying atop the bedcovers. She gripped the ornately gilded leather and took a deep breath. 'Yes.' This time more strongly. 'Mr Praxton wished to show me an interesting botanical species that grows close to the river.' *Or so he said.* 'My parents and their friends were following in a walk of their own.'

One dark eyebrow raised in a minuscule motion.

Georgiana saw it and found herself swamped in a feeling of wretched shame and anger. She knew very well the path his mind was taking. 'We were not alone for long.' *Long enough for Walter Praxton to make clear the exact nature of his intent!* She knew she was only exposing her own guilt. Drat the man, why was he looking at her like that? She had a sudden urge to confess all, tell him exactly what Mr Praxton had done and why. But when all was said and done, Nathaniel Hawke was a stranger and a man…a very attractive man. And she couldn't reveal such sordid details, especially not to him.

'And what was it that you were doing to come to land in the river, Miss Raithwaite?' He stepped closer to the bed and lowered his voice.

'I…I was…' She glanced up to meet the strength of his gaze.

'Examining the botanical specimen?' he suggested.

'No.'

'Then what?'

She could give him no answer that would not compromise herself and she did not think that she could bear to see the condemnation in his eyes that was sure to follow. So she said nothing, just shook her head.

'And what was Mr Praxton doing to allow you to fall?'

I didn't fall, I jumped! And Mr Praxton was doing precisely as you suspect! she wanted to shout, but couldn't. 'We had a disagreement, and…that is when I went into the river.' Subconsciously her fingers slid to tug at her ear lobe.

Nathaniel took another step closer. He made as if to reach his hand out to her, then checked the action. 'Miss Raithwaite,' he said quietly, 'I have the notion that you're fearful of returning home. Who are you afraid of?' He waited, before prompting, 'If Mr Praxton has done aught that he should not have…'

The beautiful grey-blue eyes widened in shock and for the briefest moment he thought she was about to tell him something of the greatest significance. Then she faltered, and the moment was gone.

'No.' The temptation was great. She wanted to tell him. The words had crept to the tip of her tongue before she'd had the sense to restrain them.

'Then, your father?'

The intensity of his gaze made her shiver. It was as if he could see past her defences to the truth. She willed herself to stay calm. 'Why should I be afraid of my papa?'

'Perhaps he does not approve of your friendship with Mr Praxton.'

If only that were the case! Had she imagined his subtle emphasis on the word 'friendship'? She bristled at the implication. 'I have no *friendship* with Mr Praxton. My papa is more approving of our betrothal than you could possibly realise.'

Hell's teeth, but the girl was infuriating. He'd come here to assail the nagging doubt that there was more to Georgiana's story than she was telling—something that wasn't quite right. Fear, desperation, anger, indignation, he was sure he'd seen them all marked clearly on her face. Damn it, he hadn't even known her this time yesterday. Now here he was, behaving like the village idiot, in the chit's bedroom of all places, with the foolish chivalric notion that she needed his help. So Mirabelle had been right. Miss Raithwaite had been indulging in some compromising behaviour with the man and she was to marry him. The thought irked him more than it should have. 'You are betrothed to Mr Praxton?' He struggled to keep the scowl from his face.

'Mr Praxton is very determined to marry me.' She spoke so quietly that he struggled to hear her answer, strange as it was.

He thought he saw her lower lip tremble, but before he could be certain it was caught in a nip by her teeth. Praxton was clearly capable of eliciting strong emotion in her. Again that surge of disquiet made itself known.

Nathaniel looked at the girl with her flushed cheeks and glittering eyes for a moment longer. 'Then, you have my felicitations, Miss Raithwaite. I will leave you to your rest.' He bowed and strode from the room as if it was a matter of the smallest consideration. Georgiana Raithwaite's future was none of his concern. But he could not rid himself of the unsettled feeling for the rest of the day.

Chapter Two

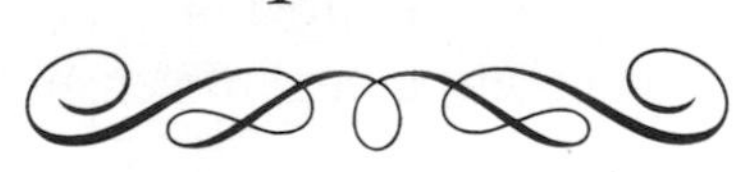

Nathaniel Hawke dropped a chaste kiss on to his brother's wife's cheek, only to find himself embraced in a bear hug. Mirabelle's arms barely stretched around him and she stepped on the tips of her toes to reach up to him. 'Dearest Nathaniel, promise me that you'll take care on both your journey to Portsmouth and your voyage, wherever it may take you.'

His mouth opened to reply.

'And make sure that you send Henry back from Collingborne. He's been away for an age and I'm sure that your father will manage perfectly well with Freddie instead.'

Nathaniel's eyes crinkled with amusement. 'I'm quite sure that—'

'Shall we see you again soon?' Mirabelle disengaged her hold and launched herself in Freddie's direction.

'I'm afraid I haven't received my sailing orders yet so I cannot answer your question.'

Freddie suffered a similar mauling at Mirabelle's hands and grimaced when she pinched his cheek. 'You grow more like Henry every day!'

He groaned. 'Mirabelle!'

'Well, fortunately for you it's true. Now, off with you both. It's time for my visit to the nursery and I can hear Charlie and Richard bawling from here. Such lungs!'

* * *

Having taken their farewells of Mirabelle, their nephews and a rather wan Miss Raithwaite, the brothers headed out at a steady pace south along the Gosport Road.

Freddie screwed up his face. 'The prospect of an increasing similarity between Henry and myself is most depressing!'

Nathaniel laughed. 'Why? Surely a marked resemblance to our distinguished sibling can be nothing but good? I mean, Henry has wisdom, good judgement and a deal of sense. What more could a fellow want?'

'A sense of humour springs to mind, along with a number of other criteria. Henry's a fine chap and all that, but he's a trifle dull. All work and no play, *et cetera, et cetera*!'

'Beneath that stuffy exterior is a good man.'

'I know, I know. But can you imagine Henry jumping into the River Borne to rescue Miss Raithwaite? Poor girl would have drowned, and I wouldn't have had the pleasure of carrying her back to Farleigh Hall.' A wicked expression crossed Freddie's face. 'Delicious! Quite a figure beneath all those clothes!'

Nathaniel affected shock, but laughed just the same. 'Frederick Hawke, that's no way to speak of a lady.'

Freddie's grin deepened, and his eyes twinkled. 'But if Mirabelle is to be believed, our Miss Raithwaite is hardly a lady. Lucky Mr Praxton.'

'Ah, Mr Praxton. I'd lay the blame for Miss Raithwaite's misdemeanours firmly at his door. Taking advantage of the girl he is betrothed to.' Nathaniel looked directly at his brother. 'There's something rather unsavoury about the man, wouldn't you agree?'

'He seemed perfectly fine to me. Rather a fashionable good-looking chap. I wouldn't have thought he'd have too much trouble with the ladies, if you know what I mean.' Freddie winked.

'Perhaps you're right. But my instinct sets me against him, however unfair that may seem. Still, what's it to us? We shall likely never set eyes on Mr Praxton or Miss Raithwaite again.' He twitched the reins beneath his fingers. 'I wonder if she knows what she's getting herself into, tangling with such a man?'

Freddie snorted. 'You're growing suspicious in your old age. I think it must be time that we stopped for some refreshments to soothe your poor addled brain. The George Inn isn't far ahead. I'll race you to it!'

It seemed to Mirabelle Farleigh that Georgiana's health had suffered not so much from her plunge into the River Borne, but from the visit of her father and the man to whom she was betrothed. Subsequent to their leaving the girl appeared pale and listless. Scarcely a morsel of food had passed her lips since and she declined to be drawn by the brightest of conversation that her ladyship had to offer. Not that any sign of fever or pain could be seen to account for her behaviour. But something was wrong, very wrong. Georgiana wore the air of a woman condemned, not of one about to marry her lover. Lady Farleigh, who had an innate interest in such things, had every intention of getting to the bottom of the mysterious affair.

'My dear Georgiana, I've spoken to your stepfather's man and explained that you're not sufficiently recovered to travel home today. Why, such a journey would be sure to leave you with a chill, and is quite out of the question. The carriage has departed with a letter to your stepfather explaining my decision.' Mirabelle did not miss the brief flicker in Georgiana's bleak eyes.

'My father did not come in person?'

Mirabelle shook her head. 'No, my dear. I'm sure he must have important matters to deal with that prevent his presence. Don't concern yourself over it. It's well and good that he didn't come here himself, as he's clearly busy, and gentlemen do so dislike a wasted journey.' She adjusted her skirts and sat herself down on the bed. Taking hold of Georgiana's hand, she studied the girl's face with undue attention. 'I understand that you would be much happier to be going home today.'

A careful guard slotted in place over the white features.

'But can you reconcile yourself as a guest at Farleigh Hall for a few more days?'

The grey-blue eyes widened in surprise.

Mirabelle saw the blatant relief, felt the lapse of tension in the hand positioned beneath her own.

'Of course. Thank you, Lady Farleigh…Mirabelle. I have been feeling a little unwell,' Georgiana lied. The river experience had caused exhaustion, bruising, a sore throat and some cuts to her hands, nothing more. But the knowledge that Walter Praxton had tricked them all to force her into marriage affected her far more deeply. And the loathing that it engendered made her wonder just how she could endure such a thing. He stood for everything that she despised and now she had no choice but to marry him. 'No choice at all.' The mumbled words had escaped her before she realised what she was about. Her eyes slid to Lady Farleigh's in a panic and she pressed her fingers to her lips as if to stopper any further traitorous disclosures.

Her ladyship's bright blue eyes looked back, and Georgiana could have sworn that they held in them an understanding that belied the lady's blithe manner. She held her breath and waited.

'If something is wrong, Georgiana, you need only tell me and I will try to help.' Her small face was unusually still.

Georgiana pressed her palms to her forehead. Dare she trust Mirabelle Farleigh? 'I'm afraid that it's a matter of some delicacy, ma'am.'

Lady Farleigh gently touched Georgiana's arm. 'I thought it might be, my dear. Rest assured I won't discuss your story with anyone else.'

She so desperately needed to speak to someone, to tell another of Walter Praxton's lies. She remembered Nathaniel Hawke's concern and how he'd offered her the opportunity to confide in him. But he was a man, and a very attractive one at that. And she didn't doubt that he had mistaken her situation with Walter Praxton entirely. Why else had she been forced to reveal the wretched betrothal? Lady Farleigh was different altogether. She undoubtedly liked to chatter. That wasn't what worried Georgiana. The nature of her concern lay more in whether the lady's preferences stretched to gossip. She twisted her fingers nervously together and contemplated further. If that was the case, then the damage was already done, for Georgiana was certain that the conversation witnessed by Lady Farleigh could do nothing but lead her to conclude that Georgiana had indulged in grossly inappropriate behaviour with Mr Praxton. And that man's—she could no longer say *gentle*man's—manner had done everything to foster the impression that he was her suitor. Heaven forbid that Lady Farleigh thought Georgiana and Walter Praxton lovers as Lord Nathaniel had done! The greatest harm had happened. Telling the truth couldn't make it worse, and might even go some way to helping her situation. The prospect seemed appealing.

All the while Mirabelle Farleigh had sat, quietly watching the play of conflicting emotions on Georgiana's face. 'If you choose not to speak of what's bothering you, then I'll say nothing further on the matter other than there's always a choice, no matter what you might think, and you must always remember that.'

The words confirmed Georgiana's decision and with a sigh she uttered, 'There's so much to tell, I scarcely know where to begin.'

Mirabelle's curls swayed as she lowered her head. 'You must start at the beginning, it is usually the best place.' And, so saying, she made herself comfortable upon the bedcovers and prepared to hear Georgiana's tale.

It was some considerable time later that Lady Farleigh had heard it all. Her ladyship was fairly bursting with indignation. 'I cannot conceive that a gentleman could be so profoundly dishonest and despicable. Indeed, his actions are most definitely not those of a gentleman and I refuse to call him that.' She paced up and down the bedroom, her hands pulling at her skirts, her cheeks a blaze of furious colour. 'Of course you won't marry him.' She honed her gimlet eye upon Georgiana, who was already feeling much better for having unburdened herself.

'No. I had no intention of accepting his addresses when he indicated that his affections lay in my direction. I made sure that he fully understood that I wouldn't look favourably upon him—that's why he resorted to this scheme.' She had swung her legs from beneath the covers and was sitting on the edge of the bed.

Lady Farleigh struggled to understand the motivation behind such a dastardly deed. 'He must be mad for love of you; when he realised that you'd no intention of accepting his suit, it forced him to take desperate measures. What other explanation can there be?'

'I don't know.' Georgiana shook her head. 'But I cannot believe that he loves me, for all his declarations.' She moved her bare toes across the rug. 'Indeed, I cannot believe that he loves anyone other than himself. My friends, Sarah and Fanny, can barely contain themselves in his presence. They swear that he's quite the most handsome man they've seen. Their response seems ludicrous to me, for I cannot find him handsome in the slightest. He's a cruel and unfeeling man with no regard for the welfare of others.'

The small woman was regarding her quizzically. 'Have you seen evidence of his nature to reach such a conclusion?'

Georgiana stood up and found herself a full head taller than her hostess. 'Mirabelle,' she implored, casting her hands out before her, 'I've seen it with my own eyes. He owns the paper mill in Whitchurch and, because of his friendship with my family, invited us to visit. I attended with my mama and papa and explored all through the mill. Oh, Mirabelle, you wouldn't believe how that man treats his employees. It's truly awful. I saw one poor boy, who couldn't have been more than five years old, running around gathering any rags that had fallen on the floor. He was as thin as a stick and couldn't stop coughing. The child had the misfortune to drop a piece of material close to Mr Praxton—not that it touched him in any way at all. And do you know what that man did?' Georgiana's facc contorted with anger. She swept on heedless of Mirabelle's reply, fuelled by wrathful indignation. 'He struck the boy hard across the head with his cane. Can you believe it?' Her breast heaved dramatically, leaving Lady Farleigh in no doubt as to the extent of Miss Raithwaite's feelings. 'Blood ran from the child's crown and the boy didn't dare to utter a sound. Not one sound. That is the essence of Mr Praxton's nature. Nothing excuses such callous behaviour.' Georgiana's eyes flashed with all the fervour of the stormiest sea, grey and green lights shimmering in their depths. 'These people have nothing, Mirabelle. They steal bread to feed their families, such is their plight. And for that crime, Walter Praxton would have them flogged as thieves. He was the one who reported Tom Jenkins, and you know what fate that poor soul met.'

Lady Farleigh nodded. 'Flogged through the streets before transportation for seven years.' She pursed her lips. 'Theft is indeed a crime, but the punishment seems a trifle harsh.'

'Harsh?' The word erupted from Georgiana with all the force of Mr Trevithick's new *Wylam* locomotive. 'That must be the greatest understatement I've heard.'

'Georgiana, I understand that you feel sorry for these people, but you're becoming distracted from the point. Mr Praxton is reprehensible to you. He's behaved abominably and it's quite clear that you cannot allow your stepfather to believe his lies.'

The fire surging through Georgiana's blood mellowed and she let out a sigh. 'I've tried. He won't listen.'

'Perhaps if you spoke to your mama, she would intercede for you.'

Georgiana wrung her hands miserably. 'Mama loves me dearly, of that I'm sure, but she would never stand against my stepfather, not for anything in the world. She says that a good wife must do her husband's bidding, for he always knows best.'

Exactly what Mirabelle Farleigh thought of that statement was written all over her face, but she made no mention of it.

'Please, Mirabelle, do not blame her. My own dear papa died when I was fourteen years old, leaving Mama and me quite alone. After his death she was so lonely and afraid…and then she met Mr Raithwaite, and everything changed.'

Mirabelle laid a hand across Georgiana's white knuckles and said gently, 'Try to speak to your stepfather again. I'm sure that, once the truth is revealed to Mr Raithwaite, he'll send Walter Praxton packing with a flea in his ear. You must speak to him, Georgiana, even if he doesn't want to listen.'

Later that night, as Georgiana lay snug beneath the blankets within the four-poster bed she mulled over Mirabelle's advice. It was the most sensible approach of course. No more moping. No more lying in bed. Mirabelle was right. Papa would be horrified to learn that Walter Praxton had used them both miserably and all talk of marriage would be dismissed. But first she just had to make Papa listen; knowing what she knew of her stepfather, that was not likely to prove an easy prospect. It was very late before Georgiana finally found sleep.

Two days later, and Georgiana had left the sanctuary of Farleigh Hall. The clock ticked its frantic pace upon the mantelpiece as she faced her stepfather across his study. She stood tall with her head high, her hands held tightly behind her back, trying hard to convey an air of confidence that she did not feel. From the moment of her entry to the room, it was clear that Mr Raithwaite's annoyance with his stepdaughter had not mellowed since their last meeting in Farleigh Hall. He continued to write, refusing even to acknowledge her presence, never mind actually look at her. Georgiana waited in silence. The only sound in the room was the frenzied ticking. And still Edward Raithwaite concentrated on the papers lying neatly on the desk before him. Some fifteen minutes passed.

'Papa.' She uttered the word softly, as if to diffuse any notion of confrontation or insult it might contain.

Mr Raithwaite's flowing script did not falter, his hand continuing its steady pace across the page.

She thought he had not heard or was intent on refusing any means of communication with her when he placed his pen upon the desk with the utmost care. Finally he raised his eyes to meet hers and they were filled with such unrelenting severity as to almost unnerve Georgiana before she even started.

'Have you come to apologise for your appalling behaviour and the lack of respect with which you treated me the other day?' His thick wrinkled hands lay calm and still upon the polished wood veneer, a stark contrast to Georgiana's fingers, which were gripping onto each other behind her back.

'I meant no disrespect to you, sir, and I'm sorry if my words sounded as such.'

Mr Raithwaite's austere demeanour relaxed a little. 'No doubt the shock of falling into the river was responsible for your harsh words. And now that you've had time to reflect upon the whole affair, you see the error of your ways.' The elderly brow cleared a little more. 'Mmm.'

A woman was expected to be obedient and unquestioning, first to her father, and then to her husband. Her stepfather was an old-fashioned man, fully supportive of the view that his wife and children were merely chattels. Nothing would be gained by antagonising him, or so Georgiana reasoned. The best strategy was to agree with most of what he said, even though it rankled with her to do so, and then, when he was at his most amenable, to reveal Mr Praxton's lies. Not for the first time, Georgiana wished that she'd been born a man. The feeble weapons of women were not those she would have preferred to use. But they were the only ones available to her. She forced her face into a smile. 'Indeed, Papa. I didn't mean to be ill mannered with you. I know that you only have my best interests at heart.'

The old man nodded and looked at her with a strange speculative gleam in his eye. 'Never a truer word has been spoken, Georgiana. Your welfare lies at the heart of all of my actions of late. It's well that you realise that.' And then he looked away, and the peculiar intensity of the moment had vanished.

It was precisely the opening Georgiana was looking for. 'I never should have doubted it, and it's with such an understanding in mind that I must speak with you. I ask only that you listen to me, for what I have to say is the truth. I would never lie to you, Papa, you must know that.'

He cleared his throat, rose, and meandered over to stand before the window. 'Then say what you must, child, and be quick about it.'

The time had come. Now she would reveal Mr Praxton for the man he truly was. She pressed her cold clammy palms tighter and began to speak in what she hoped was a calm and controlled voice. Any hint of emotion could condemn her as a hysterical female, not worthy of Mr Raithwaite's attention. 'I'm aware that Mr Praxton has spoken to you regarding what happened prior to my accident.

And I also know that you hold that same gentleman in high regard.' She swallowed hard. 'But I must tell you, sir, that Mr Praxton has not spoken the truth. I would never entertain an improper dalliance with any gentleman, let alone Mr Praxton. You know that I've never encouraged his attentions. Why should I then behave in the absurd manner he's claimed? I swear that I'm innocent of his charges. He's trying to make fools of us both.' Her heart was pounding and her lips cracked dry. She waited to hear his understanding, his proud belief in her virtue, his condemnation of Walter Praxton.

Silence, save for the clock's incessant ticking.

Georgiana longed to still its maniacal movement, but she waited with restrained patience.

Eventually her stepfather turned from the window to face her. 'No man, or *woman* for that matter, makes a fool of me.' His voice was slow and measured.

The breath escaped her in a small sigh of relief. The deed was done, the truth told. Mr Praxton would be banished from her life.

'How could you even think it?' He surveyed her with a closed look. 'Whether you did, or did not, indulge in unladylike behaviour no longer matters. Your marriage to Mr Praxton has been arranged and in time you'll come to see that it's a good thing for both our families. Mr Praxton thinks very highly of you and I trust you will endeavour to become a good wife.'

A strangled laugh escaped Georgiana's lips as she stared at her stepfather with growing disbelief. 'He lied to you, tried to destroy my reputation. Does that mean nothing? You would still have me wed him?'

Edward Raithwaite's manner was carefully impassive. 'There was never any threat to your reputation until you started your foolish twittering in front of Lady Farleigh. Any damage to your reputation was effected by your own hand, my dear. But your forthcoming marriage will rectify any harm that has been done.'

'You cannot seriously expect me to marry him!' Georgiana's voice increased in volume and she placed her hands against the desk's cool wooden surface, leaning forward towards her stepfather.

'Sit down, Georgiana,' he snapped, 'and do not raise your voice to me.'

Georgiana took a tentative step backwards, but remained standing.

Mr Raithwaite's face darkened. 'I said, sit down,' and his enunciation was meticulous.

Her legs retreated further and she stumbled into the closely positioned chair.

Gone was the bumbling genteel man. Mr Raithwaite's eyes focused with a shrewd clarity. 'A woman must marry as her father directs, to consolidate power and wealth, to open up new opportunities for the family. It's the way of the world. If you're labouring under some childish notion of love or romance, then I'm here to tell you that it's nonsense. I didn't send you to that expensive ladies' academy to learn such foolishness. No, Georgiana. Walter Praxton is as best a match as can be expected. You will marry him and behave as behoves a decent young lady. And that, my dear, will be an end to the matter. Forget all else.'

Georgiana stared at Edward Raithwaite as if seeing him for the first time. A tightening nausea was growing within her stomach and she could feel the sweat bead upon her upper lip. The terrible sinking sensation arose not so much from what her stepfather had just said, but rather from that which he had not. Her scalp prickled with unease as she struggled to comprehend the enormity of what she had just learned. All his talk of childish notions and nonsense was a distraction, an attempt to divert her from the real issue. But Georgiana would not be distracted so easily. Her mind had grasped the problem in full. 'You knew,' she said in a quiet voice, and never once did her eyes leave Edward Raithwaite's face. 'You knew all along.'

Mr Raithwaite sent her a look that held nothing of affection. 'The water has sent a fever to your brain.'

The harsh chill of the truth seeped through to scrape at her bones. Now that she had started she could not stop. 'It was an agreement between the two of you. That's why you were so content to allow me to walk alone with him in Hurstborne Park, even when you knew that I didn't want to go. The seduction was planned.' She stared at him, the full extent of the horror uncoiling. 'And Mama...surely she could not have known too?'

'Your ranting renders you fit for nowhere but Bedlam, an amusing spectacle for the aristocracy, nothing more. Be careful what you say, Georgiana. I would not have your mother any further upset than she already is. I must warn her to watch for any signs of a brain fever in you.' He sighed and, removing his spectacles, pinched at the bridge of his nose. 'Both Mr Praxton and I only want what is best for you.'

Her mouth cracked to form a cynical smile that did not touch her eyes, eyes that faded to a bleak grey-blue. 'How my leap into the River Borne must have dismayed you both.'

'You jumped?' Raithwaite's brow lowered.

Georgiana's smile intensified. 'Oh, yes, dear Papa, I'd rather face death in a swollen river than submit to Walter Praxton's cruel lips.'

'You're mistaken about him. It's a measure of your youthful ignorance, and I won't let you throw away the chance of a good marriage because of it. You're one and twenty, and in danger of being left on the shelf. This is the best opportunity you'll get.'

She shook her head sadly. 'He is not a kind man, Papa. How can you justify what you've done?'

Edward Raithwaite slowly sat himself down in the comfortable chair behind his desk. 'I said that my actions are for the best, and so they are. The end justifies the means, my dear. You'll thank me in the years to come. Now, our discussion is at a close. It would be well if you did not mention that of which we have spoken to your mother. I will not have you run bleating to her. Do not seek to flout my judgement, Georgiana, for, if you refuse to marry Walter Praxton, then I'll have you deemed of unsound mind, and I don't need to explain what the consequences of that would be.' His mouth shut in a tight grim line.

Indeed, he did not need to offer any explanation at all. It was with a very heavy heart that Georgiana made her way out of the study.

* * *

Nathaniel propped himself against the sturdy wooden gate and was content to enjoy the view before him. Collingborne was set amidst the soft rolling splendour of the Hampshire countryside, close to Harting Down. The green velvet of fields stretched ahead, dotted periodically with prehistoric mounds. Above yawned a rich russet canopy, its seasonal castings rustling gently around his feet. The air was damp and still, the sky grey with cloud. Within the hour the light would fade to darkness and the gentle patter of winter rain begin…and he would be back within the great house to suffer the hatred of his father. A robin flitted between the branches overhead, singing its distinctive call, alone in a field of crows and starlings and magpies. It was a feeling that Nathaniel knew well, and not one on which he wished to dwell. This was his respite, his time of peace, and from it he gathered the strength to face the sombre house once more. He would be gone tomorrow, and he could endure all that his father would throw at him until then. The leaves crunched beneath the soles of his riding boots as he strolled with purposeful resignation towards the place he could not call home.

'Mirabelle?' Nathaniel halted in surprise upon the gravel drive.

'Nathaniel!' His sister by marriage clambered down from the travelling coach. 'You'll think that I'm following you! But I couldn't wait four more weeks for that dratted brother of yours to return. He sent me a letter saying that he couldn't leave until then. So I decided right then and there to come. And here I am. Won't Henry be surprised?'

Nathaniel thought that perhaps surprise might not be Henry's primary sentiment when he viewed the arrival of his wife and children. Not that his brother did not care for them, it was just that Mirabelle's presence was not entirely conducive to performing matters of business. Quite how the relationship between his straight-faced sibling and Henry's vivacious wife worked was something that Nathaniel was often given to speculate upon. Mirabelle certainly brought happiness to his brother. Perhaps there was more to the lady than her chatterbox ways would suggest.

Behind Lady Farleigh a stout woman had just emerged from the carriage carrying one small child wrapped within a blanket, and holding another by the hand. 'Unc Nath!' The child loosed Nurse's hand and threw himself towards Nathaniel. On reaching the now mud-splattered high boots, the small boy stopped, looked solemnly up with his big pansy-brown eyes, and raised his chubby arms towards Nathaniel. 'Up, please, sir,' he said in a polite voice, and waited patiently for Nathaniel to respond.

Nurse tutted and stepped forward to reclaim her errant charge.

But without a further thought Nathaniel lifted the child against him, unmindful of the buckled shoes scraping against his smart country coat, and the small sticky fingers pressing against his cheeks. 'Have you missed your uncle Nathaniel?'

The curly head nodded seriously.

'And have you been a good boy, Charlie?'

Again the head nodded and the arms tightened around his neck, rendering his carefully arranged neckcloth a mass of crushed linen.

'Then I think we'll have to play a game of horses.'

A broad grin spread across Charlie's face and he uttered with reverence, 'Horses, yes, play horses.'

To which Nathaniel set the boy upon the ground, turned around and crouched down as low as he could. Charlie clambered upon Nathaniel's back, gaining a firm hold around his uncle's neck. He was secured in place by Nathaniel's arms and then the pair were off and running, galloping up the broad stone stairs in front of Collingborne House, accompanied by Mirabelle's laughter and Nurse's snorts of disapproval.

Charlie's giggles reverberated around the ornate hallway, up the splendid sweep of the staircase and along the full length of the picture gallery, through the green drawing room and back down the servants' stairwell. The boy squealed with delight as his uncle attempted some neighing noises and stamped his boots against the marble floor to simulate the clatter of hooves. Just as they rounded the corner to head back to the blue drawing room and Mirabelle, Nathaniel stopped dead in his tracks. For there, not two feet in front of them, in imminent danger of being mown down by

Nathaniel and his small passenger, stood the Earl of Porchester and Viscount Farleigh. Both heads swivelled round to view the intruders, the old man's face haughty with censure, the younger's gaping with shock.

'Charles?' Henry managed to utter, as he regained a grip on himself. His countenance resumed its normal staid facade and he raised his eyebrows in enquiry to his brother.

The earl said nothing, only looked briefly at Nathaniel with sharp brown eyes. His cool, unwelcoming expression altered as his gaze shifted to his grandson, and although it could hardly be described as a smile, there was a definite thawing in its glacial manner.

'Papa!' Charlie's sticky hands reached out towards his father.

Nathaniel shifted the child round and handed the small squat body to his brother. 'Mirabelle and the children have just arrived. She wanted it to be something of a surprise for you. I left her in the blue drawing room.'

'Quite.' There was no disputing the disapproving tone in the earl's voice. He did not look at Nathaniel.

'We had better take you to find your mother, young man.' Henry tried unsuccessfully to disengage his son's arms from around his neck. 'Be careful of Papa's neckcloth, Charles.'

Charlie completely ignored the caution and pressed a slobbery kiss to his father's cheek.

Henry sighed, but Nathaniel could see the pride and affection in his brother's eyes as he turned and headed off to meet his wife.

The two men stood facing one another, an uneasy silence between them. Up until this point they had managed to avoid any close meeting.

'You'll be leaving tomorrow?' the earl said sourly.

Nathaniel inclined his head. 'Yes, sir. My ship sails in one week and there's much to be prepared.' He looked into the old man's face, so very like his own, knowing as he did before every voyage that this might be the last time he looked upon it. 'I'd like to speak to you, sir, before I leave Collingborne, if that's agreeable to you.'

'Agreeable is hardly a word I'd use to describe how I feel,

but—' he waved his gaunt hand in a nonchalant gesture '—I'm prepared to listen. Get on and say what you must, boy.'

'Perhaps the library would be a more suitable surrounding?' Nathaniel indicated the door close by.

The earl grunted noncommittally, but walked towards the door anyway.

Once within the library, Porchester lowered himself into one of the large winged chairs and lounged comfortably back. He eyed his son with disdain. 'Well? What is it that you want to say?'

Nathaniel still stood, not having been invited to sit. He knew his father was cantankerous with him at the best of times. He moved towards the fireplace and eyed the blackened grate before facing his father once more. 'Will you take a drink?'

The old face broke into a cynical smile. 'Is what you have to say really that bad?' When Nathaniel did not reply, he continued, 'Why not? A port might help make your words a trifle more palatable.'

Nathaniel reached for the decanter, poured two glasses and handed one to his father. 'Your good health, sir.' He raised his glass.

The earl pointedly ignored him and proceeded to sip his port.

Despite his father's blatantly hostile manner, Nathaniel knew he had to try. The ill feeling between them had festered unchecked for too long, and was spilling over to affect the rest of the family. He knew that it had hurt his mother and that was something he bitterly regretted. But with her death it was too late for recriminations on that score. Her going had taken its toll on the earl. Porchester had aged in the last years. For the first time Nathaniel saw in him a frailty, a weak old man where before there was only strength and vitality. And it shocked him. They had always argued, his mother blaming it on the similarity in their temperaments. Nathaniel thought otherwise. The matter with Kitty Wakefield had only brought things to a head. He could not go away to sea without at least one more attempt at a reconciliation.

'Is it money you're after or do you find that you need my influence with the Admiralty after all?' Porchester's insult was cutting in the extreme.

The corner of Nathaniel's mouth twitched and the colour drained from beneath his tanned cheeks. He controlled his response with commendable restraint. 'Neither. I wish to have an end to this disagreement. The…incident…with Kitty Wakefield happened a long time ago and she's since married. I'm sorry that it has led us to where we're at now.'

The earl looked at him, a hard gleam in his eyes. 'You weren't sorry then, as I recall, seducing a young innocent girl and then refusing to marry her!'

'Kitty Wakefield was no innocent, whatever her father led you to believe. She engineered the situation to her own ends, thinking to force a marriage.'

The earl gave a cynical snort and took a large gulp of port. 'So you claim. Where's your sense of honour? If you didn't want to wed the girl, you should have controlled your appetite.'

The glass stem slowly rotated within his fingers and he let out a gentle expulsion of breath. 'If you won't forgive me on my own account, won't you at least agree to some kind of reconciliation for my mother's sake?'

The Earl of Porchester became suddenly animated. His previously slouched body straightened and he leaned forward in his chair. 'Don't dare to utter her name. It was the scandal associated with your debauchery and gambling that drove her to the grave!' He shouted the words, then collapsed back against the chair. His voice became barely more than a whisper. 'You broke her heart, lad, and that is something for which I'll never forgive you.'

The muscle twitched again in Nathaniel's jaw and his eyes hardened. 'That's unworthy of you, sir.'

'Unworthy!' the old man roared. He struggled upright, leaning heavily upon the ebony stick beneath his white-knuckled fingers. 'That's a word descriptive of yourself, boy! How dare you? Get out and don't come back here until you've changed your ways. You'd do well to take a leaf out of Henry's book. He's not out chasing women, drinking and gambling. Thank God that at least one of my sons can face up to responsibility. He knows his duty, has settled down and is filling his nursery. It's about time you grew up enough to do the same.'

The accusation was unfair. The earl's estimation of his character was sadly misinformed, but Nathaniel knew that any protestations would fall on deaf ears. The discussion was at an end and he had succeeded only in making the matter worse. He should have let the words go unanswered, but he could not. Such was the hurt that he stuffed it away and hid it beneath a veneer of irony. 'There's hardly a proliferation of suitable ladies available to court upon the high seas, and, as that's where I'll be spending most of my time, it's unlikely that I'll be able to meet with your suggestion. I'm sorry to disappoint you yet again.'

'It's nothing other than I've come to expect,' came the reply.

They finished their drinks in silence before Nathaniel took his leave.

Chapter Three

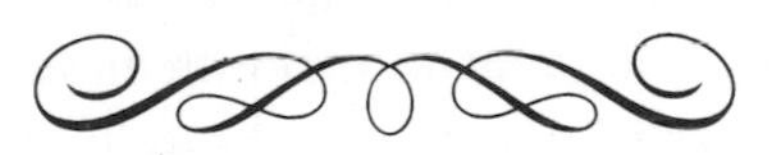

Georgiana urged the mare to a canter and looked around for her groom. The news that Lady Farleigh had gone to Collingborne and was not due to return for at least two months had come as a severe disappointment. It felt as if yet another door had slammed firmly shut in Georgiana's face, for if there was anyone who could help her out of her present predicament it was Mirabelle Farleigh.

The interview with her stepfather the previous day had left her shocked and disillusioned. The faint nausea of betrayal lingered with her still. Never could she have entertained the notion that he would have used her so, even if he was labouring under the misapprehension that he was doing what was best. She'd been so sure of his understanding, so confident of his support. All of those beliefs had shattered like the fragile illusions that they were. Her stepfather had clearly misread Walter Praxton's character to have agreed to such a devious plan. She swallowed down the pain as she recalled his zealous principles in which he had instructed them all. His actions made a mockery of them. She did not doubt for one minute that he would make good on his threat. He had made it clear what would happen if she made any appeal to Mama. And, if she refused Mr Praxton, her life was effectively over—her papa's influence would see to that. She would be an example to Prudence so that he would never have to deal with such insurgent behaviour from her little stepsister, or from Francis or Theo for that matter. The dapple-grey mare shied away from the street hawkers' carts, forcing

Georgiana to leave her troubled thoughts and concentrate on Main Street and its normal chaos. It was not long before they reached Tythecock Crescent and home.

Immediately that she entered the house Harry, the youngest footman, directed her to her father's study.

'Where have you been?' Her stepfather was standing by the window and had obviously witnessed her return.

She smoothed the midnight-blue riding habit beneath her fingers and tried to appear calm. 'I called on Lady Farleigh. She asked if I would visit and I wanted to thank her for her kind hospitality.' Georgiana was just about to explain that the lady had not been present when Mr Raithwaite interrupted.

'I hardly think such a trip is in order. If you remember correctly, my dear, you left Lady Farleigh with rather a tawdry view of your reputation and it wouldn't do to remind her of that until we've remedied the affair. Once you're married then I've no objection to your seeing her, and I don't suppose that Mr Praxton will have either.' He touched his hands together as if he were about to pray, moving them until the tips of his fingers rested against his grizzled grey beard.

What would he say if he knew the extent of that which she had confided in Mirabelle? Georgiana looked directly at her stepfather, unaware that distaste and pity were displayed so clearly on her face.

Edward Raithwaite saw the emotions and they stirred nothing but contempt and frustration. 'In fact, it would be better if you remained within this house until the day of the wedding. We don't want to encourage any idle chatter, now, do we?'

'I'm to be a prisoner in my own home?' Georgiana could not prevent the words' escape.

'Let's just say confined for your protection, and in *my* home, Georgiana.'

She glowered at him, but said nothing.

'The wedding will take place in two weeks' time at All Hallows Church. Your mother has arranged for a mantua-maker to attend you here tomorrow to prepare your trousseau.' He looked away and picked distractedly at the nail on his left thumb. 'That will be all, at present.'

And with that summary dismissal Georgiana made her way to her room.

The moon was high in the night sky and still Georgiana lay rigid upon the bed. Thoughts of her stepfather's and Walter Praxton's treachery whirled in her brain, ceaseless in their battery, until her head felt as if it would burst. Such a tirade would not help her situation. She must stop. Think. Not the same angry thoughts of injustice and self-pity, but those of the options that lay before her. What options? Marry Mr Praxton and ally herself with the very devil, or have her sanity questioned and be sent to the Bethlehem Royal Hospital in London? Neither choice was to Georgiana's liking. She calmed herself and set to more productive thinking. Why had Papa confined her to the house? What was it that he was so afraid of? And quite suddenly she knew the answer to the question—a runaway stepdaughter. With the realisation came the seed of an idea that might just prove her salvation.

Within five minutes she was standing alone inside the laundry room, her bare feet cold against the stone-flagged floor, the candle in her hand sending ghostly shadows to dance upon the whitewashed walls. It did not take long to locate what she was looking for and, stuffing her prize inside the wrapper of her dressing gown, she crept back up to her bedroom. After her booty had been carefully stowed under the bed, she climbed once more beneath the covers, blew out the candle and fell straight to sleep. A smile curved upon her lips and her dreams were filled with her plan to foil Papa's curfew and his arrangement for marriage.

During the subsequent days, it appeared that Georgiana was content to pass her time in harmless activity, and all within the confines of the house in Tythecock Crescent. She amused her youngest siblings Prudence and Theo and spent some considerable time conversing with her stepbrother Francis who, at fourteen, had been summoned home from school to attend the wedding. Surprisingly Francis's bored manner, while still managing to insult his sister at any given opportunity, did not seem to annoy Georgiana, who was the very model of a well-bred young lady.

Mrs Raithwaite was much impressed by this novel behaviour, attributing it to Mr Raithwaite's firm stance. It seemed that her daughter had at last overcome her initial reservations to an alliance with Mr Praxton. Not that Clara Raithwaite had an inkling of comprehension as to just why Georgiana had taken such an apparently unprovoked dislike for that perfectly respectable gentleman. He seemed to Clara a most handsome fellow with commendable prospects. *And* he had so far managed to ignore Georgiana's stubborn tendencies.

Mrs Raithwaite's delight abounded when her daughter entered a conversation regarding Madame Chantel and her wedding dress. Quite clearly Georgiana had resigned herself to the marriage and the Raithwaite household could at last breathe easy. They, therefore, were most understanding when two days later Georgiana complained of the headache and was forced to retire early to bed. Mrs Raithwaite ascribed it to a combination of excitement and nerves, which she proclaimed were perfectly normal in any young lady about to be married. And when Georgiana hugged her mother and told her that she loved her and hoped she would be forgiven for being such a troublesome daughter, Mrs Raithwaite knew she was right. For once, Clara Raithwaite's diagnosis of her eldest daughter's emotional state was accurate.

Georgiana had forced herself to lie still beneath the bedcovers, feigning sleep when her mother came in to check on her. Only once the door had closed and her mother's footsteps receded along the passageway did she throw back the covers and set about her activity. With all the precision of the best-planned ventures, Georgiana moved without sound, aided only by the occasional shaft of moonlight stealing through her window. Her actions held a certain deliberation, a calm efficiency rather than a frenzied rushing.

From beneath the bed she retrieved her looted goods and set

about stripping off her night attire, never pausing even for one minute. Time was of the essence and there was none to spare. With one fell snip of the scissors, purloined from Mrs Andrew's kitchen, her long braid of hair had been removed. Georgiana suppressed a sigh. This was not the time for sentimentality. At last she had finished and raised the hand mirror from the dressing table to survey the final result. An approving smile beamed back at her, and deepened to become a most unladylike grin. The effect was really rather good, better even than she had anticipated. Now all she had to do was hope that the coachman and postboys would not see through the disguise.

She loosed the few paltry coins that she could call her own upon the bed and, gathering them up, tucked them carefully into her pocket. The rest of her meagre provisions were stowed within a rather shabby bag that she'd managed to acquire from one of the footmen. Everything was in place. It was time to go.

She could only hope that Mama would forgive her. It wasn't as if she was just running away. No. She'd never been a coward and didn't mean to start now. It was advice and help that she needed, and Lady Farleigh had offered both. The trouble was that Mirabelle Farleigh had gone to Collingborne. And so it was to precisely that same destination that Georgiana intended to travel. Fleetingly she remembered Nathaniel Hawke's concern. *Who are you afraid of? If Mr Praxton has done aught that he should not have...* Would it have come to this if she'd told him the truth? Too late for such thoughts. One last look around her bedroom, then she turned, and slowly walked towards the window.

If a casual observer had happened to glance in the direction of Number 42 Tythecock Crescent at that particular time, a most peculiar sight would have greeted his eyes. A young lad climbed out of the ground-floor window, a small bag of goods clutched within his hands. From the boy's fast and furtive manner it could be surmised that he was clearly up to no good, and was acting without the knowledge of the good family Raithwaite, who occupied that fine house. Alas and alack that the moral fibre of society was so sadly lacking.

Georgiana sped out along the back yard, down Chancery Lane, meeting back up with Tythecock Crescent some hundred yards down the road. Even at this time of night the street was not quiet, and she was careful to keep her head lowered in case any one of the bodies meandering past might recognise Mr Raithwaite's daughter beneath the guise of the skinny boy. It was not far to her stepfather's coaching house, the Star and Garter, and she reached its gates within a matter of minutes. Fortunately for Georgiana, there was still room upon the mail to Gosport, and she soon found herself squashed between a burly man of indiscernible age, and a well-endowed elderly lady. Ironically, no member of the Raithwaite family had ever travelled by mail, and it was not far into the journey when Georgiana came to realise the reason. The burly man was travelling with two other men seated opposite; all three smelled as if they had not washed in some time and insisted on making loud and bawdy comments. As if that were not bad enough, the straggle-haired one opposite Georgiana spotted the young woman positioned further along and proceeded to eye her in a manner that made Georgiana feel distinctly uncomfortable, and profoundly glad that she had had the foresight to disguise herself in Francis's clothes.

'Come on, darlin', give us a smile.' The man flashed his blackened teeth at the woman who, seemingly completely unaffected, did not deign to reply.

The burly chap beside Georgiana sniggered. 'Won't even smile at some fellows that are bound for sea to keep out that tyrant Boney! It's us seamen that saves the likes of you, missy, our bravery that lets you sleep easy in your bed at night.'

'Yeh!' his companion grunted in agreement. His beady eyes narrowed and his expression became sly. 'If you won't give us a smile, darlin', maybe you'll give us one of your sweet kisses instead?'

Georgiana felt a rough elbow dig into her ribs, and a boom of laughter. 'What do you 'ave to say about it, young master, eh?'

Georgiana's heart leapt to her chest and she didn't dare to look round.

The man persisted. 'Oi, with all that fancy clobber, he thinks he's too good to talk to the likes of us. Is that it?'

'No, sir.' She forced the voice as a low rumble, and shook her head.

'Want to give that lass a kiss?'

Georgiana looked at the floor and shook her head. 'No, sir.'

The third sailor spoke up at last. 'Leave the lad alone, Jack. He's still wet behind the ears, just a young 'un. Let's get some sleep on this bloody coach while we can.'

'I was only 'avin' a laugh,' Jack protested, 'weren't I, lad?'

The journey seemed long in the extreme, although it took little more than three hours. By the time they arrived in Fareham, close by Portsmouth, Georgiana was cold, hungry and tired, having been exhausted by excitement and nerves. And she had yet to travel to Havant from where she could catch the mail in the direction of Petersfield, thus allowing her to make her way to Collingborne. To make matters worse, the first stagecoach to Havant did not leave until early the next morning. After all this she could only hope that at the end of her travels, she would not be turned away from Collingborne House and that Mirabelle Farleigh would offer her the help she so desperately needed. Pray God that it would be so.

Captain Nathaniel Hawke stood on the quarterdeck of the *Pallas* and surveyed the busy commotion on his ship. The *Pallas* was a frigate, a long, low sailing ship, the eyes and ears of the navy. Before the quarterdeck a chain of men were hauling spare spars, placing them down beside the rowing boats on the open deck beams. Others scoured water casks ready for refilling. Shouts sounded from those up high checking the rigging, climbing barefoot and confident, white trousers and blue jackets billowing in the strong sea breeze. The smell of fresh paint drifted to the captain's nose, as the men dangling over the bulwark on their roped seats, brushes in hands, applied the last few strokes of black across the gunport lids of the broadside. The black coloration contrasted starkly with the ochre yellow banding around the gunports themselves, setting up the smart so-called 'Nelson's Chequer'. In the distance, beyond the forecastle, the finely carved lion figurehead glinted proudly in the sunlight. 'How fares Mr Hutton with his repairs?'

'He's completed all of the gunports on the starboard broadside and is halfway through those on the larboard. Mr Longley is continuing with caulking the hull and estimates that the job will be complete by this evening.' First Lieutenant John Anderson faced his captain, resplendent in the full naval uniform that he had so recently purchased. He held himself with pride and eyed Captain Hawke with a mixture of respect and admiration. 'The men are working hard, Captain, and all should be ready in two days. We'll meet the sailing time.' There was a strength and enthusiasm in his voice.

Nathaniel turned from his view of a chaotic Portsmouth Point and faced his second-in-command. The lad had everything that it took to make a good first lieutenant except experience. And that was something that would not be long in coming if Nathaniel had his way. 'Indeed, Lieutenant, they've worked like Trojans, we all have. You're right in your estimation of the work. But it's not the repairs that threaten to postpone our departure.' He glanced away, out to where the open sea beckoned. 'We both know the real problem—our lack of manpower. We've not enough crew to properly man this ship and I cannot take her out as we currently stand. The men that we have are good and true, all came forward willingly to serve on the *Pallas* because she's widely known to be a fair and lucky ship.'

Don't be misled, sir. The men are here because Captain Nathaniel Hawke is reputed to be one of the best post captains to sail under and all that have sailed with him previously have been made rich with the prizes he captured. But the lieutenant knew better than to speak his thoughts.

Nathaniel's face had grown grim. 'But for all that, we've insufficient numbers to sail. It seems that we're forced once more to turn to Captain Bodmin to supply the extra men needed.' The knowledge curled his top lip.

Lieutenant Anderson sensed the captain's reticence in the matter. 'Most of the ships that sail from here require Captain Bodmin's services and a good proportion of their crews comprise pressed men. It's no reflection on you, Captain. Be assured of that.'

'Thank you, Mr Anderson.' He clasped his fingers together. 'It seems that we've no choice, for if we're to sail we must have men, even pressed men who've never set foot off land before and lack any seafaring skills. Not that that is what presents the biggest problem. They've no desire to be on board and so will cause any manner of trouble to illustrate the point. Little wonder when they've been forcibly deprived of their freedom. God knows, Mr Anderson, the Press Gang is very much a last resort. Better one volunteer than three pressed men.'

Both men turned and looked once more out across the crowded harbour of Portsmouth.

Georgiana was not feeling at her best as she huddled in the yard of the Red Lion. She felt as stiff as an old woman and she'd long since eaten any vestige of food contained within the bag pressed against her chest. The delicious aroma of hot mutton pies wafted from the pie seller just beyond the courtyard gates.

'George, fancy a pie?' The gruff voice surprised her.

Georgiana looked down and shook her head. 'No, thank you, sir,' she uttered in as manly a tone as she could manage. Her stomach protested with a fierce growl.

Burly Jack, as she'd taken to calling him, although not to his face, whispered to Tom, 'Lad's not the full shilling, but he's 'armless enough. Reminds me of me nephew.' He straightened up and raised his voice in Georgiana's direction. 'Come on, now, boy, don't be too proud for your own good. You must be starvin'. I 'aven't seen you eat nothin' all night.' Jack advanced, carrying three steaming pies, and thrust one towards her.

An audible rumbling erupted from Georgiana's stomach.

Tom laughed. 'Don't try tellin' us you ain't hungry. They must have heard that stomach growl in the streets of London!'

The pie loomed before Georgiana, all hot and aromatic. She felt her mouth fill with saliva and could not help but lick her lips.

'Come on, lad.'

The pie danced closer, calling to Georgiana with an allure that she had never experienced before. Her hand reached out and enclosed around the vision of temptation.

Burly Jack delivered an affectionate blow to her arm before the trio headed off towards the closest tavern.

Georgiana slumped against the wall. She bit through the pastry until delicious gravy spurted into her mouth, so hot that she could see the wisps of steam escape into the coolness of the surrounding air. Squatting down, she leaned her back against the rough-hewn stone behind her and chewed upon the heavenly chunks of mutton. It was strange just how contenting the simple act of filling one's empty belly could be. Gravy trickled down her chin and she lapped it back up. She was just wiping the grease from her fingers down Francis's brown woollen breeches when it happened.

Yells. Thuds. The sound of Burly Jack's voice raised in anger and fear.

Georgiana started up like a scared rabbit, peering all around. The voices came from the other side of the wall. Darting through the gate she ran round and into the narrow alleyway. 'Jack!' Her voice rang out clear and true.

In the gloom of the alley her travelling companions had been set upon by several men. There was much flying of fists and kicking of legs, but Georgiana could just see that Burly Jack was being thoroughly bested. Without pausing to consider her own position, she launched herself upon Jack's attacker, ripping at his hair and boxing his ears for all she was worth.

'Run, lad!' Jack's voice echoed in her ear. It was the last thing she heard before she was felled by a hefty blow to the back of her head. And then there was nothing.

Georgiana awoke to a giddy nauseous feeling. There was an undoubted sensation of swaying that would not still whether she opened her eyes or closed them. Not that it made any difference to what she could see within the dense blackness of where she now found herself.

She tried to sit up, but the throbbing of her head increased so dramatically that she thought the remnants of the mutton pie would leap from her stomach.

'George, is you awake yet?' The unmistakable tone of Burly Jack's voice sounded.

'Yes, sir.' She groaned. 'Where are we? I can't see anythin'.'

A hand landed on her thigh and she let out a squeak.

'There you are, lad. Did them bastards 'urt you? Looked like they landed you a right good 'un on the 'ead.' Jack's hand moved up to her arm. She prayed it would stray no further.

'I'll mend,' she uttered, trying to quell the queasiness rising in her stomach, and struggled to a sitting position.

Jack's hand patted her arm. 'That's the spirit. Tom and Bill's 'ere too. Bastards got us all, and two others by the name of Jim and Rad.'

'The lad sounds young,' Rad's voice came out of the gloom. 'Voice ain't broken yet.'

'He *is* young, so don't be startin' nothin' with 'im or you'll 'ave me to answer to.' Burly Jack's voice had lost its soft edge.

It seemed that Georgiana had found something of a protector within the smelly dark hovel. Would he remain so if he fathomed her secret? It was not a question that she wished to test. The rocking motion seemed to be getting worse, just as her eyes had adjusted to see grey shapes within the surrounding darkness. And with it grew her nausea. 'Dear Lord!' The curse escaped her as the retching began.

'Easy, lad.' Burly Jack's voice sounded close. 'You'll get used to it soon enough and then it won't never come back. Seasickness ain't a pleasant feeling, but there ain't nothin' can be done about it.'

'Seasickness?' Georgiana questioned with a feeble tone.

'Oh, aye, lad. What d'you think them fellows wanted with us? They're the bloody Press Gang and you're aboard ship now.' Jack's words had a horrible nightmarish quality about them.

She blinked her eyes into the darkness. 'You must be wrong, sir.'

'Nope,' Jack replied with a definite cheery tone. 'You're a ship's boy on the *Pallas* now, young George, whether you like it or not. Best get used to the idea before the bosun comes to fetch us.'

Georgiana let out a load groan and dropped her head into her hands. She was once again in a diabolical situation as the result of her own foolhardy actions. But this time there would be no handsome Lord Nathaniel Hawke to jump headlong in and save her.

'You've interviewed them all, Mr Anderson. So what do we have?' Nathaniel continued in his stride towards the small group of men standing at the far end of the main deck.

Lieutenant Anderson walked briskly alongside. 'Good news, Captain Hawke, sir. There are five men, three of whom have plenty of experience at sea. I've rated them as able seamen, sir. The other two are landsmen, never set foot on a ship before, but I estimate that they'll be quick to learn. All are now registered on the *Pallas*' books.'

Nathaniel's face was grim. 'It sickens me to the pit of my stomach that I'm forced to resort to such a thing. I'd rather have them here willingly or not at all.'

'You're only following orders, Captain,' the first lieutenant pointed out. 'And I fancy that they'll soon change their minds as to a life at sea once they've sailed on the *Pallas*.'

Nathaniel remained unconvinced, but he had a job to do and he had best get on with it, no matter that having pressed men aboard his ship left a bitter taste in his mouth. 'Three able seamen, you say?'

'Oh, and there's a lad of fourteen as well. It seems that he was with the sailors when they were taken by Captain Bodmin's men. We're still short on ship's boys, so I've rated him as a third class. Mr Adams is under the impression that the boy is dim-witted; indeed, I did notice that he keeps his head down and mumbles when spoken to. But I thought…well, with the need to leave port that…' John Anderson struggled to find the words.

Nathaniel came to the rescue. 'Given the right instruction I'm sure that the boy will learn. You did right, Mr Anderson. Better that he ends up here with his friends than alone aboard another ship.' He pushed the stories of what had happened to lone youngsters on certain other ships out of his head. Not while Nathaniel Hawke had breath in his body would any such depravity take place on the *Pallas*.

The pressed men stood separately from the rest of the crew, forming a small distinct group. As Nathaniel and John Anderson approached, the group stiffened and stood to attention.

'Stand at ease, men,' Lieutenant Anderson commanded.

The men responded.

Nathaniel stood before his crew and surveyed the latest additions. 'Welcome to the *Pallas*. Some of you may not be here by your own free choice, but you're here to serve your king and country nevertheless. Our voyage may be long and difficult. Indeed, we will be exposed to many perils and threats. But as men of England I know that you will fight, as we all fight, to retain our freedom. For if our great navy does not fight, we may as well collect Bonaparte ourselves and deliver him to London's door.'

He looked into each man's eyes in turn.

'This voyage is not an easy walk. I demand your obedience, your loyalty and your diligence.'

The first two faces in the line were pale, their skin tinged with a greenish hue—the landsmen, no doubt. They were listening despite their rancid stomachs.

'In return I offer you adventure, and the chance of wealth. There are prizes out there, gentlemen, and they are ours for the taking.'

The next three were ruddy and vigorous. Two fellows of medium build and one large bear of a man. All were intent on his words.

'But with the biggest prizes come the biggest dangers. And only the best crews will win them in the end. With drilling, with perseverance, with determination, gentlemen, we can be the best of crews; we can win the best of prizes.'

He swung his arms in a wide encompassing gesture to the massed crew. 'Gentlemen, I give you the best of me, and I demand the very best of you, each and every one of you. We sailed yesterday under sealed orders. We have reached the specified longitude and latitude and I can reveal to you all that the *Pallas* will proceed to the Azores and cruise there to capture any enemy vessels encountered. The pickings will be rich indeed. What say you, men, will you give me your best?'

The deck resounded to raucous cheering. Even Burly Jack, Bill and Tom clapped one another on the back and raised their voices. Jack laughed down at Georgiana and spoke out of the corner of his mouth. 'This is much better than the poxy vessel we were bound for. We'll be rich, lad, rich!'

Nathaniel's voice sounded above the din, and an immediate hush spread. 'Then let us commence our voyage as we mean to finish it.' As the crowd dispersed, Nathaniel glanced at the boy hovering by the elbow of the large man. Lieutenant Anderson had been accurate in his description, for the lad's gaze was trained firmly on the wooden floor, his head bent low. 'What's your name, boy?'

The boy's head bent lower, as if he wished the deck to open and swallow him up. 'George, Captain, sir.'

Nathaniel had to strain to catch the low-pitched mumble. 'And your family name?'

The small boots standing before him shuffled uncomfortably. 'Robertson, Captain, sir.'

'Well then, Master Robertson, my first command to you is that you stand up straight at all times and look whoever may be talking to you directly in the eye. Do you understand?'

'Yes, Captain, sir,' the faint reply came back.

The boy's head remained averted.

Perhaps Mr Adams had been right in his estimation of the boy's wits. Nathaniel frowned. 'Master Robertson,' he said somewhat more forcefully.

The large sailor nudged the boy and hissed between blackened teeth, 'Do as the Captain says, George. Stand up straight. Look up.' He turned back to the captain. 'Sorry, Captain, he's a bit slow, but he's a good lad.'

Nathaniel's gaze drifted back to the stooped figure.

Slowly but surely Georgiana straightened her shoulders and raised her face to look directly at Captain Hawke.

Nathaniel blinked. There was something familiar about the dirt-smeared little face that looked up at him. A memory stirred far in the recesses of his mind, but escaped capture. Surely he must be mistaken? The boy was clearly no one he had ever seen before. He tried to shrug the feeling off. And all the while George Robertson's youthful grey-blue eyes were wide with shock. 'That's how I prefer to see you at all times, Master Robertson. A seaman should be proud of himself, and as a boy aboard my ship, you've much to be proud of.' Captain Nathaniel Hawke returned to his cabin with a faint glimmer of unease that could not quite be fathomed.

Georgiana's knees set up a tremor and she pressed her hand to her mouth. She thought that her nausea had subsided with the fresh sea air of the open deck. The sight of the gentleman striding purposefully towards them brought it back in an instant. Dear Lord, but he bore an uncanny resemblance to Lord Nathaniel Hawke. It was a complete impossibility, of course, or so she told herself. Many men were tall with dark hair that glowed red in the sunlight. But as he came closer, and Georgiana was able to look upon those brown expressive eyes, fine straight nose and chiselled jaw line, she knew that her first impression had not been mistaken.

Her sudden gasp went unnoticed as Lord Nathaniel addressed the surrounding men. Shock gave way to relief. Providence, in the guise of Nathaniel Hawke, had helped her before and was about to do so again, or so it seemed. Even as her spirit leapt, the stark reality of her circumstance made itself known to her. Only two kinds of women came aboard ships, the wives of officers, and those who belonged to what she had heard termed the oldest profession in the world. Georgiana belonged to neither group. Yet the *Pallas* had sailed from Portsmouth two days since. Her position was precarious in the extreme. The very presence of an unmarried lady aboard Nathaniel Hawke's ship was likely to place him in a difficult situation. Her own reputation no longer mattered, but she had no wish to cause trouble for the man who had saved her life. There seemed to be no other alternative than to continue with her deception as the simple-minded boy. She dropped her gaze to the spotless wooden decking and played her part well, hoping all the time that Nathaniel Hawke would not recognise any trace of Miss Georgiana Raithwaite.

'Oi, dopey!' The rough-edged voice sounded across the deck. 'Have you got cabbage for brains or what?' The fat gunner's mate delivered a hefty slap to Georgiana's ear. 'Get this bloody place cleaned up before Mr Pensenby arrives. If he sees it in this state, you'll be on reduced rations again. Now get a bloody move on.'

In the two weeks that had passed since the *Pallas*' departure from Portsmouth harbour, Georgiana had managed to avoid the worst of trouble and had retained her disguise. All trace of seasickness had vanished thanks to her daily consumption of grog. It might have tasted foul, but it had settled her stomach when she thought it would never be settled again. Her hands still bore some open blisters, although most had healed to calluses upon her palms. Her hair was matted and itchy beneath the dirty black woollen cap that she permanently wore and her feet were rubbed and sore from clambering barefoot over the slippery decks. As if that were not bad enough, she seemed to be covered from head to toe in a layer of filth from her newly appointed position of gunroom servant. Heaven only knew quite how scrubbing floors and tables, washing plates and glasses, and being at the beck and call of every officer and young midshipman, as well as waiting at their dining table, could have got her into such a state! It was not an easy job, but it was infinitely preferable to that of the 'Captain of the Head', young Sam Wilson, who had the unenviable task of cleaning the lavatories at the head of the ship. Sam was only eight years old and she had taken the little lad under her wing.

She saw little of Jack and the others except at the odd meal time, when his hearty laughter allowed her to find him amidst the rows of rough wooden tables and benches set between the guns that transformed the upper deck into a mess each mealtime. As Georgiana grew accustomed to daily routine on board ship, she began to think that perhaps she might just survive the voyage in the guise of George Robertson, but she had reckoned without the interference of the second lieutenant, Cyril Pensenby.

'Lieutenant Pensenby, sir!' The gunner's mate straightened and saluted the poker-faced young gentleman who had just strolled into the room.

'Holmes.' Georgiana watched as the officer's snowy white breeches brushed inadvertently against one of the narrow wooden benches. The lieutenant glanced down and stopped dead still. He raised his eyes and looked accusingly at Georgiana, whose own gaze remained riveted to the discoloured smear that now sullied the material stretched across the gentleman's leg. 'Master Robertson,' his cultured voice lisped, 'you will scrub this room from top to bottom until it has not one grain of dust, not one smear of dirt. And when you've finished you shall scrub yourself clean in a similar fashion. There is a bathing cask up on deck. See that you make use of it. I shall return before the first dog watch to inspect the work you've undertaken. I hope for your sake, boy, that it meets with my approval.'

Georgiana stared wordlessly at the retreating figure.

The gunner's mate eased his corpulent frame on to the bench. 'Best get started, lad. The lieutenant ain't a man to be trifled with and he won't cut you no slack on account of your simple-minded ways. Gunner won't be best pleased either.'

Three hours later the gunroom was shining like a new pin. *Please don't let anyone mess it up before he sees it,* Georgiana prayed, before setting about cleaning the worst of the ingrained muck from her face and hands in a small wooden basin. Most of the dirt had been brushed out of her blue culottes and jacket before Lieutenant Pensenby returned.

He perused the gunroom down the end of his long thin nose, saying nothing, before turning his scrutiny to Georgiana herself. 'Roll up your sleeve, Robertson,' the curt voice commanded.

Georgiana did as she was told, holding one grubby arm up for inspection.

'You have not bathed.'

'Beggin' your pardon, Lieutenant, sir, but I cleaned myself just as you told me.' Georgiana tried to retrieve her arm from beneath the gentleman's fingers.

Cyril Pensenby's thumbnail scraped against her skin, releasing a layer of blackened grime. 'The evidence speaks for itself, boy.'

'No, sir, you're mistaken, sir,' Georgiana mumbled in as low a tone as she could muster.

Mr Pensenby's brows lowered and he thrust Georgiana's arm angrily away. 'Are you calling me a liar, Robertson?'

What had started as a small matter was rapidly escalating out of control. 'No, Lieutenant, sir.' She bit at her bottom lip and focused on the decking around Mr Pensenby's feet.

Pensenby turned to the gunner's mate. 'See that this boy is scrubbed clean in a cask bath. Immediately, Holmes.'

'Aye, Lieutenant Pensenby, I'll see to it personally, sir.'

Georgiana's eyes widened in terror as she realised what was about to happen. 'No!' She made to run past the two men, but fat fingers closed cruelly over her wrist and dragged her back.

'Come along, Master Robertson, ain't nothin' so very bad about havin' a bath. Let's be havin' you up on deck, lad.'

Georgiana wriggled and squirmed, but nothing, it seemed, could dislodge the gunner's mate's firm grasp. By the time they had reached the deck she could scarcely catch her breath.

'Hoist up the cask!' the gunner's mate instructed, and attempted to remove the simpleton's jacket.

Georgiana yelled for all she was worth, her voice rising higher in her panic. 'Jack! Jack!' She plunged her teeth into the fat man's hand and kicked as hard as she could at his shins.

'Ouch! You little bugger!' Holmes released the skinny arm to deliver a weighty cuff to the lad's ear.

It was the opportunity that Georgiana had been waiting for and she needed no invitation. Before the gunner's mate could recover, she legged it straight up the rigging of the main mast. She didn't dare look down, just kept on climbing up towards the topgallant mast. The wind blasted cold and icy, contriving to knock her from her precarious perch, but she clung to the ropes until her fingers hurt. Voices murmured from far below, their words lost to the wind. Her heart pounded in her chest and she watched with rising misery as the light diminished in the surrounding sky.

'What the hell is going on?' The men scattered before Captain Hawke.

Lieutenant Pensenby stepped forward. 'Ship's boy Robertson disobeyed a direct command, sir. He attacked Holmes here when he tried to effect that order.'

'And what exactly was the command, Mr Pensenby?'

Pensenby's thin face flushed. 'The boy and the gunroom were filthy, Captain. Indeed, it wasn't possible to enter the place without soiling my own uniform. As I am adverse to having such a dirty specimen serve the food upon my plate, or, indeed, to sup in unclean surroundings, I instructed that he clean both himself and the room. He complied with the room, but is most reticent to bathe himself, sir.'

Nathaniel groaned to himself. This was the last thing he needed. That half the ship's company was lacking in personal hygiene could not have escaped Pensenby's notice. Indeed, most of the men saw bathing as something undertaken only by eccentrics. But flouting of any order was not something that could be taken lightly, especially when it had been issued by the second lieutenant. 'And where is the boy now?'

All eyes looked up into the rigging.

'Ah,' the captain murmured by way of understanding. 'Fetch able seaman Grimly.'

Someone was coming up to fetch her. She dared a look and saw Jack not far below.

'What the 'ell 'ave you been doin'?' the gruff voice queried. 'Pensenby's got his dander up about you and no mistake and I ain't gonna be able to stop 'im.' Burly Jack sighed. 'Bathin' ain't exactly my delight, but couldn't you 'ave just 'ad a quick duck in and out?'

Georgiana's hands wove themselves tighter through the ropes.

'No, Jack. Don't make me go down. I won't have a bath. I can't.' The words were barely more than a hoarse whisper into the wind.

'If you don't come down with me they'll just send someone else to get you. Come on, lad, don't make it worse than it already is.'

He was right. Pensenby would never leave her be. There was nothing else for it, she would have to throw herself upon Nathaniel Hawke's mercy and hope for the best.

Chapter Four

'Master Robertson, no man or boy on this ship is exempt from the line of command. To disobey an order from an officer is an offence, and one that merits disciplinary action.' A chill wind blew hard across the deck, carrying in its wake the damp smell of rain. Darkness was closing in fast, and the lanterns were being lit. Nathaniel felt a pang of sympathy for the lad; nevertheless, it was the first direct contravention of an order and his response was likely to set a precedent amongst the men. 'Lieutenant Pensenby has instructed you to bathe and bathe you shall. See to it, Mr Holmes.'

'Aye, aye, Captain.' The boy was so pale he looked as if all the blood had left his body. Holmes quelled the thought, he had a job to do. 'You ain't got nothin' different from the rest of us, lad. Let's get on with it.'

Panic constricted Georgiana's breathing. 'No! Wait!'

Holmes's hand clamped upon her shoulder and Captain Hawke made to walk away.

'Captain Hawke, please wait, sir. I can explain.' Her usual hushed mumble was forgotten. She lashed out at the man beside her. 'Leave me be!'

It was imperative that he remain indifferent to the boy's pleading voice. Such scenes were always difficult for Nathaniel, but he could not back down. He continued towards the forecastle.

'You will not address the captain, Robertson, it is not your place to do so,' Pensenby interrupted.

Her jacket had been removed and Holmes was tugging at her culottes. Georgiana bellowed as loudly as she could, and tried hard to maintain the slight edge to her accent. 'I must speak with you, Captain, sir. Please, sir!'

Still she saw only the receding view of his deep blue coat, his shoulders squared, his golden epaulettes glinting in the lantern light.

'It concerns Farleigh Hall, sir.'

Nathaniel ceased his measured steps and swung round. Surely he had misheard? 'What did you say, boy?' He drew his brows together in perplexity and walked slowly back to where the gunner's mate held the boy in a neck lock.

'Farleigh Hall,' Georgiana managed to choke the words out.

Something was most definitely amiss. How did a simpleton third-rate ship's boy know of his brother's house? An uneasy feeling was gathering in his gut. 'Release the boy, Mr Holmes. I would hear what he has to say.'

With considerable relief Georgiana lurched forward, her hand pressed to the bruising on her throat. 'It's private, Captain, sir. I must speak with you alone, sir.'

If Nathaniel observed that his previously tongue-tied ship's boy had suddenly developed a clear and coherent manner of speech, he forbore to mention it.

Pensenby's countenance was growing tarter by the minute. 'How dare you?' he spluttered with the indignation of a man who could not quite believe what he had just heard. 'I've never seen a more audacious manner in a boy.' The second lieutenant's temper was wearing dangerously thin. 'You will be punished for this insolence.'

'Make 'im kiss the gunner's daughter,' a coarse voice added from the background.

The prospect of being bent over one of the long guns and caned on the backside was enough to make Georgiana's hair to stand on end. 'Lady Mirabelle,' she squeaked in defiance, and, 'Lord Frederick,' just for good measure.

Nathaniel's mind was decided in an instant. 'I'll interview the boy in my cabin. Have him brought down immediately.'

Georgiana's knees almost gave way with relief as Holmes dragged her along in the captain's wake.

'But...' Lieutenant Pensenby's jaw dropped.

'Thank you, Mr Pensenby. Continue with your duties.' Captain Hawke's clipped tones floated back to reach him.

The captain's cabin, positioned at the rear of the gun deck, was incredibly large in comparison with the cramped conditions endured by the rest of the crew, and furnished well, if not luxuriously. As well as a desk, captain's chair, dining table, six dining chairs and a small chest of drawers, there was a large and very fine oil painting depicting Lord Nelson's victory against the French Admiral Brueys at the Battle of the Nile. Amidst the elegance of the décor were two large eighteen-pounder long guns, shone to a brilliant black finish. Nathaniel Hawke leaned back against the desk, stretching his legs out before him. The cocked hat was removed and positioned carefully on a pile of papers to his left. An errant lock of hair swept across his forehead and his eyes glowed deep and dark.

'Well, young Robertson, tell your tale.'

Georgiana felt the tension mount within her, and quickly slipped on the torn jacket that Holmes had replaced in her hands. An extra layer of protection against what was to come. And what *was* to come? She had no notion what Captain Hawke's reaction would be. No notion at all. She licked her dry, salt-encrusted lips and began. 'Thank you for agreeing to my request for privacy. I'm sure that you'll agree to its necessity once you've heard the truth.'

'Indeed?' One winged eyebrow raised itself. 'You suddenly have a most eloquent turn of phrase, Master Robertson. The prospect of a bath seems to have overcome your tendency to the whispered mumbling of a simpleton.'

Georgiana cleared her throat and clutched her hands together. How did one go about imparting such a revelation? 'Quite,' she muttered softly.

The silence stretched between them.

Nathaniel's hands stretched flat upon the desk and he leaned forward. 'I believe that you have something to tell me.'

Such long strong fingers, so representative of the power within the man himself. An image of those fingers stroking her cheek popped into her mind and she flushed with guilty anger. How could she think such a thought, and at a time like this? A warm blush rose in her cheeks and she rapidly averted her gaze.

Nathaniel did not miss the emotions that flashed so readily across the boy's face, nor the telltale rosy stain beneath the dirt-stained cheeks. He waited, curiosity rising.

'I... You...' She paused, unable to find the words. Oh, heaven help her! Taking a deep breath, she launched into the story. 'There's no easy way to say this, Captain Hawke, so I'll strive to be brief and to the point. Please remember throughout that I...that I never intended the position in which I now find myself. Such a possibility never entered my mind.' She looked up at him suddenly, her eyes wide and clear, her voice elegant and polite. 'The fact of the matter is that I'm not who I appear to be.' She paused, her breathing coming fast and furious, almost as if she had ran the length of the ship.

'I'd gathered that much. And you're now about to do me the honour of revealing your true identity.' His tone was dry, but there was an encouraging gentleness in his eyes and Georgiana knew that Nathaniel Hawke was a fair man. The knowledge gave her the confidence she so desperately needed to continue.

'Yes.' The single word slipped softly into the silence of the cabin.

Nathaniel experienced a reflexive tensing of his muscles and an overwhelming intuitive certainty that the next words to be uttered by the ragamuffin boy standing so quietly before him would change his life for ever.

The boy's chin forced up high. The grey-blue eyes met his without flinching. The narrow chest expanded with a deep breath. 'I am Miss Georgiana Raithwaite, recently of your acquaintance at Farleigh Hall.' Still the breath held, tightly squeezed within her lungs. She waited. Waited. And never once did her gaze wander from those dark eyes that were staring back at her with an undisguised disbelief.

Silence.

The blood ran cold in Nathaniel's veins and a shiver flitted down his spine. It was not possible. The ragged boy, Miss Raithwaite. 'You cannot be Miss Raithwaite. You're a...'

Georgiana endured the roving scrutiny of his eyes without moving. 'Now you understand why I couldn't comply with Lieutenant Pensenby's command.' She raised her eyebrows wryly and bit her bottom lip.

'Hell's teeth!' Nathaniel cursed and stood upright. A horrible sinking sensation was starting within his stomach, for beneath the grubby urchin face he could see what had previously eluded him—the fine features of the young woman he had pulled from the River Borne. 'Your hair... Have you—?'

'Naturally,' replied Georgiana. 'It wouldn't have been much of a disguise otherwise.' She whipped the cap from her head to reveal her sheared and matted locks.

'Dear God!' Nathaniel could not suppress the exclamation.

'Yes, quite. It's in a horrible filthy state, as is the rest of me. How ironic that my present trouble has arisen from my refusal to bathe when that is one of the things I've longed so ardently to do these two weeks past.' She smiled then, a smile that lit up her face.

Nathaniel stared, and stared some more. Inadvertently his eyes dropped lower, as if he would see what lay beneath the torn blue jacket. 'You show no external signs of...of, um...'

'Bindings. Terribly uncomfortable things to wear, if you must know,' she said stoutly.

Captain Hawke's swarthy complexion flushed. 'Yes, quite.'

'But it wouldn't have done at all for Burly Jack or the others to have discovered otherwise.'

'Burly Jack?' Nathaniel's brows knitted.

'Able Seamen Grimly, sir.' She sighed. 'He's been looking out for me, you see, since we became acquainted on the mail-coach to Fareham.'

There was a definite pain starting behind his eyes. The tanned fingers rubbed at his forehead. 'No, Miss Raithwaite, I don't see at all. I think you had better explain all that has happened since I saw you last.' He gestured towards a wooden chair and said politely, as if they were both in the drawing room of Farleigh Hall, 'Please be seated.' He then lowered himself into the red leather captain's chair and prepared to listen.

Georgiana started to talk and, with only the occasional interruption from the captain, continued to do so for some considerable length of time.

'So let me check that I have understood you correctly, Miss Raithwaite.' He watched her with a quizzical expression. 'Following a disagreement with your father, you ran away from home, by mail, to seek refuge with a friend who lives near Portsmouth, and were mistakenly taken by the Press Gang?'

'Yes.' She folded her hands before her and tried to look composed.

He wasn't fooled for an instant. Nathaniel Hawke knew guilt when he saw it. 'And may I enquire as to the nature of your disagreement?'

Her fingers pressed to each other. 'I cannot reveal that, my lord. It regards a personal issue.'

'Such as your betrothal to Mr Praxton?' he asked softly.

Her eyes met his, then dropped to scan the mahogany surface of his desk as colour flooded her cheeks.

'Yes,' she whispered.

A small silence elapsed.

'Then I'll write to your father and at least let him know that you're safe.'

'No!' Georgiana was out of her seat and facing him with a look of pure horror. 'No, I beg of you,' she pleaded. 'If you have the smallest consideration for me at all, my lord, please do no such thing.'

He felt her distress as keenly as if it were his own. 'Very well, but if I'm to help you I must ask that you tell me the truth, all of it.'

The moment had come. She swallowed hard and squared her shoulders. The truth, whatever it was, had affected her dearly. He watched her gather her courage, watched her sweet lips open in preparation. 'When I said that my father approved of my betrothal to Mr Praxton, I was not telling you the whole story. He…he and

Mr Praxton…' It seemed that she could not find the words. 'After what happened in Hurstborne Park with Mr Praxton's…plan, Papa was so angry with me, and I with him. I just couldn't believe what he meant to do. Papa knew how I felt and still he didn't care. He was determined to have his own way, wouldn't even listen to me. In my heart I knew that I couldn't do as he bade, so…so I decided to run away.'

A horrible sensation was settling on Captain Hawke. He thought he could see exactly where Miss Raithwaite's tale was leading. And that somewhere was in the direction of a disapproving father and an elopement. There would be no friend near Portsmouth, of that he was sure, only Walter Praxton waiting at their chosen place of assignation. Damn the scoundrel! He schooled the emotion from his voice. 'Your father's response to Mr Praxton's actions in the park is understandable. No man would condone such treatment of his daughter. It's hardly surprising that he won't have you wed Praxton. The man is a knave.'

'No, you misunderstand. Mr Praxton—'

'Is no gentleman to behave as he did. I cannot think you would believe anything other. Think, Miss Raithwaite, what kind of gentleman would have encouraged you to such actions? Deserting your family, dressing as a boy, travelling across country alone, and on the mail of all things. Why, anything could have happened to you!' He raked his fingers through his hair with mounting exasperation. Hell, but did the girl have no inkling as to what sort of man Praxton was? Little idiot! The thought of Miss Raithwaite allowing Praxton liberties made his blood boil.

'Captain Hawke, you're mistaken in what you think. Mr Praxton is indeed a—'

Nathaniel knew exactly what Praxton was. He didn't want to hear the woman before him plead the wretch's case. 'I suppose you mean to tell me next that you love him and that is excuse enough.' It was a brutal statement, brutal and angry and disappointed.

Her mouth gaped open and beneath the dirt he could have sworn that her skin had drained of any last vestige of colour. She gripped the edge of his desk, leaned forward towards him and said in her most indignant voice, 'I beg your pardon, sir!'

'If you speak a trifle louder, Miss Raithwaite, you need adopt your guise no longer, for every man on the ship will have heard a woman's voice from within my cabin.'

The grey-blue eyes closed momentarily before fluttering back open. 'I'm sorry, Captain Hawke. I'm trying to tell you that your beliefs concerning Mr Praxton are quite wrong. The incident in the park was not how—'

But Nathaniel had no intention of listening to Miss Raithwaite defend the scoundrel. It was hard enough knowing that she had feelings for him. 'I do not wish to hear your thoughts on Mr Praxton. Whatever your plans were, they can be no more. We must concentrate on the situation we now find ourselves in.'

Those clear fine eyes stared at him with such wounded disbelief as to render him the cruellest tyrant on earth.

'It seems that you have made up your mind on the matter and nothing I can say will change it.'

There was a melancholy in her voice that he had not heard before. Why did he have the sudden sensation that he had just made the worst blunder of his life? Damnation, the truth was harsh, but it was kinder than letting her believe Praxton's lies. And she was right, nothing *would* make him warm to the rogue. 'The Atlantic Ocean lies between you and Mr Praxton now. You had best forget him, Miss Raithwaite. He cannot reach you here.'

When she bowed her head and did not answer, he knew that nothing he could say would affect the girl's affection for the villain. He battened down his own feelings and moved to deal with the practicalities of disguising a lady's presence on board his ship, all the while oblivious to the relief that his last comment had wrought in Miss Raithwaite.

Quite why Nathaniel was so adverse to hearing the truth about Walter Praxton escaped her. If only he had let her explain. But perhaps it was better this way, for heaven only knew what a man like Nathaniel Hawke would do if he understood exactly what Mr Praxton and her papa had been about. And that was sure only to make matters worse, for them all. Let him think the worst if it would prevent him becoming embroiled with Mr Praxton. Besides, he was right. That she had set out to seek Mirabelle's advice no longer mattered, for she was far beyond any help that lady could now offer. On a social standing, even Mr Praxton's loathsome attentions paled in contrast to the circumstance into which she had now stumbled...well, thrown herself. She was under no illusion as to exactly what she had done to her reputation just by running away. And then there was the small matter of being pressed aboard a naval frigate...as a boy.

At least her papa's evil plan had been foiled. No man, not even Mr Praxton, would wish to wed her now. Even so, she could not help but be glad at Nathaniel's words: *the Atlantic Ocean lies between you and Mr Praxton... He cannot reach you here.* The hairs on the back of her neck prickled. Somehow, she doubted that she had heard the last of Walter Praxton.

The door opened to reveal Captain Hawke's head. 'Morris, organise that a large tub of warmed sea water be brought to my night cabin. And also a jug of warmed fresh water.'

'Aye, Captain.' As the captain's head disappeared once more the young marine sent a look of bewilderment to his opposite sentry, shrugged his shoulders and scurried off to do as he was bid.

Neither did the captain's steward or his valet blink an eyelid when he requested fresh bedding and clean clothes of a size to fit Master Robinson. But it did not take long for the news to spread far and wide aboard the *Pallas*. Indeed, in a matter of hours, both Lieutenants Anderson and Pensenby had heard the rumours.

'I cannot credit that he's treating the boy in such a way.' The tip of Mr Pensenby's long nose trembled at the very thought. 'There is no doubt some unsavoury motive at play. Robertson openly flouted my command and what does he receive in return? A flogging? Reduced rations? Crow's nest watch? Oh, no. Master Robertson is treated to a private warmed bath within the captain's own cabin. There's something very much amiss.'

John Anderson's brow furrowed. 'I'm sure that there must be

some perfectly reasonable explanation for what has happened. We shouldn't jump to conclusions. No doubt the captain will inform us of anything that we should know.'

'Mark my words, Mr Anderson, only trouble will come of this. Trouble and nothing else.' His wide thin lips compressed. 'We both know the direction the men's thoughts will take.'

Lieutenant Anderson said nothing, but turned his attention once more to the log he was writing.

The water lapped warm and luxuriant against Georgiana's naked skin. She sighed and relaxed back within the captain's personal hip bath, bending her knees until her soapy head submerged beneath the surface. When the worst of the lather had been removed, she reached for the jug and poured its freshwater contents over her cropped hair. The ebony locks squeaked clean, and Georgiana marvelled at Nathaniel Hawke's generosity. Freshwater was precious; she did not know how long it would be before they would have an opportunity to replenish the supply. And yet he had not expected her hair to suffer the coarse drying effects of seawater. As she stepped dripping from the tub and wrapped the cloth around her, she looked with curiosity at the small room around her, marked so clearly as belonging to Captain Hawke. Besides the furniture she'd already noticed, there were a case of books, a small table and chair, a heavy sea chest, a basin, shaving accoutrements, a mirror fixed upon the wall…and the cot. A shiver ran down her spine and she dried herself briskly, stepping into the clean clothes that Nathaniel had provided for her.

She folded the cloth and could not resist inspecting her reflection in the mirror. A pale face with short dark hair stared back at her. There was a purple bruise to the side of her right eye and a cut upon her lip. Now that the dirt was gone, she felt naked, exposed, as if anyone who looked at her would know *who* she really was, *what* she really was. She arranged the straggle of hair as best she could using only her fingers, then stepped away with deliberate care towards the flimsy connecting door, and paused. He believed that she loved Walter Praxton, that her father had forbidden her marriage to the man. As if anything could have been further from the truth! How could he even think that she would let that rogue so much as touch her? Her gorge rose at the memory of Walter Praxton's roving hands, his greedy mouth. She swallowed it down, pushed the shame and disgust away, determined never to think of it again.

Nathaniel Hawke was a good man, a man that attracted her in a way she'd never felt before. She'd tried to tell him, wanted to shout the truth when he'd misunderstood. But she couldn't, not if she wanted to stop him challenging Mr Praxton and her papa. She was nothing to Captain Hawke save a problem, a thorn in his side, turning up at the worst of times, like a bad penny. It was bad enough that he'd already risked drowning to save her. And now here she was, on his ship, in the middle of the sea, alone, and in the guise of a boy! Little wonder that he was angry. Best to remember her place, quell such inappropriate feelings for the man and get on with surviving the consequences of her own foolish actions. With this resolution in mind, she knocked softly upon the wooden panels and passed through from Captain Hawke's night cabin to the one that he used during the day.

The man himself was sitting at his desk, a glass of brandy held loosely in his hand. Grey winter light from the large windows behind the desk contrasted against the stark outline of his broad shoulders. He appeared to be deep in thought, a distant gaze in his eyes. Georgiana's resolution wavered at the sight of him. The errant curl still dangled temptingly on his forehead and her fingers itched to smooth it back to its rightful place. She suppressed the urge, blushed that she should have thought such a thing, and sat down in the chair across from Captain Hawke.

'Thank you, sir, I feel so much better now that I'm clean. And I'll no longer be a cause of offence to Lieutenant Pensenby.' She smiled and felt suddenly shy.

Nathaniel could have groaned aloud. How could he have ever thought that the girl before him was anything other? The delicate bone structure, straight little nose and full pink lips. Her eyes twinkled blue washed with shades of grey, and her eyelashes were sooty and long. How could any man fail to see what was right in front of his very eyes? The dirt had camouflaged her well and now that it was gone he wondered if the rest of the crew would see what he did. And that wasn't all the dirt had hidden. He frowned and, reaching forward, gently clasped his fingers to her chin.

'How did you come by these marks?' His voice was gruff, belying the careful touch of his fingers as he tilted her face to view the bruising near her eye. He couldn't help but notice how white her skin was next to the brown of his hand. And soft…so very, very soft.

Her skin burned beneath his touch, and a strange light-headed feeling came over her. For some inexplicable reason she found herself unable to reply, unable even to think of anything other than his strong warm fingers that touched like a feather to her face. The pulse leapt to a frenzy in her neck, so that she was sure that he would see it. But still she could not move, frozen by her own response to the man sitting before her.

Nathaniel looked down into Miss Raithwaite's shimmering eyes and experienced an urge to pull that slender body into his arms and kiss her. And not in the least chaste or polite manner. The kissing that he had in mind was of an extremely thorough nature. He watched as her lips parted, almost as in invitation. His fingers caressed her chin, moving up to capture the smoothness of her cheek. His heart thumped loudly within his chest, he lowered his mouth towards hers and—'

A short sharp knock sounded at the door.

Brandy splashed on to the captain's desk. Georgiana jumped so high that Nathaniel's hand brushed against her breast. Even through the depth of her bindings she felt his warmth. She gasped. Blue eyes held brown in confused horror.

'Quickly, slip into the night cabin and don't make a sound,' Nathaniel whispered in her ear. His large hand covered hers, gave one brief squeeze of reassurance and was gone.

She reacted instinctively, moving quickly and quietly to the connecting door.

When Lieutenant Anderson entered, it was to find the captain engrossed in some charts, and no sign of ship's boy Robertson.

* * *

'First Lieutenant Anderson.' Nathaniel's voice was laconic and mellow, betraying nothing of the turbulent emotions simmering so recently in his breast.

'Captain Hawke, sir. I beg your pardon for the intrusion, but my hourly report is due.' The young man's face appeared a trifle flushed.

Nathaniel leaned back in his chair and surveyed his lieutenant. 'Indeed, it is, Mr Anderson. Please proceed.'

John Anderson cleared his throat and recited his list. 'All stations have been checked. The first dog watch passed without event and the first watch proper commenced. All is in order. Ernie Dobson's tooth has been extracted and he's been allocated an extra quart of grog. There's no change in the weather and we are continuing on course as per your instructions. That is all I have to report, sir.'

'Thank you, Mr Anderson. That will be all.'

But the first lieutenant stayed firmly rooted to the spot, an awkward expression plastered across his face.

'Was there something else, Mr Anderson?' Nathaniel had a fairly accurate idea of what was causing John Anderson to linger.

'No, Captain... Well, perhaps...' Mr Anderson appeared to be finding a spot upon the cabin floor of immense interest.

Nathaniel decided to put the officer out of his misery. 'Would you care for a brandy, Mr Anderson?'

The first lieutenant looked up in surprise. 'Yes, thank you, sir.'

'There's been talk of my dealings with ship's boy Robertson.' It was a statement, not a question. He passed the glass to Anderson.

'Yes, sir.' His cheeks were glowing with all the subtlety of two beacons.

Nathaniel's jaw clenched grimly. That the captain had ordered a private bath for the boy within his own cabin would be known by every man on the *Pallas* by now. He was under no illusion as to what the common interpretation of his action would be, and that was something that would have to be dispelled as quickly as possibly. Nathaniel was thinking and thinking very fast. John Anderson's green eyes had raised to his in quiet anticipation. Whatever

Nathaniel told him, it could not be the truth. 'It's a delicate matter over which discretion is required. I trust that I have your complete confidence in the matter?'

'Of course, sir!' Lieutenant Anderson had drawn himself up to his full height and was regarding his captain with more than a little curiosity. He sipped at the brandy.

'The boy, Robertson, is not who he seems.'

Anderson's eyes were positively agog. 'No?'

'No.' Nathaniel's tone was conspiratorial. 'Indeed, Robertson is a pseudonym he's used to his own ends.'

John Anderson nodded triumphantly. 'I knew that all wasn't as it appeared, sir.'

'Master Robertson—we'll continue to call him that for reasons that will soon become apparent—should not be aboard the *Pallas* or any ship. Mr Anderson, the boy is my nephew.' He paused for effect. 'My brother, Viscount Farleigh, has strictly forbidden George a career at sea. The boy, naturally, wants nothing else. He has therefore run away from home to pursue his dream. He didn't, of course, anticipate a brush with Captain Bodmin's men. I don't need to impress on you, Mr Anderson, exactly what my brother's response would be should any harm come to George while he's in my care. It's bad enough that I failed to recognise the wretched boy beneath his disguise of filth and rags and halfwit trickery.' Nathaniel sighed and took a gulp of brandy. 'I suppose Henry's overprotectiveness is understandable, given that George is his oldest son and therefore ultimately heir to the earldom of Porchester.'

'Dear Lord!' Mr Anderson exclaimed with feeling.

'Puts me in a bit of a quandary and no mistake. Until I can deliver the boy back to my brother, I'll have to keep a very close eye on him. If Henry knew that his son had been sleeping in a hammock squashed amongst those of the midshipmen, he'd have a fit!'

The lieutenant saw an opportunity to solve the captain's problem. 'The boy may share my cabin, sir, and I'll see to it that he's kept safe.'

The thought of Miss Raithwaite sharing a cabin with the most personable First Lieutenant Anderson brought an uncommonly disgruntled feeling to Nathaniel Hawke. If he had not known better, he would have thought it reminiscent of jealousy. 'An admirable offer, Lieutenant, but quite unnecessary. I mean to have the boy as my personal servant. He shall sleep within my own cabin.'

Georgiana, whose ear was pressed firmly to the wooden connecting door, almost fell against the supporting structure at Captain Hawke's words. She had to admit that the story Nathaniel had concocted at such short notice was reasonably believable; in fact, she'd been admiring the gentleman's quick wits and imagination—up until his last utterance.

Nathaniel continued, blissfully unaware of Georgiana's rising indignation at the other side of the door. 'This apparent favouritism is bound to lead to supposition by the men. And it will be all the worse if the true nature of our relationship is not known.'

Mr Anderson's sharp intake of air at Captain Hawke's remark led to an inhalation of brandy and a subsequent plethora of coughing and spluttering. 'Quite so, sir.'

'Perhaps I could rely on you to see that the men are informed, by covert means, of course. A chance remark in Mr Pensenby's ear should suffice.'

The first lieutenant smiled. 'I'll see to it right away, sir.' He finished the brandy without coughing. 'It'll be all round the ship by lunchtime tomorrow.'

Captain Hawke raised his glass in salute. 'That will do nicely, Mr Anderson, very nicely indeed.'

By the time First Lieutenant Anderson exited Captain Hawke's day cabin, Georgiana was adamant that there was no way on earth that she would share a cabin with Nathaniel Hawke. She had even rehearsed a polite refusal of his offer, for undoubtedly he thought it the gentlemanly thing to do. *Thank you, Captain Hawke. You are most kind in your offer, but I cannot comply. It would be quite unseemly behaviour for a lady.* But then, Georgiana reflected, hadn't the vast majority of her behaviour of late come under that description? She sat down on the bed, touched her left hand to the lobe of her ear and worried at it as she set about thinking what her best course of action should be. In truth, there were not a great many options available. She was still mulling over various scenarios when Captain Hawke entered. Georgiana jumped up from the bed.

'You didn't knock,' she said, and her voice sounded breathless within the small confines of the cabin.

Nathaniel's eyebrow lifted and a tiny smile tugged at the corners of his mouth. 'I didn't mean to startle you, Miss Raithwaite—or should I say George? Now that I've revealed to Mr Anderson that you are in truth my nephew, Lord George Hawke, it's advisable that we stay in our respective roles at all times. Just think what he would say if I mistakenly referred to Miss Raithwaite!' Nathaniel pulled such a comical expression that the ponderous burden of anxiety eased itself from Georgiana's shoulders and she laughed.

'Should I then call you Uncle Nathaniel?' A mischievous light shone in her eyes.

Nathaniel grinned provocatively, as he stepped forward. 'Only when we're alone.'

She was so close that he could smell the clean soapy aroma arising from her jagged riot of ebony locks. She was still laughing as she turned her face up to his. Long sooty lashes swept up to reveal those magnificent eyes. Quite suddenly the laughter had gone and an arc of tension leapt between them. Georgiana was not a small woman, but the top of her head only met with Nathaniel's shoulder. He experienced an urge to pull her into his arms. It was absurd and completely unreasonable. And no matter his father's thoughts to the contrary, Captain Hawke was too much of a gentleman to take advantage of a lady in any situation. Calmly, deliberately, he moved back and looked away, pretending to examine the books lying open upon his table. 'But as you are pretending to be my nephew, and my nephew is pretending not to be my nephew…' he twitched his brow comically '…then it should suffice to call me Captain Hawke.'

A flicker of excitement exploded in Georgiana's belly the minute she looked into those dark smouldering eyes. Eyes that seemed to enchant her will, so that she could not remain unaffected whatever her resolve. No. Sharing a cabin with this man would be positively dangerous. And as the night was drawing in they had best resolve the issue here and now. She moved the chair to the far end of the tiny cabin and sat herself down on it in a ladylike fashion.

Nathaniel tried not to notice her legs that looked to be long and shapely within the culottes.

She pressed her hands demurely together and began. 'Captain Hawke, I couldn't help but overhear your words to First Lieutenant Anderson.'

'You were eavesdropping?' He looked up with surprise.

Georgiana had the grace to blush. 'It couldn't be helped, sir. The wall is so very thin.'

Nathaniel raised a cynical brow in her direction.

'It's very clever of you to play a double bluff so that the crew think they have discovered that I'm your nephew.'

The deep dark eyes regarded her, but he did not reply.

'I'd like to thank you for helping me. I'm aware of the difficulty my presence must present to you.'

He sincerely doubted whether Miss Raithwaite fully understood the precise nature of the difficulties that she presented, and he was not about to enlighten her. 'It's nothing that cannot be surmounted.'

'Nevertheless, would it not be more sensible for me to continue as before? It would certainly be less problematic to you, and is the option that is least likely to attract attention.'

'You've underestimated Mr Pensenby's preoccupation with naval regulations. You've slighted him before the crew. Direct disobedience with no punishment. And all seemingly because you're my nephew. The matter won't sit well with my second lieutenant. Indeed, he's probably worrying himself into a frenzy over the blatant breach in protocol. The man has a nose for subterfuge. Can sniff it out at twenty paces. Why do you think I want you under my command? Reverting to your previous role would be too risky, and I cannot allow it.'

She tossed her head in exasperation, even though she knew that he spoke the truth. Pensenby had the tenacity of an elephant, he would never forget and his curiosity had been roused. The prospect of such a man discovering her real secret was too dangerous, for who knew what Pensenby would do with the knowledge, being such a stickler for conformity and, according to Nathaniel, the nephew of Rear Admiral Stanley. 'Yes. I believe you're a good judge of character.' She looked at Nathaniel shrewdly. 'Then I'm to act as your servant?'

Nathaniel gave a brief nod of the head. 'It's the best I can think of to protect you,' he said simply. 'It will keep you close to me.'

A faint blush stole over Georgiana's cheeks at his words. She cleared her throat and attempted to look nonchalant while not meeting his eye. 'What of the sleeping arrangements? I know that you don't wish me to continue in my place down in the midshipmen's berth, but…'

'Surely you must have heard my comment to Mr Anderson? You heard everything else.' His eyes held a twinkle and his lips the glimmer of a wicked smile. 'You will sleep here, Miss Raithwaite.' He gestured towards the cot taking up most of the small cabin space.

It seemed that her heart lurched to a halt within her chest before setting off again at full tilt. She stared at him, shocked, horrified at the words he had just spoken, but beneath it all crept a tiny sliver of desire. And it was this that caused Georgiana to exclaim in a tone so frosty that it could have frozen the Thames, 'I beg your pardon, Captain Hawke. I believe I must have misheard you.' All thoughts of the polite refusal she had rehearsed were forgotten.

Nathaniel's eyes glowed even more wickedly. 'Your hearing cannot be faulted, nephew George. You will sleep in my bed.' He tried hard not to laugh at the expression of fury that was forming upon Miss Raithwaite's normally sweet face.

'Captain Hawke—' she stood up quite suddenly '—no gentleman would suggest such a scandalous arrangement. You cannot honestly expect me to… I assure you that it's quite out of the question. What kind of woman do you take me for?' Miss Raithwaite's eyes flashed with the violence of the stormiest sea. With her head held high and her hands planted firmly on her hips, she presented an admirable sight.

Nathaniel's fingers touched to his breast, and he feigned a look of total astonishment, which soon turned to one of most convincing wounded insult. 'Miss Raithwaite,' he gasped. 'You cannot think…? You did not…? Heavens above, dear girl, what kind of man do you take me for?'

The hurricane dropped out of Georgiana's sails. She looked suddenly very unsure of herself.

'You will sleep in here, Miss Raithwaite, and I—I will sleep next door.' Nathaniel was modelling his manner on the pompous Mr Pensenby. 'Anything else would be most unseemly behaviour for a lady, most unseemly indeed.'

Her skin burned the fiery red of embarrassment. 'Of course… Please accept my apologies, Captain Hawke, I thought—'

'I know very well what you thought, Miss Raithwaite,' replied Nathaniel with a grin. Something of Georgiana's excruciating discomfort showed in her face and it tugged at Nathaniel's heart. A pang of guilt smote him. 'I have a confession to make.'

Georgiana's heart trembled a little. He was in earnest. She looked at the captain with escalating suspicion.

Nathaniel's grin cracked wider. 'I'm teasing you.'

Her mouth opened wide. 'Why, you… That was a most ungentlemanly thing to do!' She stepped towards him.

'I couldn't resist it. You're so very charming when you're angry.' He laughed aloud.

'You, sir, are a rogue!' announced Georgiana with force, but her eyes had calmed to a tranquil blue and her mouth turned up at the corners.

It was Nathaniel's turn to look sheepish. He held out his hands towards her. 'You're right. I shouldn't have tricked you. I do beg your pardon.'

'I shall have to think about it, Captain Hawke,' she said in her sweetest voice.

'I fear the worst, sir, it's as we thought. The hank of hair beneath her bed, the kitchen scissors within her bedroom, and the missing clothes belonging to Francis—all evidence points in one direction only. The wretched girl has brought disgrace on us all.' Edward

Raithwaite pinched the skin between his eyes and crumpled back in his chair.

The man seated opposite him rose. 'If I may be so bold, Mr Raithwaite, as to suggest that some brandy is required.' When Edward Raithwaite nodded limply, the man set out two balloon glasses and dispensed the tawny liquid. Passing the measure to the older man, he sat back down before resuming the conversation. 'It's not too late to discover her direction and halt her progress, but we must not delay our action, for every minute that we wait she travels further from the security of your home, and closer to danger.'

Mr Raithwaite's heavy-lidded eyes had succumbed to the temptation to close. He sipped at the brandy without trying to open them. 'How dare she do this to me? It's just reward for the selfish pampering by her mother. Clara was always too soft with the girl. And now look where it's got us. We shall all bear the brunt of her silly action. To be the subject of such petty gossip and infamy when all I am guilty of is living my life as a decent upstanding man of business. What have I done to deserve such a daughter, when I have struggled to do nothing but my best for her?' He seemed content to wallow for a little longer in a quagmire of self-pity.

'You've done nothing sir, save to act as a father. All of your actions have been only with Miss Raithwaite's best interests at heart, even to the point of sending her to Mrs Tillyard's Academy for Young Ladies. It seems that, despite your aspirations, all that she learned was to follow her own will.'

'A stubborn and self-gratifying will at that,' added her father.

The man inclined his golden head. 'She is perhaps a trifle strong-willed, but, in the hands of the right husband, such a flaw could be remedied.' He smiled, revealing a row of perfect white teeth to offset the pretty looks of his face.

'Our plans fade to dust, Praxton. What desire have you for a woman whose reputation is tarnished? She has absconded, dressed as a boy! For all we know she's run off with a lover!' He clamped his large loose-skinned hands over his face. 'Oh, heaven help us, for we're soon to be a laughing stock throughout the town, and wherever else this story travels.'

Walter Praxton examined his nails before replying. 'All is not lost, sir, for I have it on good authority that a young boy matching your daughter's height and build was observed to take the evening mail to Gosport on the night in question. A boy that no one of the town knew, and who didn't alight from any other coach. He was quite alone amidst the travellers, no sign of any possible *lover.* I rather think—' his mouth twisted to a crooked semblance of a smile '—that the reason for Miss Raithwaite's flight was due to her determination not to become my wife.'

Mr Raithwaite's eyes opened at that. 'Surely you're mistaken, for, no matter what she thinks she feels, Georgiana would not disobey me so blatantly.'

'I doubt that your daughter views the situation in quite the same way.'

The grizzled head shook once more. 'I'll put it about that she's gone to stay with an elderly relative in Scotland. At least that may buy us some time with which to attempt to remedy this damnable mess. When I get my hands on her—'

Mr Praxton swiftly interrupted. 'The betrothal is still binding. If I can discover her location, then the situation might be resolved if I were to immediately marry Miss Raithwaite. That way she could return here as my wife, with all threat of scandal avoided. Do I have your permission to force her to a speedy exchange of vows by whatever means are required?'

'You would still wed her, after all she's done? What if she's dishonoured? A fallen woman? Would you take her even then?' Edward Raithwaite's tired eyes focused with a new clarity.

'I would take her whatever the circumstance, provided that any threat of ensuing scandal could be extinguished.'

The older man leaned forward and with a deliberate and careful manner said, 'Well, in that case, Mr Praxton, you must do whatever you deem necessary to resolve this matter satisfactorily. You have my full support.' One fleshy hand thrust forward and clasped Mr Praxton's in a firm shake. 'I wish you Godspeed, Walter, and may you save the situation for us all.'

* * *

Mr Praxton glanced back only once at Tythecock Crescent, and as he did anyone close by would have heard him utter softly, 'I will have you, Georgiana Raithwaite. One way or another, you are mine.'

Chapter Five

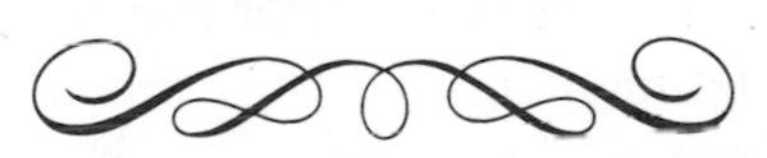

Captain Hawke was taking the noon sight with Lieutenants Anderson and Pensenby, and the young midshipmen. The murmuring hush of their voices lapped against his ears as, armed with their sextants, they compared measurements and subsequent calculations of the ship's latitude. Across the breadth of the forecastle he could see Jenkins, the quartermaster, at the great steering wheel, hands firm upon the burnished wood. Canvas flapped and ropes creaked as the wind moved to catch the sails. He stifled a yawn and, turning to look out across the great expanse of the cold grey water, thought of the previous night spent sitting upright in his captain's chair. Little wonder that he'd only managed to catnap through the long dark hours, and had been up on deck before the bosun had piped the hands just before dawn. In truth, he had pondered long and hard over the matter of Miss Georgiana Raithwaite.

It was unfortunate that for this trip none of the officers had brought their wives along for company. Indeed, there were no women aboard, only one hundred and eighty-five men. Nathaniel grimaced and corrected himself. One hundred and eighty-five men and one lady. A lady whose ability to place herself in quite the worst situations possible was equalled by none. To have almost drowned in the River Borne was one thing. To have run away from home, been taken by the Press Gang and worked, disguised as a boy, undetected upon his ship for two weeks was quite another. That the captain of that ship could have failed to notice such an absurd thing was preposterous.

He glanced once more at the group of young men behind him. Such enthusiasm, such commitment. If any one of them learned of Miss Raithwaite's secret, she would be well and truly ruined—if she wasn't already. And despite what his father thought, that was something Nathaniel could not let happen. The girl affected him far more than he was willing to own—her courage in the face of what for her was most definitely a disastrous situation, the transparency of emotion upon her face, those eyes that mirrored the colour of the sea before him. That he was attracted to her was obvious. He'd felt it since the moment she opened her eyes and looked up at him on the riverbank, her long hair dripping river water, her body relaxed and trusting in his arms. It had obviously been too long since he'd had a woman. A physical need, nothing more. But even as the thought formed, he knew it wasn't true. What he felt for her was much more than that, more than he was ready to admit.

Quite how Miss Raithwaite had escaped detection was nothing short of a miracle. He gripped the smooth wood of the quarterdeck rail with tense hands. It was imperative that no one should discover the true identity of Lord George Hawke or, indeed, Master George Robertson. He walked back to the small group of would-be officers without a hint of the worry that plagued his mind or the fatigue that pulled at his body.

Georgiana was helping Mr Fraser, the captain's valet, in cleansing the great man's clothes. She struggled to hold back her laughter at the reverential voice that Gordon Fraser constantly adopted when speaking of Captain Hawke.

'Now, Master Robertson,' Mr Fraser said in his lilting Scottish tones, 'it is vital that *Captain Hawke*'s shirts—' he lowered his voice as he uttered his master's name '—are treated exactly to his liking. Gather up the washing tub and follow me.' He marched off across the deck with the manner of a schoolmaster who would brook no nonsense.

Georgiana did as she was bid, scooping the wooden basin under one arm and holding three of Nathaniel's shirts in the other hand.

They stopped before a large wooden cask. 'Off with the lid and fill your basin.' Mr Fraser stood well back.

'Yes, sir.' Georgiana prised the lid off and promptly dropped both the basin and the shirts in her hurry to scramble away. 'Dear Lord!' she mumbled beneath her breath and retched.

Mr Fraser pursed his lips. The boy had to learn, even if he was the captain's nephew, perhaps even more so. 'We haven't got all day, laddie. Now, retrieve your basin and *Captain Hawke*'s shirts, and do as you're bid.'

The hard biscuit and apple eaten for luncheon were threatening to make a reappearance upon the deck. Georgiana's stomach heaved. 'What on earth…?'

'That's quite enough, Master Robertson. Stop behaving like a namby-pamby and get back over there.' He twirled at his grey moustache.

Georgiana held her nose, approached the cask, and fulfilled Mr Fraser's requirements as quickly as she could. The liquid slopping within the basin was dark brown in colour and stank to high heaven.

'Submerge the shirts and scrub around the cuffs and collar to remove any marks.' He handed her a small brush.

The thought of plunging her hands into the vile liquid brought Georgiana's stomach back up into her throat. 'Yes, Mr Fraser,' she managed to croak.

'When you're sure there are no stains left, you can start using the soap. Then give them a good rinse in sea water from the cask over there. Ring them out and then peg them on to the line fixed at the far corner. After that I'll instruct you in the care of the *captain*'s boots.' Mr Fraser was clearly used to giving orders.

The stench was unbearable and her hands were soon red raw with the scrubbing. It occurred to Georgiana that perhaps a gunroom servant hadn't been such a bad job after all. Finally the chore was done and she was just pegging the shirts on the line when Captain Hawke and the boatswain wandered by, deep in conversation. Nathaniel's eyes held hers for a moment, although he gave no other outward sign of having seen her, and in the next instant he had passed by. Irrational as it was, Georgiana felt a pang of annoyance. What did she expect him to do? Execute a tidy bow at his ship's boy? Enquire as to her health this fine afternoon? Georgiana grumped back down to Mr Fraser.

'You managed then, boy?' Mr Fraser's single jaundiced eye was trained upon her.

She stifled the words that so longed to jump off the tip of her tongue. 'Yes, Mr Fraser, sir.' The old man was kind enough for all his stern ways.

'You'll soon get used to the washing stench. Stale piss is never fragrant. And it'll have grown a mite more pungent by the time we reach our destination.'

The blood drained from Georgiana's face, leaving her powder white. 'Stale piss?' she uttered faintly.

'What else did you think it was?' retorted Mr Fraser with a snort. 'There's nothing better for shifting dirt.' He noticed his assistant's pallor. 'You've a lot yet to learn, laddie, a lot to learn.' Shaking his head, he went to fetch the revered Captain Hawke's boots and shoes.

The pillow was plump and soft and smelled of Nathaniel Hawke. Sandalwood and soap and a distinctly masculine aroma. Georgiana snuggled beneath the covers and marvelled at the luxury. No choir of snores, wheezes and coughs, no foul odours from a multitude of youthful male bodies, no scuttle of rodents. Bliss! During her two weeks in the midshipmen's berth she had failed miserably in her attempt to grow used to the narrow hammock strung so closely between those of Mr Hartley and Mr Burrows. Each night had seen her lying rigid and afraid to move, lest she fell out, until she found sleep by virtue of sheer exhaustion. The alternative of sleeping on the dampness of the deck below, amidst the spiders and the rats, was too awful to contemplate. She stretched out her spine, unmindful of her bindings, and pulled the sheet up to meet her nose. A contented sigh escaped. Such warmth, such comfort. She sighed and wriggled her legs around.

It was wonderful to be able to relax, to drop her vigilance of trying to disguise her voice, her manners and all feminine tendencies, which, she had come to realise, were too numerous to count. A space of her own. Privacy. Safety from discovery. Heaven only knew what Mama would do if she knew her situation. Swoon, no doubt. It was the first time that she'd allowed herself to think of Mama, of little Prudence and Theo. Even her stepbrother Francis with all his teasing and impudence did not seem so bad. Please God, keep them safe. She felt her eyes begin to well and took a deep breath to allay the tears that threatened to fall. Mama would be worried sick, not knowing where she was, and Papa… Papa would be livid. In her rush to escape marriage to Mr Praxton, she'd only succeeded in making things difficult for her family. There would be gossip, and worse. Denigration, castigation, direct snubs. Poor Mama. She wept silently, stifling her sobs in Nathaniel Hawke's pillow. Sleep finally found her with swollen eyelids and the taste of saline upon her lips.

It was still dark. Georgiana's eyes strained against the gloom. It seemed barely five minutes since she had laid her head on the pillow. Nathaniel's soft tread sounded from the adjoining cabin. A dull pain thrummed around her head. She groaned, dragged her fatigued body from the bed and started to dress herself. Late, she was late. What would Mr Fraser say? No time for boots.

Nathaniel sipped at the brandy and stared at the charts laid on the desk before him. It was a little after two o'clock and he still could not find sleep. The lantern light flickered as he moved to peer blindly from the windows. He had stood there some time when he heard the noise, and turned with confusion to look at the connecting door. Therein lay the reason for his insomnia. The indomitable Miss Raithwaite, who had not the slightest notion of the precarious position into which she had thrust herself. He smiled at the memory of her determined face—she certainly did not enter into anything faint-heartedly. Even as he thought it the door creaked open and Miss Raithwaite—or should he say Master Robertson?—stumbled out fully dressed. 'George?' he quizzed lightly.

'On my way to my station, Captain, sir,' she pronounced through tired lips and dragged herself towards the door. She had reverted to her 'boy's' voice even though they were alone.

Nathaniel's eyes opened wide, suddenly alert. 'George,' he said again and moved to grab at her shoulders.

Georgiana's sleep-fuddled mind could not comprehend what had happened, only that she now found herself staring up into Nathaniel Hawke's handsome face. 'Late, I'm late,' she mumbled, and tried to disengage herself.

He gathered her slender body into his arms and held her against him. She did not protest further, just laid her head against his shoulder. Nathaniel swallowed hard. She was warm and soft. The effects of the brandy swam through his brain. His hand swept across her back, moving up to touch the delicate nape of her neck. No woman had ever felt this right. He pressed a kiss to the top of her head, revelling in the sweetness of her smell and with great reluctance held her away. 'You're sleep-addled, George. It's the dead of night, and you should still be asleep.' His winged eyebrow twitched as he smiled down at her.

'But I heard the hands piped.' Her voice was sleepy and low.

Nathaniel drew his thumb gently against her cheek. The skin was still soft and white. 'Perhaps in your dream.'

Georgiana could not move. Still heavy with sleep, she felt mesmerised by the man in whose arms she stood. His voice was gentle, and there was such kindness in his eyes that it gladdened her heart. Couldn't her stepfather have desired to marry her to a man such as this? A man who was just and fair, a man who had risked his life and now jeopardised his career to save her. She sighed, as his warm hands held her from him. He would never be interested in the likes of her, even if she hadn't made such a mess of things. Not when his father was the Earl of Porchester. For all his standing, Nathaniel Hawke would always do what was right.

'Let me help you back next door.' His voice was soft in her ear as he lifted her up fully into his arms, her bare feet brushing against his breeches.

Georgiana was surely dreaming, and it was the same stuff that had filled all her nocturnal thoughts of late. His arms were strong and he carried her as if she were the merest featherweight. She laid her head against the hard muscle of his chest and felt the rhythmic beat of his heart. A lady would not have done such a thing, Georgiana knew that implicitly, but still she did nothing but revel in the warm languor that was spreading throughout her body.

Nathaniel pushed open the connecting door, pulled back the covers and carefully laid Miss Raithwaite upon the bed. The strength of the feeling she invoked shocked him. She should not have to suffer the rigors of ship life in the guise of a fourteen-year-old boy. The sight of her washing his shirts had worried him and he had resolved to speak to Mr Fraser to go easy with the lad. Her head sank into the pillow and he made to release her. It certainly would not do to linger in such a situation.

Suddenly, without any warning whatsoever, even to herself, Georgiana succumbed to the mad impulse to wrap her hands around Nathaniel Hawke's neck.

Nathaniel froze, the breath caught in his throat.

She thrust her fingers through his auburn locks as she had so longed to do, trailing them down to feel the taut muscles in his neck. 'Closer, come closer.' The words escaped as a whisper. The dream felt very real.

Nathaniel stared down at where he knew her face to be. He knew without seeing that her eyelids would have swept shut. Through the darkness he felt her rise beneath him, touching her lips to his cheek in a chaste kiss.

'Oh, God!' The blasphemy tore in a gritty hush from his throat. Never had a man been so tempted. Her soft cheek pressed to his and his body responded instinctively. His lips turned to seek hers and, upon finding them, possessed them with a gentle insistence. Their lips writhed in a torment of ecstasy until his tongue could no longer resist the sweet allure of her mouth and raided within, seeking its hidden intimacy with an increasing fervour.

Georgiana floated in a blissful haze of delight. Her hands slid of their own accord across the broad muscle of his back, basking in the heat of his skin through the fine lawn of his shirt. More, she wanted more of this strange enchanting feeling.

The cot swayed as he clambered upon it and lay his length against her. The wool of his breeches could not disguise the feel of her legs beneath him. He fumbled with her shirt and soon felt the satin skin beneath his hand. She made an inarticulate little noise, but did not draw back. His fingers wove their sensual magic across her stomach, swirling up towards her breast, only to meet with the coarse linen wrap of her bindings. It was enough to bring Nathaniel crashing to his senses. In that single instant he realised their predicament, and stopped.

'Nathaniel?' Miss Raithwaite's sleepy whisper sounded through the darkness.

Hell's teeth, it was enough to tempt a saint! Slowly, gently, he disengaged himself from the slender soft arms surrounding him. 'You're sleep-addled. Miss Raithwaite. I must not take advantage of a lady in my care.' His teeth gritted in determination. 'Please forgive me.' And, so saying, he turned and strode briskly from the cabin, closing the door firmly behind him.

In the weeks that passed Captain Hawke took considerable care that just such a situation did not arise again. He threw himself into his work upon the *Pallas* and struggled to think of his ship's boy as George Robertson rather than Miss Raithwaite. The task proved difficult, but not impossible. His illicit actions of that night had shaken him more than he cared to admit. For in acknowledging the young woman's allure and his own inappropriate response, he felt that he had behaved as the singular debauchee his father thought him. He had embraced the role willingly for those tender few minutes, had revelled in Georgiana Raithwaite's warm caress, until he'd realised the shamefulness of what he was doing. And the thought repulsed him. He thrust it away, determined to think no more of that night. Mercifully Miss Raithwaite had made no mention of the incident, and continued to adopt her guise of the ship's boy, revealing nothing more by her outward demeanour. Perhaps the fates had been kind to him, and robbed her of the sleep-laden memory. It was a prayer uttered most fervently by Nathaniel, although he was not naïve enough to believe that it would be answered.

Georgiana had woken to a heaving frenzy of conflicting emotions. Not only did she have a very clear and precise memory of her actions of the previous night but she also had to admit to having experienced a distinct pang of disappointment when Nathaniel Hawke had behaved like the gentleman he was and refused to continue his interest. She, on the other hand, to her extreme chagrin, had behaved like a wanton and was subsequently reaping a much-deserved vengeance of guilt. It was her first kiss, the first tentative touch of a man's body. How could Miss Georgiana Raithwaite have behaved like a veritable slattern? With her fancy schooling, formidable parenting and proper Christian upbringing, she was nothing but a drab. She cringed when she thought what she had tried to do, the blatant seduction of a man who had done nothing but sought to help her. What must he have thought of her? Utter abhorrence, nothing less. Especially in view of what he thought she had been about with Mr Praxton in Hurstborne Park. Oh, Lord! She still had to face him. Confusion, fear and guilt vied in her breast.

With frank determination Georgiana pulled her fragmented emotions together, squared her shoulders and decided that she would pretend that the incident had never happened. It seemed the only way to survive the months that lay ahead. In all the days and weeks that rushed past with gathering momentum she threw herself body and soul into the role of the captain's boy. Georgiana Raithwaite no longer existed, only the juvenile George Robertson. And through the boy she learned to quell the attraction she felt for Captain Nathaniel Hawke.

'Take in all the canvas until she's bare. We'll have to try-a-hull. Have the galley fire extinguished and check that the magazines are secured.' Captain Hawke lowered the small brass spyglass from his eye and turned to face Mr Anderson. 'There's a storm brewing, and from the cloud formation I'd say it'll have its way with us if we're not careful.'

'Aye, Captain. It doesn't look good.'

'With the wind the way it is we can't tack safely into it and any other move would have us well off course, or worse. Our best option is to weather the storm until it passes.'

John Anderson nodded his head. He'd trust Nathaniel Hawke above all others. The man had an uncanny ability for choosing wisely, even if it did appear sometimes slightly questionable to those who had neither his knowledge nor his experience.

The deck heaved beneath their feet as the white-crested waves buffeted the bow of the *Pallas*. The wind howled above the roar of the waves. All around them timber groaned and creaked as the sails were retracted. Men climbed fast, loosing the ropes, securing them again when the canvases had been taken in. Spray stung at their faces, dripped from their hair, soaking their clothes and drenching the decks.

'All men to stay below other than are absolutely necessary up here. I'd say we have twenty minutes at the most before it reaches us.' Nathaniel's face was grim.

'Yes, sir.' Lieutenant Anderson watched his captain's determined stance, a shiver of apprehension snaking down his spine. 'What's so bad, sir? We've suffered storms before and faired well enough.'

He did not want to frighten the young man, but forewarned was forearmed. 'Never a storm like the one that's coming for us now. Pray to God, Mr Anderson, that it passes quickly.'

'Promise me, George, that you'll stay in my day cabin until the storm has passed.'

She could see the anxiety in that determined glare. For a moment she thought that it was true what they said—the eyes were the windows to the soul, and Nathaniel Hawke's soul was concerned by whatever he had seen sweeping down towards them across the ocean. He cared no more or no less about any man aboard the *Pallas*. Each was a member of his crew; he saw every one of them as his responsibility. 'Yes, sir. There's darning to be done and I'll keep myself busy with the linen repairs.'

Still he seemed restless and uneasy. 'Promise me,' he said, his voice quiet and insistent. Seawater dripped from dark, sodden hair to run down his cheeks.

'I'll give you no cause to worry more over me than any other man or boy aboard this ship. I promise I'll do as you command.'

Lines of tension were deeply etched into the flesh around his mouth, his coiled energy palpable within the confines of the small cabin. She longed to give him some measure of comfort, some little encouragement in the task that lay ahead. Wanted to touch her lips to his and tell him that all would be well. But George Robertson could not. She forced a smile to her mouth.

He stood still, silent, and regarded her for a minute, a single long minute, with an unreadable expression upon his face. Then turned and walked towards the door, shouting over his shoulder, 'Fraser and the others will keep you company. It's going to be a very long day and an even longer night.'

The waves grew larger as the wind set up a banshee howl. Through the windows in Nathaniel's cabin, ship's boy George Robertson watched the cold grey sea whip into a fury of froth and lashing fingers. It attacked the ship with violence as the sky darkened to a deep lifeless hue, chasing the light away. Only three bells had sounded, but already they could scarcely see within the captain's cabin. The *Pallas* pitched and rolled at the mercy of the roaring ocean, her pine structure creaking and groaning under the strain. The holed bed linen slithered to the floor undarned as Georgiana clung to the unlit candle sconce. Waves battered at the feeble glass of the windows until she thought they surely must shatter beneath the hostile assault. A single lantern swung from the ceiling, lurching and swaying with the convulsions of the ship, illuminating the captain's servants as monstrous distortions.

'How're you doin', laddie?' Mr Fraser's lilting voice enquired. He raised his head from the game of cards that he was enjoying with Bottomley, the captain's cook, and Spence, the captain's steward.

'Survivin', thank you, sir. Will the storm last long?'

The grizzled grey head concentrated upon his hand of cards. 'As long as it has a mind to last, no' a moment less.'

A wave battered the stern, sending Georgiana hurtling across the room.

'Steady, lad!' the valet exclaimed, reaching out a gnarled old hand and hoisting the boy back by the scruff of the neck.

Three books fell off Nathaniel's desk and a silver wine goblet rolled across the floor. Bottomley stopped it dead with his toe. Just when Georgiana thought that things could not possibly get any worse, a torrent of rain was released from the heavens to beat the *Pallas* into submission. A sheet of driving shards lashed the frigate without mercy and a rumble of thunder cracked loud. Somewhere across the deep darkness a tiny flicker lit up the sky, then it was gone as quickly as it had appeared. Dear Lord, nothing could hope to survive against such ferocity.

Fear twisted at Georgiana's gut. 'Where's the captain?'

'Up on deck.' Mr Fraser's single eye focused upon the boy and softened a little. 'No need to worry, laddie. The captain knows what he's doin'. Been through a hundred storms, he has, and never got caught yet.'

'But shouldn't we be helpin', sir?' The thought of any man, let alone Nathaniel Hawke, out facing the wrath of the heavens was worrying in the extreme.

Mr Fraser shook his head. 'We'd only create more hindrance than help. The captain'll send for us if he needs us. Best to just stay out the way and look after his cabin.' The boy's eyes looked huge in the whitened pallor of his face. Poor lad. 'It'll pass soon enough, laddie. Best turn your mind to other things.'

A pile of papers slid off the desk and landed with a thud by her leg. She grabbed them and crawled along the floor to stuff them inside a drawer. Mr Fraser was right. There was nothing any of them could do about it, other than wait for the storm to pass, and pray that the *Pallas*' crew remained safe.

The thunder rolled across the sky, masking the muffled knock at the door. A drenched seaman staggered in, dripping water across the polished wooden floor. 'Man overboard,' he said through gasping breath.

'Who?' Mr Fraser's single eye widened at the news.

'Midshipmen Hartley.'

'Are we needed?' His ancient tone was clipped, determined.

'Not yet.'

And the sailor was gone.

Time dragged by. And still the storm showed no sign of abating. Georgiana hoped that Mr Hartley had been saved, but even as she turned her gaze once more to the large sea-battered windows she knew it was unlikely that anyone plunged into such a furore of indomitable wave power could survive. Drowned beneath the towering waves, or smashed like a weightless puppet against the hull. Dear God protect them all, she prayed like she never had done before, protect them all, but especially Nathaniel Hawke. Fear that he might be injured or, God forbid, die, pierced a pain through her heart. Never that, please Lord, never that. Why should she care so much for him? Was it his kindness or his strength, or the way he was just and fair? Maybe it was because he made her laugh, made her want to be with him? She laid her head against the edge of Nathaniel's desk, clinging tightly to the wooden leg with one hand, worrying at her ear lobe with the other. Whatever the answer, ship's boy George Robertson had no right to such feelings. Whether Georgiana Raithwaite did was another matter altogether.

Georgiana awoke to the stern tones of Mr Fraser and a vigorous shaking of her shoulder. 'Robertson, waken yourself now, laddie. There's plenty work to be done. It's no time to be nappin'.'

The violent heave of the frigate was no more. No batter of rain, no riot of waves, no screaming darkness. She crawled out from beneath the captain's desk and made for the windows. A calm leaden sea and colourless sky stretched endlessly ahead.

She turned to the elderly valet. 'Mr Hartley, sir?' The question had to be asked.

'They fished him out alive, if not well.'

'Thank God!'

Mr Fraser's eye narrowed. 'There'll be no takin' the Lord's name in vain on this ship.'

'And the captain?'

Fraser mellowed slightly at the anxiety-edged voice. 'In fine mettle as ever. Come on, laddie, you're gabbin' like a fishwife. You youngsters would do anythin' to avoid work. Got to keep my eye on you!' His single eye stared large and cod-like at Georgiana.

'Yes, Mr Fraser, sir.' She breathed her relief and watched while the cod eye delivered her a hearty wink.

Nathaniel was exhausted, but he knew that there was still much to be done before he could rest. Jeremiah Hutton and his assistants were already sawing up wooden spars to repair the damage done to the mizzen topgallant mast. Debris strewn across the decks was in the process of being cleared. And midshipman Hartley had apparently survived his ordeal with little more than a scratch to his arm.

Georgiana clambered upon the forecastle and surveyed the damage. 'Set to it, lad.' A basin was pressed into her hands. 'Gather up seaweed and all else, exceptin' fish, heave it over t'side. Look smart, now.' She felt a thrust in her back and the voice was gone.

Pieces of wood, shells, dead and dying fish and stinking seaweed covered the floor before her. She scanned up towards the quarterdeck for any sign of Nathaniel. The seaweed squelched cold and slimy beneath her fingers. Sam Wilson's thin body emerged ahead, gathering up the fish in his basin.

'Sammy!' she hailed.

The little lad looked round. 'George! Place ain't been the same without you.'

'It's good to see you too.' She embraced the skinny body, glad that the orphaned youngster had survived the storm unscathed. Sam Wilson worried her more than she let anyone know. 'Have you been helpin' Jack like I told you to?'

'Yeah, I'm Jack's mate. He's learning me knots for the riggin', and he don't let no one cuff me, or take me grog.' Sam gave her a gap-toothed grin.

'What happened to your teeth?' Georgiana held the lad at arm's length and inspected his small grubby face.

He trailed a dirty hand across his runny nose. 'Fell out when I was eatin' me biscuit. Jack says more'll grow.'

Georgiana smiled at the small ragamuffin before her and ruffled his matted hair. Poor little mite, thank goodness Burly Jack was looking out for him.

'Master Robertson,' a curt voice sounded. 'Much as I hate to interrupt your little reunion, there's work to be done aboard this frigate. And that means for all of us, no matter who we might happen to be.' The veiled snub hit home, causing Georgiana to blush and resume her debris collection with renewed vigour. Lieutenant Pensenby leaned back against the railing and watched the boy's progression with shrewd eyes. There was something strange about George Robertson, something very strange indeed. The way that he'd hugged ship's boy Wilson, the clear, fine-boned face. It smacked of something unnatural, even if he was the captain's nephew, or at least purported to be. Perhaps Captain Hawke was not quite the hero everyone thought. All was not as it presented itself, of that Cyril Pensenby was sure, and, one way or another, he meant to get to the bottom of the puzzle.

Captain Hawke worked solidly for the next two days, ensuring that every last speck of storm damage on the *Pallas* was repaired. He had already left the day cabin when Georgiana awoke and slipped through to pass to the station call for drill each morning, not returning until long after she had fallen asleep within the comfort of his cot. On the third day she had entered the captain's cabin with a pile of freshly pressed neckcloths to find him poring over charts with both his lieutenants. The great stern windows striped pale winter daylight across the three men. Crossing quietly to his great sea chest, that he had had moved from the night cabin, she made to stow the linen safely and retreat without notice. Their voices mumbled in conversation, but she kept her head down and her eyes averted. She had almost reached the door when Nathaniel spoke out.

'Wait behind, Robertson. I want to speak with you before you continue with your duties.'

She had no choice but to do as she was bid, hovering awkwardly near the exit while the captain finished his business with the lieutenants. Both men's gazes washed over her, but the weight of Pensenby's stare drew her attention. She glanced up to catch his regard, and the look within those small overly-curious eyes made her wary. Captain Hawke had not been wrong in his estimation of Second Lieutenant Pensenby. And the knowledge released in her a small spasm of worry.

The door closed.

'Sit down, George.'

She glanced once more at the cabin door as if to make sure Pensenby was gone, and moved to one of the chairs positioned beside the captain's desk.

'Captain Hawke,' she said quietly, inclining her head like some great lady, and composedly sat herself down.

Nathaniel watched the graceful figure before him. He cleared his throat and adjusted his neckcloth. 'I just wanted to be sure that you took no hurts from the storm.'

Georgiana bowed her head to hide the smile that leapt to her lips. Nathaniel Hawke had been worried about her after all, and the thought, inappropriate as it was, brought a gladness to her heart. 'None at all, thank you for your concern, sir. Mr Fraser looked after me most admirably.'

'It must have been a frightening experience for you, all the same.' There was a concern in his eyes that he could not entirely mask.

Gcorgiana shrugged her shoulders slightly in a dismissive gesture. 'Yes, but not as fearful as the thought of those of you facing the storm up on the deck. When I heard that Mr Hartley had been washed overboard…'

'His rope snapped, carrying him over. Fortunately we were able to retrieve him.'

She smiled at him. 'It seems that on this occasion luck was on your side.'

'Luck plays her part, but experience, skill, a decent ship and a good crew of men are the foremost defences against a stormy sea.' He raised his brow, and the corners of his mouth tugged up in a crooked smile. 'I sound to be singing my own praises, but that isn't my intention. Your acclaim should be for the men who did their jobs so well in the face of the storm.'

Laughter played on her lips. 'Captain Hawke, an arrogant man? Who would have thought it?'

His eyes creased with the boyish grin, but beneath it she could see the toll fatigue was taking upon him.

'There's a tiredness in your face. You're bone weary and should rest.' The thought was spoken aloud. She glanced down in embarrassment, unwilling that he should guess the truth of her feelings for him. 'Forgive me, Captain, I shouldn't have spoken.'

One long tanned finger gently tipped her chin up. He was still smiling. 'Could it be that my nephew has a thought for my welfare?'

Georgiana could not prevent the colour that flooded her cheeks. 'Yes…no…I…' then exclaimed, 'You're teasing me again, sir. I should be about my duties.' She made to pull back, but he stopped her.

'Maybe so, but not before you've answered your captain's question, ship's boy Robertson.' Nathaniel's eyes shone wickedly.

He had not removed his hand from her chin, and in truth had no compulsion to do so. What was it about the dark-haired girl before him that attracted him so? Even during the long hours of work he had found himself desiring her company, to hear her clear voice, watch the rose blush grow in her cheeks when he teased her, witness her enthusiasm for learning anything and everything she could about the ship. She had a good mind, that much was evident. A mind wasted as a third-class ship's boy. And the marriage mart of today would view it as a mind wasted on a woman. But Nathaniel did not think so.

When she looked at him her eyes were a cool, calm grey blue. 'I'm concerned for every man upon the *Pallas*, including her captain.'

'Even Mr Pensenby?' It seemed he was willing to say anything to prolong the conversation, anything to prevent her leaving. He had missed her these past days. The realisation hit him with the force of a mid-Atlantic gale.

The light in her face dimmed and a frown crept between her eyes. 'My concern is *about* Lieutenant Pensenby rather than *for* him.' Her fingers stole to worry at the lobe of her ear. 'It would seem that the second lieutenant does not quite believe our story. There's something in the way he looks at me, as if to say he knows something is amiss. Perhaps I'm just being fanciful, but it leaves me uneasy.'

'Yes.' Nathaniel looked pensive. 'My thoughts flow in a similar direction. We had best have a care where Pensenby is concerned. He has a scholar's mind for analysis and a passion for a puzzle. The sooner that his focus is trained on Bonaparte's forces, the better.'

They looked at each other, without further speech. And within each breast stirred disquiet and beneath it something else warm and joyous.

He touched his thumb to her cheek with gentle reassurance. 'Don't worry, I won't let him discover our secret, whatever it takes.'

A sense of unity blossomed between them, as if it were just the two of them together, against the world.

The severity of his gaze softened.

A knock at the door revealed Mr Fraser.

'There you are, laddie. If you're finished with the boy, I'll be off with him, Captain.'

Captain Hawke nodded his compliance. 'Go ahead, Mr Fraser.' But the dark eyes did not leave Georgiana's slender frame until she had departed his cabin.

'Mr Fraser,' he called as the grizzled head disappeared around the door.

'Aye, Captain?'

He looked at his valet meaningfully. 'Keep the boy within your sight at all times.'

Fraser's lone eye glared unblinkingly back. An unspoken understanding passed between them and he nodded. 'That I certainly will, sir.'

And he was gone, leaving Nathaniel to contemplate how best to deal with Lieutenant Pensenby.

Chapter Six

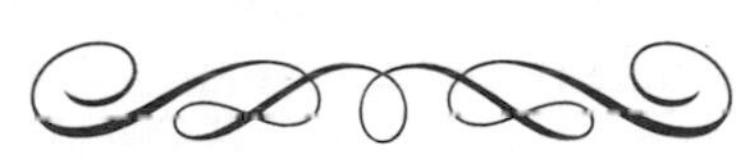

It was not long before they arrived in the warmer waters of their destination. Despite it being so late in the year the seas surrounding the Azores were clear and calm and of such a bright coloration that Georgiana never ceased to marvel at their beauty. The cold dark skies of England had been left far behind, replaced instead with a cloudless expanse of blue. Even more incredible was the temperature, for, as those novice members of the *Pallas*' crew discovered, it was pleasantly warm. Indeed, such was the sun that an awning was positioned over the quarterdeck each morning to protect the officers about their work. The men did not take such precautions from the heat, preferring instead to divest themselves of their shirts at any excuse. On first sight the exposure of masculine flesh rather shocked Georgiana, who tried to avert her eyes from such indecency. She was thus engaged one morning when she tripped over a large coil of rope, landing face down on the swabbed and holystoned deck. Mr Fraser had hauled her up, dusted her down and given her a good tongue lashing for not watching where she was going. Thereafter, Georgiana had learned to take the seminaked sights in her stride, much to Captain Hawke's disapproval.

As they travelled further south past Madeira, the sun grew stronger and the smothering heat sapped the strength of them all. Even Nathaniel wilted a little beneath the dark blue wool of his dress coat, perspiration soaking through from his shirt to his waistcoat. And as Mr Fraser put it, with the captain having such a peculiar compulsion for clean clothes and bathing, Georgiana was kept busy with the laundering. Not her most favourite of duties. Indeed, she could steadfastly avow to the truth of Mr Fraser's earlier prediction concerning the pungency of the stale urine. It was while filling her basin with the well-matured fluid that Georgiana heard the captain's voice suddenly close behind her.

'Just what do you think you're doing, Master Robertson?' he demanded in a whisper. His annoyance was plain.

Georgiana, who had been daydreaming sweet and pleasant thoughts as a diversion from the rather distasteful task at which she was employed, jumped as if she'd been scalded. This had the unfortunate effect of spilling the aromatic contents of her basin down the length of her, soaking her jacket, waistcoat, shirt and culottes. Even her feet did not escape the frothy brown deluge.

A yell wrought forth. She spun round to see Nathaniel looking at her, an expression of undisguised horror set clearly on his face. 'Captain,' she ground out through gritted teeth. 'I didn't hear your approach, sir.'

'Evidently not,' uttered the captain.

If looks could kill, Nathaniel knew without a doubt that he would have lain mortally wounded upon the deck. For Georgiana was eyeing him with an accusing look of 'it's all your fault'.

The urine dribbled down the bare flesh of her stomach and was soaking its way through her bindings. She grimaced at Nathaniel. 'You wanted to know about my actions, sir?'

'This is not your duty,' he hissed.

Georgiana opened her eyes wide and stared at him incredulously before muttering drolly, 'I beg to differ, sir, but it surely is.'

By this stage Mr Fraser was travelling towards them at a fair rate of knots for an elderly retainer, and several of the crew had noticed the boy's state.

'I'll speak to you later,' was all he managed before the valet was within earshot.

'Laddie!' Fraser bellowed. 'I turn my back for two minutes and you've landed yourself in mischief!' As he stepped closer the stench assailed his nostrils. 'In the name of…' He retreated rather quickly, his eyes watering. 'You'd best stand down wind of us, laddie, the captain'll not be wanting to smell that.'

Georgiana pressed her lips firmly together and moved to where Mr Fraser was pointing. 'I wouldn't want to inflict anythin' so horrible on the captain, sir.'

Nathaniel did not miss the murderous glint in her eye, even if Mr Fraser remained oblivious.

'Quite so, laddie, quite so.'

The baking heat of the sun caused steam to rise from Georgiana's sodden clothes, magnifying the smell acutely.

Nathaniel coughed once and Mr Fraser set about a loud and raucous choking sound.

'Have someone else finish this job, Mr Fraser, I rather think that Master Robertson is in need of a change of clothes.' A smile twitched at his face. 'Either that or we've found the perfect weapon to inflict upon our enemies.'

Guffaws sounded all around.

Georgiana's eyes darted daggers. 'Yes, sir, right away, sir,' she muttered, and made her way below, leaving behind a trail of smelly wet footprints.

'Beast!' the word escaped Georgiana as she huddled within the hip bath, washing her limbs with cold seawater. Anger had given her the strength to fetch and fill the bath herself. With the chair wedged firmly beneath the handle of the interconnecting door of her cabin—or should she say the *captain*'s cabin?—she stripped naked and balled the stinking wet clothes in the corner, ready to be rinsed once she had removed every last trace of the offensive odour from her own person. *If he thought he could just come upon her and cause such a mishap...* How she fumed. *He was rude and uncaring, the antithesis of a gentleman, and...* And he was none of these things. Georgiana plummeted off her high horse and acknowledged the truth. Nathaniel Hawke was everything to be respected in a good man. It was only her pride that was smarting, as well it might, having been soaked in the stale urine of one hundred and eighty-five burly members of the King's Navy. Ugh! She shivered at the very thought. And no matter how hard she scrubbed, it seemed that she could detect the faint whiff of that unsavoury excretion. By the time she had completed her ablutions, the tablet of soap was very small and she was once more fragrant and cleansed. Her clothes lay clean and ready to be hung out on deck. At least they would dry quickly in the warm breeze. All except her bindings, which she could not risk revealing to any other eyes. They dripped alone, a saddened state in the corner.

Georgiana looked down at her newly donned shirt and took a sharp intake of air. It would not do, it just would not do at all. Pulling on the waistcoat and jacket she inspected herself further. The problem still manifested itself in a rather obvious way. She would have to wait some time before facing the crew of the *Pallas* once more.

There was a tap at the door.

'George.' Nathaniel's voice sounded through the wooden panels.

She did not answer.

The handle shifted beneath Nathaniel's hand, but the door stuck fast. 'George,' he persevered. 'I shouldn't have laughed at you. It was an unfortunate accident. You're not hurt, are you?'

'No. I'm quite recovered from the incident, sir.'

'Open the door, I wish to speak with you.' His voice sounded a little impatient.

Georgiana's gaze scanned the empty cabin. 'I cannot.'

'Why not?' She could hear his perplexity.

She paused, thinking quickly. 'I…I'm not suitably dressed.'

'Well, put some clothes on and be quick about it.' Nathaniel Hawke could be a persistent man when it suited him.

A pool of water was collecting on the floor beneath the bindings. It would be some hours before they would be dry enough to wear again. Neither Captain Hawke, nor any other member of the crew, would believe that it took that length of time to bathe and dress. 'It will take some considerable time, sir.'

'I've letters to write. Come out when you're ready.' He listened for her reply, as his boots echoed across the wooden floor to his desk.

There was nothing else for it. She would have to tell him the truth. 'Captain Hawke, are you still there?'

'Yes.'

She pictured him sitting serenely at his desk, quill in hand, a sheet of paper in readiness before him. 'Are you quite alone, sir?'

She felt his gaze shift from the paper to the door. 'Yes. Is something the matter, George?'

A small silence.

'Yes, sir.'

The boots had risen and were making their way back over to the other side of the doorway. 'George?'

More silence.

Then, 'I cannot leave the cabin until tomorrow, sir.'

'Why ever not?'

She chewed on her lip. 'It's rather difficult to explain, sir.'

Nathaniel's apprehension was mounting by the minute. The girl must have hurt more than her pride. Worry pulled at his brow. 'Open this door at once, George.'

'I cannot.'

'If you don't, I'll take the whole damn wall down.' What the hell had happened to make her afraid to open the door? Had Pensenby accosted her? Nathaniel felt suddenly apprehensive at the thought. 'George!' The door handle rattled uselessly in his fingers. He contemplated dismantling the flimsy structure—it was, after all, designed to be removed into storage during battle situations.

Georgiana leapt up off the bed and placed her hands against the door. 'Please do not, sir. I beg of you.'

The girl was clearly distraught. He forced his voice to sound calm, reassuring. 'I cannot help you if you won't speak to me. Just open the door.' And all the while the knot of worry within his stomach expanded.

Silence.

She sighed. It was no use, her rebuttals and half-explanations were just making things worse. For all his efforts, she could hear the unease in his voice. Slowly she removed the chair and opened the door.

'Georgiana,' Nathaniel uttered with relief and stepped through the portal. Nothing seemed to be amiss. She appeared fully dressed and uninjured. He grasped her shoulders and scanned her face. 'What's wrong? Why wouldn't you open the door?'

He watched the rosy hue rise in her cheeks as she would not meet his gaze. It was quite unlike her normal behaviour. 'Georgiana,' he whispered again and pulled her into an embrace. He touched a kiss to the top of her head and soap and seawater tickled his nose. His hand slowed its caress across her back as he looked down into her eyes. 'Is it Pensenby? Has he questioned you?'

The blush deepened. 'Oh, no, nothing of that nature.' She tried to pull away, but his arms only tightened around her. She swallowed hard. 'Perhaps, it's not so much of a problem as I'd imagined if it's not apparent to you.' Easing herself away from him, she stood back and, despite the mortification she was suffering, held herself open to his perusal. 'Do you notice no change in my appearance, sir? Please be truthful.'

His brow wrinkled in puzzlement as he scrutinised her hair and face, his gaze dropping to examine her newly donned clothes. Was it his imagination, or had she, was she…? Brown eyes met blue and a dark winged eyebrow raised its enquiry. 'Take off your jacket.'

'No, indeed I will not!' Two pink spots burned brighter upon her cheeks.

At last Nathaniel experienced a glimmer of understanding of his ship's boy's strange behaviour. 'Come now, George, it's better if I see the full extent of the problem.'

Embarrassing though it was, she supposed him to be right. The jacket was quickly thrown upon the bed. 'Perhaps it's not as obvious as I'd thought. If I were to keep my jacket on—'

'It would not hide the fact that you have a most admirable figure, nephew George, a fact that would not go unnoticed by the entirety of the company.' He raised appreciative eyes to hers. 'Yes, I believe I understand your dilemma.'

She snatched the jacket back against her breast. For, once freed of its restraining bindings, Georgiana's bosom was clearly apparent and in complete defiance of her ship's boy status. The reappearance of the hitherto forgotten attribute rendered Miss Raithwaite uncomfortably self-conscious. 'Captain Hawke, if you would kindly refrain from staring,' she said.

'I do beg your pardon, nephew George,' replied Nathaniel, executing a small bow in her direction. 'But the view is uncommonly good.'

'Nathaniel Hawke!'

A broad smile spread across Nathaniel's face. 'Forgive me, George. It's quite clear you must remain cabin bound until your, um, bindings are wearable once more.'

'That,' said Georgiana with some exasperation, 'is what I've being trying to tell you.'

'I'll inform Mr Fraser that you're assisting me with my letter writing and we're not to be disturbed.'

A shiver tickled at the nape of Georgiana's neck. The prospect of remaining undisturbed in the company of Captain Hawke seemed remote indeed.

The white of the marine sentry's crossbelts and facings stood out starkly against the scarlet of his coat. He gripped his musket and looked at the second lieutenant indifferently. 'Orders is orders, Lieutenant Pensenby. If the captain says no disturbances, that's what he means.'

'I beg your pardon!' Cyril Pensenby was annoyed to find the captain could not be interrupted. 'I'm quite sure that the order did not include Lieutenant Anderson or myself, and—' he puffed his chest out in self-importance '—given the importance of my news, he will want to know.'

The sentry looked unimpressed.

'Has he someone in there with him?' Pensenby snapped.

The marine's shoulders shrugged, and he scratched at his head beneath the brim of his tall black hat. 'Only the servant boy Robertson. But it makes no difference to my orders, sir.'

Cyril Pensenby's face took on a sharpened expression. 'Indeed. Well, I'm afraid I must override your orders and insist upon seeing the captain. There's no time to waste, man.' Without further ado, Lieutenant Pensenby rushed past the marine and straight into Captain Hawke's cabin.

Everything around the cabin seemed perfectly in order. In the middle of the room the polished mahogany of the cleared dining table glinted in the sunlight. Six ornate chairs were tucked beneath it, awaiting the time it would be set for dinner. The desk was positioned closer to the windows lining the back wall of the cabin, its surface littered with papers and charts. Three pens lay beside the inkwell, a small sharpening knife in front of them. The red leather captain's chair behind the desk was empty. Nathaniel was standing, arms behind his back, peering out of the stern windows while he dictated a letter. Ship's boy Robertson was seated at the near side of the desk, neatly transcribing the captain's words on to paper. Both faces shot round to stare at him.

The marine stumbled in at Pensenby's back, musket raised towards the lieutenant. 'I told him you wasn't to be disturbed, Captain, but he wouldn't listen.'

'Mr Pensenby?' Captain Hawke turned a glacial eye upon his subordinate and moved swiftly to shield Georgiana from the men's view.

Georgiana's hand surreptitiously stole to cover the front of her neatly buttoned jacket as she shifted in her seat to present both the second lieutenant and marine with a fine view of her back.

'Forgive me, Captain Hawke,' Pensenby looked over the captain's shoulder at the rear of the boy's head. 'I thought you would wish to know that the look-out has sighted two French frigates heading in our direction.'

'Very well, Lieutenant.' Nathaniel hid the shock well. 'I'll join both Lieutenant Anderson and yourself on the quarterdeck shortly. That will be all.'

He waited until both men had left the room before turning to Georgiana. She looked so young, so vulnerable. He ignored the urge to take her in his arms, protect her for ever. 'Lock yourself in the night cabin—' a key passed between them '—and open the door for no one except myself. I'll instruct that it should be left intact when we ready the guns. Do you understand?' He wondered at the degree of concern he felt for her. If anything happened to her, he would never forgive himself.

A brief nod before she touched her hand to his arm. 'Be careful.'

They looked into each other's eyes before Nathaniel swept a feather kiss to her lips and was gone.

Through the magnification of the spyglass he could see that they were both large frigates, loading forty guns apiece, with the French tricolour fluttering boldly at the stern and a pennant at the topmast. He glanced at Pensenby, saw the shadow of fear in his small shrewd eyes. The stiff northwesterly wind would lead them directly to the *Pallas,* of that there could be no mistake.

'They'll be within range in approximately one hour, sir.' Lieutenant Anderson was pale, but his blue eyes glittered with excitement.

Nathaniel knew what he must do. 'Let out each canvas in full, we move with top speed in a southeasterly direction.'

'But that would take us towards Santa Cruz and the Canary Islands, both of which are held by Spain.' Lieutenant Pensenby frowned his disapproval.

'Indeed, it will, Mr Pensenby. It's what they'll least expect. Before reaching Santa Cruz, we'll turn and head out towards the mid-Atlantic, before sailing back up to the Azores.'

John Anderson was looking somewhat crestfallen. 'We are to run?' In his mind's eye he was already valiantly engaged in the dramatic glory of battle, annihilating the French ships, and all for the sake of King and country.

Nathaniel saw the slumped shoulders and read the reason correctly. 'In a straight confrontation we don't stand a chance against them. They each carry forty guns to our thirty-two, both are made of oak to our pine. The *Pallas* simply cannot withstand the pounding she would receive. Hit for hit we would suffer vastly more damage than they, not to mention the injury to the men from the splinters. They would have us down in a matter of minutes.'

'Then all is lost and we should strike our flag,' said Lieutenant Anderson miserably.

'Quite the contrary, Mr Anderson. We must look to our advantages and make the best use of them.'

Pensenby piped up, 'But you said that the *Pallas* is no match for them in battle.'

Nathaniel closed the spyglass with a snap. 'No, Mr Pensenby, that is only the case in direct confrontation. There are many other types of battle.'

'But we're to run.' John Anderson looked puzzled.

'For now, until the conditions favour us rather than our enemy.' Both men regarded him in silence. 'The *Pallas* is smaller, and at only 667 tonnes, significantly faster. She should easily outrun them. Then it's simply a matter of waiting until the timing is right.'

Lieutenant Pensenby seemed reassured by this. He was not a man suited to the bloody physicality of war, and the prospect of escaping what would undoubtedly prove to be a crashing defeat beckoned appealingly.

Captain Hawke strode across the quarterdeck to shout orders to the ship's master. He paused momentarily, looked back over his shoulder, and said, 'Rest assured that I'm not Byng, Mr Anderson.'

John Anderson thought of Admiral Byng who had been executed for failing to engage the Spanish Fleet with sufficient vigour. No, he did not doubt Captain Hawke's courage. He would do better to watch and learn.

With the sails set fully to capture the wind the *Pallas* skimmed across the surface of the water with a deftness of speed that could not hope to be matched by her bigger, bulkier opponents. Heading further south into Spanish waters, they had lost sight of the two large French frigates before Nathaniel gave the order to change direction.

Georgiana could feel from the rolling motion that the ship was fairly flying across the waves, and concluded with relief that they were fleeing from the French. Although she did not know the size or manner of the enemy, common sense warned her that two against one did not offer good odds of a favourable result. This, coupled with what she had learned: the *Pallas* was experimental in design, being unusually small for a frigate and built entirely of lightweight pine rather than sturdy English oak. It did not take a genius to surmise that any big gun fire would tear the ship apart.

Although Georgiana had no direct knowledge of exactly what naval battle involved, she had spent many an evening listening to Burly Jack's reminiscences, tales of glory and honour, descriptions of blood and gore, death and decay. She shivered and drew her jacket closer around her. Nathaniel Hawke could be the best damn naval captain in the world, but, outnumbered and disadvantaged by his ship, there was little doubt as to the outcome of any encounter. And the thought of it brought a shiver to her soul. If she were to lose him now… She bit at her lip and wrung her hands together. She knew what would happen if the French were to catch up with them. For the second time in Georgiana's life she was sailing dangerously close to a watery grave, poised to topple. She dropped to her knees and prayed for a gale that would spirit the *Pallas* with wings, far, far away from the long guns of the French.

A dense sea fog shrouded the *Pallas*, as she swept slowly, steadily on, cutting a path through the vast Atlantic Ocean, blind but for her trust in her captain's charts and compass. Silently stalking her prey through the muffled cloud that enveloped her. All calls had been stifled, all pipes quelled. She floated as a ghost ship ever closer to her quarry, ears straining, guns readied. Then they heard it, an eerie shout through the gloomy miasma. Fingers moved to cock their muskets, hands to quietly draw their swords. Captain Hawke whispered his orders and the *Pallas* responded mutely, slipping into position. A bell sounded close by, its clang deadened by the blanket of fog. Nathaniel waited. Waited. Biding his time. Breath by breath. Second by second. He only hoped his calculations were correct, there would be no room for error. One chance, and one chance alone, to take the prize or be damned in the process.

Even as his hand clenched, poised to give the final command, his mind flitted to the girl locked below in his cabin. Like a moth to a flame he was drawn to her. Could no longer deny his compulsion.

Was glad even that she was here on his ship, in his care, for all the danger that it brought. He knew he was a scoundrel to think such a thing. Hadn't he learned his lesson with Kitty Wakefield? He had no right to gamble with Georgiana's life, none but the knowledge of her likely fate at the hands of a French captain, or, even worse, a French crew. That was if she survived the wrecking of the *Pallas*. They were all supposedly governed by the gentlemanly rules of warfare. But Nathaniel knew that these were employed as and when it suited. Georgiana would stand little chance against either the Atlantic Ocean or their French opponents, and the thought lent strength to his resolve. There could be no failure. Not for her. Not for any of them. He could only hope that the *Pallas* would live up to her name—the Greek goddess of victory. With a steady hand and a courageous heart, Captain Hawke gave the order.

The full force of four carronades on the *Pallas*' forecastle blasted at close range upon the hapless and unsuspecting French frigate *Ville-de-Milan*, inflicting substantial damage to the hull. In the lull that followed Captain Hawke personally led the small boarding party to secure the ship. In a matter of minutes the task had been completed. Nathaniel returned to the *Pallas*, ready to engage the second frigate positioned close by. The yells of her crew alerted him as to her precise position and he swung the *Pallas* round to hide her bow. The French guns fired before the manoeuvre was complete, shattering the foremast and splintering the bow. The *Pallas*' carronades roared again, delivering their massive twenty-four-pound round shot with a snarling ferocity. The *Coruna* slipped behind the *Ville-de-Milan*, but Nathaniel had anticipated the move and was already leading his men across the barren boards of the first frigate to reach the second. Nothing could stop him, Georgiana would be safe and the prize his.

Georgiana shivered at the unnatural hush that surrounded her. No voices, no banging, no footsteps, no pipes, no bells. Only the gentle lap of water and the weary creaking of timber. Foreboding prickled at the nape of her neck and she was aware of a tight smothering tension. She sat rigidly in the small chair within the night cabin and waited. Sweat trickled in slow rivulets down her back. Fingers grew cold and numb. Silence. Suddenly an enormous explosion ricocheted around her, the blast echoing in her ears. Even locked below within the tiny cabin, the unmistakable odour of gunpowder pervaded. She leapt up from her seat. The *Pallas*' guns were firing. Nathaniel must be cornered, under attack. Dear Lord! The ship shuddered violently, landing her forcefully to the floor. Men's screams, voices shouting. Georgiana struggled to her feet. Fear rippled through her, but it would not stop her. She could no longer stay hidden and safe while the rest of the crew faced death and capture. Ship's boy Sam Wilson needed her, able seaman Jack Grimly needed her, and then there were the others. And the most important name of all held close to her heart—Nathaniel Hawke. She would do what she must to help those that she had come to think upon as friends. For Nathaniel she would lay down her life. Without further ado she slid the key into the lock and turned the handle.

Scenes of mayhem greeted Georgiana as she ran along the gun deck. Surprisingly the long guns were run in and silent, gun teams at the ready. Neither was the usual screen of pungent blue smoke hanging in the air, but she scarcely had time to ponder upon it. Two massive holes gaped on both the starboard and larboard sides where a round shot had ripped its way through and fortunately departed again. Not so fortunate was the devastation it had reaped on its route. Part of the capstan had been destroyed and enormous splinters of wood lay all around. Worst still, Georgiana could see the surgeon tending a blood-soaked figure on the floor. Several other men slumped nearby, their faces ashen, their clothing ripped and red-stained. Blood pooled invisibly upon decks painted red for just such a purpose. She ran to the surgeon's mate kneeling over a prone body.

'Mr Murthly, can I assist you, sir?'

Robert Murthly, a sturdy young man with untidy red hair, looked up at the boy. 'Captain wouldn't be best pleased to find you here, Robertson—or should I say *Lord* George? Shouldn't have thought you'd have wanted to dirty those fine letter-writing hands of yours.'

The gossipmongers had been busy. She looked beneath the sneer on the surgeon's mate's face and saw fear and fatigue. Little wonder he despised her, thinking her a pampered brat to be coddled in the captain's cabin while the rest of the ship risked their lives. Surreptitiously she fastened her jacket, and hoped that the surrounding chaos would draw Murthly's full attention. With so much blood and carnage she doubted that any man would have the time to notice the subtle change in Lord George Hawke's appearance. Besides, the crew were about to learn there was a whole lot more to the captain's nephew than they supposed. 'I'm here to help, sir, just tell me what to do.' Her voice was harsh and gritty, its tone as low as she could manage.

The surgeon's mate wiped the sweat from his brow with bloodied fingers and regarded her with deliberate consideration. Most of the men were busy securing the French frigates, and the gun crews were not permitted to leave their stations. An extra pair of hands, even aristocratic ones, would come in useful.

'Murthly!' bellowed the surgeon. 'Have a table shifted over here and quickly.' He gestured to the mess tables that interspersed the long line of guns. 'This man won't make it below, losing too much blood. We'll have to operate here. Run and fetch my instruments.'

Murthly looked at Georgiana. 'Move the table like he says.' Then the squat figure was off and running.

Georgiana, helped by one of the nearby powder boys, dragged the rough wooden structure that passed for a table across to the surgeon.

The surgeon scarcely looked at her, just dumped the haemorrhaging body down on to the surface that had so recently served up a dinner of salted meat and biscuit.

The seaman's face was chalk-white and smeared with sweat, his lips trembling as he tried to suppress the moans of pain. She skimmed down and saw the ragged stump where what had been his hand hung. His breathing came fast and shallow and his pupils shrunk to pinpricks. No time for rum, nor for the opiates which would have deadened his agony.

Nimble fingers loosed the belt from her waist and looped it

around just below the sailor's slack elbow. She tightened the tourniquet and held the injured arm aloft. Her other hand touched to the man's brow, its cool fingers wiping the sweat from his eyes.

The surgeon looked at her then, a suspicious expression of enquiry on his face.

She said nothing, just focused on the injured man lying so helplessly before her.

Murthly's feet clattered back along the gun deck. He threw open the wooden box that he carried and handed the surgeon a large and wicked-looking knife. 'Tourniquet already in place,' he observed, and saw the surgeon's eyes flit to the captain's nephew.

'Yes,' he said drily. 'Speed is our saviour,' he proclaimed, 'let's not waste any more time.' He paused before the blade contacted the bloodied pulp of reddened tissue and addressed Georgiana. 'See what you can do for the others. There are clean linen strips within the box.'

She did as she was bid, using the knowledge she had gleaned from her furtive reading of Mr Hunter's *A Treatise on the Blood, Inflammation, and Gunshot Wounds*. A fascinating book, if not one of which her stepfather would have approved for either her or Francis. Thankfully her stepbrother's secret medical ambition had led him to lodge the book safely beneath his bed. When the last of the men had been transferred to the sick berth down on the lower deck, Georgiana slipped away to discover what had become of Nathaniel. She had just made her way up the companion ladder when the answer to her question appeared most suddenly, for, as she stepped from the last rung up on to the uppermost deck, she practically collided with Captain Hawke.

'George!' The word escaped unbidden, as his hands closed around her upper arms. His gaze swept over her, taking in the dried blood streaking her face, the pale fragility of the skin beneath and the dark stained clothing, and a pulse of horror beat in his breast. Behind him Lieutenant Anderson cleared his throat, and with a start he came crashing back down to the reality of the situation. Not only had Georgiana blatantly disobeyed his order, but she was now risking her secret in an awkward situation. Perdition, but the girl seemed utterly determined to destroy her own reputation despite all his efforts. His eyes darkened. 'Get back down below, Robertson,' he barked.

Georgiana blinked, the breath caught in her throat. He was safe, unhurt. Her heart leapt at the sight of him. Thank God. But even as she relaxed with relief she saw the change wash over his face. And the tide that it brought with it was not one of love or even affection, but one of blazing fury. 'Nathan…' She remembered herself in time. 'Captain Hawke,' she amended, deepening her voice.

'That is an order.' His words were hard and angry, a stranger to her ear. Just as she turned to retreat she caught sight of the two smartly dressed French captains standing proudly behind him, their intense, dark eyes trained on Nathaniel. For one awful minute she froze, suddenly aware of how close she'd come to betraying herself. Wandering about the ship without the protection of her bindings, almost calling the captain by his given name, and all in full view of not only their own men, but also the French!

It was Nathaniel who recovered first, releasing his rather overtly intimate grasp on his ship's boy's shoulder. The breath had stilled in his throat, alarm bells ringing in his head. But the face he presented to the captives was calm and self-assured. 'Lieutenant Pensenby will escort you both to your quarters. Those of your men taken aboard will be held below, the remainder will be well treated upon your own ships. Please make your needs known to Mr Pensenby. I shall endeavour to call upon you in a short while.'

Only when his prisoners had been removed from earshot did Captain Hawke turn to his ship's boy. 'I'll have the key, if you please.' The handsome features appeared completely devoid of emotion. He did not trust himself to reveal a hint of the torrent that raged within him.

'Yes, sir.' From within her pocket she produced the cabin door key and held it to him.

He grasped it, taking care great care not to brush against her still bloodstained fingers. The dark eyes remained carefully shuttered as he turned away. A muscle twitched in the firm line of his jaw. 'Lieutenant Anderson, escort my nephew to my night cabin. See to it that the door is locked, from the outside, and return the key to me.'

Georgiana's turbulent blue eyes swung to meet his, but his gaze remained fixed hard and uncompromisingly ahead.

'I'll be in the sick berth with the surgeon, Mr Anderson.' With that the tall figure climbed down the companion ladder and strode off to check upon the injuries his men had sustained.

A cold breeze raked across the deck, rippling the British flag above. And below John Anderson moved quietly to take hold of the boy's arm.

Walter Praxton lifted the tankard before him and sipped at the ale. The Crown was quiet on account of the Impress Service's activity in the area. Only once the *Leander* had sailed would the men return from the surrounding villages. A warm fire blazed in the hearth, lightening the grey misery of the cold December day. He barely noticed the slant of winter rain that pattered against the mullioned glass windows, so intent was he on the small weasely man seated opposite.

Bob Blakely was five foot in height, of skinny build with hair the colour of the rats that meandered leisurely through the streets of Portsmouth. A short ragged moustache perched upon his upper lip, and a peppering of stubble added to the impression that washing did not constitute one of Mr Blakely's favourite pastimes. He sucked on a long pipe and regarded the rich gent with small glassy eyes.

'Like I said, Mr Praxton, sir, me contact saw the boy you're after pressed aboard a frigate that was then in dock. They don't normally take boys, but he wasn't alone, was he?'

Walter Praxton raised an enquiring brow that did not so much as crease the perfection of his handsome face.

'Was with them three seamen from on the mail. It was them that the Press Gang was after. Expect they took the lad 'cos he was there in the wrong place at the wrong time, so to speak.'

'Which frigate?' The ale tasted smooth and mellow to Mr Praxton's jaded pallet.

A grubby hand displaced the runny discharge seeping from his nose before Bob Blakely saw fit to continue. He swigged at the ale, smacking his thin chapped lips as the last of it slid like nectar down his throat. 'Could do with another of those.' He eyed Mr Praxton hopefully.

As the ever-parched Bob had proved himself efficient in obtaining the information that he was so eager to learn, Walter averted his eyes from the black grimy fingernails cradling the empty tankard and gestured for the serving woman to fetch another jug of ale. 'We wouldn't want you going thirsty. Drink up, my good man. Remember the payment we've arranged.'

Bob Blakely tapped his nose and gave the rich man a sly wink. 'You're a gentleman, Mr Praxton, and if I don't have the info that you're after, me name's not Bob Blakely.'

Walter stifled a retort and forced a smile to his face.

'Was the *Pallas*, as sailin' under Captain Hawke, sir. Left here start of last month, but under sealed orders. No one knows her destination, but me *friend*—' he stressed the word most forcibly '—in a certain place, heard tell that she's due back before Christmas. Ain't that 'andy. Not long to wait for that boy of yours, if he's still alive, that is.'

In a furtive gesture Praxton slid three guinea pieces to the man and bid him good day. Pulling his hat low and turning up the collar of his great brown coat, he braced himself to face the onslaught of the hostile English weather.

'Nice doin' business with you, gov,' came the contented reply, and Bob Blakely settled down to the comfort of another night within the snug warmth of the tavern.

Chapter Seven

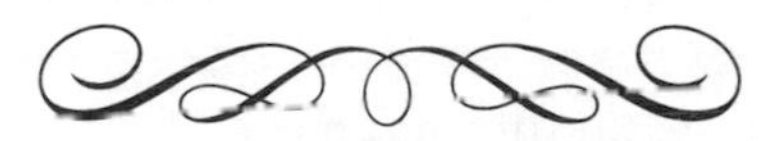

It was the aspect of war that Nathaniel hated. The price to be paid for victory and defeat alike. Admiralty might issue the orders, but it was not the old men in their elaborate uniforms that met the round shot, or took the splinters. They did not shield the ship with their bodies, or run with valour into a fracas of whirling cutlass and musket. Men that had been pressed to the service against their will, men who risked all in the hope of sharing in the prize, a financial salve to the poverty that afflicted their lives—it was a tragic necessity of war, and it never failed to cut Nathaniel to the quick. His ship, his men, his responsibility. And just as he rejoiced in their victory, so he suffered with their loss. Each death remained scored within his mind, each fallen seaman rendered immortal by Captain Hawke. Compassion. It was his biggest strength, winning the men to his cause, buying their loyalty for a lifetime…and also his gaping weakness, to feel for ever their torment.

He touched the sailor's shoulder. 'Well done, lad. Bravely fought. How fares your leg?'

'It'll mend, Captain. Now that t'surgeon's had his way, splinter's out. Says I should keep t'leg, and gain a limp.'

'No shame in that, Brown. There's always a place aboard my ship for a willing seaman, limping or not.' The captain moved on to the midshipman whose face had been sliced open by a flying splinter. 'Mr Hartley.'

The young gentleman nodded his head, the jagged stitching on his cheek already turning a purple coloration.

'You did a good job, Hartley. We've taken the day and the prize is rich indeed. A small scar won't do your future within His Majesty's Navy any harm. Your courage has been noted.'

Mr Hartley's smile pulled at the weeping wound. 'Thank you, Captain, but I fancy my young lady won't see it that way.'

'I have it on the best authority,' retaliated Nathaniel, his dark eyes lightening, 'that ladies see such marks as a badge of bravery. I'm sure it will do your reputation no harm at all.'

Captain and midshipman laughed together before Nathaniel moved on to visit the rest of his men.

'Captain Hawke.' The surgeon hurried over to him and walked some way along the deck beside him before raising the subject foremost in his mind. 'Ship's boy Robertson, sir, seems to have a wealth of medical knowledge. With whom did he study?'

Nathaniel looked at the surgeon in surprise. 'I don't know what you mean, Mr Belmont.'

The surgeon blinked back at him. 'Your neph— I mean, the boy, clearly has treated wounds before. Such knowledge is not come by easily. He must have experience of working in the surgical field. I wondered whom it was he assisted? Some of the techniques he employed were specialised to say the least. Almost as if they came straight from the pages of one of John Hunter's medical texts.'

A vision of a blood-soaked Georgiana drifted into Nathaniel's mind. So that was where the blood had come from. 'Am I to understand that the boy helped in the treatment of the wounded?'

'Why, yes. Robertson was a marvel. Young Richardson would have bled to death without his quick thinking. Foot completely severed, you know. The boy's got a feel for surgery, Captain, and it would be a shame to see it wasted. I'd be happy to have him help down here.'

Georgiana Raithwaite had quit the security of his cabin amidst the pounding fury of battle to help tend the wounded! Nathaniel reeled. The girl was incredible, infuriatingly disobedient, without a thought for her own safety, or indeed the discovery of her secret, but incredible all the same. He knew that he would have defied the First Lord of the Admiralty himself had he been ordered to lie useless within a cabin when all around a battle was sounding. A sigh escaped his lips. They were not so very dissimilar after all, the captain and his ship's boy. Even if that slim dark-haired waif was hellbent on ruining her reputation. With a heavy heart he made his way steadily towards the cabin that housed the woman in question.

Georgiana was sitting in the wooden chair, reading by the light of the flickering lantern. Or that at least looked to be what she was doing, by virtue of the book balanced carefully before her. She did not move upon Nathaniel's entry to the cabin, only glanced up at him with questioning eyes.

Somehow she had managed to cleanse the blood from her hands that were folded neatly before her. The same could not be said for the rest of her uniform. The darkened jacket had been hung over the back of the chair, leaving him a clear view of a blood-splattered shirt and the shapely figure it failed to conceal.

Two voices spoke at once. One mellow and deeply masculine, the other clear and soft. 'I'm sorry.'

They stared at each other in surprise.

'I should not have treated you so, Georgiana.' His lips shaped a wry smile, finding the motion unexpectedly easy despite all that had happened, in view of what he knew he must do.

The angular line of his jaw, those firm full lips, and black winged brows all held an indefinable tension, and in his eyes lurked fatigue tumbled with relief. Such responsibility of command demanded a high price. That he paid it in full was clear to see. She had not anticipated his apology. Indeed, from the carefully controlled, impassive countenance he had last presented she could have sworn he would give her a thorough verbal lashing. 'Perhaps, sir, your anger was understandable given that I appeared before you at the most inopportune of moments, and in complete defiance of your orders. My only defence is that I was concerned for your welfare, if you'd taken an injury in the attack. I'm afraid that I acted without proper thought or consideration.' Her nose wrinkled up and her eyes squeezed shut at the memory conjured by the confession. 'Indeed, I almost called you by your given name. Most unseemly for a ship's boy to his captain.'

'A floggable offence,' Nathaniel assured her with mock severity.

When she opened her eyes it was to see a bemused expression.

The thought of Georgiana Raithwaite being concerned for his safety was really a rather pleasant one. 'I'm touched by your concern, Miss Raithwaite, and can assure you that I'm quite unhurt.' He made as if to reach his hand to her face, but checked the motion just as it began. Best wait to discover her response first.

A rosy glow spread over her cheeks. 'Yes. For that at least we must be thankful.'

'And what of you? The shock of seeing you appear drenched in blood did me more damage than the *Coruna*'s guns!' More damage than he was willing to admit even to himself. 'I thought for one horrible moment that you'd been injured.' A little line of worry creased between his eyes.

It was really rather endearing, or so Georgiana thought. 'Not me, sir,' she said.

'What were you up to, to become so blood-soaked?' The dark eyes narrowed suspiciously. 'Mr Belmont has some strange notion that you're accustomed to assisting in surgical procedures. He requested your transference to the sick berth!'

Miss Raithwaite looked suddenly a picture of pious innocence. 'I cannot think why.'

'And the blood?' He indicated her attire.

She sighed. 'I couldn't just sit here and listen to their screams, Captain Hawke. I heard the guns and didn't know what was happening. At first I thought that we were under attack. Those men... Such hurts as I've never seen the like of. Oh, Nathaniel...' She closed her eyes as if to block the memory. 'There was so little I could do for them.'

His fingers touched lightly to her shoulder, unable to bear her distress, wanting to pull her into his arms and protect her from the world. 'Mr Belmont tells quite a different story, and so, I gather, would the men that you helped. We've lost none. All survived.' Gently he pulled her upright, looking down into her face. 'There's another matter that we must discuss, Georgiana.' A matter of honour, a matter of doing what was right even when his father thought that he was all wrong.

The deliberate use of her given name sent a delicious little shiver through her body, but something in his tone forewarned her of the gravity of his intent.

'Truly I didn't know that the Frenchmen were aboard,' she explained. 'Moreover, the blame for my foolish actions rests entirely with me, for it was I who directly disobeyed your command and I who presented myself in full view of your captives. Now I fear that I may have jeopardised my position.'

The girl had unwittingly stumbled directly upon the heart of the problem. A rumble of apprehension rattled through him. Somehow he doubted that his forthcoming proposal would meet with such sweet compliance. It was, after all, Walter Praxton that she loved, not himself.

'Georgiana, the presence of the French captains has served to highlight the risk we're running. It will only take one man to see through your disguise and we're done for.' He could be nothing other than frank in his explanation. Miss Raithwaite needed to face the truth.

Georgiana's fingers found her ear lobe and started to fidget. 'But we've been safe until now.'

'Yes. Lady Luck's been on our side, but she won't be for ever.' Nathaniel's voice was grim. He saw the anxiety in her eyes and misinterpreted its cause. 'Don't be distressed, Miss Raithwaite, for I swear that no harm will come to you. You're an innocent in all of this…debacle, and…'

The smooth brow crinkled in bafflement. *Innocent?* What was the man talking about? She was the singular cause of all that had happened.

'Through no fault of your own, you've been placed in a compromising—no, ruinous situation.'

No fault of her own? Georgiana's sooty long lashes batted in astonishment. Who was it, then, that had cut her hair, dressed her in

Francis's clothes and forced her upon the mail to Fareham? Didn't he realise that it was all her own fault? 'Captain Hawke.' She held her hand up to still his flow, gentlemanly and eloquent though it was. 'I fear that you're ascribing an innocence to me that's quite unwarranted.'

Nathaniel, who had been on the point of delivering his *fait accompli*, stalled, regarding her with an expression of shock. Had Walter Praxton then stolen more than a few kisses that day in Hurstborne Park? It was like a kick to the gut. He hesitated over the words to express himself. 'You…you're no longer an innocent? Are you trying to tell me that you've…that you and Mr Praxton—?

'Dear God, no!' Georgiana's face flushed scarlet. 'However could you think such a thing?' She made to step back from his looming figure, caught her legs against the chair and stumbled. In an instant his arms enveloped her, saving her from the fall, pulling her upright and against the length of his muscular body. He held her, a peculiar expression of relief on his face, before setting her back on her feet and retreating to the far end of the cabin.

'Then what do you mean, Miss Raithwaite?' Everything about him was static and still, the calm before the storm.

Exasperation and embarrassment lent an edge to Georgiana's retort. Why was it that each time she tried to remedy a situation she only succeeded in making it worse? 'I'm merely trying to tell you, Captain Hawke, that we are in this ridiculous situation because of my actions and my actions alone. *I* ran away from home. *I* disguised myself as a boy, and I didn't exactly hide myself from the officers of the Impress Service. No sir, I cannot, in good conscience, stand here while you describe me as the innocent victim. The terrible truth is that the fault is mine.' She turned stormy eyes to his, raised her voice in impassioned plea. 'Please believe me when I say that I had no thought that matters would unfold as they did. I didn't mean to ruin you, Nathaniel.'

He stepped towards her boldly, disbelieving. '*You* have ruined *me*?'

She shook her head and lowered her eyes. 'I'm sorry sir, that you've suffered when your only crime has been to help me.'

'Georgiana…' his voice gentled and he was so close she could feel his breath upon her hair '…you seem to be under a mis—'

'No, Nathaniel. Don't make excuses for me. My reputation is ruined. I know that.' She raised her head and looked him directly in the eye. 'I'm prepared to live with the consequences of my actions. But please believe me when I say that I didn't mean to risk your position, sir.'

He watched her intently. 'You've no idea of how your life would be affected if you were found aboard this ship, unchaperoned amidst all these men. A ruined reputation is easily said. It's not so easy, Georgiana, to live with. To be ostracised by society, shunned by respectable women and subjected to the worst kind of attention from those who would call themselves gentlemen.'

'I will bear it.'

She felt his forefinger touch her chin, tilting her face up to his. 'You need not. There is another way.'

The muscles tensed beneath his fingertip. 'Not for me, there isn't.'

He could see the stubborn determination in those clear grey blue eyes, knew that she would never accept him for her own sake. Nathaniel had no intention of allowing her wilful pride to condemn the rest of her life. And in that moment he knew just the ploy to use. If Georgiana thought her presence a threat to his career, then who was he to correct the misunderstanding? 'There's only one thing that we can do, given the circumstances. I know that you don't want to, but it's with both our welfares in mind that I ask it.'

The breath stilled in Georgiana's throat. Everything stopped, or so it seemed, except the loud rhythmic thud of her heart.

Rich dark eyes held hers with a burning intensity. His fingers moved softly to caress her cheek. 'Will you do me the honour of accepting my name in marriage?'

In that split second Georgiana's world turned upside down. He wanted her for his wife? She felt suddenly light-headed. 'M-marriage?' she uttered faintly.

'Indeed.' His breath was warm upon her face. His eyes watchful, waiting.

She was conscious of the gentleness of the long fingers that had stilled upon her skin, of the sheer strength of the man, and his determination to do what he thought was right. 'Would it set matters right with the Admiralty?' They stood so close yet without touching, save for the featherprint of his fingers on her cheek. Across that small space the heat of his masculinity scorched the full length of her body, pulling her like a magnet. 'I mean—' she glanced away '—how could you be saved simply by marrying me?'

'Saved by marriage.' The words were soft, whispered almost as if he were thinking them aloud. His fingers moved to stroke her silken ebony locks.

She stood entranced, unable to move.

'To have a woman steal unknowingly upon a ship, disguised as a boy, and subsequently employ her as a ship's boy, having her sleep each night within one's own cabin is enough to condemn any captain. But if that same captain were to wed his betrothed in a distant British base, and transport that lady back to England as his wife, then that is an entirely different matter. It would, of course, be frowned upon, a slap on the wrist and all that. Nothing more. My captaincy would be safe.'

The explanation made sense. 'I see,' she replied a little breathlessly. The proximity of Nathaniel Hawke's large and manly body seemed to be having rather a strange effect upon her. She struggled to retain a modicum of her common sense before it all deserted her.

His deep melodic voice sounded again. 'I wouldn't be the only one to benefit from a matrimonial arrangement. When I thought to wed you, Georgiana, it was not only the salvation of my own reputation that I had in mind.'

'No?' What, then, did he have in mind? Some measure of the same affection that she felt for him?

'A good marriage would remedy any blight on your reputation.' He smoothed her hair behind her ear, his fingers slipping down to capture the soft lobe that she worried so frequently at. 'I know that I'm not your choice, Georgiana.' He thought fleetingly, and with considerable discontent, of Walter Praxton. 'But I would endeavour to make a good husband.'

The shimmering grey-green lights within her eyes dimmed, and she looked away to hide her disappointment. It was clear that her fondness was not returned.

When she still did not answer, he prompted, 'So, Miss Raithwaite, will you consent to marry me?'

'To save us both?' she questioned in a small flat voice, so unlike her own.

'That's certainly one way of putting it.'

She raised her chin a notch. 'Then, sir, my answer must be yes.'

But the bleakness in her eyes did not escape Nathaniel's notice.

Since the prisoners had come aboard Nathaniel had confined Georgiana to the night cabin. Soon they would reach the British station at Gibraltar, where he meant to deposit the *Ville-de-Milan* and *Coruna*, and both their crews. Such a net of prizes would at least secure a decent financial recompense for them all. And he would see to it personally that his men were amply rewarded. Only when his precious French cargo had been unloaded would he be truly at ease. Nathaniel dared take no chances when it came to Georgiana. She would not be safe until they were married.

Married. He still did not fully understand how it had come to this. A mixture of honour and guilt and determination to prove his father wrong. But he had to admit that the prospect of marrying Georgiana was not altogether unattractive. Indeed, the more he thought on it, he could see that it would have a significant number of positive advantages. The girl was intelligent, and could engage him in interesting conversation more than any other female he knew. And, although she was shy, she was certainly in possession of a wicked sense of humour. For all her youth she seemed to have a certain maturity of spirit that appealed to him. Not to mention her attributes of a more physical nature. There had been a tension between them since first he'd pulled her from the River Borne, a thread of attraction that bound him to her in ways he could not hope to understand. He wanted her, all of her, from the ripple of her laughter to the endearing way she worried at her ear lobe, from her strength of courage to the fire in her eyes. Yes, indeed, marriage to Miss Raithwaite would be no bad thing.

Captain Hawke was definitely in a good mood. First there was the humming, followed by the marked spring in his step and his uncommon lightness of spirit. Lieutenant Anderson eyed him with mounting suspicion.

'Does Master Robertson show no sign yet of a possible recovery?' the first lieutenant enquired with concern.

Captain Hawke appeared supremely unaffected by his nephew's unfortunate condition. 'No, none whatsoever, Mr Anderson. Such a pity.' He leafed through the pages of the book before him. 'Have you spoken to the purser yet? I want to be sure that we've adequate provisions for our journey back to England. Plenty of lemons and vegetables. I don't want the men succumbing to scurvy. Perhaps some extra livestock to bring a bit of relief from the salted beef.'

'All is in order with Mr Tufton. He's produced his lists of provisions to procure and all his records are up to date and accurate. May I be so bold as to suggest that you speak to the surgeon?' John Anderson shuffled his boots together rather uneasily.

'Regarding the food rations?' A perplexed look crossed Captain Hawke's face. 'Shouldn't think he's got too much to say on the matter, as long as the men are reasonably well fed.'

The lieutenant examined a spot on the toe of his boot. 'No, sir. I was thinking more for the boy. He's been unwell for some days now.'

'Oh,' replied his commanding officer, in rather hearty tones, 'no need for that. Running a bit of fever. Nothing serious enough to bother Mr Belmont with. Now, as to those repairs on the gun deck…' and the captain continued in his chipper tone.

A knock sounded at the door.

'Enter.'

'Ah, Captain Hawke. I was just wondering whether young Robertson is feeling any better?'

Nathaniel barely raised his eyes. 'No improvement yet, Mr Fraser. You'll be the first to know if there's any change.'

The elderly valet's head shook in disbelief. 'Poor wee laddie. Sick to the bottom of his stomach. And him being such a help to Mr Belmont on the gun deck an' all.'

'Sickness, you say, as well as the fever?' the lieutenant piped up.

The pale eye widened. 'Has the lad a fever on top of the terrible vomiting? You never said so, sir.' Mr Fraser was looking accusingly at the captain.

When Nathaniel raised his head it was to find one and a half pairs of worried eyes trained upon him. Heavens above. What was their sudden fascination with George Robertson? 'Mr Anderson,' he said through gritted teeth, 'Mr Fraser, Master Robertson has a slight fever and a little sickness. It is nothing to overly concern yourselves with. The boy is fine.'

By the time Nathaniel was *en route* to visit Mr Tufton, the purser, his good mood was wearing a trifle thin. Not only had he been visited by both the surgeon and his mate, to enquire as to the rumour they had heard concerning ship's boy Robertson and his failing health, but Lieutenant Pensenby, yes, Cyril Pensenby, had accosted him on the quarterdeck to ask of the boy's welfare. Had his whole crew become obsessed with George Robertson? What the hell was going on?

It was a large captain of somewhat surly disposition that finally reached the orlop deck and the purser's store. 'Mr Tufton,' he began.

The purser, a short, extremely round man, was squashed within the dimly lit, caged store, directly between the sacks of flour and oatmeal and the small wooden casks of suet and butter. 'Captain Hawke. Am I pleased to see you, sir. Couldn't help wondering how the young lad Robertson was faring. Heard he's been a bit poorly of late.' An aroma of dried fish and vinegar filled the air as Mr Tufton moved forward.

The captain turned a jaundiced eye on him. 'I've suddenly remembered a most pressing appointment elsewhere. I bid you good day, Mr Tufton.'

He had almost made it back safely to his day cabin, striding past the numerous bodies busy in cleaning and checking the great long guns, when a gruff voice assailed him. 'Captain Hawke, beggin' your pardon, sir. It's about the lad, George. Has the swelling spread? Will he lose the leg?'

Nathaniel stared wordlessly at the huge figure of Burly Jack, before managing to mutter, 'The leg?'

'Aye, sir, the bad leg, like, what's got the swellin'.' The big man wrung his hands together. 'He's a good lad, even if he is your nephew, sir.' He winked broadly, 'But I'll mention nothin' of that to the others.'

Captain Hawke decided to accept this comment in the vein in which it was offered. 'His legs are quite uninjured, although he does have a mild fever and sickness, nothing serious. Why are you so concerned about him?'

Able seaman Grimly looked the captain level in the eye. 'Lad got lifted by the Press Gang when he was trying to help me. George charged in when they set about me. He didn't care nothin' for his own safety. Like I say, he's a good lad, a loyal lad.'

It was a very pensive Nathaniel Hawke that returned to his cabin.

Georgiana sat alone in the night cabin. The book sagged heavily in her hands. She closed it with a snap before standing to stretch out her back. It had been some days since she had agreed to become Nathaniel Hawke's wife, yet her feelings on the matter had not changed. He was kind, courageous and caring. Never one to shirk responsibility he would do what he knew to be the right thing, in spite of every adversity. He made her laugh, never spoke to her in the condescending manner of which her papa and Mr Praxton were so fond, and was possibly the most attractive man she had ever set eyes upon. Quite simply, she loved him. She'd known it from the moment the French guns had fired. It was strange how the risk of death brought a clarity to one's feelings. Indeed, had she not secretly wished to marry such a man as he, even at their first acquaintance in Farleigh Hall? That meeting now seemed a memory from the long distant past, so much had happened in the interceding weeks. Too much. Now her wish had been granted and she was to marry Captain Hawke. Betrothed to such a man, a glorious man, who gladdened her heart and warmed the blood in her veins. She sighed and wriggled her arms in an attempt to regain sensation in her numbed fingers.

The prospect of her forthcoming nuptials curiously saddened her, for he had left her with no illusions as to the reason for the wedding. It was nothing more than a means to salvage both their reputations. At least he'd had the decency to be honest with her, even if that honesty had wrecked those daydreams of which she had grown so fond—Nathaniel declaring his undying love, whispering sweet words in her ear, kissing her fully on the lips… She clamped the thoughts down, labelled them as childish and silly and unrealistic. He was kind to her, and undoubtedly concerned for her welfare. But it was quite clear that he did not experience the same battery of overwhelming emotions that afflicted her on his mere touch. The thought of his kiss was enough to bring a gentle glow to her cheeks, and the memory of that one stolen night when she'd… Blazing heat engulfed her body. Yet he'd never even alluded to the incident. Burly Jack's words echoed in her mind: *When a man's been at sea long enough he ain't too fussy over women, George. Anythin' will do, as long as she's willin'*. It was not a pleasant realisation.

When Nathaniel entered the cabin, it was to find a rather pale-faced ship's boy sitting glumly on his cot. 'Dinner will be here shortly.' It had become their usual custom to eat together at his table, waiting until Bottomley, the captain's personal cook, had departed before Georgiana emerged from the night cabin. Let his officers think it strange that their captain no longer invited them to the splendour of his dinner table once or twice a week. His concern rested more with the woman before him. 'Have you a little more appetite than last night?'

With Georgiana shut away from the world, the sun-kissed pale golden hue on her face had begun to fade. She was naturally of a white complexion, but within the dim light of the night cabin the pallor of her fragile skin seemed exaggerated and a little unhealthy. 'I'm afraid that my idleness has sapped my hunger.' She saw the worry ignite in Nathaniel's dark eyes and sought to reassure him.

'But I'm sure that your cook's excellent skills will tempt my appetite.' A smile lit up her face. 'You're spoiling me with all this good food. I should be dining on hard biscuit and salted beef stew like the others.'

Nathaniel crooked an eyebrow. 'Imagine the outrage if it became known that Captain Hawke had offered his betrothed a diet consisting of weevil-clogged biscuit and salted beef. Why, I should be barred from entry to all the fashionable places!' He held a limp-wristed hand to his brow as if he were London's greatest fop.

'You're teasing me again!' She laughed, then, holding herself with regal dignity, affected to fan herself in the manner of a lady at a high-season assembly. 'La, Captain Hawke,' she said in her best imitation of the flirtatious tones she had heard those same ladies employ, 'do you not know the latest *on dit?* Why, weevilly biscuit and salted beef are quite the rage in all the most fashionable establishments!' Her long raven lashes batted seductively and she delivered him a most artful look through them.

If the marine posted outside the captain's day cabin thought anything unusual in the peels of laughter that emanated from within, he was wise enough not to comment upon it. The most he allowed himself was a little sidelong glance at his fellow sentry.

Only when Bottomley had delivered the dishes did Georgiana emerge from the tiny room that had become her prison. The table had been covered with a pristine white tablecloth and laid with a finely decorated dinner service and plain silver cutlery. The flickering light from the branched candlestick centrepiece reflected in the silver serving dishes, casting a warm glow around the cabin. Chicken cutlets, a leg of mutton, gravy soup, puréed potatoes, fried potatoes and even a seed cake. Nathaniel had brought his own provisions as well as those for his officers. The food was indeed tasty but, in truth, she had no appetite despite Nathaniel's obvious efforts to cajole her.

'Perhaps a little wine?' Nathaniel made to fill her glass from the heavy crystal decanter.

Normally she declined, knowing that her papa had never allowed such a thing. Indeed, she'd not grown used to the daily ration of a gallon of beer and the strange-tasting grog in all the time that she'd been aboard the ship. She drank what she could, but Georgiana's generosity with sharing her ration had soon made her popular amongst her shipmates. But strangely tonight, in a daring gesture of defiance, she accepted the captain's offer. 'Yes, thank you, sir, that would be very nice.' She sipped the wine delicately, wondering what her stepfather had caused such a fuss about. The contents of her glass were not particularly pleasant and had, in fact, a slightly sour taste, not that she would admit as much to Nathaniel.

Captain Hawke lounged back in his chair, watching Georgiana with an unreadable expression upon his face. After a little silence he said quietly, 'Are you going to tell me what's making you so miserable?' He took a small sip from his own glass.

His question was so unexpected that Georgiana inhaled the mouthful of wine she was in the process of swallowing, and then proceeded to cough and splutter its remains down the front of her white linen shirt and waistcoat. One warm large hand clapped her heartily upon the back. By the time the coughing had subsided enough for her to speak, Georgiana had regained some measure of composure. 'Miserable? Whatever makes you think that I'm miserable?' she queried in a still-croaky voice.

Nathaniel fixed her with a knowing stare. 'I've seen men face flogging around the fleet with a cheerier countenance. Come, tell me what ails you.' His hand squeezed her shoulder reassuringly.

Still seated, she glanced up at the concern clearly writ upon his face. She wanted to say, *I'm betrothed to a man that I've come to love, and he would marry me only because I've pushed him to such a dire situation that he has no other option to escape complete ruination of his beloved career. And, because I've done such a terrible thing, I fear that he'll grow to hate me.* But all she actually managed was, 'I fear you're mistaken, sir. I'm only a little anxious over your position if my identity was to be discovered.'

'You mustn't worry, Georgiana.' He stroked the errant lock of hair from her brow. 'It will all be over soon. Hold fast until then.'

Georgiana's spine tingled with the closeness of his presence behind her. And the warmth radiating from his light touch on her shoulder had ignited a spark of inexplicable excitement within her. In a few days she would be his wife. His wife, no less. And the knowledge set the pulse racing in her neck. She tried to concentrate on what she was saying. 'How do you propose to effect this replacement of George Robertson? Won't anyone notice that I'm gone?' She took what could only be described as a swig of wine.

'Notice? Georgiana, you've been hidden next door too long. Every blasted man on this ship has expressed a profound interest in your state of health!' Nathaniel placed his other hand on her opposite shoulder and began to massage the taut muscles beneath.

A slow warm delicious sensation had started within the core of Georgiana's body. She allowed the magical motion that his hands were weaving to continue, even though every shred of common sense warned her otherwise. Burly Jack's words slipped far from recall. 'Really?' Her blue eyes opened wide.

'Yes, really,' retorted her captain. 'Can't be working them hard enough if they've time to dwell on the welfare of m'ship's boy.' He tried, and failed, to sound strict.

One small hand touched to where his were still so busily working on her shoulders. 'You don't suppose that they have an inclination that I'm not a boy, do you?' Another gulp of wine descended.

'Most certainly not.' A butterfly kiss flitted to the crown of her head. 'They're steadfastly convinced that you're my nephew. It seems that they regard the dratted boy with some affection.' The long tanned fingers paused in their ministrations. 'I can't think why!' he added with an impudent glimmer. 'Can you?' Glossy dark locks parted to reveal the soft white flesh at the nape of her neck. His thumb moved to caress it in a slow sensual circle.

She sat rooted to the spot, unable to move. Touched as if by Midas to cold static metal, except the blood pounding through her veins and the rampant heat rising through her body proved she had not turned to gold. 'Nathaniel,' she whispered slowly, 'I don't think that you should be doing that.'

'Doing what?' he enquired with a tone that belied innocence.

Her words were hushed and breathy. 'Your fingers, touching... touching my neck.'

'Yes,' he said solemnly, 'you're quite right. I shouldn't be doing this with my fingers.' And he bent lower until his mouth met her neck.

'Oh!' exclaimed Georgiana in a soft moan. 'I...I didn't mean...' Words ceased as he nuzzled the tender skin with the full force of his lips.

She melted beneath the flame of his touch, a silky smooth sensation washing over her, dragging her down into a spiral of leaping desire.

'Georgiana...' Her name escaped his lips as he pulled her gently up from the chair. She felt the warmth of him against her. 'Sweet Georgiana.' His hands slid over her shoulders, down over the coarse linen of her shirt, and down further still to close around her buttocks.

'Nathaniel,' she gasped, 'we must not...' Her thoughts struggled out from beneath the feathery down of his embrace.

He moved his hands in a sensual massage, sliding his fingers against her hips, stroking with an increasing intensity.

'Nathaniel...' A yawning need was growing within her. Every caress, every touch, banked the fire higher until she thought she would expire for want of his hands upon her skin, for his lips to claim hers.

His mouth nibbled the soft lobe of her ear as his fingers found passage beneath her shirt, basking on the smooth satin of her back. 'Georgiana!' His words were low and husky, stirring her blood to run faster, wilder.

Her skin tingled beneath his touch, ached for more. The long tanned fingers fluttered against her stomach, then traced a path higher, to splay against the coiled linen strips that hid her breasts. Even through the thickness of the bindings her nipples tightened. She arched, driving herself against his palms, clutching his hands harder to the coarse wound cloth. His tongue lapped against her neck, sucking the sweet nectar of her skin. At last his fingers found the knotted end of linen strip. She reached her searing lips to his—

A knock sounded against the door.

Georgiana's heart lurched in her chest.

'Wait where you are,' Nathaniel ordered loudly.

A voice floated through the wooden panelling, sounding suspiciously like Lieutenant Anderson's dulcet tones. 'The prisoners are requesting your presence, sir.'

Nathaniel stared down at her, his eyes darkened to a smouldering black, the starkness of reality intruding on their passion. His breath came harsh and ragged and the glisten of sweat showed upon his skin.

Georgiana tensed in his arms as the lieutenant's voice delivered her back down to earth. The sparks extinguished within her flashing eyes and her cheeks glowed hot and pink. She could still feel the warm press of Nathaniel's hands in a place they most certainly should not be. She glanced up at him, suddenly afraid.

'Lieutenant Anderson?'

'Yes, sir.'

'Make them wait. I shall be along presently.'

The footsteps receded.

She relaxed in his strong arms, daring to breathe again. 'Nathaniel, we should not have…' Her face burned scarlet.

'The fault is mine. *I* should not have. But you're a very tempting woman and—' he crooked a smile '—we're soon to be married. I'm very much looking forward to that day.' He raised one dark winged eyebrow, and delivered a chaste kiss to her forehead. 'Until then I shouldn't take advantage of you. Please—' he touched a kiss to the rosy swell of her lips '—forgive me.' Finally, and with some considerable reluctance, he prised his hands from her body, fixed her shirt neatly back into place and escorted her back to the night cabin. 'Hold fast, sweetheart, just a few more days to wait.' He executed a bow, hastily donned his undress coat and strode from the cabin.

Chapter Eight

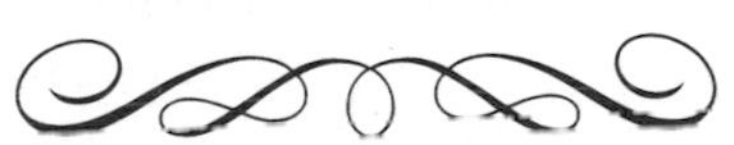

How could a girl of one and twenty survive undiscovered amidst a crew of seafaring men? For the umpteenth time Walter Praxton pondered the conundrum, returning again to his ultimate conclusion that it was impossible. That led him to extrapolate two possible scenarios. Firstly, that on the remote chance she had managed to hide her fair sex, she was likely to have expired from the hardship of life at sea. Secondly, and perhaps even worse, if it was known that she was a woman, then what men in the confines of a ship at sea would not rejoice in the comfort that her body offered? Mr Praxton allowed himself the indulgence of remembering just how very appealing Georgiana Raithwaite's soft curves were, her slim body pressed to his. No matter that she had spurned his kisses, had thrust herself from him. Even the memory of that heaving bosom, those flashing eyes, drove him instantly to a state of arousal.

What would he do if she had been badly used, had fallen, as Edward Raithwaite so aptly put it? Would he still want her then? But Walter Praxton knew the answer before even the question had formed in his mind. Her image obsessed him, goaded him. The one woman who seemed immune to his handsome looks. The one, alone, who had not succumbed to the enticement of his charm. How ironic that it was she above all others that he wanted. More than wanted, for want did not come near to describing the utter determination that burned in Walter Praxton's breast. He would have Georgiana Raithwaite if it was the last thing he did.

* * *

Georgiana lay alone on the bed, reliving her shocking conduct of earlier that same evening. Now that Nathaniel was no longer present she was able to think clearly and with a good deal of sense. She could not deny that their encounter had been more than pleasurable. Indeed, it had left her with a most unladylike appetite for more. Her eyelids shuttered and she pressed her palms to her forehead. Dear Lord, was it really the prim and proper Miss Raithwaite who had encouraged Nathaniel Hawke in his…his…? The word would not form upon her tongue. The same Miss Raithwaite who'd readily thrown herself into a fast-flowing river to escape similar attentions from Mr Praxton. It seemed that common sense was long forgotten when Nathaniel turned his charm on her. And therein lay the problem. She could not blame the man, for she knew with absolute certainty that had she repulsed him at any point he would not have pressed her, would have behaved as the perfect gentleman. Not only had she failed to deter his actions in any way, but had positively encouraged him. When Lieutenant Anderson's interruption had sounded, it was not relief that had flooded her senses, but disappointment.

Mama had once alluded to wanton women who, without a shred of decency, undertook illicit and intimate relations with men. How horrified she would be to realise that her own daughter was now of that ilk. And Papa? Why, he would beat her senseless and disown her if he ever discovered that truth. Georgiana felt guilty at what she had done, and afraid of the powerful emotions that seemed to have the ability to turn her into a pathetic heap of quivering jelly. So much for all that she'd learned!

Nathaniel Hawke was a good man, a man of honour, and a man who had been some months at sea without the company of women. She had no idea how he amused himself back on land, no idea if he kept a mistress, or had affairs. No doubt he did, didn't all gentlemen? His affection seemed real enough when he kissed or even touched her. Surely the hoarse desire gravelled through his voice could not be feigned? Yes, he wanted her—even through all her naïvety she understood that. But now, beneath the cool light of her calm analysis, she realised that any man starved of women for such a time might behave in the same manner. Jack was right. *Anyone'll do, as long as she's willin'*, and hadn't she proven herself to be more than willing?

Anger clenched at her teeth, compressed the fullness of her bruised lips. He'd called her a very tempting woman—wasn't that proof that the nature of his affections lay with a woman, any woman, rather than Georgiana herself? Tears welled in her eyes, and she blinked them back furiously. She would not cry. Never. She had plunged herself into this ridiculous situation, and therefore she would deal with it the best she could. Rallying her courage, she held her chin high and carefully, calmly weighed up the evidence.

Her history proved that such wantonness had never previously assailed her. Indeed, she'd found Walter Praxton's kisses repugnant. Coupled with this was the fact that she'd drunk two whole glasses of wine, ignorant of their possible effect. Perhaps an excess of such a beverage could produce unladylike behaviour. Her head did feel rather light and fluffy since consuming the sour liquid. Finally, she had been virtually imprisoned within the tiny night cabin for days, and could not such a confinement result in a type of brain madness that might explain the strange effects Nathaniel Hawke was having upon her person? Yes, indeed, the evidence was strong and glaringly obvious. Georgiana felt rather less guilty and a little more woolly-headed. Now that she thought about it, the ship seemed to be rocking in a dizzy, uneven manner. It was shortly after this observation that the brilliant idea made itself known to Georgiana. Brilliant was perhaps not the word that Nathaniel Hawke would have chosen to describe it.

The moon was full and high in the night sky when Georgiana stole silently from Nathaniel's cabin.

'Feeling better, Robertson?' the marine sentry enquired.

She pulled the hat lower over her head. 'Yes, thank you, sir, a bit. The captain thought some fresh air might help.'

'Does he know that you're up and about?' Suspicion creased the marine's brow.

'Yes, sir,' she lied in her deepest mumbling voice. 'Bade me not be out too long, sir.' She prayed that Nathaniel's business on the lower deck would keep him occupied for some time.

The sentry did not appear entirely convinced, but before he could question her further Georgiana had disappeared in a swift flurry of steps. She made for the uppermost deck, keeping to the shadows, avoiding those of the watch. Silver moonlight glistened over the water, lighting its gentle undulation. All was quiet save for the tranquil lap of waves against the hull. Water slapping softly on wood. And best of all was the subtle night breeze, fresh and clear. It nipped at her cheeks, chased the foggy clouds from her head and soothed the worry from her shoulders. She drank in the sight of the beautiful nocturnal seascape, tasted salt upon her lips, felt the wind rake her skin, smelled what had become a welcome and familiar scent. Carefully and methodically she impressed the scene upon her memory. *If I lose all else, I'll remember what's before me for the rest of my life. For it is of such captivating clarity as to remind me how fortunate I am to live to witness it.* The thought lingered even as she made her way back down to the cabin. For although the freshness of the air had cleared the stuffy confusion from her head, it had brought with it the realisation that she was jeopardising Nathaniel's plans. And that was something she did not want to risk.

The days passed quickly and the comfortable companionship between Captain Hawke and his erstwhile ship's boy grew, but it was not long before Nathaniel eventually brought the *Pallas,* the *Ville-de-Milan* and the *Coruna* to dock within the harbour at the great Rock of Gibraltar.

Four boats rowed ashore from the frigate. The launch and two cutters carried the French seamen, as well as the bosun, his assistant and several marines. The crew left imprisoned upon the French frigates would be transported in their own vessels. Captain Hawke and his landing party travelled in the pinnace and consisted of Lieutenant Anderson, four marines, two midshipmen, the surgeon, the purser, both French captains and, of course, Captain Hawke's ailing servant George Robertson.

'You look a little better, Master Robertson. Do you feel somewhat recovered?' Lieutenant Anderson enquired as the pinnace was rowed towards the shore.

Georgiana tugged nervously at her ear. 'Yes, sir, much better, thank you, sir.' Then, following a rather black look from Nathaniel, hastily amended the report upon her health. 'That is, except for the headache, sir.' She averted her eyes to the shoreline.

Mr Belmont leaned forward, his perceptive surgeon's eye peering at her face before turning to address the captain. 'Captain Hawke, I don't profess to be a physician, but I have some little knowledge that may help the boy's condition. Perhaps, if I could examine him when we return to the ship? I know that you did not previously deem it necessary, but the sickness has persisted for quite some time.'

Nathaniel nodded briefly as if the subject was of little consequence. 'Of course, Mr Belmont, do as you see fit. Mr Tufton, use the launch to transport the provisions back to the *Pallas*; my business ashore will take some time and I'll return with the pinnace later.'

'Aye, sir,' replied the purser.

Rear Admiral Tyler was only too happy to welcome Captain Hawke and his party to the station on Gibraltar—his joviality perhaps due, in part, to his profound love of receiving captured vessels. With the necessary documents completed, Admiral Tyler was keen to invite Nathaniel and his officers to a celebratory dinner the following evening.

The main town, or city as it was termed on the Rock, was bright and busy. Despite the advancement of the year, the sun was shining and the temperatures mild. In the background loomed the dominating huge stark purple grey of the rocky terrain. Within the city matters were less severe. Both men and women in colourful clothing called from behind their street stalls set out in the commodious market place. Small flat-roofed houses crowded from the sea wall up the steep elevation towards the Rock, their walls whitewashed and clean, splashed with the vibrant reds and pinks of the strong-smelling flowers that clambered upon them. Mules, laden with large cylindrical bags, trotted in small troops to and from the harbour, competing with the rumble of the wooden carts. Colonel Drinkwater's fine library stood proud in its newly completed building, proclaiming the cultured interests of the Gibraltarians. In the distance, at the northern extremity of the hillside, were the ruins of a Moorish castle. In the centre of the city was Commercial Square, across which more pedlars displayed their wares. But the most astounding sight that met the officers of the *Pallas* was two small Barbary apes lounging at the edge of the city, nibbling on a large pile of bread and fruit. Mr Belmont and Lieutenant Anderson were quite taken with the creatures, so much so that they set to sketching the scene before them. Thus it was that Nathaniel found himself able to slip discreetly away, accompanied only by his ship's boy.

Through the narrow back streets they wove, following the directions that the man had relayed to Nathaniel. Georgiana grinned as she thought of the wary suspicion on the fellow's face. But then it wasn't every day that he was accosted by a captain of His Majesty's Navy asking where he might find a lady's dressmaker.

'Keep up, George, we haven't got all day.' Nathaniel reached an arm round to catch the rather out-of-breath ship's boy straggling behind.

She had been taking too much of an interest in her surroundings. 'My legs aren't as long as yours,' she grumbled.

'And my eyes aren't so big as yours,' came the droll reply.

She had just rallied a spurt of energy to keep up with the tall figure along Waterport Street when he turned down an alleyway and came to an abrupt halt. Georgiana panted mercifully at the rear.

'Here we are, Master Robertson. Let's just hope that Mrs Howard is prepared to help us.'

Mrs Evelina Howard was a lady of large proportions with kind grey eyes and the most artfully *coiffured* grey hair. Originally from Brighton, she had arrived on the Rock some ten years ago, as the wife of an elderly naval officer. Since being widowed, she had established a small dressmaking service to cater to the ladies of Gibraltar, a business that had proved lucrative in the extreme. If the sudden appearance of a tall dark-haired naval officer with a boy by his side startled Mrs Howard, she was too polite to show it. She observed the golden epaulettes on both his shoulders, the gold-edged lapels and collar, and the embroidery upon the cuffs and pocket flaps of the smart dark dress coat.

'Good day, Captain. How may I help you?' She eyed him serenely, wondering as to the woman who had obviously prompted his visit to her establishment. Wife or mistress? Mrs Howard speculated that the man before her would never lack for the attention of female admirers.

Nathaniel bowed. 'Captain Nathaniel Hawke, of His Majesty's Navy, at your service, ma'am.'

The grey head inclined graciously.

'Mrs Howard,' he began, 'it's on a matter of some delicacy that I seek your help. A matter that demands the utmost discretion and for which, if you are prepared to assist, I will recompense you most generously.'

Mrs Howard felt a quiver of curiosity. 'You intrigue me, Captain Hawke. Are you asking me to undertake something illegal, immoral, or both?' Everything about her bespoke a calm still.

'Neither, madam. My request is, however, unusual and, were it to become widely known, would prove injurious to the lady concerned. It is somewhat urgent.' He had not moved and yet the sheer height and power of his frame dominated the surroundings.

She walked to the door and turned the key within the lock. 'Then you had better tell me, Captain, with all speed.' Rustling back across the room, she faced him and waited composedly for the story to unfold.

For just a moment, one single moment, Evelina Howard's usual aplomb deserted her as she stared slack-jawed at the boy. The serene grey eyes flicked back to Captain Hawke questioningly.

'Miss Raithwaite is both a lady and my betrothed,' he said firmly, irrefutably.

Mrs Howard smoothed her hands over her skirts. 'Of course.' And, when she looked up, there was nothing upon her countenance to betray the shock. 'Then you had best be about your business, sir, and leave the lady to me.' She did not miss the fleeting touch of his hand to the boy's, or the concerned reassurance he muttered in his ear before he departed.

'So, Miss Raithwaite, I think we had better begin with a bath.'

'But that's not—'

The older woman's voice interrupted. 'You smell of ships and the sea. Perhaps not the most desirable of fragrances for a young lady. Blunt words, but pray do not take them unkindly. We've much to do if we're to fulfil Captain Hawke's requirements.'

And so the day progressed and did not end until Georgiana had been scrubbed, rinsed, perfumed, poked and pinned into an endless variety of costumes. The transformation had now entered its final stages.

'It would be indelicate of me to enquire as to how you came to be in your present circumstance, miss, and therefore I won't. But I couldn't live comfortably with my conscience if I didn't offer you my help to escape a situation that may not be of your making.' The capable fingers coaxed ebony curls to frame Georgiana's face.

Georgiana looked up into the kind eyes that held hers in the mirror. 'Thank you, ma'am, for your concern. I fear that my appearance had misled you, for my fate is entirely of my own making.' She looked away, blinking, unable to say what would follow next. *As, I'm most ashamed to admit, is Captain Hawke's.*

'*Entirely* of your own making?' queried Evelina. 'In my experience, no lady's fate ever is. Women have so little say in the shaping of their lives, bound as they are by the constraints of their fathers and husbands.' When the girl did not reply, the modiste continued, 'When is the wedding?'

A blush spread across Georgiana's complexion. 'I'm not sure of the precise date.'

Mrs Howard regarded her with a knowing look, but said nothing.

'It's not what you think,' she protested. 'Captain Hawke has not ruined me!'

The pale eyebrows raised a notch and lowered demurely. 'Then it's a love match?'

'Yes…no…I cannot…'

'Do you love him?' Evelina asked quietly.

Georgiana's head drooped. 'Yes.'

'But you fear he doesn't love you?'

The ebony curls shook beneath her fingers. 'No. I know he doesn't.'

Mrs Howard moved round to take the girl's hands. 'From what I've seen, Miss Raithwaite, I believe you're very much mistaken. Captain Hawke most definitely had the look of a man in love.'

Georgiana sighed. 'Dear Mrs Howard, I know you're trying to help me, but you wouldn't if you knew what I'd done.'

The matronly lady patted the small hands within hers. 'Surely it cannot be so very bad?'

'Oh, but, ma'am, I very much fear that it is.' Georgiana said solemnly.

'Do you wish to tell me about it?'

Stormy blue eyes met peaceful grey. 'Yes, I believe I do.'

The sun had dropped low in the sky when Nathaniel Hawke returned to the modiste's establishment to collect Georgiana. He soon found himself ushered through to a small parlour.

'Captain Hawke.'

'Your servant, Mrs Howard.' Nathaniel bowed, his eyes scanning the room for a sign of Georgiana.

The plump pleasant face smiled. 'You are no doubt keen to make the acquaintance of Miss Raithwaite once more.'

'Yes, indeed.' Nathaniel tried to quell his rising impatience.

Mrs Howard sat down on a pink scalloped chair and fussed with making herself comfortable before facing her visitor once more. 'Forgive me, Captain Hawke. Won't you take a seat?'

Nathaniel did as she directed.

'Do you plan to stay long in our little town, sir?'

'No, no more than a se'nnight.'

The cool grey eyes watched him.

'We return to England, having fulfilled our duty, ma'am.' He glanced towards the closed door and back at Mrs Howard.

'Something at which I understand you're quite adept, Captain.'

Nathaniel's gaze swung to hers. The skin prickled at the nape of his neck. 'As is any naval officer, ma'am.'

Silence.

Evelina Howard spoke quietly. 'No, Captain Hawke, I don't believe that every officer would have acted as you have done.'

His heart set up a gallop, a tiny muscle flickered in his cheek. 'Please be direct, madam. Of what do you speak?' Precisely what had Georgiana told the woman, and where was his betrothed? His fingers resisted the urge to drum on the arm of the chair.

'Why, of Miss Raithwaite, of course.' She smiled at the frown descending upon his brow. 'You were quite right in what you told me, sir. Miss Raithwaite is a lady…a young and naïve lady.' She waited for the captain's response.

His eyes darkened. 'She is also the lady promised to be my wife before we leave this place.' He paused. 'You'll be well paid for your silence, Mrs Howard. Don't seek to destroy her reputation by a careless word.' His gaze narrowed. 'Where is Miss Raithwaite? She should be ready to join me by this hour.'

Satisfied by his response, Evelina raised herself and walked to the doorway. 'Miss Raithwaite!' Her voice raised just enough to carry upstairs. She turned to face Nathaniel once more. 'I thought it prudent to allow the servants the day off. They do so love to gossip, and we wouldn't want today's events to be discussed around the Rock.'

Any response Nathaniel might have uttered was forgotten as he gaped at the figure moving into the room. Dear God, he'd forgotten just what she looked like as a woman. Leaping to his feet he stepped towards her, noting the pink tinge in her cheeks and the embarrassed little smile playing upon those voluptuous lips. 'Georgiana!'

Mrs Howard watched as Captain Hawke stared at the young woman who stood rather self-consciously before them. The girl's face illuminated with a radiant smile as she moved to throw herself into the captain's arms.

'Hmph…hmm!' Mrs Howard developed a sudden irritation in her throat, respectfully reminding the love-struck couple that they were not alone.

'Oh!' Georgiana remembered herself just in time, skidded to a halt on Mrs Howard's best rug and managed to stutter, 'Captain Hawke!'

'Miss Raithwaite!' gasped the erstwhile supremely confident captain. He looked, thought Mrs Howard, a little shaken.

They stared at one another, a palpable flow of attraction between them.

Evelina Howard's mouth curved into a smug smile. She clearly had not been mistaken in her first appraisal of Captain Hawke's feelings for the girl. Why, he was looking at her with such tenderness it would have moved Mrs Howard to tears, if she had been of such a silly disposition. One small dry cough echoed in the room. 'So, Captain Hawke, do you find Miss Raithwaite's appearance satisfactory?'

Nathaniel recovered himself, dragged his eyes from the vision of loveliness before him and addressed the dressmaker. 'Indeed, Mrs Howard, it's much more than satisfactory. Let's discuss payment before Miss Raithwaite and I leave.' He removed a purse from his pocket.

Mrs Howard gestured Georgiana to be seated. 'Where do you intend to stay this evening?' A closed expression had descended upon her face.

'Miss Raithwaite will be safely lodged at an inn.'

Her eyebrows raised. 'Alone and unchaperoned?'

An uneasiness stole over Nathaniel. 'Yes,' he replied harshly. 'We have little choice.'

'That, Captain Hawke, is where you're mistaken. May I be so

bold as to make a suggestion that could prove mutually beneficial to us all?'

Thus it was, having discussed the matter in detail, that Nathaniel returned to the *Pallas* without his ship's boy George Robertson. Tomorrow would see the introduction of his betrothed, Miss Georgiana Raithwaite, to Gibraltarian naval society, and all under the chaperonage of the highly respectable Mrs Howard.

The next evening when Nathaniel called upon Mrs Howard's establishment, it was to discover two immaculately attired ladies patiently awaiting him in the parlour. Georgiana's skin glowed with an opalescent sheen beneath the pale aquamarine of her shot-silk gown. The satin ribbon sash around the high waist served only to draw attention to the gentle curve of her bosom above. The neckline was plain with a low, but not indecent, décolletage. Matching long gloves and a finely worked shawl completed the ensemble. Small curls of dark glossy hair kissed the edges of her face and a beaded bandeau triumphed as her crowning glory.

His eyes swept over her as if seeing her for the first time, feasting upon each detail.

'Miss Raithwaite, you take my breath away,' he said at last, before turning politely to Mrs Howard to compliment her own silver-grey outfit.

Elation glowed in those calm grey eyes. 'I do not think that we have to fear that your officers will recognise George Robertson,' she said.

'No, indeed, Mrs Howard, you've worked a miracle,' conceded Nathaniel.

Georgiana smiled up at the tall dark captain smartly clothed in his full dress uniform. In truth, she thought she had never seen him look so devilishly dashing, and longed to press a kiss to the stark line of his jaw. 'Mrs Howard has been a wonder. Even I was surprised when I looked in the mirror.'

'We had best leave, for it wouldn't do to be late for Admiral

Tyler's party. I have taken the liberty of hiring a carriage to transport us the short distance to the admiral's house.' Nathaniel gestured towards the door. 'Ladies.'

Admiral Tyler was a jovial bluff sort of fellow, who had grown rather rotund with the comfortable ease of life in Gibraltar. His wife, a little pudding of a woman, buzzed around him like an industrious bee. The old admiral's eyes lit up on sighting the young lady following in Captain Hawke's wake.

'Sir, may I present my betrothed, Miss Raithwaite, and of course her chaperon, Mrs Howard, with whom, I'm sure, you're already acquainted.'

Before her husband could reply, Lady Tyler ejected a nervous titter. 'But of course, dear Mrs Howard, quite the best modiste on the Rock. I do so rave about her designs. Always such a pleasure to meet with you.' She lavished a huge smile on Evelina and turned her attentions to the young woman at her side. 'Miss Raithwaite, what a positive delight.'

Georgiana, knowing herself to have been suddenly thrust into the spotlight, anchored down her quivering apprehension and managed her devoirs with a surprising calm confidence. It seemed that Lady Tyler could have rivalled Mirabelle Farleigh when it came to the chatterbox stakes. For, once Lady Tyler started to talk, she apparently found it difficult to stop. Not that Georgiana complained—it was much safer to allow their hostess to draw the focus of attention away from her own nervous self.

'How did you come to arrive without my notice? Mrs Howard has kept you hidden all to herself. For that I must chastise her most thoroughly.' A plump white hand reached forward and tapped an elaborate turquoise-coloured fan upon Mrs Howard's substantial arm. The modiste bore such patronage with a steadfast spirit, betraying not one inkling of her true opinion on Admiral Tyler's feather-brained wife. 'And, Captain Hawke, such a fine young captain. Haven't I always said that the navy needs just such men?' she cooed up at him, batting her lashes in an unbecoming flirtatious manner, which she managed to employ when in the company of any man of good breeding.

Nathaniel suffered her attentions admirably well, so much so that the falsetto of her laughter soon penetrated every nook and cranny of the drawing room.

'La, Captain Hawke, I declare you are a gentleman of hidden talents. To land so magnificent a prize, and with such little effort.'

His eyes fleetingly sought Georgiana across the crowded room. She shone, outstanding amidst the ladies of Gibraltar, and his heart swelled with tenderness and possessive pride.

Lady Tyler's shrill laugh raked across his musings, dragging him back to face her. 'You naughty man, that was not the prize of which I spoke, as well you know.' She delivered him a teasing tap of her fan.

'Indeed, but Miss Raithwaite is a prize above all,' he responded gallantly.

Lady Tyler shrieked even louder. 'That's quite the most romantic speech I've heard.'

The admiral joined them, intent on relieving Captain Hawke of his wife's presence. There was only so much that any one man could be expected to suffer.

'Ronald, dear—' she beamed '—I was just commenting on how very romantic Captain Hawke is concerning his betrothed.'

'Quite so, quite so. Couldn't help noticing that Lieutenant Pensenby is looking rather down in the mouth over in the corner. See if you can't coax him along, Jane.' He turned to Nathaniel, one large veined hand patting Lady Tyler's consolingly, 'M'wife's the best hostess on the Rock. Got something of a reputation to uphold within our little society.'

Jane Tyler screeched appreciatively.

'Off you go, m'dear.' He surreptitiously gestured towards Pensenby, and Lady Tyler headed off in the direction of the unsuspecting lieutenant. 'A damned fine accomplishment, Captain Hawke, well done, m'boy. That's what I like to see.'

'Thank you, Admiral Tyler.'

Ronald Tyler swirled the wine in his glass and looked towards Georgiana Raithwaite, who was now engaged in a conversation with Lieutenant Anderson and Mrs Howard. 'Fine filly of a gel,' he exclaimed. 'No wonder you've stored her quietly with the charming Mrs Howard. Too many ships in port to take any chances, what?'

Nathaniel saw the opportunity beckon before his eyes. 'Indeed. I wished to seek your advice on a related matter, sir.'

Admiral Tyler puffed out his chest and pretended not to be flattered. 'What is it that you need to know, young Hawke?' The admiral had adopted a distinctly paternal attitude to the man before him. For all his bravado, he recognised a good sea captain when he saw one.

Nathaniel met his enquiring gaze directly. 'I have a mind to marry Miss Raithwaite before we set sail for England once more. But the *Pallas* cannot linger here—we must reach Portsmouth before Christmas.'

'Say no more, say no more, Captain.' The admiral tapped the side of his nose in a sly fashion. 'No need to tell me how deuced an uncomfortable journey it would make, confined to ship with Miss Raithwaite when the lady is not yet your wife.' A suggestive wink issued from the wrinkled eye. 'Leave it to me, Hawke. I'll have a word with the chaplain, Mr Hughes. The licence will be ready and waiting before the week is out. Of course, you'll allow Lady Tyler to arrange the wedding in the King's Chapel, and the breakfast here in Belstone House. She would stop speaking to me if it were any other way. Come to think of it, that might not be such a bad thing!' He chortled and emptied the contents of his glass down his throat, none the wiser that Nathaniel Hawke knew exactly the difficulties of just such a journey with his young lady.

At the other end of the elaborate drawing room Georgiana was fencing Lieutenant Anderson's polite enquiries. 'Yes, thank you, Lieutenant Anderson, I am enjoying my visit to Gibraltar very much. The climate is so much milder, and drier than England's.'

John Anderson was having difficulty in drawing his eyes away from the enchanting young woman before him. 'Please don't think me bold, but I have the strangest notion that I've seen you before. But I'm quite sure that we've never been introduced, for I wouldn't have forgotten you.' A hint of pink crept into his cheeks.

'Perhaps I remind you of someone.' Georgiana's heart fluttered fast and furious.

'A *lady* of your acquaintance in England?' added Mrs Howard emphatically.

Lieutenant Anderson puzzled over the matter a moment longer. 'That must be the explanation, but memory fails me for the minute.' Suddenly memory was no longer a consideration, for Georgiana bestowed her most dazzling smile upon him.

'I would be most grateful if you were kind enough to explain exactly how you captured your prizes.'

John Anderson's cheeks flushed deeper. 'It was all Captain Hawke's doing, Miss Raithwaite.'

But Georgiana had no intention of allowing the first lieutenant to return to his musing of why he found her face familiar. 'I'm quite sure that he didn't perform such a task entirely alone. Won't you tell me an account of the ship's adventures?'

'Of course, miss, if you'd truly like to hear.' Lieutenant Anderson would not have refused the delectable Miss Raithwaite anything that she desired, and was soon in his element, describing the method by which the two French frigates were taken.

Nathaniel had the honour not only of taking Lady Tyler in to dinner, but also the delightful prospect of sitting beside her for the duration of the meal.

Georgiana was seated farther down the table between the vying attentions of Lieutenants Anderson and Pensenby.

One fleeting conspiratorial glance passed the length of the table between the grey-blue eyes and the deep brown, then was gone.

'Captain Hawke didn't mention your rendezvous here. I had supposed the presence of the *Pallas* within these waters to be solely because of her prizes.' Cyril Pensenby was attacking the roast beef with increasing vigour. He raised inquisitive eyes to hers.

Mrs Howard made her presence known. 'Miss Raithwaite's trip

had long been planned. She's enjoyed a most interesting visit in the weeks since her arrival.'

'Indeed, I wasn't suggesting anything to the contrary.' Although the girl seated by his left side was not what he considered a beauty, he had to admit that she possessed a certain inexplicable quality of attraction. A dewy fresh complexion and lips shaped to tempt a kiss from a man of stone. But that wasn't what held Cyril Pensenby's attention at the minute. His gaze fastened firmly upon her *décolletage*, on the glinting jet beads surrounding her neck, and lower to the swell of her bosom. It was evident that he had been too long from port. 'I can quite understand Captain Hawke's desire to collect you and take you back to England.' The remark was addressed to the curve below Georgiana's neckline.

'Are you one of the Pensenbys of York?' enquired Mrs Howard, determined to draw the man's attention from her charge.

With some reluctance Lieutenant Pensenby remembered his manners and entered into conversation with the formidable woman, leaving Miss Raithwaite to be monopolised by Mr Anderson.

At last the evening was done and Georgiana was making her way to the safety of the carriage, Nathaniel's reassuring presence close by. For all that she had enjoyed the dangerous game they played, she could not be sorry that the night was at a close. It was more of a strain than actually pretending to be George Robertson! She was just poised to climb into the carriage behind Mrs Howard when the hushed tones of Lieutenant Anderson sounded.

'Please excuse me, Captain Hawke, I wondered if I might speak with you before you return the ladies to their residence?'

Nathaniel was not best pleased by John Anderson's interruption, especially as he was desperate to gain some time with Georgiana, something that had so far evaded him throughout the evening. 'Mr Anderson?' He turned a glacial eye upon the officer.

'It's Master Robertson, sir, I'm concerned for—' The lieutenant halted abruptly as Miss Raithwaite missed her footing on the steps.

With a lightning reflex Nathaniel's arms were around her, lifting her up and against him, concerned eyes scanning her face.

'Georgiana!' he whispered, a look of intense urgency tensing his jaw.

'It's nothing. I'm a little tired and careless, and somehow missed my footing. No damage done.' She blushed profusely, aware of both the close heat of his body and Lieutenant Anderson's fixed interest. To make matters worse, Admiral and Lady Tyler had noticed the rumpus and were making their way steadily to the epicentre of the commotion.

Mrs Howard hurriedly removed Georgiana from Captain Hawke's arms, guided her into the seat, and fixed her firmly into position by means of a blanket across the knees.

The strain of Lady Tyler's high voice carried to the carriage. 'So romantic, so in love!'

Georgiana blushed the colour of port wine. Captain Hawke clambered aboard, bid his lieutenant meet him at the pinnace in half an hour, and escaped into the blackness of the night.

Chapter Nine

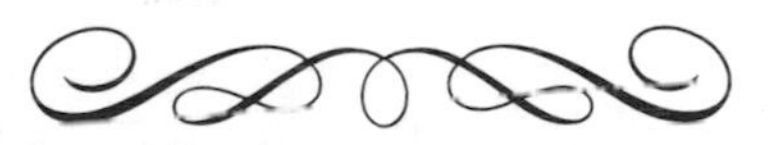

Georgiana sat at one end of Evelina Howard's parlour. Nathaniel sat at the other. The clock on the mantel sounded its slow and steady rhythm in measured ticks.

Mrs Howard stood beside the doorframe. 'All that chatter has rendered me quite thirsty.'

It occurred to Georgiana that no one could possibly describe Mrs Howard's articulate conversation as chatter. No, chatter was a word that could only be ascribed to the likes of Lady Tyler and Mirabelle Farleigh, although she had rapidly revised her opinion on any similarities existing between those two women.

'I'm sure, Georgiana, that you would benefit from a dish of tea. Captain Hawke, may I offer you some refreshment?' Her serenity spread like ripples in the room.

'Yes, thank you, tea would be most acceptable.'

The soft rustle of grey silk and they were alone, separated by space and Mrs Howard's elegant furnishings. Each gaze fixed on the other, intense brown deepening to a dangerous dark smoulder, stormy blue lit with sparks of the translucent silver of the sea.

Nathaniel broke the silence first. 'Well done, Georgiana, you were wonderful tonight. I'm quite sure that nobody suspected in the slightest. You weren't too uncomfortable I hope?'

'No.' The long ebony ringlets of the hairpiece tickled the skin of her neck. 'Indeed not. It was really rather exciting, apart from Lieutenant Anderson's insistence that my face was familiar.' A grin spread across her cheeks. 'And, of course, his overt reference to George Robertson. I must confess to being surprised at that, and at the most inopportune of moments! Your officers and Admiral Tyler will pity you that you're promised to the most clumsy-footed of women, not knowing that I've yet to find my land legs!'

Nathaniel laughed, flashing white teeth against the subtle blue shadow of his jaw. 'I promise you, it's not pity that they feel!'

'Whatever do you mean, sir?' she countered, rising from her chair, hands on hips.

'You know very well and I don't mean to make your head swell with too many comments on the extent of your beauty.' His eyes glinted dangerously and his mouth had moved to a lopsided grin.

The sight of his powerful athletic figure encased in the magnificent full dress uniform was impressive. Georgiana tried not to stare. 'You're teasing me again, you wretch.'

He moved playfully towards her. 'That's a fine way to address the captain of your ship, and your betrothed—a wretch, indeed! I should have you strung up and flogged for the very mention of the word.' Reaching her, he pulled her to him with mock severity. He knew it was a mistake from the minute that his fingers wrapped around the bare skin of her arms, between the end of her short puff sleeves and the start of her long silken gloves. So soft and smooth, so warm and inviting.

A harsh intake of air. He was so close that she could smell his scent—soap and sandalwood, and something unique and masculine. The skin on her arms burned beneath the touch of his fingers and a pulse leapt in her throat. The dark smouldering eyes were filled with tenderness and a look that Georgiana knew now to be desire. She wondered if her own face betrayed her rising emotions as clearly as his, for then Nathaniel would not mistake what he saw there. Her hands moved of their own accord to gently cup the roughened skin of his face, tracing the outline of his jaw with infinitesimal care.

'Georgiana!' he breathed, and the name was pained on his lips. 'My own sweet Georgiana.' His hands slid round to the soft silk of her back, gliding over the curve of her hips. His head turned to capture her gloved fingers to his mouth, nibbling on their tips, lapping against them with his tongue.

At last she could bear it no longer and, rising onto the points of her toes, replaced her fingers with her lips, meeting his tongue with her own until they arced in a sensual lightning of passion.

China chinked on china and the thud of Mrs Howard's suddenly heavy footsteps sounded outside the parlour. Nathaniel thrust his betrothed back down into her chair and, by the time their hostess entered the room, was examining a small porcelain vase on the mantelpiece. Silence echoed loudly.

'Your tea, Miss Raithwaite.' Mrs Howard passed the delicate dish and saucer to an extremely red-faced and breathless Georgiana. Amazingly Mrs Howard appeared to notice no change in her charge's appearance and busied herself with supplying the same beverage to Nathaniel. 'Captain Hawke,' she said politely. The steady silver gaze slid to his, and Nathaniel inclined his head in a silent salutation.

The deep mellow voice sounded within the room, his words halting Georgiana's sip of tea midflow. 'Miss Raithwaite and I were just discussing Admiral Tyler's kind offer to hold our wedding breakfast in Belstone House. I'm hopeful that everything shall be in place to allow our marriage before the week is out.'

It was Mrs Howard's turn to acknowledge his response, which she did most amiably with a smile and a nod of her immaculate head. 'That,' she said smoothly, 'is something I'm very relieved to hear.'

Georgiana squirmed within her seat, acutely aware of the unrefined hurry of her forthcoming nuptials, and the magnitude of the obligation she had thrust upon Nathaniel Hawke. Whether he wanted to or not, he could not reasonably do anything other than wed her. She reminded herself that he was taking such drastic action to save his own reputation as well as her own, but what if… A shadow of cold wheedled its way through the warmth that blazed within Georgiana's breast. It was a matter that deserved nothing less than the foremost consideration. She looked up to find herself the focus of both Nathaniel and Mrs Howard, and realised that she had paid no heed whatsoever to the conversation. 'Please forgive me, I was wool-gathering.'

'So it's settled, then,' concluded Mrs Howard. 'We look forward to seeing you tomorrow, Captain Hawke. Until then we'll bid you good-night.'

Captain Hawke took his leave as the most gracious of gentlemen, entrusting his precious prize to the safe care of the dressmaker.

'Sir, I wondered if I might be so bold as to enquire of Master Robertson's condition?' Lieutenant Anderson spoke in a quiet voice, but not of sufficiently low volume to prevent the remainder of the boat from pricking up their ears. He was seated beside the captain as the pinnace rowed back out to the *Pallas*. The gentle murmur of conversation died out. Only the sweep of the oars through the water sounded in the warm night air.

Nathaniel resisted the urge to ask just what damn business it was of Anderson's and answered as if it were not a matter of concern at all. 'Oh, the boy has taken a turn for the worse, I'm afraid. Presently he's lodged with an acquaintance of mine in the town and will be attended by a physician tomorrow.'

'I cannot help but overhear your words, Captain,' exclaimed the surgeon, who had in truth been straining to listen from his position at the other side of the small wooden boat. 'Allow me to offer my services, humble though they are. I'll happily attend the boy tomorrow and assist the local physician in any way that I can.'

'Thank you, Mr Belmont, but that won't be necessary.' Captain Hawke made to turn the talk to another subject, an aim that was to be thwarted by the tenacious interest of his officers.

Mr Pensenby spoke up. 'Sir, I saw the like of Robertson's symptoms when I was in the East Indies. Sweating, fever, pains within the stomach and a terrible sickness. Not a pretty sight, and many of the afflicted men did not recover. Ran rampant amidst the crew, lost a third of the men. Still, it's unlikely to be the same thing, different part of the world and all that.'

Nathaniel suppressed a smile. Cyril Pensenby may well just have handed him the very excuse to leave poor George Robertson behind on Gibraltar. 'Let's leave it to the expert and pray that such a plague is never visited upon the *Pallas*.'

'Amen to that,' came the unanimous response.

Alone in the cosy bed in the largest of Mrs Howard's visitor bedrooms, Georgiana lay wide awake. For all her fatigue, sleep was proving elusive, in part due to the lack of the habitual rhythmic roll of the *Pallas* to which she had grown so accustomed. But that was not all. For the tiny seed of a thought revealed to her prior to Nathaniel's departure had taken hold and germinated. And with it she knew a method that would release Captain Hawke from the prospect of an enforced marriage. A cold and hard knowledge that would not let her sleep, relentlessly straying into her mind each time she drove its discomfort to the dark and distant recesses.

It was twenty minutes after two o'clock when Georgiana decided that a dish of tea was required to remedy the situation.

The house was quiet and lit only with the silver beams of a full moon flooding through the unmasked windows of the landing and lower rooms. Bare feet tiptoed step by step downstairs and on to the cold stone floor of the kitchen. Breathing her good fortune that none of Mrs Howard's maids actually lived in, she had just set the kettle of water to boil when she was interrupted by a soft padding and a gentle voice.

'Georgiana, whatever is the matter? What are you doing down here at this time of night?'

She wrapped the dressing gown tightly across her chest, trying to warm herself against the nocturnal chill. 'I'm sorry if I woke you, Mrs Howard. I couldn't sleep and thought some tea might help. Would you like some?'

'Perhaps a small dish.' Mrs Howard's grey hair was plaited tidily into a braid that swept far down her back. She paused, before adding, 'And you will, of course, tell me what it is that is troubling you, my dear.' No one would ever think of disobeying the quiet command intrinsic in that voice.

An ear lobe suffered several pulverising squeezes between thumb and forefinger before Georgiana could find the words to answer. 'It's Captain Hawke and our forthcoming marriage.' She glanced rapidly at Mrs Howard before resuming her watch on the kettle.

'A watched pot never boils,' quoted the modiste. 'Georgiana, come and sit at the table with me.' Grey eyes observed the girl's cold bare feet. 'On second thoughts, run and fetch your slippers, my dear, before we continue, or you're bound to catch your death of cold.' A clucking, tutting noise filled the kitchen as Georgiana rose to do as she was bid, and eventually they were settled comfortably with their tea.

The steam rose from the dish as Georgiana sipped gingerly.

'Now,' said Mrs Howard, 'you were about to tell me precisely the nature of your concerns with marrying Captain Hawke.' She drank her tea and waited with her usual patience.

Georgiana fiddled with her ear. She sipped some tea. And adjusted her slippers. And her dressing gown. 'Well…it's just that…oh, it sounds so feeble when it comes to transfer thought to spoken word!'

'I'm sure that it's no such thing,' said Mrs Howard reassuringly. 'Perhaps you are worried as to the nature of your wifely duties? You are far from home, and your mama, but have no concerns, my dear, for I'll tell you all that you need to know. And they're nothing to worry about. Indeed, you are likely to find them really quite pleasurable.'

A furiously blushing Georgiana gulped the rest of her tea, hot though it was, and tried not to think of what Mrs Howard was alluding to. Unfortunately the memory of intimacies shared with the captain came flooding back all too readily. She cleared her throat. 'Thank you, ma'am, for offering such advice, but that isn't the cause of my quandary.'

'Do you find the thought of wedding Captain Hawke distasteful?' The modiste asked the question even though she had witnessed its answer with her own eyes.

'No, indeed, there is no other man whom I'd rather marry.'

'You said that you love him, and you really do, don't you? Any fool with eyes in his head can see that.'

'Yes,' she said simply.

Mrs Howard took Georgiana's hand between her own. 'Then, tell me, dear girl, precisely what is the problem?'

'I don't want him to sacrifice himself by making a marriage that's not of his own free will. He will wed me to save both our reputations. Can you imagine what would be thought of Captain Hawke if the truth were to emerge? A woman creeps aboard his ship, serves as a ship's boy, before being transferred to the position of captain's boy, sleeps within his own night cabin, while the captain lies to the crew that the lad is his nephew! Through my folly, and nothing of Captain Hawke's fault, I've placed him in a position that could ruin his career, something that he's worked long and hard to attain. I've forced him to a marriage. Nathaniel Hawke doesn't love me, and I fear that eventually he'll grow to hate me.' She turned saddened eyes to Mrs Howard. 'How can I marry him, knowing all that I do?'

The older woman was quiet for a little. 'I take it that Captain Hawke himself told you of the threat to his captaincy?'

'Nathaniel only confirmed what I already knew. It's the reason I agreed to marry him.'

'I see,' said Mrs Howard. 'Not because your own reputation is ruined and you love him?'

Georgiana darted a startled look at her chaperon. 'Nathaniel is of the aristocracy. My father's an inn-owner. I bring no dowry, no contacts, nothing that could be of any use to a man like Nathaniel, nothing except Georgiana Raithwaite. I would never agree to wed him to save myself.'

Evelina Howard smiled. 'But you'll do so to save him?'

'Of course.'

'Would you believe me if I told you that Captain Hawke holds you in very great affection?'

The girl slowly shook her head.

'I'd wager that you've misjudged his true feelings. Many gentlemen can be a little reticent to convey their romantic sensibilities. It doesn't follow that they don't care. Besides, you're forgetting, I've seen the way that he looks at you!' She raised one perfectly shaped eyebrow and turned up the corners of her mouth.

'I'm afraid you're mistaken, ma'am.' Georgiana sighed. 'Although it pains me to admit the truth, I must. Captain Hawke is not indifferent to me. Indeed, I do believe he actually feels some element of—' she paused, blushed, and completed her sentence '—of desire for me. But living amidst one hundred and eighty-five men these past weeks has certainly been educational. For I've learned that when a man is at sea for any length of time, confined with other men, and away from women, he's liable to desire the company of any woman. And I stress the word *any*.'

Mrs Howard fixed a determined look upon her young charge. 'Georgiana Raithwaite, I dread to think what manner of education you've been exposed to. Suffice it to say that men do have certain, shall we say, appetites, but if Captain Hawke was of such a mind he would have taken advantage of you long before the *Pallas* docked in Gibraltar. And as you've assured me that the captain has not...ruined you, then we can be confident that it's not his carnal appetites that are driving him to marry you.' She did not add that a man with the looks and position of Nathaniel Hawke would have no difficulty finding any number of women within the port to satisfy those needs.

'No,' agreed Georgiana, 'it's his sense of honour and the fact that his back is against the wall that propel him.' She shook her head. 'There's no way to postpone the wedding and save face, so I thought that perhaps after the ceremony I could stay here with you while Nathaniel sails for England. He could then obtain an annulment, leaving him free to marry as he wills. I, of course, would wait some time before returning.'

Evelina Howard carefully placed the fine porcelain dish upon the saucer. 'To resume your place in the bosom of your family? To stand once more within the marriage mart, and wed a man other than Captain Hawke?'

'No, I could never do that! I'll stay in Portsmouth and become a paid companion.'

'You think to have it all worked out,' said Mrs Howard smoothly. 'But—' she raised her cool grey eyes to Georgiana's '—you've omitted to consider one vital fact.'

Georgiana's brow furrowed.

'I leave Gibraltar for England after your wedding. I've a notion to return to my roots, and Captain Hawke has been kind enough to offer me transport upon his ship. We shall make the journey together, my dear, and arrive in Portsmouth before Christmas.'

'But…'

Mrs Howard's firm hand patted Georgiana's. 'Life as a poor miserable spinster at the beck and call of arrogant old women, or marriage to Nathaniel Hawke—I wouldn't have thought the choice a difficult one. The man loves you, Georgiana, as you love him. Be happy with the chance that fate has dealt you, take the risk, and you'll see that I'm right.' She rose and, leaving the empty dishes still upon the wooden table, moved slowly across the moonlit room. 'Now, I, at least, am for bed, and so too should you be.'

With Mrs Howard's words echoing in her mind, it was some time before Georgiana finally found sleep.

Walter Praxton tutted at his fingers stained with ink from the quill held tightly between them. He scrubbed at them with his handkerchief before continuing with his carefully constructed text.

Portsmouth
December, 1804

My dear Mr Raithwaite

I write to apprise you of the latest knowledge that I have ascertained concerning your daughter. It is with a degree of trepidation that I reveal that Miss Raithwaite conspired to travel to the town of Fareham, unaccompanied upon the mail and dressed in the attire that we previously discovered. However, I am afraid to report that upon reaching her destination, she was pressed into service as a boy upon a naval frigate, which has since left dock. I cannot be certain as to the fate she has suffered upon her journey, but reassure you once again that, if there is any way that the situation can be resolved, I will endeavour, with every ounce of my being, to bring that about. I understand your distress in the matter and can only implore you to hold fast in your resolve until my return to Andover. Although your heart is breaking with sadness, I know that your concerns must now lie with the prevention of any ensuing scandal. Therefore, take some small crumb of comfort in my promise that I will return with Miss Raithwaite as my wife or not at all.

The ship she was stowed upon is due to return to this port in the next weeks. Thus, the truth will soon become apparent, and our waiting is nigh at an end. I have a man watching the port at all hours of the day and night, so fear not that the girl will elude us for a second time. No matter the expenditure, I am committed to my duty, and remind you of the freedom that you granted me when last we spoke.

When next you see me, I am confident that it will be in the capacity of your son. Miss Raithwaite shall learn the error of her ways if she has not already done so.

For now I bid you adieu.

Your faithful servant,

Walter Praxton

The week had passed almost as a blur for Nathaniel, caught as he was between completing the preparations for his wedding and ensuring that all on the *Pallas* was in order prior to the commencement of her return journey to England. On top of this he was required to fashion and reveal a clever tale to account for the sudden disappearance of Master George Robertson, a task that was proving rather more difficult than his initial estimation because of the overt interest his crew seemed to have taken in the matter. Indeed, he had barely had time to visit his betrothed. Wednesday had seen a rushed affair when he'd called at Mrs Howard's to inform the ladies that the ceremony would take place two days hence. Georgiana had expressed a wish to converse with him, seemingly at length, but, due to a pressing appointment with Rear Admiral Tyler, Nathaniel had been unable to comply. Thus it was that he found himself on Friday morning waiting with a growing sense of pleasurable anticipation for the arrival of his bride before the altar in the King's Chapel.

Lieutenant Anderson smiled nervously as his second by his side. Around the splendid interior Lady Tyler had organised the hanging of garlands of small white flowers, artfully interspersed between vivid green foliage swags on the ends of the pews. The chaplain hovered nearby, looking unwell, but insisting that he was able enough to perform the marriage ceremony. On one side of the church a clutch of finely attired ladies and their smart naval husbands, Admiral Tyler's officers, were seated on the heavy wooden pews. On the other, the officers of the *Pallas* sat rigidly upright. It appeared that Miss Raithwaite's preference for punctuality might, on this occasion, have failed. No doubt putting the finishing touches to her wedding gown, or some such matter. Or so Nathaniel thought. Not for one minute did he consider that the object of his affection's delay could be due to another reason all together—that perhaps the strong-willed Miss Raithwaite was suffering a late resurgence of conscience.

'I cannot marry him,' avowed Georgiana with surprising force. 'He must not make such a monumental self-sacrifice.' She sat herself down abruptly in the parlour chair, oblivious to the crushing of the delicate pale pink silk of her train. The tiny rosebuds and pink pearls clustered around the neckline heaved dramatically with the agitated thrust of her bosom. 'No, it won't do at all.' Her fingers seized upon her ear lobe setting the single pink pearl earring dipping and diving in a veritable frenzy of motion.

Mrs Howard, far from lapsing into hysterics at the sudden change of mind in her charge and the rapid ticking of the clock, calmly faced Miss Raithwaite with a steely eye. 'No, indeed, it won't,' she said, swaying the intricacies of her classically styled hair with a delicate shake of the head. 'Of course you must not marry him if you feel that it would be a mistake to do so.'

Georgiana glanced up, somewhat surprised at the modiste's agreement. She had expected at least some semblance of persuasion.

'Captain Hawke will already be present and waiting in King's

Chapel. Shall I send a maid along to inform him by way of Admiral Tyler that you're jilting him at the altar?' Her voice was silky smooth, her eyes flashing the colour of sword blades. 'Don't concern yourself that he'll suffer overly much from the pity of his own officers—oh, and, of course, Admiral and Lady Tyler, and the rest of Gibraltarian society. He's a strong man, and one who is, after all, due to sail tomorrow morning.'

Georgiana opened her mouth to argue, but promptly closed it again when Mrs Howard returned, 'No, Miss Raithwaite. Kindly do me the honour of allowing me to finish what I have to say.' And so she continued. 'The scandal shall be short-lived. And I'm sure that his honour will still guarantee you a passage home aboard the *Pallas,* so there's no need for you to worry on that score either. Perhaps the journey within such confinement will give you time to explain to the captain how your treatment of him is a fitting reward for all that he's done. Risking his very position within His Majesty's Navy for a woman, only to have her jilt him, and in such a very public way. No, you're quite right, Georgiana, one's conscience must always be clear, no matter the consequences suffered by others in its purging.' She rose in one fluid movement and made to ring the bell. 'I'll dispatch the maid immediately. No point in prolonging Captain Hawke's ordeal.'

'No!' Georgiana cried. 'Your words have shown my thoughts as shallow and petty. I've been absorbed with myself, never thinking of the harm I may do Captain Hawke with my childish notions. Mrs Howard, please forgive my foolishness. My mind has been quite overcome with selfish emotion.'

Mrs Howard reached for Georgiana's hands. 'It's common for young ladies to experience such doubts just before their marriage. Cast them away, hold your head high, and with a stoic countenance do what you must to complete what this day has started.'

'Thank you.' Georgiana's voice was small, her heart suitably chastened, as she accepted Mrs Howard's embrace. 'Mrs Howard, I do believe we have a wedding to attend.'

And with that the ladies made ready to depart the modiste's establishment for the very last time.

* * *

Nathaniel's hands were growing somewhat clammy and a gnawing feeling of unease had developed within his stomach. It appeared that Miss Raithwaite's outfit must be in need of complete restyling or something else was very much wrong. John Anderson was shifting his weight between both feet, small beads of perspiration collecting upon his upper lip and brow. He pulled nervously at his neckcloth before glancing for the umpteenth time at his commanding officer. A murmur of disquiet had set up within the party as they sat bathed in the colourful light from the great stained glass window. Nathaniel had just made up his mind to send a messenger to Mrs Howard's residence when he spotted the lady herself.

Georgiana looked splendid in a pseudo-Greek classical gown of the palest pink coloration. With her dark hair swept up and adorned with a bandeau of pink rosebuds, she looked nothing but beautiful. Her ivory skin seemed to have been carved from alabaster and the single row of fine seed pearls fastened around her neck mirrored those sewn so painstakingly around the neckline of her dress and upon the three-quarter-length gloves that covered her arms.

She looked down the aisle and saw Nathaniel's tall tense figure. Even as her eyes rested upon him he turned and looked at her. In that single moment time stopped for Georgiana. For her, there was no one else in the church. Even across the vast distance of the aisle she could see the relief in his eyes, and she cringed that she alone had set such a worry there. Had she really contemplated jilting the man? Surely only madness could have prompted such an idea? For Georgiana knew without a doubt that she could wish for nothing more than to be the wife of Nathaniel Hawke. She loved him, it was as simple as that. Her silly fears and idle threats had centred around depriving herself of that which she most desired. Yet Evelina Howard had forced her to see that, in denying herself, not she, but the very man that she cared most for would reap the cruellest of punishments. A shudder rippled down her spine at the thought of what she had almost done in the folly of her anxiety. Now, here, in this church, in his presence, she felt no fear, no worry, no imaginations of the future or gloomy speculation of what it would mean for them both. There was nothing. Only Nathaniel Hawke. And the woman that loved him. She took Admiral Tyler's arm, smiled, and walked slowly, steadily towards the one person that she wanted most in the world.

Captain Hawke's eyes swept down over the woman seated by his side and felt a swell of possessive pride. His wife. His sweet Georgiana. And not for the first time wished that the wedding breakfast might soon be over so that he could speak with her, and more. She was smiling, a picture of youthful vivacity, captivating, polite, everything a man could wish his wife to present to society. Quite deliberately he moved his thigh beneath the table to brush against hers. Watched with pleasure when those sea-blue eyes met his with surprised delight. A secret smile meant only for him. And he revelled in it, the desire to hold her to him, to protect her from any hurt, growing strong and deep within him.

Georgiana conversed admirably with all present at the table, the very picture of the happy bride. She had remembered to apologise for the tardiness of her arrival, a matter that was waved inconsequentially away by a magnanimous Admiral Tyler and his lady wife. Lady Tyler seemed in such high spirits, spouting forth maxims of romance and love at such regular intervals as to suppose that she herself might have been the bride. Amid responding graciously to her hostess and exchanging pleasantries with Lieutenant Pensenby, Georgiana still found time to watch the man beside her, the man who was now legally, and in the eyes of the Church, her husband. The dark dangerous eyes frequently swept in her direction, and in them was such indisputable affection that the breath almost caught in her throat. Perhaps Mrs Howard had been right, and Nathaniel Hawke had a care for her after all. For surely there could be no mistaking the message so clear in his gaze? Excitement fluttered in her chest, and when the strong warmth of his thigh brushed hers she felt the blood rise to her face and smiled up at him. A promise between them sealed. Secret, honourable, binding, for ever.

Georgiana pushed the curtains further back to uncover the window from which she had been examining the view of the town below. Beyond the streets of illuminated houses a smoky sky smudged with the onset of night, the horizon highlighted in a golden glow that deepened finally to a rich burnished red. Waves lapped gently upon a tranquil darkening ocean, and the topmasts of the *Pallas* were silhouetted in the distance.

'It'll be a fine day tomorrow, just right for us to set sail. When I was young my nurse taught me a saying: "Red sky at night, shepherds' delight; red sky in the morning, shepherds' warning." Look at the sunset, it's beautiful.'

Nathaniel came to stand behind his wife. 'But not as beautiful as you,' he murmured against the shell of her ear. His arms enclosed around her waist, feeling the soft silk of her gown and the warmth of the woman beneath. His lips nibbled insistently at her ear lobe.

She sighed and relaxed against him. 'It was kind of Admiral and Lady Tyler to let us spend the night here.' The thought of them both squashed within the cot in Nathaniel's night cabin with the entirety of the crew knowing full well what they were about brought a blush to her cheeks. 'I can scarcely believe that we're married now. It seems so strange to bid farewell to both Master Robertson and Miss Raithwaite. I'm fast running out of personas!'

He heard the laughter in her voice. 'That's just as well,' he replied, 'for you'll be no other than Georgiana, Lady Hawke. You had best grow to like it, as I don't intend to let you use any other.' He chuckled and pressed his lips to her neck. The subtle aroma of roses tickled his nose, and he inhaled against the soft white skin. 'You smell rather different to George Robertson. Did I ever tell you that my nephew-cum-ship's boy, emitted the most robust odour of the sea? Indeed, on laundry days it was wise to stay upwind of the boy!' Mirth creased his eyes.

'Oh, you exasperating man!' Georgiana exclaimed and swatted the muscular arms encircling her waist. 'I didn't smell any worse than the rest of the crew, and well you know it!'

'Even on a laundry day?' he teased.

She wriggled round to face him. 'And whose clothes was I commanded to scrub in that foul-smelling fluid? I'll be happy never to see that barrel ever again!'

He dropped a kiss to the top of her carefully arranged curls. 'And neither you shall. The captain's wife will find her journey to England somewhat different to that of poor George Robertson, that I promise you. Indeed, I'm quite looking forward to resuming the comfort of the cot in my night cabin.' One dark eyebrow angled dangerously.

A delicate hue of tender pink suffused her cheeks at his mention of the intimacies that lay ahead. 'You're quite incorrigible, Captain Hawke.'

'What's all this *Captain Hawke*? Next thing you'll be saluting me! We're married now, you must call me Nathaniel, as I will call you sweet Georgiana.'

She snuggled in closer to him, laying her cheek against the hard muscle of his chest. 'Nathaniel,' she breathed, listening to the thud of his heart, 'you're so kind to me, even after all the trouble I've dealt you. I must confess I feel guilty that I've forced you to this marriage against your will. Can you ever forgive me?' She stood quite still, not daring to move her face or meet his gaze, just waiting, waiting, for his answer.

Nathaniel gently held her from him and stared down into her face. His voice was soft and melodic. 'What makes you think that I didn't want to marry you?'

'Why, given the foolish position in which I'd placed us both, marriage was the only way for you to save my reputation, and protect yourself from a possible court martial. I know you to be a man of honour. Twice you've saved me from death or worse, without thought for your own situation. And for your pains you're rewarded with the burden of an unwanted wife.' Eyes the colour of the Atlantic on a wild day regarded him solemnly, huge within the pallor of her face. Tension racked her shoulders and the swell of her bosom raised and lowered with a steady control.

His dark head gently lowered to hers, moving until the tips of their noses just touched. And once there he gently rubbed against her. 'Georgiana, I know that you didn't plan to land upon the *Pallas*. It's true that your presence aboard the ship presented us both with difficulties, and that neither of us had anticipated such a situation arising. Believe me when I tell you that this marriage is very much of my making. As a gentleman I was honour-bound to wed you, but as Nathaniel Hawke—' his lips moved softly to brush hers '—I *wanted* you as my wife.'

'But…' Georgiana regarded him in bewilderment, afraid to allow herself to believe what she thought he might be saying.

'No buts, sweetheart, never any buts. In the time I've come to know you, I'm persuaded that no other lady could fulfil that role quite so well. So, you see, if anyone should feel remorse it should be me, for it was I who took advantage of a young and innocent lady within my care.' Warm breath tickled upon her skin as he traced the line of her jaw with a myriad of butterfly kisses.

The magical allure of his mouth's motions served to render her a trifle light-headed, but she could not let him take the blame so gallantly for something that she herself had encouraged. Indeed, had she not dreamt of his kisses from their very first encounter? 'Nathaniel.' His name sounded silky smooth to the roll of her tongue. 'You did nothing that I didn't want, took nothing that I didn't give freely. And know this—' her palms pressed against the strength of his body '—I would have given you much more than you took.'

A small rumble started from deep in his throat, and his mouth captured hers with an insistent passion. Lips sliding together, moist, hot, in desperation. 'Georgiana,' he whispered.

His kisses enlivened her, emboldened her beyond a level she had reached before, goaded her to tell him the truth she had sworn never to reveal. 'Indeed, that night, that single night, when you lay upon me in the cot and kissed me, I didn't want you to leave, only to stay the whole night beneath the covers in my arms.' She felt wanton, giddy, but strangely unashamed. 'Are you shocked and disgusted with me?'

'Never!' he murmured against the soft lobe of her ear as he feasted on its tender flesh. 'You don't know what it is you would have asked.'

She twisted against him, moving her lips to press a line of small hot kisses against his throat. 'Not then, but I do now. Mrs Howard has warned me of my wifely duties.'

His voice guttered low, a hoarse whisper and no more. 'It's no duty, in truth I'll force nothing of you. Given freely or not at all.'

Slender fingers touched to the roughness of his chin, pulling it lower, so that she could look directly into those burning brown eyes. 'You're a good man, Nathaniel Hawke. I've known it since you plucked me from the Borne. I'm yours, I'll always be yours.'

His lips caressed her cheek, moving to claim the tender-shaped form of her mouth. She opened to his touch, meeting the entry of his tongue with her own. Sensation flickering down her spine, sparks of desire rising from the banking heat growing within. Those long tanned fingers traced magic upon her skin, leaving in their wake a path of awakened sensitivity. For all the time that Mrs Howard had taken to fit the elegant rosebud wedding gown to Georgiana, Nathaniel Hawke removed it deftly and with the speed of a sailor retracting the sails in the path of a burgeoning storm. The petticoats and stays were laid carefully upon the chair, leaving her female form clearly visible beneath the sheer material of her shift.

'Georgiana!' The word sounded guttural in his harsh expiration of breath. And when his hands reached out to touch her she could feel the tremble within them. He pulled her to him, his strong fingers sweeping the length of her back to cup her buttocks.

The neckcloth tugged once beneath her hands before she tossed it to the floor and returned to pull at his shirt. In a flurry of impatience he disrobed all except his fine midnight-blue breeches, which, mindful of his new wife's innocence, he determined to retain so as to save her from any fright. He had reckoned without Georgiana's blossoming passion. As he kissed her, her back arched against the poster of the bed and he felt her fingers move to the fastening on his breeches. 'Take them off.' Her voice was low and throaty with escalating desire.

Nathaniel did not need to be told twice. He watched her eyes as they dropped lower. 'Don't be afraid,' he whispered. Strong fingers slipped the fine woven shift to pool upon the Oriental rug, touching where he had ever longed to trace. Along the smooth flesh of her stomach, sweeping over the rounded curves of her hips.

The peaks of her finely formed breasts teased against the dark hair matting of his chest, causing her to gasp in an agony of spiralling need. His taut manhood probed her belly, and she wriggled against him. She felt his intake of breath before she heard it. And his strong arms moved to sweep her up on to the bed. He knelt over her, licking kisses down her neck, moving ever closer to her breasts until at last his wet tongue flicked against the rosy peaks. Georgiana's thighs burned hot and hard, even while her insides elicited a curious melting sensation. Her fingers wove between his dark glossy curls, his hair sleek and glossy to her touch. Soap and sandalwood and something that caused her to cry out his name. He slid lower, kissing the silky hidden skin of her thighs, his breath scorching other hidden places until she trembled from the need rising within her, knowing nothing but her love for the man above her and the rising pleas of her body. At last he moved away, his lips skimming her before he uttered his warning, pausing even in the depths of his passion to reassure her. With one thrust she was his, the pain dispersed by the gentle words in her ear and the soft touch of his thumb teasing her lips. He lay quite still until she eased around him and only then did he reveal to her the age-old game that escalated in such a fountain of pleasure for both its players.

Georgiana lay sated and content. Nathaniel's arms curled around her, the light touch of his sleeping breath rhythmic upon her shoulder. This night had changed her for ever, for she knew with irrefutable certainty that she loved the man beside her, the man who was now her husband. And for all that he had not uttered the words, she had seen in his eyes, his deep dark eyes, that she had captured a place close to his heart.

Chapter Ten

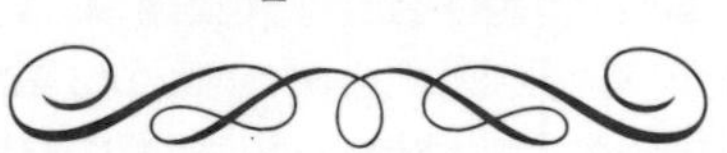

Georgiana was doing her best to alleviate Mrs Howard's seasickness. The poor woman had been unable to retain one morsel of food within her stomach since leaving the port at Gibraltar. Indeed, they had been only thirty minutes into the journey when her normally creamy complexion paled. By the Saturday afternoon her skin had taken on a greenish tinge and had stayed that way ever since. None of Georgiana's ministrations seemed to make the slightest difference and even Nathaniel declared he had never seen such a bad case. Such was the lady's malady that Georgiana was unable to leave her, spending the night-times in a hammock strung close by Mrs Howard's narrow cot in the first lieutenant's cabin. John Anderson had gallantly offered to share with Cyril Pensenby since the ladies had come aboard. The small room was crushed enough with only Georgiana and Mrs Howard in it. Heaven only knew how Lieutenants Anderson and Pensenby were coping. The hammock reminded Georgiana of her time amidst the midshipmen and ship's boys, with only fourteen inches separating each man, or boy for that matter. But she did have to admit that, even when sleeping in a hammock, the captain's wife commanded softer, warmer bedding than that of any ship's boy. Her mind flitted briefly to young Sam Wilson.

She rubbed a small spot of tension on her forehead and allowed Nathaniel to massage her shoulders.

'You must not take it all upon yourself, my sweet, you're wearing yourself out. Much more of this and *you* shall be ill. Take a break, she'll be safe alone for one night.' Nathaniel pressed a tender kiss to the nape of his wife's neck and slid his arms down to capture her waist. Even as he made the suggestion he knew that Georgiana would never default in her duty to Mrs Howard, determined in the knowledge that she owed the modiste so much. They both did. But fatigue showed clearly on Georgiana's wan features, from the shadows beneath her lacklustre eyes to the faint droop in her normally erect shoulders. 'I'm worried about you,' he uttered against the softness of her skin.

'Well, you mustn't be,' came the reply. 'Save your worry for Mrs Howard, for I fear that if she doesn't improve she'll be gravely ill, or much worse, by the time we arrive back in Portsmouth.' Georgiana stood on her toes and kissed that full firm mouth.

'In that case we had best have Belmont examine her.'

Where her lips had lingered she now traced a delicate finger. 'Mrs Howard will not like it,' she argued. 'She could scarcely endure the glance of his eye upon her.'

'Captain's orders,' pronounced Nathaniel in a masterful tone. 'It is for the lady's own good. And we shouldn't risk her health for the sake of her sensibilities. If you are present during the examination, I think her reputation will withstand it!'

Georgiana nodded. 'You're right, but she won't like it.' And, so saying, she dragged her tired body off to prepare Evelina Howard for the arrival of Mr Belmont.

Mrs Howard fared no better despite suffering the indignity of a physical examination under the surgeon's hands. In her weakened state it was all she could do to force a little water down, and she knew that it would not be long before that small luxury would grow stale and slimy. Thus, she finally succumbed to Georgiana's suggestion to try a little grog, which, surprisingly and much to her chagrin, proved to be the tonic that settled her stomach like no other. Although she was still of a nauseous disposition and kept to her cabin, the utter wretchedness of her situation eased, allowing Georgiana a little time to herself. It was therefore at the earliest opportunity that the captain's wife sought out the company of ship's boy Sam Wilson down in a darkened corner of the gunroom.

The boy was staring at her rather uneasily. What did the captain's lady want with him? Scared that he had said or done something to insult her exulted person, he said nothing, waiting for her to reveal what she wanted with such a lowly being as himself.

'Master Wilson, Sam,' she began. 'I wished to enquire as to your welfare. Is the food to your liking? Are the slops you wear warm enough against the increasing cold?'

Sam stared at her as if she'd grown two heads. Why did Lady Hawke care about as poor a boy as him? 'Yes, thank you, m'lady.' He bowed his head.

The lad was plumper than when he'd left Portsmouth, an observation that brought the hint of a smile to Georgiana's face. 'You must tell me if you're unhappy, do you promise?'

'Yes, m'lady,' he said slowly, still puzzled. She smelled sweet like flowers in summer, and glossy black ringlets peeped from beneath her fancy bonnet. Even in the faint light filtering through from the gratings in the deck above he could see that her skin was white and smooth. He thought it would feel soft to touch, but did not dare to even move towards her.

'Are the others kind to you?' she asked.

As if he could say nothing else he repeated the same words.

'And have you not a best friend aboard the *Pallas*, one who helps you, and looks out for you?'

The little lad nodded vigorously, apparently forgetting his shy reserve. 'Oh, yes,' he replied. 'I'm mate to the best sailor on this ship, able seaman Grimly, m'lady.'

She smiled at that.

'That's on account of George being taken poorly like. He was my friend before Jack.'

The name sounded slowly into a question. 'George?'

'George Robertson, m'lady. Jack said he got taken on as captain's boy 'cos he was the captain's nephew. He got sick and we left him behind. He was a good friend to me.' Sam's voice had taken on a wistful quality.

Georgiana placed her hand stoutly on the boy's shoulder. 'Don't worry, George will get better and come home to England. I'm sure he much prefers the sunshine of Gibraltar to the stormy skies that lie ahead.'

'That's what Jack said. But he didn't look too happy about it. I heard 'em talkin, when they didn't know I was listenin'.'

'And what did they say?' A horrible suspicion was forming deep within Georgiana's gut. She tried to keep her voice light as if Sam's answer wasn't so very important.

Sam wiped his nose on the back of his sleeve and leaned forward conspiratorially as he'd seen men do when they said anything of any importance that they did not want all and sundry to hear. 'That the captain had no choice, that George would have spread the disease to us all.'

Relief swamped her and the tight coil of gathering tension sprang loose.

He sniffed again. 'But they all said that the captain didn't care a stink about George once he met you, m'lady. Never even called to see him, or let Mr Belmont treat him once. Right sore they are about that.' It did not occur to young Sam that a lady might take insult at learning such a rumour regarding both her husband and herself.

Foreboding was a fine thing, especially once you'd let yourself be lulled into a false sense of comfort. 'Thank you for telling me, Sam.' She thought quickly. Discontentment below decks was the last thing Nathaniel needed right now. She wetted her lips and offered as best an explanation as she could think of. 'Captain Hawke couldn't visit George for fear of bringing the disease back to the *Pallas*. But I've seen with my own eyes his concern for the boy. He sent for word of his condition every day and was greatly worried about him. He didn't want to cause panic amidst the crew, so was careful not to speak of it.' Without thinking she pressed her arm around the boy's thin shoulders, looking down kindly into his face. Poor little lad, he was scarcely older than Prudence and Theo. 'And now you alone have the truth of it, Sam, and the next time you hear the men discussing the matter, you'll be able to set them right.'

He nodded sagely, liking the feel of the lady's soft arm around him. 'Yes, m'lady,' he said and saluted.

Georgiana pressed a small kiss to his forehead while he stared up at her with great round eyes. 'Now I'd best return to my work, Master Wilson.' And she walked away, leaving young Sam basking in the glory of her rose-scented fragrance and intrigued by the discovery that even the captain's wife worked.

Seated within the captain's cabin, Evelina Howard managed a small crooked smile when Georgiana relayed what she had learned from young Sam Wilson. Still pale, she was at least contriving to keep down the breakfast she had eaten. 'It seems that ship's boy Robertson made quite an impression with the crew. They must be an unusual lot if they show such concern over the boy.'

Captain Hawke attempted an explanation. 'It's not so much that they cared overly for George, rather it's more a matter of loyalty and of fair treatment, Mrs Howard. The men are as one family when this ship is at sea. The welfare of each depends on the co-operation of all. Each man must do his job and do it well, so that we all survive. The captain is no exception to that truth. His decisions are difficult to make, sometimes requiring the sacrifice of one for the benefit of many. Life at sea is harsh, they all know that. I had thought they'd understand that a boy suffering with what looked to be yellow fever couldn't possibly take his place aboard the *Pallas,* even if he were the captain's nephew. To do so would be to place the entire crew at risk. Besides, Gibraltar is the best place for him as the Rock suffered a pestilence not four months since, and the hospital will know well how to treat him.' Nathaniel looked stern, unbending.

Georgiana looked up into her husband's face with its angular dark brows pulled low over the burnt umber of his eyes. It seemed that with each passing day she loved him more. 'Perhaps their disgruntlement stems not so much from the fact that the boy was left behind, but more from the secretive aura that surrounded the affair. Mr Belmont was never permitted to examine him, and you never spoke with them to inform them of the situation.'

'To reveal my suspicions that he carried yellow fever would have caused panic on this ship. Mr Belmont, as a surgeon with little training in the skills of a physician, would have been quite unable to treat the boy, and such a visit would only have served to expose him to the possible contagion.' Captain Hawke's hands were clasped behind his back, allowing the ladies a full frontal view of the fine white shirt, neatly tied neckcloth and white embroidered ivory waistcoat. 'I'll have a subtle word with Anderson, that should do the trick.'

A small laugh emitted from Mrs Howard. 'I declare that I've not had so much entertainment in many a month. You two would do justice to one of Mr Shakespeare's plays!'

Husband and wife turned to look at her, expressions of puzzlement upon their faces.

'I merely meant that to hear you converse, one might be mistaken in feeling some element of sympathy for that poor boy left behind on Gibraltar. A boy who does not exist,' Mrs Howard explained.

'I feel as if he did,' said Georgiana. 'The friends that I made, the way that people treated me… It gave me a glimpse of a life outside my own, of a life that I could never possibly have hoped to understand. It was a valuable experience that I'll never forget.'

The silver eyes glowed with compassion and Mrs Howard pressed a large hand to Georgiana's. 'I didn't mean to distress you, my dear.'

A smile lit Georgiana's face. 'You must think nothing of it, ma'am, as I'm not at all distressed. I'm grateful that I've seen life from another's perspective.'

'There's a very good reason why we must continue to refer to George in such terms. It would be too easy to forget ourselves and speak otherwise in the company of the men or the officers. The last thing we need is for an incriminating comment to be carelessly overheard. And there's always the risk that someone will see a resemblance between Georgiana and George. No, the sooner we reach Portsmouth the easier I'll rest.'

Captain Hawke's last comment left the little party feeling somewhat perturbed. The man himself strode off to communicate with his lieutenants. Mrs Howard retired to her cabin with the headache. And Georgiana suppressed the glacial feeling that someone had just walked over her grave.

It was just three days later that Georgiana had very good reason to recall the words of concern that her husband had uttered.

Surprisingly the day was dry, the absence of rain corresponding to a marked decrease in the temperature. The air fairly crackled with cold across a clear blue sky. Although the sun had not yet made an appearance the light was bright, a welcome change from the dismal murky skies that had recently plagued them. Ice had formed upon the rigging and on the casks, rendering the simplest of jobs difficult, not helped by the fact that the cold had forced the men to squeeze their callused feet into shoes that slipped so easily upon the deck. Despite donning as many items of clothing as they could, they were pained by the extreme bite in the air. Fingers and toes burned red raw, and breath caught as smoke shuddered from chilled lungs.

Given that the sea had calmed its white frothed swell a little, Georgiana and Mrs Howard decided to take some fresh air by a short walk along the quarterdeck. Evelina's demeanour had markedly improved since taking her daily ration of grog—not that she would have admitted to drinking such a thing to any other living person. Indeed, it was only by explaining that the medicinal properties were most probably due to the lime juice rather than the water, the sugar, or, heaven forbid, the rum, that Georgiana had persuaded the lady to continue with her consumption. The cold nipped two patches of pink to her cheeks, endowing her with the most healthy appearance since the *Pallas* had left Gibraltar. As there had been insufficient time to prepare an entire wardrobe, Georgiana had few warm clothes in her possession. She was dressed, therefore, in a sturdy walking dress of a bottle green with a cashmere shawl wrapped snugly around her shoulders. The cream bonnet, with dark green ribbons, tied firmly to her head, and matching gloves offered little protection against the ferocity of the temperature, but as the ladies did not intend to dally long upon the open deck Lady Hawke was not too disconcerted by the rasping cold.

The view was spectacular, all yawning clear sky above and icy swirling water below. Gulls hovered on air currents unmindful of the chill and the sun emerged to light the pale white blue of the waves. Georgiana and Mrs Howard were just making their way back across the main deck to retreat towards their cabins when they heard the shout.

'Man overboard!'

Georgiana's heart set up a patter, the wintry freeze seeping from her skin through to the pit of her stomach. Images of the cold blue ocean leapt in her mind. No man could survive immersion in that. Her eyes met Mrs Howard's horrified stare. She stopped, paused for a heartbeat, and then without having exchanged as much as a single word the two women turned and ran to where they could see a small crowd amassing. Nathaniel was there before them, his cheeks ruddy from the bite of the weather.

'Bare the masts and lower the cutter!' he yelled.

Beyond the polished outer rail, out amidst the silver blue swell of water, a small figure bobbed, tiny arms flailing, the faint strains of a voice carried away by the wind.

Forward progress halted. The *Pallas* bobbed on the undulating waves as the boat was lowered to meet the bitter waters. Men had gathered, watching, praying, while Jack Grimly and Billy Todd rowed closer to where the figure had disappeared. Tension tightened, time ticked by, the deck of the *Pallas* so quiet as to hear a pin drop. Against the silence a roar went up, cheering, men slapping one another on the back. A limp figure pulled from the icy depths, hoisted back aboard.

Georgiana felt Nathaniel close behind her. His strong voice sounded quietly in her ear. 'Go below, Georgiana. This may not be a pretty sight.'

She turned her head to where he had been, but he was gone, striding across the deck to meet Jack Grimly and his sodden parcel.

Georgiana's insides turned to ice, her husband's warning forgotten in an instant. Nausea quickened in her gut, for across the distance she could clearly see the small thin body, the sandy hair flat and dark with water, and the white pinched features.

'Sam!' The name erupted loud and distraught from her lips, but she had no notion that she had spoken, running as she was to close the space between them.

He did not move, his face a carved effigy, white, waxen, his mouth edged with a gild of blue. Water trickled down the elfin chin as Nathaniel rolled him to his side and back again, touching his fingers to the stalk of a neck, shaking his own dark head as he did so. He rose and spoke quietly to able seaman Grimly.

'No! No!' she whispered. Her frozen fingers tugged at the ivory shawl, wrapped the cloth around the boy. She pulled the chilled wet body to hers, giving her warmth, taking his cold. Against her cheek, where his breath should have been, was stillness. 'Turn him upside down, quickly!' She glanced around her for a man large enough to do so. They watched her quietly with pained eyes. 'What are you waiting for?' she yelled.

Nathaniel stepped forward and took the body from her tender grasp. He moved to hand the boy to Jack.

'Nathaniel!' Her voice was urgent, high-pitched, panicked. 'Please!'

'It's too late, Georgiana. His heart doesn't beat nor does he breathe.' His voice was solemn, quiet in tone. He made to take his wife's arm, but she resisted.

'Please, Nathaniel,' she whispered. 'Please try. I've read of a man pulled from beneath an ice sheet who appeared to be dead; within the hour he had recovered enough to speak. What have we to lose?'

The men were watching him, compassion in their eyes. The boy was dead. The captain's wife grasping at straws, unable to face the fact, her softness serving only to highlight the tragedy of the situation. An ordinary seaman sniffed aloud, the bosun's mate cleared his throat, and tears trickled from Jack Grimly's roughened cheeks down on to the bundle within his arms. It heartened them to know that a fine lady could care so much for a dirty ship's boy whom she barely knew. They waited to see what the captain would do.

'Turn the boy upside down. Hold him by the ankles,' instructed

Captain Hawke. He then delivered two hearty wallops to the boy's back. The figure dangled limp and unresponsive. Jack lowered him to the deck.

Mr Belmont raked a path through the crowd, dropped to his knees and examined the boy. Shocked eyes locked with the captain's. 'A heartbeat, albeit a faint one, but a heartbeat at that. And he breathes.'

A murmur sounded through the surrounding men.

'Thank God!' uttered Georgiana, and promptly knelt beside the surgeon, holding her hands around the thin flaccid shoulders, peering down into the deathly white face. The warmth of her breath whispered against the cold wet skin.

The eyelids flickered, a feeble splutter sounded.

'Sam, you're safe now. Mr Belmont will look after you and make you better.'

His clear tawny eyes opened, 'George.' The word was weak, gravel upon his injured throat. 'George,' he said a little more strongly, unable to move his numbed exhausted body. The curve of a smile played upon his pale lips and his eyes shuttered once more.

Georgiana smiled back and, removing her sodden glove, touched her palm to cup the boy's cheek. 'Sleep now, Sam, all will be well.'

It was not until she turned to Mr Belmont and saw the strange expression upon his face that she realised exactly what had just happened. The surgeon said nothing, just stared, eyes fast upon her, looking and looking as if he would peel back her very skin to find what was beneath. A quiver of fear darted in her chest and she raised her gaze to the men surrounding them, eyes scanning faces that for the main showed only relief and joy. But not Jack Grimly. The sailor was regarding her with a combination of disbelief and horror. Silent. Static. All of a sudden she felt chilled to the marrow, a terrible cold that seeped through, freezing, pervasive. She could not move. The breath caught in her throat. Blood pounded in her head. Dear Lord, what had she done? All of her fear and dread welled up, bursting forth in a surge of riotous emotion that threatened to overwhelm her. But the fear was not for herself, and neither was the dread. Only one person mattered. And if she was not very much mistaken she had just thrown that man's reputation to the wind. She stumbled to her feet, only to find a pair of strong arms engulf her. Deep dark eyes met hers momentarily before he pronounced in a voice that would tolerate no defiance, 'The lad is babbling. Take him below, Mr Belmont, and see that he gets the best of care. For I had not thought that any man, let alone a boy, could beat the sea today.'

The crowd dispersed, the surgeon directing able seaman Grimly to carry young Sam. Jack looked directly into Georgiana's eyes and then was gone.

The green velvet of her dress hung heavy with frozen seawater, dragging her down to meet the dark-stained planking. Her head ached, a searing pain. Her eyes closed against it. She heard Mrs Howard's words, but they made no sense, just sounds buzzing distantly in her ears. It was so cold, so very cold. And to her added mortification she felt her knees buckle before someone somewhere lifted her up and she knew no more.

Captain Hawke touched a hand to the boy's brow and spoke quietly. 'Will he live?'

The surgeon wiped his hands upon the cloth and moved to spread another blanket over the small form. 'No reason why he shouldn't.' Mr Belmont's eyes met the captain's and looked away again. 'With his hammock strung close to the galley fire he's as warm and dry as he's going to get aboard this ship. He's young and a hardy little thing.'

'Good. I don't want to lose the lad.' Nathaniel made to walk away.

'Is Lady Hawke recovered, sir? She seemed to have suffered a little in her bid to help the boy.' All the while Belmont's eyes did not leave Sam Wilson.

Nathaniel held himself taut, just waiting for the man to say what he knew he would. From the minute that the boy had uttered George's name to the sudden realisation dawning in the surgeon's eyes, he knew. Now he must do what little he could to salvage the situation. Let them say what they would—he was still the captain of the *Pallas,* and, as his wife, Georgiana still deserved their respect. And so he waited for what was to come.

'Captain—' Mr Belmont's voice sounded clear and loud enough for the men working around them to hear '—it's very common in cases of exposure to extreme temperatures for the patient to become dazed and confused. The boy is likely to confuse names, faces, people, but hopefully the effect will soon be remedied.' His gaze held Nathaniel's with a profound intensity. A silent promise, an affirmation of allegiance.

Nathaniel bowed his head in a small gesture of acknowledgement. 'Thank you, Mr Belmont,' was all he said, but those few words contained a wealth of gratitude and respect. They looked at one another a moment longer before the captain walked away to be about his business. He almost made it past the long guns with their open ports when a voice stopped him.

'Captain Hawke, may I speak with you, sir?' Lieutenant Pensenby appeared by his side.

Nathaniel gritted his teeth and waited for the second lieutenant to say the words.

Pensenby's voice lowered in volume. 'In confidence, sir.'

The two men climbed up and headed to the forecastle out of earshot of the crew.

'I saw what happened over there, heard what the boy said to Lady Hawke.' Pensenby's long face was gaunt in its austerity.

Nathaniel watched him carefully. 'What do you mean to do about it?'

The slight hint of colour rose in Lieutenant Pensenby's pale thin cheeks.

Seagull cries sounded overhead, the murmur of men below, creak of timber, lap of waves. Pensenby said nothing.

Nathaniel would not ask the question again. The wind ruffled through his hair, nipping at his face, but it was neither the wind nor the falling temperatures that drew the shiver down his spine.

When Pensenby eventually spoke there was an unusual stillness about him and his shrewd sharp gaze rested not on Captain Hawke, but far out to sea. 'I know what you think of me, sir. That I hold my position only because of who my uncle is.'

'I choose my own crew, Pensenby, you know that. Whatever Admiral Stanley might have done for you, he didn't secure your place aboard the *Pallas,* your own merit did that.' His gaze shifted to where Pensenby's lay.

'For the first time in my career,' replied the second lieutenant.

'But not the last.'

'We shall see.' The narrow lips pressed firm. 'It wasn't me that I came to speak of.'

'No,' said Nathaniel quietly.

Pensenby didn't turn his head, didn't even move his eyes from their distant focus. His words were slow, stilted. 'I knew from the first that there was something about George Robertson, something that wasn't right, but I never took him for a woman. Indeed, I must confess, Captain, to having thought the worst…about yourself, sir.' He looked at him then, with direct and bold eyes. 'It's a blessed relief to learn that my suspicions were wrong.'

'Indeed, it is,' said Nathaniel wryly.

'I wanted to tell you that you need not worry over the matter. Lady Hawke's reputation is quite safe. Most of the men will not have noticed, and I'll ensure that those who did never speak of it.' One bony hand extended. 'You have my word, Captain.'

A firm handshake, and Pensenby was gone.

Darkness had closed in upon the sky before Nathaniel returned to his cabin. Everything lay just as he'd left it that morning. Charts neatly stacked in a tidy pile, the log book, his quills… But everything had changed in the hours since. He found his way to the thin wooden door that led to the night cabin and knocked.

The room within was dark, the lantern unlit, the only light spilling in from the adjacent cabin. He could see her slender form seated upon the small wooden chair, her head held upright, her shoulders squared. She rose in a graceful motion, her figure too far recessed in the darkness to see her features. There was silence and the trace of summer roses. One strong long-fingered hand snaked forward and, enclosing her wrist, gently pulled her forward. The faint edges of the warm yellow lantern light glowed upon her face, revealing eyes that were trained steadily on his own. Standing there within the darkness, he felt the fatigue wash over him, pulling at his muscles, dragging at his mind. He leaned down to rest his cheek on the top of her head, inhaling the sweet fragrance of her hair, as his arms wound around the softness of her body.

'Georgiana,' he whispered into the silence, and the word dripped heavy and tired.

He seemed so weary, exhausted with disappointment. She closed her eyes tight to stop the fall of the tears that welled too readily. Little wonder that he was so saddened when she had just unwittingly undone all of his hard work. His cheek was warm and light upon her hair, as if even now he sought to hold the full weight of the burden from her. She turned her face up to his, noting the dark play of shadows. 'I'm so sorry,' she said. 'I thought only of the boy, nothing else.'

Still he said nothing, only holding her close, their two bodies merging as one within the amber flickering shaft.

And now that he was here, at last, she wanted to tell him that she would rather have ripped her heart from her breast than hurt him in any way, that yet again, through her own folly, some aspect of his life was at risk, that he deserved so much better—all the thoughts that had flooded through her head since that fateful moment. But those words would not come, tucked tight and deep inside. Instead, she found herself chattering on with all the indiscretion of Lady Tyler.

'He's only eight years old. Eight. Lived in Portsmouth all of his short life. His father was a man of the navy, died at sea six months since. Mother's a widow. Fond of the gin. Six little sisters. Sam thought to follow in his father's footsteps. That's why he joined the navy, that and the fact that his mother couldn't afford to feed him. God knows what will happen to all those little girls.' She paused as if to ponder on the question. 'When I saw him there, so pale and lifeless, I thought I couldn't bear it. Such injustice. How did he come to fall overboard? What was he doing?'

Nathaniel's deep voice rumbled low beside her ear. 'Helping the men to clear ice from the lower rigging. It seems that his shoes slipped on the ice, and unfortunately the safety rope around his waist came loose.'

She shook her head slowly. 'I didn't think any further than to save him. That life would breathe again in his frail little body, and when Mr Belmont said he was alive, I rejoiced. That small dear face. I didn't even notice that he'd called me George. Only saw his smile and was glad.' Her hands crept up to grip the top of his arms. 'Why should anyone take note of Sam's words? He was cold and shocked. Surely no one will take that one slip of the tongue seriously? He's just a child.' Her stormy dark eyes were pleading, her fingers biting. But even as she said it she knew what she'd seen in the surgeon's face, and Jack Grimly's.

'No one took Sam's mistake seriously, Georgiana. But by saying what he did, he exposed that inconceivable thought for the merest fraction of a second, and that, I'm afraid, was long enough to do the damage. Any association between the image you present now and that of George Robertson would be enough to alert those who'd dealt closely with my servant. The suggestion alone was our undoing.'

'Do they all know?' She clung to him, felt his muscles tense beneath her hands.

His long fingers slid to her shoulders to where her skin was bare and cold. 'It's too early to say. Mr Belmont does, but he won't speak of it. Of the others I'd guess Mr Anderson and Mr Fraser to have realised. Cyril Pensenby most definitely so. The men are an unknown entity. Only those close enough would actually have heard Sam's words.' He omitted to mention that gossip would soon inform those who had not. 'But it seems that you have something of a champion in my second lieutenant.'

'Lieutenant Pensenby?'

'The very one. He means to silence the men and protect your reputation.'

'Pensenby! I can hardly believe it.' Her eyes opened wide and round. 'But what of his uncle? Won't he tell Admiral Stanley?' She couldn't bear to think what that would mean for Nathaniel.

'No, Georgiana, I don't believe he will.'

Even if Nathaniel was right, gossip had a way of reaching those that it should not. 'Jack Grimly knows. He gave me such a strange look before he took Sam away. It was as if I'd betrayed him, which of course I did. I lied to him, to them all. It's not something of which I'm proud.' A shiver rippled down her spine.

Nathaniel wrapped his arms around her. 'You're cold, let me warm you.'

'I've ruined you after all,' she whispered so quietly that the words almost missed her husband's hearing.

'No, never that. Let's just wait and see what emerges. Fate has a strange way of contriving the outcome she always intended. Don't worry, Georgiana. You're my wife now, and that's enough to protect you.' He kissed her forehead, smoothing the worry furrow with the sweep of his thumb.

Her eyes held his, as dark a blue as ever he'd seen them. 'But what of Captain Hawke?' she asked. 'Is marriage enough to protect him?'

'Of course.' He swept her up into his arms, and laid her gently in the cot. And throughout the night, long and cold, he held her as if he would never let her go.

If Georgiana had thought the revelation to have earned the crew's condemnation, she was to be pleasantly surprised. The following day she could sense no discernible difference in the men's treatment of her but, even so, she was not foolish enough to indulge in the belief that they did not know. There were no whispers following in her wake, no utterances of George Robertson's name in her hearing, no stares, no cat calls. Even when she braved the elements to appear upon the forecastle in her woefully inadequate plain blue dress and matching pelisse, the men did not stare, only nodded their usual greeting in her direction. Nathaniel, who had been scanning the horizon with his spyglass, chided her for her presence.

'Georgiana, you'll catch your death up here, go below at once.

Even Mrs Howard has had the sense to stay within her cabin.' A frown marred the strong angular face.

The weather was his excuse, of course. She knew that. Knew that he thought her appearance following yesterday's revelations to be foolish in the extreme. But she had to see for herself the damage she had caused, and for that small task she would have walked quite willingly into the very jaws of hell. He was regarding her with an expression of displeasure, his dark brows brooding and low. A shiver stole through her. It seemed that an icy coldness had beset her since Sam's unwitting utterance, and she could find no warmth to thaw it. Nathaniel might say that he did not blame her, but he was too honourable a man, too kind a man, to do such a thing. For, despite the words he shaped to comfort her, Georgiana was aware of the change within him. A wariness, a fatigue that had not been there before. The blame lay quite firmly with herself, she needed no other soul to tell her that. Her husband—the very words brought a sear to her heart—was right in his dictate to wait and see. It was quite naturally the sensible course to take. But the lack of action, amid the stretch of time ahead, wound Georgiana's nerves taut as cheese wires around a block. Waiting was not an activity at which Miss Raithwaite had ever excelled. She was a woman used to striking while the iron was hot. It had always been her way, much to the irritation of her papa.

She did not speak, merely turned and retreated from his domain, walking briskly down towards the hatch that led to the gun deck, a new determination in her step. Georgiana Raithwaite had not been content to sit back and meekly accept her stepfather's injustice. And neither would Georgiana Hawke. She loved Nathaniel, of that she was certain, and if she had gone to such ridiculous lengths in an attempt to thwart Walter Praxton, what more would she do to save the man that she loved? No matter the cost, no matter the sacrifice, Captain Hawke would not suffer the humiliation of a court martial, nor would he lose the *Pallas*, which he so loved. Georgiana would see to that.

Unaware of the burgeoning resolve within his wife's breast, Nathaniel was navigating the ship through worsening weather, creeping ever closer to their destination. With two further injuries from accidents in the rigging, the stormy seas, dark skies and pressing time, Nathaniel worked hour after hour, intent on making it home safely in time for Christmas. The torrential rain and lashing winds had delayed their progress, and although they had made up a little time during the subsequent cold snap, he could be nothing less than vigilant to meet his goal. For despite the short duration of their trip his men were tired, wrung out by the ferocity of the weather. The capture of their prizes seemed a long distant thing, and Nathaniel was keen to press the prize agent so that the men received their payments promptly.

They were good men, loyal to the last. Hadn't the incident with young Sam Wilson proven that? For all his denials to Georgiana, the matter did worry at him. It would be an impossible task to silence a whole crew, and the exact manner of their courtship would make interesting telling throughout the taverns on the cold winter nights ahead. Georgiana was his wife now. The damage had been limited. But that didn't mean he was about to stand back and allow any aspersions to be cast her way. Come hell or high water, he would do what he could to protect her.

Chapter Eleven

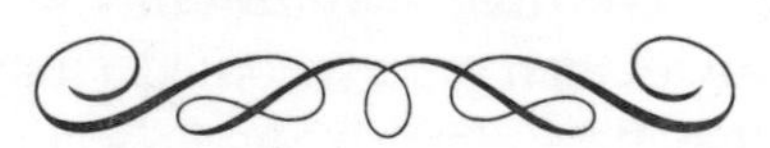

It was late in the day when Georgiana finally found an opportunity to converse with Jack Grimly alone. The orlop deck was deserted and in shadowy darkness as she silently dogged his footsteps along to the tools store. The smell of stale dampness hung heavy in the air. Just as his fingers reached towards the storeroom door she spoke. 'Mr Grimly, I wondered if you might spare me a few minutes of your time.'

His large body started and his head swung round in alacrity. 'Bloody 'ell! You nigh on gave me a right turn!' Then, recovering himself, he added, 'Beggin' your pardon, *Lady* 'awke, I've no wish to offend your ears with such language.' Without waiting for a reply he moved to wrench the door open.

'Mr Grimly.'

Jack's hugely broad back presented itself. He made no sign as to having heard.

'Jack!' The word was like a sigh on Georgiana's lips. 'Please. Won't you even listen to me?'

He turned and faced her then. 'If the captain's wife commands my attention, who am I to disobey?' His gaze was cold and hard, his tone no better.

What right had she to feel aggrieved at the contempt in his eyes? She'd taken what he had offered in good faith and given back nothing but dishonesty. No wonder she now suffered under his condemnation. 'Jack, I'm sorry that I lied to you. I'm sorry that I pretended to be someone that I wasn't.'

'Not 'alf as sorry as I am.'

She forced herself to look him directly in the eye. 'You trusted me and I betrayed you. I know that nothing can excuse such behaviour. I deserve your contempt in full, but Captain Hawke does not.'

Jack stood silent, waiting, a shadowed figure behind the flicker of his single lantern.

Taking a deep breath, she steeled herself to the task. 'I have no excuses. All that I can offer is my trust in return for the trust that you once had in me.'

She saw the cynicism, heard the utterance, 'Your *trust*?'

Refusing to give up, she stumbled on. 'When we met on the mail coach, I was fleeing my home. It seemed safer, at the time, to dress myself as a boy. I thought it would attract less attention and let me reach my destination unhindered.'

'Your destination?' he mocked. 'Running off with a lover, most like.'

'No!' Georgiana's denial was swift and determined. 'There was a lady who offered to help me…' The sentence trailed off unfinished. 'It doesn't matter now. All that I'm trying to say is that I had no notion that I would end up aboard this ship. It was never my intention to involve you, or Captain Hawke, or anyone else for that matter, in my harebrained scheme. But…well…somehow it happened.'

Something of the frostiness thawed from Jack's manner. 'Not *somehow*. You ruddy well jumped on that Press Gang Officer's back and tried to box his ears!'

'Only because he was punching you while you lay on the ground!' Her indignation was clear. 'What did you expect me to do, just let the two of them half-kill you?'

'Yes!' he shouted back, then shook his head and gentled his voice. 'It was bad enough when I thought it was a soft-brained lad who'd come to my rescue, never mind a slip of a *girl*!'

'Well, I don't see what difference it makes.'

Jack's eyes rolled firmly up into his skull before reappearing. 'You bleedin' well wouldn't!'

A rat scuttled by Georgiana's foot, but she resolutely held her ground. 'Regardless of that, once I found myself to be on the *Pallas* we had sailed and were out at sea. I couldn't just suddenly say, *"Please can you turn the ship around on account of my mistakenly being on board,"* especially when I saw who was captaining her. There seemed nothing else for it but to keep up the pretence.'

Jack's brow lowered suspiciously. 'What do you mean, *especially when you saw the captain*?'

Georgiana sighed and looked down into the darkness surrounding Jack's feet. 'Captain Hawke was not unknown to me. He'd already saved me when I ju…fell into a river.'

'God in heaven! What kind of lady are you? Running away from home, attacking officers of the Press Gang, nearly drowning?'

'I know that it doesn't sound good, but—'

'That's putting it mildly!'

'Urgent situations call for urgent actions.'

He looked at her soberly. 'Like the one where you shinned up the mast rather than 'ave a bath?'

'Yes,' she said simply, then added, 'I must admit that the sight of the cask bath being hauled up from the water was not a pleasant one.'

One bushy brown eyebrow raised. 'No, 'appen it wasn't.'

'My presence on board places Captain Hawke in a very difficult situation. He's never acted as anything other than a gentleman. Indeed, he even married me to try and repair the damage I've caused.' Her teeth gritted to prevent the waver in her voice. 'Hate me if you must, Jack, but please spare Nathaniel. He's paid enough because of my foolishness. Please don't push the cost any higher. There's nothing else that I can—'

One large hand moved to touch her arm. 'Lady 'awke—' he began.

Her eyes glittered brightly in the candlelight. 'My name is Georgiana, George to my friends.'

The silence stretched between them.

'You've 'ad a wasted journey.'

She stared disbelievingly into the big man's face. Not Burly Jack. He had a heart of gold, didn't he? 'Jack?' she queried quietly.

A soft chuckle sounded in the gloom. 'Why would you think that I'd let anything 'appen to Captain Hawke…or his wife? He's a good captain and there ain't too many of them around. Besides, Pensenby's already spoken to them that 'eard what young Sam said.'

Georgiana chewed at her lower lip. 'Lieutenant Pensenby?'

'He threatened to have us flogged around the fleet if we so much as made a whisper of it. Thought you'd know'd us better than that, George!'

The blue bonnet dipped low as the tears sprang to Georgiana's eyes. She tried to speak, but the only words that sounded were, 'Burly Jack Grimly, you are a very fine man!' And she hurled herself at the big man to embrace him in a bear hug.

Jack patted her arm affectionately before gently disengaging himself. 'Here, you'll have me in trouble for manhandling the captain's wife!'

Georgiana ignored his protests and, standing on her tiptoes, pulled his head lower to plant a small kiss on his roughened cheek. 'Thank you, Jack.'

The big man blushed crimson. 'Bleedin' 'ell, George, it's the least I can do when I'm the bloody reason you got pressed in the first place!'

Laughter filled the air, before Georgiana hurried up two decks to slip unnoticed back into the captain's cabin.

Walter Praxton sipped at his ale within the comfort of the inn, not even bothering to keep his eye on the window. Not that such an observation would have proved to be of much assistance in his plan, for the small glass panels were so steamed up that the dim light of day could scarcely penetrate the mist of condensation. Blakely would alert him as to when the *Pallas* came into the dockyard—that was, if he wanted the gold guineas that lay within the finely fashioned pockets of Praxton's forest-green coat—and Walter knew that the little man would do anything that he asked as long as the price was high enough. As if summoned by the mere act of thinking about him, the weasel-faced Bob Blakely appeared.

'Mr Praxton, sir, it's the *Pallas,* she's arrived. Best come quickly, for I don't fancy that they'll hang about for long in this weather.' Rain battered against the steamy windows just to highlight Blakely's point.

Shrugging into his many-caped great coat, Mr Praxton accompanied the sodden Blakely through the door. The streets were a muddied mess, puddles pooling to overflow into miniature rivulets. Walter's expensive leather boots strode through them all the same, splattering a pattern of mud speckles around the lower periphery of his overcoat. The stench of wet wool and filth drifted from his companion and a look of disdain flitted across his face. It was gone in an instant. Walter Praxton wasn't fool enough to upset the small smelly man. Blakely, after all, was still of potential use.

By the time they reached the allotted spot, the *Pallas* was neatly and securely anchored. A small group of men huddled as a welcome party, wet and windblown. An orderly rabble of crew started to clamber out of the first boat, a trail of rain-drenched bodies rapidly forming a crowd within the dockyard. The carts and waiting carriers and cabs poised themselves to receive their customers. Officer's sea chests were large and weighty, something that no man wished to carry far on a day like this. The boys and seamen lugged the wooden chests to the waiting recipients and, with a rapid salute, and a shake of the hand in some cases, were off.

Praxton's pale blue eyes narrowed as he scanned each figure leaving the ship. He had seen several boys, none of whom could possibly have been Georgiana. Was Blakely's information flawed? He pondered exactly what he would do if that proved to be the case. The little man's life wouldn't be worth living once Walter had finished with him. The thought spread a malicious grin across his handsome face. Never once did the narrow eyes waver from their cause, trained so obsessively on the emerging crew. A tall, well-built man came into view. Dressed smartly in a boat cloak and with his cocked hat catching the worst of the downpour, he held himself with supreme ease and self-confidence. Praxton did not doubt for a minute the man's identity, for it was abundantly clear from his demeanour that this was none other than Nathaniel Hawke, the captain of the frigate. Walter frowned— where the hell was Georgiana? If Blakely had played him false... All thought broke off thereafter as Walter Praxton's jaw gaped, slack and open. He stared as if he could not believe what lay before his very eyes. There could be no mistake. For there, walking behind Captain Hawke, was Georgiana Raithwaite, and not dressed in the guise of some ship's boy either. From where he stood he could see that she wore a dark green walking dress that matched the colour of his own stylishly tailored coat. Around her shoulders was draped a pale woollen shawl, which seemed to be absorbing the English rain with the voracious capacity of a sponge. From beneath her bonnet peeped damp ebony ringlets that were fast losing the shape of the curl. The captain turned to her, offering his arm. Beside her walked a taller woman, dressed smartly as a lady in a walking dress and cape of dove grey. The rain was gradually darkening her attire to a deep smoky charcoal.

Walter watched as Georgiana willingly took the proffered arm, smiling up into the man's rugged face. Bitter gall rose in his throat; he felt a band of tension constrict his chest and the overwhelming urge to run Captain Hawke through with the blade of his sword.

Blakely was prattling on in the background. 'Don't see the lad, gov. Not one that meets your description. Maybe he didn't make it. Like I said, it ain't an easy life out there.'

Mr Praxton ignored him, all his attention focused on the object of his desire. It was one thing to say that he would take her no matter her sullied state, and quite another to witness her play the part of another man's mistress. His teeth ground together and his lips narrowed to a thin hard line. An image of her naked white body writhing beneath the tall, powerful man at her side arose unbidden to torture his mind. He clenched his knuckles and held his breath.

'You all right, gov? Lookin' a bit pale about the gills there, Mr Praxton.'

The narrow light eyes were focused far away.

'Mr Praxton, sir,' Bob persisted, rightly concerned that his payment wouldn't be forthcoming if the gent decided to take a flaky turn.

Walter Praxton forced the wash of imaginings away, and turned to the odorous Blakely. 'The woman on the captain's arm, find out who she is,' he hissed. A cold and malevolent light sparkled in his eyes. When Blakely did not move, he snapped derisively, 'Now!'

A few minutes passed in the blissful absence of Blakely's stench, watching the captain hand both women up into a waiting hansom cab. Hawke's tall frame issued instructions to the driver before setting the ladies on their way and tracing his steps back to the ship's master and the dockyard office.

Mr Praxton began to walk in long loping strides towards the few remaining vacant cabs.

Blakely caught at his arm as he threaded his way through the thinning crowd. 'Mr Praxton, the lady is the captain's wife. It's Lady Hawke.'

A chill of pure malice traversed Praxton's heart. Hawke had not only taken her to his bed, but had married the girl! All of his dreams, all that work, all that time, destroyed by Blakely's few words. Rage erupted within his chest, but he battened it down. No one made a fool of Walter Praxton, not even the woman that he had wanted for as long as he could remember. 'Find out all you can of Captain Hawke,' he barked at Blakely, 'and meet me tonight in the Crown.' And with that he was off, his leather riding boots kicking up a pattern across the mud.

Georgiana regarded Nathaniel's town house with a little apprehension. Not because it was small and somewhat spartanly furnished, or that the few servants had yet to remove their eyes from her. Rather, it was the knowledge that this place would see the start of her life properly as Captain Hawke's wife. While aboard the *Pallas,* everything had been so much more contained, a small world of its own. Now that she was back on *terra firma*, all her problems loomed large and oppressive. No more thinking, no more planning.

Here in England she would have to act or leave Nathaniel to face the deplorable consequences of her mistakes.

Mr Fraser had accompanied them from the dockyard to the house located within St Mary's Street in Portsmouth. The elderly retainer set about chasing the gawking servants to light the fires and make the rooms ready. All this involved was a change of bedding as the house was maintained in a type of semi-ready alert, not knowing when the master was due to return. With only three bedrooms and one of these in use by the rather crotchety housekeeper, Mrs Posset, Georgiana found her few belongings delivered directly to Nathaniel's room.

Mrs Posset, a small apple-shaped woman of indiscriminate years, eyed Georgiana with obvious suspicion. No amount of reassurance from Mr Fraser seemed to alleviate the coldness from her glare. It was clear that she regarded herself as some kind of defender of her employer, and had cast Georgiana in the role of the wily strumpet who had hoodwinked a naïve milord into marriage. Not so very far from the truth, thought the new Lady Hawke rather grimly, although she would not go quite as far as to describe herself in such strong terms. The housekeeper was not so condemnatory in her attitude to Mrs Howard, sensing in that lady one who would come up trumps in any altercation into which she was drawn. Besides, Mrs Posset reassured herself, the woman was far too old to present any real threat to milord. Not that this excused her for any part she may have played in assisting the scheming young lady, if one could call the trollop so, by her side.

Thus it was that when Nathaniel returned later that afternoon to the house in St Mary's Street, he found a rather gloomy state of affairs and Mrs Posset with a face like an angry terrier.

'The house is to your liking?' he ventured, unsure of how to deal with the new-found tension.

'Quite impeccable,' replied Mrs Howard with the utmost politeness of manner. What she did not say was that she was only suffering to stay in such an abode to protect Georgiana from the worst of Mrs Posset's sniping.

Georgiana nodded and curved her lips to a smile. 'Yes, it's a fine residence,' she managed.

But Nathaniel did not miss the bleakness in her eyes, nor their stormy grey palette, that he knew from past experience to be indicative that she was in low spirits.

The evening progressed without improvement, from the dinner that was served under the direction of the rather steely-eyed Mrs Posset to Mrs Howard's early retirement due to the headache. Indeed, he could have sworn he saw the housekeeper positively glower when Georgiana announced her intention to do likewise. But Nathaniel had little time to ponder as to what lay at the root of the glumness of the ladies' mood. He supposed it to be due to fatigue, nothing more. Life at sea was hard enough for a man. The toll it had exerted upon the two women was bound to make itself known. And, besides, there was a much more pressing matter monopolising Captain Hawke's attention.

An uneasiness lay heavy across Nathaniel's soul. Tomorrow they would travel to Collingborne, a place he knew that he was not welcome. Georgiana was his wife now, come what may, and, as such, it was time she was presented to his family. The earl had told him to take a wife, and so he had. But he was under no illusion as to what his father's response to Georgiana would be. When it came to Nathaniel the earl knew only one manner of behaviour, and Georgiana would not change that. Scornful bitterness. Nothing more, and nothing less. He did not doubt that his wife would be subjected to the same. And he had yet to utter a word of warning to the woman lying upstairs within his bed. He gulped at the brandy, allowing himself the short respite that its fiery deluge offered. How exactly did one go about informing one's wife that she was married to the black sheep of the family? That his father could not stand the very sight of him—indeed, that he blamed Nathaniel for the death of the countess? With slow measured steps Nathaniel made his way to the bedroom.

Georgiana lay quite still, rolled upon her left side within the small bed, the blankets pulled high to cover her chin. She did not look round when she heard her husband enter the room. She did not need to, for the crackling fire within the grate cast the flicker of his shadow clearly upon the wall. She watched while the shadowman disrobed, folding each newly stripped article upon the storage chest at the bottom of the bed. Even in the dark silhouette upon the painted surface she could see the athletic strength in his finely toned body. Her mouth felt suddenly dry. She could hear the soft tread of his footsteps across the rugs, the rustle of his clothes as they left his limbs. The mattress tipped as his weight settled upon it and her heart tripped fast into a canter of beats. He moved to mirror the curve of her body, curling around her as if they were two spoons laid one on the other. The essence of sandalwood and soap drifted to her nose. Her heart careered to a blatant gallop and she tried to swallow down her arid throat. The touch of his naked skin seared through the flimsy cotton of her nightgown, asserting his claim over her, proclaiming their intimacy.

'Georgiana.' The hush of his words caressed her shoulder. His right hand meandered over, brushing her breasts as it traced a path to the flat plane of her stomach.

The gasp escaped her spontaneously, ejaculating into the silence of the room.

'Are you asleep?' he asked, although he must have known from the sound and the tremble of her body beneath his enquiring hand that she was not.

She wriggled round to face him, her eyes smouldering a deep dark blue in the warm glow of the fire.

His fingers slipped round to linger against her firm rounded buttocks. 'It has been a long day, sweetheart, and I know that you're tired.' Shapely lips nuzzled affectionately against her forehead.

Georgiana's body felt enlivened, as if the heavy mantle of fatigue had dropped from her shoulders. Stirrings fluttered low in her belly and a surge of excitement coursed through her veins. She raised her lips to his. 'Not that tired,' she murmured as she plucked one sweet kiss.

A dark winged eyebrow flickered, but he did not move to take her. 'Patience, sweetheart.'

Georgiana wriggled with a growing enthusiasm. This time he smiled, but when his hand moved to stroke the softness of her short feathered hair she saw that his expression was not one of desire. His jaw was stiff with tension and his dark eyes serious. Her reaction died in an instant, torn apart by a sudden trepidation. Surely the Admiralty could not know so soon? She raised herself up on one elbow and stared at him with worried eyes.

'Nathaniel?' And in that one word was the question she did not dare to ask. 'They cannot know already. We only docked today. How can they know?' It was sooner than she'd expected, too soon.

'Hush, petal.' He suppressed a pang of guilt over the white lies, knowing exactly to what she was referring. A callused thumb touched to the soft pink cushion of her mouth. 'Georgiana, there's nothing to fear from the Admiralty. Not now, not ever.' He was still looking at her, aware of the tension. 'There's another matter of which we must speak. You should be prepared for what lies ahead.'

She said nothing, just delivered a slight nod of the head and waited for her husband to find the words. The lines deepened around his mouth and a furrow etched vertically between his dark angled eyebrows. Georgiana braced herself for what was to come. A horrible possibility made itself known to her: what if he meant to put her aside after all? Was that why he was looking like a man about to face the firing squad? A sudden ball of nausea heaved in her stomach. She swallowed it down, and waited with as much courage as she could muster to her cause.

The dark eyes shuttered. 'Tomorrow we travel to Collingborne House, the seat of my father, the Earl of Porchester.'

'And he won't be best pleased that you've married the daughter of a glorified innkeeper, even if he doesn't know the rest of the truth. You don't need to tell me, Nathaniel. I never expected anything else.'

A grimace twisted upon Nathaniel's full lips. 'Nothing concerning me would ever please my father, so don't think that the reaction he may present is in any way connected to you.'

From the tautness of his musculature, she knew that he had touched upon a subject that pained his heart. In all that had happened, through all their trials, she had never seen him so patently distressed. 'I sense there's ill feeling between you and the earl. What has caused such a rift between you?' she asked as gently as she could.

He did not want to tell her. That wasn't supposed to be a part of this conversation. Just a warning, so that she would know what to expect before she arrived at the country house and witnessed the situation for herself. Yet he could not deny her the knowledge, felt that she had a right to know. If he did not tell her, she would only hear the story from another, and what guarantee had he that that person would not bias the truth?

She saw the light sheen of sweat upon his upper lip, felt his indecision. He sighed and then started to speak in his quiet and melodic tones.

'It all happened so long ago. Nine years to be precise. I was twenty and as foolish as any young man of that age. There was a house party that Henry and I attended. He hadn't met Mirabelle at that time and wasn't quite as long-jowled as he is now. On the final night our host held a ball in honour of his daughter, a girl of nineteen with a reputation for being a little fast.' He paused and shifted his gaze, his brow marring at the memory. 'I danced with her, and then she asked me to walk with her through the gardens. Said she was too hot in the ballroom. I should have declined, but I didn't. Once we were out of sight she made her intentions very clear. And I, fool that I was, responded to them. All the worse, for I knew what was being said of her.'

Georgiana said nothing, but it seemed that a heavy hand levered upon her heart.

'I don't wish to cause you pain, Georgiana, but it's better that you know the truth. There should be no secrets between us.' Brown eyes held blue with a stark intensity, and again the flutter of guilt brushed against him.

'Of course,' she murmured.

'I was kissing her when her father came upon us. Needless to say, you can fathom his response to discovering the situation. He demanded that I wed her, and I refused. She'd set out deliberately to entrap me. And it seemed rather strange that her father decided to walk through his orange house alone, at that time of night, when he was supposed to be hosting a ball. I later learned that the very same circumstance had taken place with another young gentlemen, who happened to be heir to an earldom. Dropped their sights a little when they selected me. Probably thought that my father would see to it that I married the girl. And he damn near did.' His breathing came fast and shallow, the sheen intensifying on his brow. He swallowed hard, more of a gulp, and waited for his wife's response.

'What happened?' Her voice was low and husky, her eyes overly bright.

'I explained the whole thing to my father and refused to marry the girl. I was labouring under the mistaken illusion that he would support me. Instead, he chose to believe the lies of a mere acquaintance over his own son.'

Georgiana understood the bitterness all too well.

'It wasn't as if I bedded her, excuse my blunt turn of phrase,' he uttered aside. 'But my father's a man to whom duty and honour are everything. He would have none of it. Called me a coward and worse. Said I was a disgrace to the family name and that he'd ensure that I received not one penny in inheritance if I didn't marry the girl. Well, I refused his instruction.'

Georgiana knew that feeling too, but kept quiet.

'I removed myself from Collingborne and joined His Majesty's Navy. The old man cut off my allowance and cursed me to the ends of the earth. We didn't speak for years.'

Georgiana's hand moved to cup his cheek. 'Oh, Nathaniel,' she uttered.

'That's not the worst of it. The rift between us caused my mother immense distress. She loved us both and was caught in the middle. She couldn't disobey him, but neither could she fully desert me. I still have all of her letters. Three years ago she became ill, a wasting disease that sapped her strength and eventually her life. With the little time she had left she tried to mend the breach between us.

But I was chasing Villeneuve in a frenzy of skirmishes throughout that summer and by the time I received word it was too late. My mother died thinking that she'd failed in her bid, that I'd ignored her letters. My father blamed me for her death. Said that I'd driven her to it with my scurrilous actions. Since then he can barely stand to look at me, let alone exchange a word.'

It was a heavy and unfair burden that he carried. Through the bitterness of his words and the sadness of his story Georgiana at last gleaned an understanding of what it was that drove Nathaniel so hard. Little wonder that he sought to rise through the ranks, to make something of himself in the navy. He possessed a steadfast determination to prove that he was not the unworthy cause his father clearly thought him. Nine years of a father's hatred was a lot for any man to bear. That, and an unreasonable guilt for his mother's death.

Her eyes bound to his. 'Then why do we travel to Collingborne? We could just stay here and celebrate Christmas.' She quelled the sudden image of the hatchet-faced Mrs Posset. The price was a small one to pay for her husband's peace of mind.

'No.' He shook his head in one clear defiant gesture. 'You're my wife, Georgiana, and I want my family to acknowledge you. I needn't tell you that my father won't approve of you, disapproving so adamantly as he does of me. But I'm not ashamed of you, and I don't mean to hide out with you here as if I am.' His lips were firm in their resolve, his jaw line rigid. It was not a confrontation from which Nathaniel meant to back down.

She pressed small soft kisses to the fullness of his mouth, watched the tension melt away. 'Then we'll go to Collingborne,' she whispered lightly between kisses. And when his hand strayed to caress the low hollow of her back, and his eyes darkened to a dusky simmer, she knew that the image of his father was fading from his mind. With slow deliberate boldness she leaned against his shoulders, pushing him down against the crisply laundered sheet. He showed no resistance, following where she would lead. She rolled so that the full length of her body lay on top of him, a bed of firm muscle and long limbs. Even as she lay there, calm and still, she felt his interest stir against her. A small wicked smile curved upon her mouth. Before this night was out, Nathaniel Hawke would have no further thought of his father, of that she was quite determined.

Without further warning she rose to a kneeling position, straddling his thighs in a most indecent fashion. If Mrs Posset thought her a strumpet... Her smile deepened at the disapproval her current posture would have caused the housekeeper. Teasing her fingers through the coarse dark hair across the breadth of his chest, she balanced a tip against each darkened nipple. He was watching her through eyes filled with dark and dangerous passion. An intensity of expression, a spring coiled tight and strong. Her hands slid lower to explore the defined ripples down his stomach and abdomen. He tensed beneath her and reached for her, murmuring her name with something akin to a growl. But before he could touch her she caught his hands, pressed them down to the soft rumple of the pillow above his head. When he would have moved she shook her head and stayed him with a kiss to the tautness of his stomach. He groaned and moved beneath her, eyes closed against temptation. She waited until his gaze found hers once more, then with a languorous grace peeled the nightgown from her body. It dripped slowly to the floor in a white frothy pool. She saw his eyes widen, watched her name shape upon his mouth. Slowly, surely, she moved to lower herself against the burning hardness of his masculinity. Nathaniel did not think of the earl then, or later that same night when they lay entwined together in sated contentment.

A white dusting of frost glittered in the bright morning sunshine, casting a magical feel to the landscape. The ice-clad streets and smoke-billowing houses of Portsmouth had been left far behind as Walter Praxton urged his mount on at a relaxed pace. The winter chill nipped, rouging his cheeks a ruddy red. Next to the golden curls flowing down from beneath his hat he had taken on the appearance of a beautiful cherubim, his clear light blue eyes adding the final touch to the splendid angelic visage. It was an image that had gained Mr Praxton almost everything he had ever desired in life.

Almost. For the one thing that he wanted most in the world did not seem to notice the charm that had the other ladies in a flutter. Indeed, three ladies had actually been known to swoon, such was the young man's impact on members of the fairer sex. Alas, Georgiana Raithwaite was not one of them.

Undoubtedly her appreciation of the finer things in life had been somewhat tarnished by her experiences at Mrs Tillyard's Academy. Or so Mr Praxton concluded, for what other reason could there be for her adamant refusal of him? If he had not known better, he would have sworn that the girl bore a downright dislike for his person, when he had presented himself to her in nothing other than a charming and generous light. No, the wretched Mrs Tillyard could only be to blame.

He watched the progress of the plain black travelling coach in the distance. Therein was housed the woman who haunted his dreams, alongside her husband. He could scarcely bring himself to utter the word, such was his contempt for the man. But not for much longer. For Walter Praxton had not lain idle. Indeed, he had not slept much of the previous night under the weight of his industrious scheming. He had lost her once, but the matter would soon be rectified. He just had to bide his time. Gloved fingers pulled the brim of the hat lower over his eyes to shield the glare of the sun. And such was his focus that he no longer noticed the cold stiffness in his knees or the numbness in his fingers and toes.

Georgiana felt the warm press of Nathaniel's thigh next to hers and tried to pretend that she did not feel a sear of excitement quiver through her. Immediately opposite, in the small quarters of the hired coach, Mrs Howard sat, back straight, immaculately clothed, her eyes closed. Even while dozing, Mrs Howard managed to exude an air of serene sophistication. Georgiana, who was anything but relaxed, wondered if anything ever succeeded in rattling the modiste. Not for the first time did she covet just a little of that lady's decorum. Seated beside the elegant figure was Nathaniel's valet, Mr Fraser, who, with rather less delicacy, was lounging quite happily in the corner, making a sound like the workings of one of the great wood saws Georgiana had observed aboard the *Pallas*.

Nathaniel's eyebrow raised and he cast a jaundiced eye towards his valet. 'It's thanks to Mr Fraser here that I've learned to sleep soundly through the liveliest of gun practices at sea. One becomes inured to the sound of his snoring after a while. When we first knew one another, I made him sleep at the other end of the ship!'

Georgiana laughed. 'Poor Mr Fraser. But it is a snore to outdo all others. How Mrs Howard can sleep with such a racket sounding I'll never know. I think I begin to understand why there isn't a Mrs Fraser.' She pulled Nathaniel's boat cloak more firmly around her and rubbed her fingers together. 'Indeed, I suddenly realise how fortunate I am that you do not snore nearly so loud.'

'Madam, I rebut your suggestion that I snore at all,' he said solemnly, only the quirk of the muscle in his cheek giving lie to the austerity in his voice.

'Nathaniel Hawke, you could rival the noise of an eighteen-pounder long gun on a bad night!' she exclaimed saucily.

He moved to capture her hands. 'Minx! Quite obviously I'm not tiring you out enough in bed if you imagine you hear such things in the night!' As his fingers closed around hers, he frowned. 'But you're freezing!' He rubbed her hands within his own, adding warmth with his breath. 'Come here, you'll be warmer on my knee, sweetheart.'

Before she could say otherwise, a pair of strong arms had pulled her deftly on to him, and her mouth had been robbed of one lusty kiss. 'Nathaniel!' she uttered in a furious whisper, her cheeks suddenly a picture of pretty pinkness. 'We're not alone, it's broad daylight and we're halfway across the countryside in a travelling coach!' The horrified scandal in her expression drew the devil in him.

'So?' he asked. His dark eyes opened wide and innocent, even as a wicked grin plucked at his sensual firm lips. 'I know a method for warming you most thoroughly, lady wife.' Long, lean fingers meandered over her arm in a tantalising fashion, drawing a gasp from Georgiana.

Mr Fraser chose that precise moment to stir within his sleep, mumbling in a blatant Scottish lilt, 'You can't be leaving wearing *that* neckcloth!' It was clear that Captain Hawke's rather relaxed attitude to his attire was the substance of Mr Fraser's nightmares.

Georgiana and Nathaniel exchanged conspiratorial glances, suppressed a chuckle, and reverted to a more respectable seating arrangement. And just in time as Mrs Howard shortly awoke feeling much refreshed from her short nap.

It was early afternoon when Mr Praxton stood within the woodland surrounding the grounds of Collingborne House. The trees were dark and barren, their gnarled and twisted shapes softened by the deep green gloss of the interspersed holly bushes and their abundance of rich red berries. Black birds and mistle thrushes scurried in the surrounding shrubbery, pecking at the remains of autumnal wind-fallen apples. High in an oak tree a robin sounded its familiar call. But Walter Praxton was blind and deaf to the beauty that surrounded him, his eyes and ears trained only on the scene occurring some distance away on the steps of the great country mansion.

Chapter Twelve

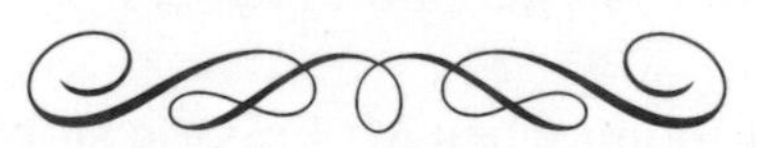

Collingborne House was more splendid than anything Georgiana had ever seen before, but its air of grand opulence could not hide the aura of sadness. With its red-coloured stone and white-bordered windows, the house was a bright jewel within the winter-darkened landscape. On arrival they had been ushered into a sun-filled drawing room while, beneath their polite façade, the servants ran around in a frenzy, informing the earl of his unexpected visitors and readying the bedrooms. It was not long before a familiar voice sounded from the doorway.

'Georgiana!' Mirabelle Farleigh, complete with baby in arms, paused by the door before rushing forward in a heady cloud of lavender-perfumed scent. 'What are you doing here? And Nathaniel? This is a surprise!' She eyed Mrs Howard with undisguised curiosity but in the most friendly of manners. Reaching forward, she clasped one of Georgiana's hands that was peeping out from beneath the swathes of Nathaniel's great boat cloak. 'My word, but you're cold, dear thing. Come and warm yourselves at the fire.' She gestured towards the yellow flames blazing within the grate. 'Don't be shy,' she added, her eyes seeking those of Mrs Howard. Baby Richard gurgled his own welcome and pointed one tiny finger at Georgiana.

'Mirabelle,' said Nathaniel, 'allow me to introduce Georgiana—' he paused '—my wife, and her companion, Mrs Howard.'

For the first time since Lady Farleigh had entered the room silence reigned supreme. Even baby Richard stopped slavering against his mother's arm. The petite flaxen-haired woman stumbled back to sit hastily on the sofa. Periwinkle-blue eyes stared like two large pennies and the perfectly formed mouth gaped round as if expressing a continuous 'O'. 'W…wife?' she managed to stutter. And then the best of her breeding declared that Mrs Howard was most welcome at Collingborne and that she, herself, could not have wished for a more amiable sister. Reaching up to embrace Georgiana, she declared it was the best Christmas present she could have asked for. 'Oh just think how delighted Henry will be! And Freddie! This is truly going to be a Christmas to remember!'

Nathaniel smiled wryly, convinced that the word *delight* would probably not describe his brothers' feelings when they learned that Georgiana was his wife. But Mirabelle was right about one thing—this certainly would not be a Christmas to forget. And just at that point a scuttle of little feet outside the door announced the small sturdy frame of Charlie.

'Unc Nath!' he yelled from the doorway and scampered across the drawing room to tangle himself around his uncle's long legs.

Laughing aloud, Nathaniel scooped the boy up high and kissed his chubby pink cheek. 'And this is your Aunt Georgiana come to visit you for Christmas.' Holding Charlie in his arms, he turned to face Georgiana, seeing the soft gentleness in his wife's face as she looked at the child.

Charlie feigned shyness for a minute, then touched a small sticky hand to Georgiana's arm. 'Ant George,' he said with the utmost politeness and smiled.

Dark eyes met grey blue, and crinkled. 'Out of the mouths of babes,' Nathaniel said, and passed a protective arm around Georgiana's waist.

'You sly dog!' Freddie proclaimed with his usual abandon. His long legs were stretched out before him as he lounged back in the winged chair. 'Telling me that Miss Raithwaite was highly unsuitable for marriage, then snapping her up for yourself.'

Henry stood by the library window, staring out at the frost-kissed lawns, a surly expression upon his face. 'Her father owns coaching inns in Andover, Winchester and Newbury. Hardly a lineage to boast of. I didn't think you'd stoop so low to spite Father. '

The hand laid so casually upon the padded arm of Nathaniel's chair curled to form a tight fist. 'Her parentage is nothing worse than mine.' He stared at Viscount Farleigh's profile, partially silhouetted against the brightness of the window. 'Believe me when I say that I'd never allow our father to influence my choice of bride.'

'No,' Henry drawled slowly. 'But you must admit, Nathaniel, that the girl is an odd choice given your situation. Father has sworn that you'll receive not one penny from him, and neither will he sponsor your naval career. If she were an heiress, I could perhaps understand it, but one could hardly describe her as that.'

Nathaniel savoured the brandy, trying desperately to control the anger banking in his chest. 'There are reasons other than money or advancement for a marriage. Georgiana's my wife whether you like it or not. We'll not beg for your blessing.' He was seated within the great winged chair opposite Freddie and turned slightly towards the windows. For all his apparently relaxed posture there was a tight whiteness around his mouth and a dark gleam in his eyes. He had known it would not be easy, and the worst was yet to come.

'Well, I say she's jolly fine,' exclaimed Freddie, his face lighting up at the memory of the delightful Miss Raithwaite. 'Would have expressed an interest myself if someone hadn't put me off the scent.' He nodded and sipped at the brandy. 'Don't be such a stuff, Henry, give the girl a chance. You haven't even spoken to her. Besides, Mirabelle likes her and will vouch for her.'

Nathaniel hoped for the life of him that neither Freddie nor Mirabelle would see fit to make any mention of Mr Praxton.

Henry turned a gimlet eye to his youngest brother. 'Mirabelle likes everyone. She's forever taking in waifs and strays and involving herself in charitable works. I cannot help but think that that is where Miss Raithwaite should have stayed—as a good cause, and nothing more. Indeed, Mirabelle spoke to me of the girl. Just because you saved her from drowning doesn't mean you're obliged to wed her, for goodness' sake!'

Freddie refilled the glasses, deliberately ignoring Henry's refusal. 'Whatever you say, Henry, you can't deny that Georgiana Raithwaite's a damned attractive woman. Nathaniel hasn't got ice in his veins, you know. What's he supposed to do after being stuck away at sea for all those months? Got to get himself a wife at some time!'

'I am not contesting that point,' Henry said with affected pomposity. 'Say what you will, she's the daughter of an innkeeper and that alone makes her unsuitable to be married to any member of this family. She's nothing but a mercenary Miss. Hell's teeth, Nathaniel, if you wanted her, why didn't you just bed her? We could have paid her off easily enough then. You weren't so reticent with Kitty Wakefield.'

The words were scarcely out of his mouth when Nathaniel was before him, his face white and bloodless. 'Cease this talk, Henry. I won't just stand by and let you insult my wife. Take back your words or I'll forget that we're brothers.' The rage that kindled in Nathaniel was akin to nothing he had ever experienced before. It was as if a red haze had descended before his eyes. His throat constricted and he swallowed hard, his fists bunched dangerously by his sides. 'Take them back.' His voice was low pitched, heavy with intent.

Henry stood resolutely silent. Then uttered, 'I will not. I speak nothing but the truth.'

'Nathaniel!' Freddie leapt to his feet, but it was too late.

'Then I have nothing more to say to you, Henry. You're no longer my brother.'

Freddie squeezed between his brothers, his hands pushing against Nathaniel's chest. 'This is absurd. What the hell are the two of you doing?'

'Defending my wife's honour,' said Nathaniel in a steady tone. 'I'll have nothing more to do with Henry until he apologises.' And the rage that consumed his body knew he would never back down from what he had begun.

Brother stared at brother, each silent in the knowledge of what had come between them.

'So be it,' said Henry and removed himself from the library.

* * *

A thoroughly chilled Mr Praxton was just about to find his way to the local village inn when he spotted Nathaniel Hawke cantering down the gravel driveway. Even across the distance that divided them Praxton could see the tension that beset the other man's body. So matters within the great house had not got off to a good start. A sneer played across his lips. Trouble within the Hawke family could only bode well for his own cause. Perhaps the earl was having difficulty accepting the facts about his new daughter. He wondered as to exactly which aspect of Georgiana's scandalous behaviour had upset the aristocrat most. Was it her running away on the mail, disguising herself as a boy, or being press-ganged aboard his son's ship? He had to admit that the choice was really rather superb. Especially in the light of the fact that Georgiana's parentage alone was enough to render her unacceptable to any of them. Matters were possibly not as dismal as he had painted them. Information on the Hawke family could only prove useful to his cause. With that in mind, he retired from the fading daylight towards the village of Collingborne. Georgiana was slipping closer towards his grasp, even if the woman did not realise it herself. And the thought of what he would do to her when he caught her fired the chill from his body.

'You did what?' Georgiana sat up, the covers of the great four-poster bed falling to her waist. The hour was late and she had almost been asleep when she heard her husband enter the room. Now her head danced dizzily as she struggled to comprehend the enormity of what he was telling her.

Nathaniel threw his finely cut coat on to the chair beside the tallboy in the corner, and stripped off his neckcloth. Even galloping the gelding full speed across country had not blunted the edge of his fury. 'No one will cast such a slur on your character and think to get away with it, even if he is my brother. Henry shall take back his vile words or I'll disown him as my brother.'

She clasped her hands to her cheeks in horror. Surely this could not really be happening? A serious quarrel with Henry and all over her honour, her damned supposed honour. 'Nathaniel, please, stop, think what you're doing.' She clambered out of the bed and stood facing him clad only in the voluminous swirl of her white cotton nightgown.

'I know exactly what I'm doing,' he said between firm set lips.

She could see by the stubborn tilt of his jaw that he wasn't going to be easy to reason with, but she had to try. Heaven only knew just how much she would. 'What did you expect when you brought me here?' she demanded, elbows akimbo. 'That they would welcome me with open arms? We both knew what this visit was to be about. I thought that we'd prepared ourselves to meet what we would find.'

He threw his shirt aside and sat down on the bed to strip off his boots, the muscles in his back rippling from his exertions. 'My father's insults are to be expected. That he has not deigned to grace us with his presence is exactly the welcome I expected. But what I'm not prepared to accept is Henry's condemnation of you.' His eyes glittered dark and dangerous as if he were recalling events from earlier in the day.

'Put yourself in his shoes. He's your older brother, Porchester's heir. It's only natural that he feels the weight of family responsibility heavy on his shoulders. He's only doing what he thinks best for you. How would you feel if matters were reversed and Henry had taken an unsuitable woman to wife? You would speak out, wouldn't you?'

'That's not the point, Georgiana,' he argued. 'The matter is not reversed and I won't allow him to speak of you in that way.' How could he explain to her the anger that stuck like a bone in his throat, when he did not understand it himself? Her words were sensible, the same advice as he would give to any other, and yet he could not swallow them, for all he knew that he should.

When he did not answer, just began to remove his stockings, she flounced round the other side of the room to face him once more. 'He's your brother. Would you lose him over a silly argument?'

'Georgiana, let it be. Henry knows how to resolve the matter.'

'And what of you?' she said with gritty determination. 'You

would throw away all that is between you, alienate yourself from your brother as well as your father, and at Christmas?'

He shrugged his shoulders with false bravado. 'If that's the price, then I'll pay it. Regardless of what people think, I have some sense of honour.'

She clutched at his shoulders, her fingers biting hard, pulling the full weight of his attention to her. 'Then hear me, Nathaniel Hawke, and hear me well. I won't allow you to lose Henry over such a pettiness. It's my honour he's insulted and therefore I'll have the say of any action taken to defend it.' Grey lights flashed boldly in her eyes as she leaned closer to him, her face barely inches from his. 'When I cut off my hair and dressed in my stepbrother's clothes I decried my honour. When I ran away to Fareham in the company of strangers I decried my honour. When I served under false pretences aboard the *Pallas* I decried my honour. And, worst of all, when I forced you to face ruination or marriage, what did I do to the little honour I had left? I'm not so high in the instep that I cannot suffer whatever words your family may choose to throw at me. And if I can suffer it, so can you.'

'Georgiana—' he started to interrupt but she would have none of it.

'No, Nathaniel, hear me out. You would deprive yourself not only of Henry, but of Mirabelle and the children too. And what of Freddie? Where will he stand with his loyalties divided? You would tear this family apart.' She saw the pain appear in his eyes. Her hands moved up to take his face between her palms. 'And what would that knowledge do to you? I don't want to lose the husband that I love.'

The last word echoed in the stillness between them. Their faces were so close that the warmth of their breath met and mingled. She saw the darkness clear from his eyes, watched them open wide and clear. 'You love me?' It was a mere whisper on a breath, but Georgiana knew what he asked.

'I've always loved you, Nathaniel Hawke, from that first day upon the river bank when you saved my life.'

He stared at her as if he could not believe the words that had just fallen from her mouth. Stared at her as if he thought never to look upon her again. His arms moved to hold her to him so that she could feel the thud of his heart against her own. Lip to lip, breast to breast, hip to hip, they lay still and heavy, each breathing the scent of the other. And all the while those dark eyes held hers, never flinching nor fading in the intensity of their focus. Silence surrounded them save for the haunting rattle of the wind against the windowpanes. When at last he moved to take her it was as if it was the first time. Such tenderness, such passion, and yet with so much more. Even as he moved over her Georgiana knew the difference. For this was a union not just of bodies but also of souls. A merging of hearts for ever. The knowledge pushed the experience into the realm of the extraordinary. It seemed that they floated clear of the bed, of the great house itself, melting together in a liquid pool of ecstasy that surpassed ordinary mortal experience. Even when Georgiana curled sleeping around him, Nathaniel knew that everything had changed. A world of difference sparked from one small innocuous word. Love. She had said it. Had spoken the truth. And in the darkness of their bedroom and the nocturnal hush of Collingborne House he lay brooding upon exactly what that meant. Truly, nothing would ever be the same again.

It was the day before Christmas Eve and both Nathaniel and Henry were still proving to be wilfully stubborn when it came to the matter of Georgiana. Henry, in his position of the older and wiser sibling, would not soften in his condemnation for all of Mirabelle's tears, tantrums and pleadings. Neither would Nathaniel withdraw his stubborn ultimatum. After that night, when she had believed him to have understood all that she had tried so hard to express, Georgiana was left lonely and confused. The man she loved seemed strangely distant, removed to a place she could not reach. That he fully intended to lose Henry over the foolish notion of her honour only fired the pain that ravaged her breast. What matter that she loved him, had bared her heart and soul, only to have it cast firmly back in her face? He did not love her, that much was clear. Indeed, had he not since taken pains to avoid her, creeping late into bed when he knew her to be asleep, and rising early in the morning?

As soon as she entered the breakfast room Henry, Lord Farleigh, departed, turning his back to meet her in a direct cut.

Mrs Howard rose swiftly from the table. 'We were beginning to worry that you'd overslept. Come and help yourself to breakfast. The choice is quite superb.'

Georgiana's normally robust appetite suddenly shrivelled to the size of a small dried pea. 'I'm not hungry, some coffee will suffice.'

'Nonsense,' replied Mrs Howard. The lady proceeded to create an assortment of devilled kidneys, eggs and bread rolls upon a plate and placed it before Georgiana. 'Take my word for it, my dear, you'll feel much better for eating.'

Georgiana's gaze met those of Mirabelle Farleigh. The small woman smiled, but it did not hide the ashen hue of her complexion or the dark shadows that smudged beneath her red-rimmed eyes. 'It isn't your fault, Georgiana. They're both as bad as each other. Henry shouldn't have said the things that he did. I'm sorry that it's come to this.'

'No, Mirabelle. It's I who should apologise. Lord Farleigh seeks only what is best for his family. His younger brother has been married in haste to a woman who cannot be described, by any stretch of the imagination, as a good match. I fully understand his feelings on the matter.' Georgiana prodded a piece of kidney with her fork.

Mirabelle pushed back a lock of hair that had escaped to sweep over her cheek. 'You're a good woman, Georgiana, and my husband's more the fool for his blindness. For all that I love him, I've never seen him so stubborn and unyielding.' She pressed the lace of her handkerchief to her mouth. 'Please excuse me, Georgiana, Mrs Howard.' A rustle of skirts and she was gone.

'Stop playing with your breakfast, Georgiana. Starving yourself shall not assist any aspect of the matter.' The silver eyes regarded her calmly, sensibly, loosening the tension within the room.

'You're right as ever, Mrs Howard,' said Georgiana. She chewed on the food thoughtfully, pondering the situation with cool composure for the first time.

Neither woman spoke, each reassured and comfortable in the other's presence. After some time, when Georgiana had scraped her plate clean and was sipping on her second cup of coffee, she asked, 'What's your opinion, ma'am? What should we do?'

Mrs Howard folded her long manicured fingers before answering. 'It's not my place to comment.'

Georgiana looked up at her, disappointment on her face.

'Georgiana,' the older woman sighed, 'I shouldn't, but...' One slow blink of the silver eyes and she continued, 'You must do whatever it takes to ensure that the disagreement is resolved. And now, please excuse me, my dear. I've already said too much.' So saying, Evelina removed herself swiftly and gracefully from the breakfast room.

Georgiana sat alone, bathed in a ray of pale winter sunshine. Mrs Howard had not told her anything other than she already knew herself. Yes, her heart was raw from Nathaniel's rejection. But a family was at stake here. Wallowing in self-pity would not prevent Nathaniel's self-imposed isolation. Whatever the outcome, the Hawkes would be destroyed, and Georgiana knew quite calmly, quite clearly, that the fault would lie with her own self. If only she had not run away, if only she had not ended up aboard the *Pallas,* if only she had not married Nathaniel... There were so many *if onlys*. On board the frigate, before they had ever come to this place, she would have staked her very life that Nathaniel could never have behaved in this way. To risk all that was dear to him, and over her. She could not stop him, just as Mirabelle could not stop Henry. The more that Georgiana thought, the more she came to realise that there was only one person who had the power to do such a thing. One man who could prevent the downward spiral of events. She squared her shoulders, took a deep breath, and determined that this was one occasion that would never merit an *if only*.

The Earl of Porchester looked up from his desk at the woman standing so doggedly before him. With her clear pale skin and short dark hair, she could hardly be described as beautiful, but there was something magnetic about her, the arrangement of her features, and those eyes. Porchester felt it, just as clearly as his sons had before him. It was, no doubt, an attribute she used to good effect—to catch a husband beyond her class, beyond her means. If she thought to manipulate him so easily, she was in for a surprise. He knew that he had been inordinately rude in refusing to meet her, and that nothing excused his appalling breach of manners. A wave of disquiet swept over him at the thought. He brushed it carelessly away. 'I did not request your presence, madam.'

'No.' Her voice was quiet but steady.

He watched her from beneath his dark hooded eyes, waited for her discomfort to grow before gesturing in the direction of the worn leather chairs by the fireplace. 'Sit down.' It was not an invitation. He moved around from behind the barrier of the desk.

'Thank you, my lord.' Georgiana settled herself into the chair and watched while the earl took the other. She noted that he was almost as tall as Nathaniel and, even if the years had not left him unmarked, he still had an impressive stature. Although his hair had turned to a distinguished silver, he did not appear old—it merely lent him an air of sophistication. For a man busy about work within his study he was dressed immaculately in a black superfine coat, under which a silver-grey waistcoat and pristine white shirt could be seen. With his black breeches and silver buckled shoes he presented a formidable image. A lavender neckcloth completed the elegant attire. She felt more than a little intimidated by the Earl of Porchester. Her gaze flickered nervously to his face, and she almost gasped aloud at what it found there. For Lord Porchester was possessed of the same expressive eyes as each of his sons and he was watching her with a cold disdain. Even the knowledge of his hostility to her husband, and therefore, by association, to herself, had not prepared her for the severity of the earl's presence. The power of speech appeared to have deserted Georgiana as she stared overawed at the man seated opposite. A vision of Nathaniel came to her aid and she forced herself onwards, and upwards.

'Please forgive my interruption, sir. I'm sorry to disturb you when you're clearly busy, but I wondered if you might spare me a few minutes of your time.' The sides of her throat were in danger of sticking together such was their aridity, and her stomach was starting to rebel against the devilled kidneys. It growled loudly in the pause after her words. A hint of colour suffused her pale cheeks and she muttered, 'Oh, please do excuse me, my lord.'

The harshness in Lord Porchester's dark eyes did not even waver, just remained trained on the woman seated before him. 'What do you want?' he asked with uncivil bluntness. 'Other than what you've already acquired for yourself.'

She felt the colour deepen in her cheeks at the insult. 'I ask only that you'll listen to my request.'

'Asking for more already?'

The muscle in her jaw twitched before she schooled it to remain impassive. 'I'm not here for myself. You will think what you want of me. I cannot change that, nor am I about to try.'

A dark eyebrow raised in response. 'Then I ask you again, what do you want?'

She swallowed hard. 'Nathaniel and Lord Farleigh have argued.'

He waited.

She swallowed again and tried to make him understand. 'It's serious. They won't speak to one another and neither is prepared to back down.'

'Over what have they disagreed?' The expression on his face was closed, but the tone of his voice suggested that he already knew.

'Over myself.' Her hands clasped firmly together. 'Nathaniel has taken exception to Lord Farleigh's opinion.'

'And what exactly is Henry's opinion?' Just how much was she prepared to reveal?

Georgiana steeled herself to say what must be said. There could be no evasion, no hiding from the truth. 'He doesn't approve of me, sir. He believes that I married Nathaniel to further my own ends.'

The earl smiled, and the slow ironic curve of his mouth was more chilling than his frown. And still those dark eyes looked coldly on. 'It's nothing less than the truth.'

The silence stretched between them.

'Nothing I say will persuade you otherwise. I'm not here to plead my case. In fact, I deserve your condemnation more than you can know. But I won't stand by and see brother against brother, or watch the destruction of my husband's family. Whatever you think of him, Nathaniel deserves better than that.' Her fingers strayed surreptitiously to worry at her ear.

The dark eyes widened, and watched as Georgiana unwittingly mirrored the habit of the earl's late wife. It was an action that had ever betrayed concentration or anxiety in his beloved countess. And in that single motion, time stripped away so that he could see Mary, bright, alive, smiling, before the pain, before the dark finality, before the bitter years of misery. When he looked again, there was only the frightened girl wearing her defiant courage like a badge. 'Nathaniel has exactly what he deserves,' he said, but there was a huskiness to his voice that had not been there before.

'No.'

Their gazes locked.

'You're wrong about him. Your son, my lord, is an honourable man. Whatever else he is, never doubt that.'

A mirthless laugh escaped the old man. 'You plead his case well. He will be pleased.'

'He doesn't know that I'm here.'

The clock ticked loudly upon the mantel.

She tried again. 'Nathaniel is a good man. He's sacrificed much in the name of honour and duty.'

Another pause.

'I'm listening,' he said, and Georgiana knew it to be the best chance she would get. To reveal the extent of her husband's sacrifices would be to declare the scandalous truth about herself. If Lord Farleigh disapproved of her because she was an innkeeper's daughter, she could only imagine the family's reaction when they learned the rest. She would have to leave, of course. For that, Lord Porchester would know that for all these years he had been wrong about his son. The price was high, but she knew she could do nothing other than pay it, and willingly so. So she raised her chin and straightened her back. 'There's much to tell,' she said quietly, 'and I'd have you know it all, my lord.' With a calm determination she proceeded to do just that, neither omitting details nor embellishing facts. And all the while the Earl of Porchester listened in studied silence.

* * *

'So now you know, my lord, how honourable a man Nathaniel Hawke is.' She sat caught in her memories, knowing, whatever the future held, she would never stop loving Nathaniel. Slowly she forced herself back to the present. 'Will you speak to him, make him see that this quarrel is utter folly?'

Those hooded dark eyes were regarding her intensely, and still he had neither moved nor spoken. 'It was ever my intent,' he said slowly.

'But you…I thought—' Georgiana broke off.

'Then you thought wrong.'

The grey-blue gaze shuttered and she bit down hard on her bottom lip to stop the tremor.

'Why have you told me this?'

She blinked in confusion. 'So that Nathaniel won't lose his family.'

'And for that you are prepared to give him up yourself?'

The question hung in the air between them.

'Yes.' The blood drained from her face. She knew what he was asking, what she'd known he would demand even before she'd told her story.

He leaned forward in his chair. 'Why?'

'Because I love him,' she whispered.

'Thank you, Georgiana,' was all he said as he released her to go. But the earl did not move from the chair in which she left him, and his thoughts lingered still on the man who had married to save a woman from utter ruin.

Walter Praxton blew misty winter breath upon his chilled fingers in an attempt to warm them. He did not dare to light a fire within the small woodsman's hut he had stumbled upon for fear that his presence would be noticed. Each night was spent comfortably ensconced in the snug warmth of the Fox and Hounds Inn within the village of Collingborne, each day in the tireless surveillance of the woman who haunted him incessantly. Whether in waking or sleeping he could think of little else, watching her as he did, hour by hour, with the aid of his spyglass.

The fact that Captain Hawke did not appear to spend any time in Georgiana's company heartened him. Obviously he had married her from some misplaced sense of honour. Walter did not allow his mind to wander to those activities that occurred during the long dark evenings when he was safely stowed within the inn. Those thoughts were liable to induce in him a fury that surpassed any he had previously known. Besides, he had already laid his plan, and tomorrow would see the start of it.

He knew the route across the fields and woodland that Captain Hawke had taken these past four mornings. The sight of the man upon the grey gelding instilled in him nothing but a jealous loathing. That he could call himself Georgiana's husband, that he was the one who had no doubt had full possession of her body. There was really nothing else that Walter could do, or so he had told himself just half an hour earlier as he tied the thin rope across the path. His selection of location was superb, the rope being positioned just after a sharp bend in the woodland track. The trap would not be seen until it was too late. Walter's pale eyes glittered at the very thought, before raising the spyglass once more to resume his vigil. The sight that met his eye brought a sneer to his face and set him off at a gallop down the hill towards Collingborne House.

The winter sun had sunk low in a pink-kissed sky but still sheathed the garden in its dazzling beauty. Frost-stiffened grass crunched beneath Georgiana's feet as she made her way down to the holly bushes, and her breath clouded as smoke in the crisp cold air. Following her discourse with the earl that morning, she worried precisely as to when she should leave and what Nathaniel would have to say when he realised just what she had done. Unable to reveal her fears to either Mrs Howard or Lady Farleigh, Georgiana had left the two ladies contentedly playing cards within the stuffy heat of the blue drawing room. She revelled in the sharp nip in the air, felt it clear her head a little. A short walk in the gardens to gather her senses together was all that was required. She had already packed the few items of her wardrobe. Before her she heard the startled warning call of a blackbird, then saw its small dark shape flutter up inside a large and seemingly dense holly bush. She rubbed her fingers to the dark spiky gloss of its leaves. Such a fountain of colour amidst the drab bare browns of Yuletide. A soft tread on grass, warm breath against the back of her neck, and a presence so close as to all but touch her.

'Georgiana.' The whisper sounded at her ear, so unmistakable that it caused a cold prickle across her skin and sent a shiver down her spine.

She spun round and looked up into the cruel handsome face she had never thought to see again. 'Mr Praxton!' she gasped, feeling a horrible tightening sensation within her chest. Her fingers crushed the enclosed holly leaf, puncturing her skin so that it bled, but she was aware of nothing save the pale blue eyes trained on hers.

'Did you think that I had abandoned you, my sweet?'

Spiny leaves needled her back as she tried to increase the distance between them.

'Never think that I would not fulfil my duty to my betrothed.' He stepped closer so that their bodies were touching.

Georgiana felt the stirring of panic in her breast. 'Sir, my circumstances have since changed. I'm now another man's wife. Please leave before my husband arrives.' She struggled to step aside.

Walter Praxton's hands grabbed her upper arms in a vicelike grip. 'Your precious husband is drinking himself into a stupor in the library and doubtless plans to stay there for the remainder of the day. No, Georgiana—' and his voice was cold and hard '—Captain Hawke is merely a temporary aberration in your life. You had no right to wed him when you belong to me, even if you were a ship's boy on the *Pallas*.'

'Dear God, no,' she cried, feeling her legs tremble beneath her.

He smiled down at her, and in it she saw the measure of his madness. 'There is nothing I don't know, my dear, but through it all I'll still have you.'

Her mouth opened to scream, but met with a sharp blow from Walter's fist. Then there was nothing but a gathering nausea and a rolling darkness.

Chapter Thirteen

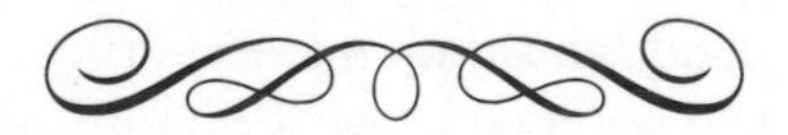

Nathaniel watched as the yellow flames engulfed the log, sending small sparks and spits cascading over the hearth. The room was pleasantly warm and the brandy had numbed the raw edge of his emotions. But still he could not make sense of the riot of thoughts rampaging through his head. He did not want to hurt Henry, never would have imagined himself doing so, not in a thousand years. There was a part of him that looked clearly at the mayhem unfolding and told himself not to behave in such a ridiculous fashion. It was the part of himself to whom he had always listened, refusing to allow his feelings affect his judgements or decisions. For once he had turned a deaf ear to its advice. Unaccountable it may be, unfathomable even, but he knew that he would never let anyone, no matter who they might be, hurt Georgiana. He did not understand the depth of his feelings, just knew that he needed her and would never let her go.

Since her admission the other night he had deliberately avoided her, for her pleas could stir his heart like no other, and he was adamant that he would not let Henry off so lightly. Georgiana deserved comfort, understanding and respect for all that she had suffered, not condemnation. And Nathaniel meant to see that she would be treated with all three. His family could take umbrage with *him*, not his wife. Her words replayed in his mind, '*...the husband that I love*', and he smiled. Damnation, how he missed her. What must she be thinking of his neglect? That he did not care for her? Never that. The thought of her suffering stirred pain in his heart. He set the brandy glass down carefully upon the table. He would go to her, explain all, beg her forgiveness. It was with a renewed vigour in his step that Nathaniel ascended the sweeping staircase.

The first things that he saw were her bags packed neatly in a small pile beside the door. His heart lurched cold as he drew his own conclusions. Within fifteen minutes he had ascertained that she was not present within the entirety of the house and was treading back up the stairs when he heard the study door open and his father's voice.

'Nathaniel.'

He paused mid-flight and turned to face the earl. 'Sir, I don't doubt that which you wish to discuss, but I've more pressing matters on my mind at this minute.' He made to turn away but was prevented doing so by the command in the tone.

'Nathaniel!'

He could not ignore it. His head nodded once and he followed the old man into the study.

'Drink?' his father asked, lifting the brandy decanter from a small round table placed close to the wall.

'No, thank you, sir, I have imbibed too much this day as it is.'

They stood facing one another, tense, waiting, and from each face the same eyes looked out.

At last Nathaniel spoke. 'I know you've called me here over my quarrel with Henry, but I cannot…will not, allow him to cast aspersions on Georgiana's character. Contrary to his opinion, and no doubt yours, she did not seek to trap me into marriage, and neither is she some kind of trollop. She's my wife and I—'

Lord Porchester interrupted. 'Save your breath. I know full well what Georgiana is.'

The gasp of incredulity that escaped Nathaniel echoed round the room. 'You go too far, sir.' He stepped forward, the closing distance between them much more of a threat than his words could ever be. 'I can bear your censure, even your contempt, but I won't let you say one word against Georgiana.'

Father looked at son. Son looked at father. Tension quivered tight and dangerous.

And then one corner of the earl's mouth raised to form a sarcastic smile. A dark brow lifted mockingly. 'You love her?'

No reply save the flare of Nathaniel's nostrils.

The earl barked a hollow laugh before the slight grimace of pain flickered across the elderly features and then was gone, masked once more behind the imperial stare. 'Sit down, for God's sake.' The utterance was little more than a tired sigh.

Nathaniel's gaze flitted once to the door before he moved to the chair.

The curve of a balloon glass was pressed into his hand, and his father sat down in the twin chair at the opposite side of the fireplace.

'This nonsense with Henry—I want it stopped—now.' Lord Porchester took a swig of brandy.

'Do you even know what the argument is over?'

Another sip of the amber liquid. 'It isn't worth losing a brother over a woman, Nathaniel.'

'But a son is a different matter entirely.'

They both knew to what he was referring.

'You judge me harshly, son.'

'As you judge me, sir.'

The flames crackled in the fireplace. The curtains rippled in the draft.

'You'll have your apology, I'll see to it. And that will be an end to the matter for both you and Henry.'

Nathaniel leaned forward. 'Why do you care? I'd have thought the fact that Henry and I are at each other's throats to have suited you.'

A soft snort of disgust issued from the chair opposite. Nothing else.

Nathaniel rose to his feet, placing the untouched brandy on the occasional table. 'Please excuse me, sir. I must find my wife.'

Porchester's eyes stared into the dancing flames, remembering the girl who had ventured here like Daniel into the lion's den. Remembering her courage and dignity, and that same betraying gesture so like Mary's across the years. God, it still hurt, hurt like hell…to lose a woman that you loved. A ragged sigh shuddered through his frame.

'Sir?'

Control resumed, vulnerability fled. 'Why didn't you tell me?'

'Tell you?'

'About Georgiana, about what happened aboard the *Pallas*.'

Nathaniel froze where he stood, his gaze widening momentarily. 'I don't know what you mean.' But the words were stiffly formed through rigid lips.

Lord Porchester looked directly at him. 'I'm sure that you do. It isn't every day that you marry your ship's boy.'

His son's lips parted.

But Porchester was there first. 'Maybe I have judged you too harshly. The girl was right.' The brandy glass touched to his mouth. 'Georgiana…' He savoured the name.

'How do you—?'

'She came to see me.'

'Georgiana?'

'She might be trade, but you're right, she doesn't deserve Henry's condemnation. As I said, I know exactly what Georgiana is, nothing but courageous.'

Shock registered on Nathaniel's face. And then the dark eyes narrowed to a cool calculating focus. 'The bags…she's packed her bags. I thought…' Long tanned fingers raked through the mahogany locks. 'You told her to leave.' The accusation was little more than a whisper. His voice raised, 'Didn't you?'

'I told her nothing,' came the tart reply.

'You would have me lose the woman that I love. And why? Because she doesn't meet your standards?' Nathaniel stared down at the man he called father. 'Because she isn't Kitty Wakefield?'

But the earl heard nothing past those few words, '*…lose the woman that I love*.' The glass slipped from his limp fingers to smash against the hearth. Blood drained from his cheeks, leaving a pallor that hid nothing of the toll exerted by heartbreak and bitterness. 'Don't say that. Never say that,' and the voice that whispered was that of an old man.

Nathaniel leaned low and looked into the haunted face. 'Father?'

The eyes that raised to his were, for once, neither mocking nor cold. 'I never realised… I didn't think…' The silver grey head shook once as if to clear the weakness of the thoughts. When he spoke again it was with the strength Nathaniel had always known. 'If her bags are still here, then so is she. It isn't too late, Nathaniel.'

The words hung between them. A two-fold meaning. One message. Hope.

'I've searched the house, there's nothing to be found.'

'Then we'll search again,' said Porchester and rose to stand by his son.

'Whatever is the matter? You look positively dreadful.' Mirabelle placed her cards on the table and rushed to Nathaniel's side. She clung to him and eyed the earl with undisguised ill ease.

Nathaniel's face was unusually pale, exaggerating the dark glitter of his eyes and the stark mahogany hairline. He took her hands in his, speaking with an urgency that Mirabelle had not heard him use before. 'Have you seen Georgiana?'

As Mirabelle's curls shook in denial, Mrs Howard stepped forward. 'She left our company some half an hour since. I couldn't help but notice that she seemed a little preoccupied with her thoughts, as if she had much to think about.'

'She's not in her room or visiting the children in the nursery. Indeed, I've searched the whole house and she's nowhere to be found.' Nathaniel could not hide his escalating concern. He did not mention the pile of baggage arranged so neatly upstairs, or what had passed between her and his father.

Mrs Howard's expression softened. Nathaniel Hawke's feelings concerning the girl could not have been clearer had he proclaimed them from the steeple tops. And whatever his reasons for avoiding Georgiana's company these past days, it was not a cooling of his ardour. Not much escaped the vigilant attention of Evelina Howard. Her gaze moved to the earl and rested a moment before gliding back to his son. 'Perhaps Georgiana has decided to walk in the gardens.

On a pleasant afternoon like this it would be the perfect setting in which to order her thoughts.'

She had scarcely completed her words when Nathaniel had gone, whirling through the door as a large dark blur.

The earl cleared his throat. 'Pray forgive my son, ma'am, he is anxious to locate Georgiana's whereabouts.' He watched the serene silver-eyed woman before him incline her head in mute agreement. 'Indeed, I must also ask your forgiveness for the tardiness of my introduction. You must be Mrs Howard.'

Mirabelle watched the discourse between Evelina Howard and the Earl of Porchester with surprise. Lord Porchester was being positively polite—and did her eyes deceive her, or was that the subtle hint of a blush creeping upon Mrs Howard's cheeks? Well, well, well, who would have thought such a thing? Mirabelle was just warming to her train of thought when the door burst open to reveal Nathaniel, with Frederick by his side.

'She's not in the gardens nor any place that I can think.' His voice was grim. 'We must find her before darkness falls.' Not one person within the room could fail to see the harsh control with which Nathaniel Hawke reined in his emotions. He turned to address his father. 'Sir, if you would be so good as to undertake a second search of the gardens and stables, Freddie and I will ride to the village in case she's walked out that way.' As Porchester gave a brief nod, a strong voice sounded from the doorway.

'No. I'll go with Freddie. You stay here.' Henry walked into the room. 'Father has spoken to me and it seems that I owe Georgiana an apology. Evidently I've been mistaken in my opinions, and I mean to tell her so.' The pain in his brother's eyes betrayed that he loved the girl, and, if what his father had said was true, Henry knew that he had been unfair in his treatment of Georgiana.

Brother stared at brother, and the silence ticked by before Nathaniel firmly clasped Henry's hand. 'Thank you,' was all he said, before the men of the Hawke family moved rapidly to action.

Georgiana came round to find herself lying on her side upon a narrow bed. Memories of Walter Praxton's leering face lurched her with a shudder back to the present. She did not move or even attempt to open her eyes, just tried to gauge her state and if the vision of her nightmare was still present. A coarse rope secured her arms behind her back and her ankles together. Although her bindings were not unreasonably tight, her limbs had grown stiff and uncomfortable from their restrictions. She was aware of a painful tenderness around her jaw and the left-hand side of her lower lip felt stung and swollen. Despite the grey blanket draped over her body the air was chilled, seeping a dampness through to her bones. All around the woody smell of decaying forestry filled her nose. Within the stillness of her surroundings she heard the cawing of crows, and the squeak and scrabbling of something else she preferred not to think of. She suppressed a shiver and slowly opened her eyes.

The hut was small and wooden, obviously the temporary abode of some shepherd or woodsman. Apart from the small truckle bed, the only other furniture comprised a stool and a wooden crate upturned to form a table. Strips of wood and sacking had been nailed securely over the single tiny window, possibly to keep out the worst of the cold or to hide the flickering illumination of the candle lantern placed on the table. On the bare wooden floor sat a saddlebag, a tankard and a bottle of wine. Clearly Mr Praxton had made liberal use of the hut, but how long had he been here, watching her? She dared not guess, only gave thanks that he was not present at this minute. Her gratitude was to be short-lived, for just as she struggled to a sitting position and strained against her bindings the gentleman reappeared.

'Ah, my dove, you're awakened once more.' He touched a hand to her bruised face, frowning as she flinched. 'Forgive my rather brutish treatment, I could not allow you to alert anyone to our plans.' His fingers slid round to cup the back of her neck, and he crouched low to look into her eyes.

Georgiana's fear squirmed inside, but she thrust it down out of sight and forced herself to face Walter Praxton with a convincing façade of calm. 'Mr Praxton, I've already told you that I'm married. Whatever plans you once had, can be no more. Cease this game now, let me go free, and I won't speak of the matter.' The firmness in her voice betrayed no trace of a tremor.

Praxton's frown vanished, replaced instead by a smirk. 'Do you think to fool me so easily? I haven't spent these last months tracing you to give you up to any man, least of all Hawke.' He leaned closer, until she could feel the warmth of his breath upon her skin. 'He only married you because his honour gave him no other option. You must be aware by now that he doesn't care for you.' Then added silkily, 'Not as I do.' The pale eyes looked deep into hers as his lips moved to claim her mouth.

'No!' Georgiana shrank back. 'No,' she said, with a little more control. 'You're wrong.' Her heart hammered within her chest and the blood pounded in her temples.

A suspicion was forming in Walter's mind, too horrible for him to fully contemplate. Surely Georgiana did not actually hold any affection for the man she called husband? He remembered her face smiling up at the captain's in Portsmouth dockyard. His fingers tightened, drawing a gasp from the woman before him. If that was her game, Walter would use it to his advantage. 'So you seek to bind a man who doesn't want you, to ruin his life, destroy his standing within his family. You're promised to me, and always have been. What of my reputation? What of my feelings in the matter?' He paused, to allow his words to hit their target. 'You are selfish in the extreme, Georgiana. What cares have you for anyone other than yourself? Not your family whom you left to face your disgrace, nor your betrothed, not even the man that you call husband.'

Georgiana's throat tightened. Every word that dripped from Walter Praxton's tongue played on the worst of her fears. She *was* selfish and thoughtless. She *had* treated them all abysmally. He only spoke the truth. She stared at him, voiceless, not knowing that her eyes betrayed all.

Walter loosed his grip on Georgiana's neck, knowing her resolve to be perilously close to crumbling. 'Let me save us all,' he whispered, his eyes softening.

Thoughts whirled in Georgiana's confused mind. She had forced Nathaniel into marriage, had inadvertently set brother against brother, and was about to be banished from Collingborne. What's more, since she had bared her heart, her husband had taken definite steps to avoid spending time in her company. But she loved him, damn it! She looked into the pale eyes before her and saw the malice and cruelty simmering below the surface. Lust and obsession stared blatantly back. Even as she struggled to hide her revulsion at the fingers caressing her shoulders, she knew she could never give herself to any man other than Nathaniel, and especially not Walter Praxton.

'Mr Praxton, thank you for your kind offer of help, but I'm afraid that I cannot accept it. I will return to my family and cast myself upon their mercy.' She felt the pressure of his fingers grow until it became almost unbearable, gnawing into her skin. A hiss sounded close to her ear.

'And I'm afraid that I cannot allow you to refuse,' he breathed, and pressed his hot avaricious mouth to hers.

Nathaniel knew that what his brothers had to say did not bode well before they even opened their mouths. Henry's expression was stern and forbidding, a sure sign that he was worried. Freddie looked unusually thoughtful.

'I take it you found no sign of her?' Nathaniel had not yet removed his caped great coat or gloves.

Henry shook his head. 'Nothing.' He watched the strain tighten his brother's face, pinching the lips white even beneath the yellow light of the candles. 'Why didn't you simply tell me that you love her?' It was a question uttered quietly, but all eyes in the room trained on Nathaniel for his answer.

Dark eyes glittered within the pallor of his face. The clock on the mantel punctuated the silence in staccato strokes. 'Because I didn't realise it myself until today,' he growled. Long fingers threaded themselves through the deep dark brown of his hair, thrusting the unruly waves back from his face. He started to speak, then stopped, cleared the emotion from his throat, and resumed once more. 'It would seem that Mrs Howard was correct. One of the maids saw Georgiana leaving the house wearing her cloak, and there were signs that someone had walked across the lawns to reach the shrubbery at the front of the house. It's dark outside and the temperature is dropping. Georgiana should have returned long since.'

'She must have met with an accident,' piped up Mirabelle. 'Perhaps she's twisted her ankle and cannot get back from where she has fallen.'

The earl spoke up. 'Nathaniel and I have scoured the grounds. She's not to be found.'

'Then maybe she walked farther than you searched.' Mirabelle would not allow herself to think the worst.

A calm voice spoke. 'Captain Hawke, may I be so bold as to suggest that you check Georgiana's wardrobe.'

'There's nothing missing,' replied Nathaniel rather tersely and moved towards the door, before pausing to address his father. 'You don't think…?'

'No, not without her bags.'

More to alleviate the awkward silence that followed his father's words than anything else, Freddie spoke up. 'Rather peculiar coincidence in the village. That chap Praxton, who visited with Georgiana's father at Farleigh Hall, has been staying in Collingborne of late.' Nathaniel paused mid-stride, but Freddie rambled on, oblivious to the spasm of tension that seized his brother's body. 'Spoke to the landlord of the Fox and Hounds. Praxton's been a good customer. Apparently has business in the area. Fancy him turning up in this neck of the woods. Strange.' He was just starting to give the matter the full weight of his consideration when he glanced up to see an unfathomable expression cross Nathaniel's face.

'Walter Praxton!' he exclaimed harshly. 'His presence might well explain the situation!' It seemed that a knife twisted in his heart, and the breath knocked from his lungs. 'Georgiana was betrothed to Praxton before she wed me.' The words scraped raw his already bleeding heart, but he refused to let his family see just how deeply the wound had pierced. 'Even now her travelling bags lie packed and ready in her bedroom,' he uttered by way of explanation.

'Ah,' said Henry softly. 'You think she has deserted you.'

Evelina Howard shook her head in denial and stepped forward

to speak. 'Captain Hawke, surely you could never believe such a thing?' And for the first time Nathaniel saw a flicker of worry cloud the woman's eyes.

'Run off with Praxton?' queried a confused Freddie.

A peel of ironic laughter sounded within the room. Five pairs of eyes riveted to the source—Mirabelle Farleigh. The small woman leapt to her feet, ringlets shaking, mouth wide and incredulous.

'Mirabelle!' Henry's voice sounded stern. He moved towards her, saying to the others as he did, 'She's overwrought and has become hysterical.' His hand closed gently over her arm but she threw it off with, what her husband thought to be, surprising force.

'I most certainly am not.' She pulled away from Henry and towards Nathaniel, who was trying and failing miserably to disguise the fact that he looked like a man who believed the bottom to have just dropped from his world. 'Men!' she snorted. 'Sometimes they've not one ounce of sense in those great oversized bodies of theirs!'

Mrs Howard was smiling and even the earl had reverted to a marginally more relaxed stance.

'Mirabelle, contain yourself!' commanded her husband with growing exasperation.

Lady Farleigh paid no regard whatsoever to Henry, who was trying to coax her away from his brother. She planted herself like a small rock before her brother by marriage. 'Nathaniel,' she said, 'remember when you saved Georgiana from drowning in the Borne?' She did not wait for his answer. 'Did you suppose that she slipped and fell? Of course you did. Well,' the lady concluded, 'you were wrong. She jumped into the river rather than submit to Mr Praxton's advances upon the river bank.'

Nathaniel's brows lowered and he stared at Mirabelle in confusion.

'Precisely why did you suppose that any woman would run away from home, alone, and by mail coach? Oh, and end up pretending to be a boy aboard your ship?'

The dark eyes shifted accusingly to his father. 'Does everyone know the entirety of the story?'

'Don't seek to change the subject,' instructed Mirabelle. Henry's hand tightened around her arm. 'Georgiana did all of these things to escape Walter Praxton.'

'But—'

Mirabelle gave him little chance to speak. 'Yes, she was betrothed to the man, but it was most certainly against her will. Her father intended to force the wedding, leaving Georgiana few options. When she fled, she was intent on making her way here to Collingborne.' She looked round at the earl. 'She wanted my help, and would have had it had it not been for the Impress Service.'

'I say, Georgiana's a bit of a dark horse all right!' Freddie had perked up substantially at the revelations. Even the quelling look pressed upon him by his father failed to staunch the flow of admiration. He whistled and exclaimed, 'What a girl!'

When Nathaniel still had not spoken, Mirabelle rounded on him. 'And aside from all of that, Nathaniel Hawke, how could you think she would run off with anyone else when it's as plain as the nose on your face that she's head over heels in love with you!'

Nathaniel's face drained of any last vestige of colour.

'And what's wrong with that?' demanded Mirabelle on seeing the haunted look flit across his countenance.

'Nothing at all, aside from the fact that, from what you say, it's growing increasingly probable that Georgiana has been abducted by Praxton.'

Georgiana choked as Walter attempted to pour half a tankard of wine down her throat. The cold liquid splashed over her mouth, cascading down her chin and neck to stain her gown dark wet. The rough fingers that had prised open her bruised mouth moved rapidly away as she set up a chorus of coughs and splutters. By the time she had regained her breath her cheeks were as red as the wine that stained them.

'Come, now, Georgiana, don't resist so. The wine will warm you against the night chill, and—' he paused and looked at her, desire clear in his eyes '—help you to relax. It will make things a deal easier for you.'

'I don't want it,' she spat at him.

A wicked leer struck his face. 'You're then as eager for me as I am for you? Come, sweet dove, let Walter warm you.' His hands slid over her shoulders, travelling slowly down to skim her breasts, outlined starkly by the clinging wet fabric of her dress. 'But first we must get you out of these wet clothes.'

Dear Lord help her! Praxton meant to ravish her here, a scant two miles from the house that contained her husband. Nathaniel! Nathaniel! She wanted to cry his name aloud, but knew that to do so would only incense Walter further. His fingers loitered by her nipples, causing the gall to rise in her throat. A thick wet tongue snaked across her lips, trying to breach the fortress of her mouth. For a moment she thought she would wretch from the sickening assault, but managed to pull herself away from his lips. 'No! Stop! Mr Praxton, we must…' The words faltered as he reached round to her back and started to unfasten the buttons of her gown. 'No!' she exclaimed as she tried to remove herself from his grasp. But there was nowhere to go and, with her hands and feet still bound, there seemed little to help her evade his attentions.

Cold air prickled the skin beneath the thinness of her shift following the trail of Walter Praxton's fingers. 'Mr Praxton, stop this madness at once!' she pleaded.

'You don't know how long I've waited for this night. How much I've wanted to plunder your soft white body.' His breathing had grown somewhat laboured and uneven.

'If you have any regard left for me whatsoever, do not use me like this. Please.' She relaxed a little as he stepped away, thinking to have found some vestige of honourable behaviour within him. But she was much mistaken. As Walter Praxton peeled off his finely fashioned coat and loosed his neckcloth, she saw the manic gleam within his ice-pale eyes and knew that all was lost. He would not stop until he had what he wanted. And the thought of exactly what it was that he wanted brought a black desolation to her soul. From deep within she drew a tiny spark of courage and fanned it with thoughts of all that Nathaniel had done to save both her reputation and her life. The flame burned brighter. She saw the bulge within

Walter's breeches, watched while his fingers moved to unfasten them, gulped as he moved towards her.

'You always were a cowardly bully, Mr Praxton. Did you never wonder why I would do anything rather than marry you?'

Walter Praxton stopped in his tracks, a frown of annoyance darkening his golden looks. 'Mutinous thoughts planted in your head by that blasted Mrs Tillyard. Even your stepfather admits his folly in sending you to her. Of course, he was never strict enough with you, always gave in to the wants of that foolish mother of yours. I won't make the same mistake.'

She held his gaze. 'You seek to inflict your will on others through the use of violence and intimidation and money. Without those three bedfellows you would have nothing!'

'I'm a successful businessman, Georgiana, rich, good looking, all in all a highly desirable catch. It seems that it's only you that cannot see what's before your very eyes. Just think, you'll be the envy of young ladies all across Hampshire when they learn that you're my wife.' He was at her side, tugging down the arms and bodice of her dress until only the rose-stained damp shift stretched across her breasts veiled her body from his gaze.

'You're mad if you think that I'll ever wed you. I'm wife to Nathaniel Hawke and there'll be no place you can hide when he discovers that you've defiled me.' She flung the words at him, knowing that, whether Nathaniel loved her or not, he would always see justice done.

He laughed, an evil sound that rasped at her taut nerves. 'Defile? I promise to have done a damn sight more than that before this time tomorrow." His hands groped at her breasts, kneading them painfully beneath his cruel fingers.

She refused to cower, had done with pleading. Her eyes met his forcefully, without fear. 'Do what you will, but know that I feel nothing for you, neither love nor hate, just the grey emptiness of nothing, which is exactly your worth. All my love lies with my husband and, whether you rape me, or beat me, or kill me, you'll never change that.'

One hand wrapped itself painfully in the dark silky ebony of her hair, pulling her up until their faces were so close that they shared the same breath. 'You have been a brave wife to him.' A smirk played across his lips, the candlelight glinting in his golden hair. 'But will you be so brave a widow?'

It seemed that her heart had ceased to beat. She gasped air into her constricting lungs. 'No!' she shrieked. 'You are no threat to Nathaniel. He's more of a man than you'll ever be!'

The blow landed hard against her temple, stunning her wits, collapsing her body. 'Bitch!' he cursed. 'How little you know.' He saw the storm clouds gather in her eyes. 'What would you give to save his life? Yourself? Would you beg me?' His mouth moved to a smile and his fingers danced around the neckline of her sodden shift.

What it was that drew Nathaniel towards the far side of Beacon Hill he could never be sure, but the growing sense that Georgiana called him urged him on. Through the blackness of the night the candle lantern illuminated little, but as the heavens smiled on him the thick cover of clouds rolled back to reveal a huge opalescent moon. Silver light bathed the countryside so that the small group of riders made good progress. The earl wanted to split up, make a sweeping check of up to old Tom's farm in one direction and John Appleton's in the other. But Nathaniel was steadfast in his refusal, adamant in his determination that they search Beacon Hill before all else. Then he saw it. The faint hint of light emanating from the woodsman's hut within the copse of trees. And even before they had spurred their horses a fraction closer, he knew that Georgiana was within.

They dismounted and left their horses, creeping quietly forward through the frozen brush until they reached their target. Through the somewhat battered looking wooden door the murmur of voices could be heard, a man's laugh, mocking and loud, a woman's denial, vehement, disgusted. Nathaniel did not wait to hear any more. The door gave way beneath the ferocity of the combined weight of his and Henry's kicks. The sight that met his eyes ignited in Nathaniel a fury and fear that escalated beyond all control.

Walter Praxton was kneeling upon the bed, golden hair glowing in the candlelight, shirtless, in the process of loosing the fastenings on his breeches. Beneath him lay Georgiana, her face white and pinched, her gown ripped open, a thin stained shift moulded to her breasts. For the merest fraction of a second Nathaniel paused to assess the scene, then moved in a fluid motion to deliver first one resounding blow and then another to Praxton. The younger man pitched to the floor, limp and helpless beneath the weight of Nathaniel's towering rage. Dark eyes glowered with implacable anger and he would have pressed his assault further had it not been for her whisper.

'Nathaniel?' Her voice was small, strained, as if she could not be sure that the man before her eyes was a mirage of her own making or of flesh and blood. All thoughts of Praxton were forgotten as he reached down, cradling her in his arms.

'Dear Lord, what has he done to you?' he uttered hoarsely, scanning the darkening bruises on her face and the ripped bodice.

She smiled then, and it banished the horror from her expression. 'You came in time,' was all she said, and a solitary tear trickled down her cheek.

He clutched her to him as if he would never let her go, touched his lips gently to her cheek, her forehead, her chin. 'Thank God you've taken no more hurts. I'd never have forgiven myself if…' He could not continue. Clearing his throat, he stood up and, shrugging off his coat, wrapped it around his wife's trembling body, before freeing her bound hands and feet. 'You're safe now and we must get you home.'

'What of him?' Henry's toe touched to Praxton's still-limp body.

'Strap him across his horse. We'll keep him at Collingborne until the High Constable can be notified.'

Nathaniel clambered upon his gelding and was in the process of lifting Georgiana up from his father's arms when it happened. Just as Henry and Freddie were placing Walter Praxton's body across his own saddle, the wretched man suddenly roused from his feigned faint, delivered Henry a solid kick in the chest, and made off at a furious gallop. Nathaniel's brothers made to follow.

'No!' he yelled. 'Let him go for now.'

Freddie turned incredulous eyes upon him. 'You would let that villain escape?'

'It's dark and freezing. He'll not get far dressed as he is. We'll find him a damn sight easier by daylight. And besides, Georgiana has suffered enough this night. We should take her back to Collingborne now.'

With great reluctance Freddie was forced to concede that his brother was most probably right.

The next morning Georgiana awoke, snuggled warm beneath the covers of the four-poster bed in the rose room within Collingborne House. Apart from a tenderness around her face and head she had sustained no other hurts from her ordeal with Walter Praxton. The image of Nathaniel bursting through the door to save her from Praxton's evil intent would stay with her for ever. She knew then that she could never leave him, despite all the trouble she had brought upon him. He would have to cast her out himself if he wanted her to go. And whatever he may have said, or more for that matter left unsaid, she knew from the look upon his face when he'd held her to him within that cold dismal hut that he would never do that. Tenderness, relief, guilt, concern, desire, and something else that she feared to name, lest she be mistaken. The thought brought a smile to her face, nipping at her bruised lip, and she cast a probing hand over the sheet in the direction of where her husband had lain all the night through. It met with the emptiness of cooled sheeting, nothing else. She sat up abruptly, alarmed at the prospect he had gone.

'Georgiana!' A deep melodic voice sounded from the other side of the room. His tall dark figure turned from the bright white light of the window and moved towards her, but not before she had scrambled from the bed to stand before him, she in her voluminous white nightgown, he fully attired in the smartest of clothes.

'It's Christmas Eve.'

He could hear the consternation in her tone. Little wonder following her ordeal at that rogue's hands. How would she take the news? he wondered. At least she would never have to worry again in the future. 'Yes,' he agreed quietly.

Her hands grasped his arms, and she stretched up on her tiptoes to look into his face. Eyes the colour of a winter Atlantic scanned his, imploringly.

'Georgiana?'

She felt the muscles contract beneath her fingers, knew the strength contained in those arms.

'What's wrong? There's nothing more to fear. Praxton is dead. We found his body this morning out by Parson's Gully. It seems that he knew I rode out that way each day and had set a trap for me across the path. We found the same rope in one of his saddlebags. No doubt he planned to make it look like an accident and then miraculously be on hand to comfort the grieving widow. In the darkness Praxton couldn't see and plunged straight into it. His neck was broken in the fall.' He moved one arm to curl around her waist, while the other hand stroked enticing circles upon her back.

Her eyes widened momentarily and she shuddered. 'Killed by his own treachery,' she said softly.

'Georgiana.'

She shook her head. 'It isn't that.' She loosed her hand to pull at her ear lobe, her gaze dropping to meet level with the breadth of his chest.

'I've written to your father informing him of our marriage and Praxton's death. I know that he tried to forcibly wed you to that scoundrel and so you need not see him again.'

'You're very kind to me, Nathaniel Hawke. But I shall not fear to visit my family with my husband by my side.'

The cloud of worry still lurked in her eyes. 'What is it, Georgiana?' He touched a finger gingerly to her cheek to raise her eyes once more to his.

'Henry. I know he was there at the woodsman's hut. But you and he… Your disagreement…'

Nathaniel stared at her as if she had run mad, then suddenly smiled. He pressed a tiny kiss to the tip of her nose and laughed. 'Is resolved, sweetheart. I should have told you last night, but there were other more pressing matters on my mind.' The twinkle in his eye brought a blush to Georgiana's cheeks. 'Henry has apologised unreservedly for his behaviour, and is desperate to beg your forgiveness.'

'But—'

'You might say family relations have never been so good.' Nathaniel traced the delicate outline of her face. Her eyes flicked towards where she had placed her travelling bags, only to find they had disappeared.

Nathaniel plucked a kiss from one eyebrow, then the other. 'I took the liberty of instructing the maid to unpack your things.'

'But your father—'

'My father is awaiting your arrival downstairs with great impatience.'

A little line of worry wrinkled between her eyes.

Nathaniel's thumb soon soothed it smooth. 'He wants you to stay. As I do, minx.'

Georgiana smiled at that.

'When I realised that Praxton had abducted you, it was the worst moment of my life. Finding you before he could inflict any more harm on you was the best.'

'Nathaniel,' she whispered, but he stilled her lips with the featherlight touch of a finger.

'No. I want you to know this first. These past days I've been a fool, avoiding your company, arguing with Henry, and all because I refused to face what was there before my very eyes. I love you, Georgiana. Always have done and always will. I was just too damned stupid to realise it until it was almost too late. Can you forgive me?' Deep dark eyes held hers with impassioned plea.

She reached up her lips so that they hovered just beneath his. 'What is there to forgive? You've saved both my life and reputation three times. I'm yours, Captain Hawke, whether you want me or not.' Her mouth slid to a wry grin. 'You'll have no more chances to rid yourself of me.'

His hands slid to her buttocks, gripping her to him so that they moulded together. 'Lady Hawke, you'll have no more bids to escape me, captain's orders!' A dark eyebrow winged high as he nuzzled his mouth to her neck.

Georgiana claimed his lips with hers, all bruises forgotten in the mounting passion. And when their tongues arced together in tantalising seduction, Nathaniel knew that it would be quite some time before they left the safe haven of their bedroom.

Henry was becoming positively worried. 'Perhaps she's taken a greater hurt than we knew. Look at the time and she still hasn't woken. Nathaniel's been up there for at least an hour. Maybe I should go up and investigate the matter.'

'I'm sure that Georgiana will join us as soon as she is able.' Mirabelle touched but one light hand to the viscount's sleeve; it was enough to bring him seated back down by her side.

Freddie smiled knowingly. 'You mean as soon as Nathaniel lets her out of bed,' he added with a wicked gleam in his dark eyes.

'Freddie!' admonished Lord Porchester. 'There are ladies present!'

Mirabelle smiled broadly in her husband's direction.

Freddie coughed and looked at Mrs Howard.

Mrs Howard's expression remained demure as she sipped her madeira and watched the snowflakes drift gently past the drawing room window. 'To Nathaniel and Georgiana, may their lives be blessed with health and happiness.'

Voices raised in hearty agreement.

And the snow conspired to wrap Collingborne House in a thick white blanket of love.

HISTORICAL ROMANCE™

Another exciting novel available this month is:

THE OUTRAGEOUS DEBUTANTE

Anne O'Brien

Eligible!

They have been summoned to London to enjoy the 'delights' of the Season, yet neither Theodora Wooton-Devereux nor Lord Nicholas Faringdon are enthusiastic participants in the game of love.

In love!

Until a chance meeting sets their lives on a different course. And soon the handsome gentleman who has captured the heart of the beautiful – though somewhat unconventional – débutante is the talk of the town!

Star-crossed...

But fate is not on their side, it seems, when a shocking family scandal rears its head and forbids that they be united. Now Thea must end the relationship before it is too late...by playing the truly outrageous débutante!

Another exciting novel available this month is:

WINTER WOMAN

Jenna Kernan

Left to face a freezing winter in the Rockies, Cordelia Channing – preacher's wife, preacher's widow – survives the deadliest season in the mountains alone. But only just.

Praying for someone to come and save her, Cordelia finds her hopes answered by Thomas Nash, an enigmatic man who stirs the deep places within her.

Nash has come to the mountains to rail at the fates that seem out to destroy him. But now he has Delia to care for – a woman who rouses his protective instincts and begins to transform his life in ways he'd thought lost for ever…

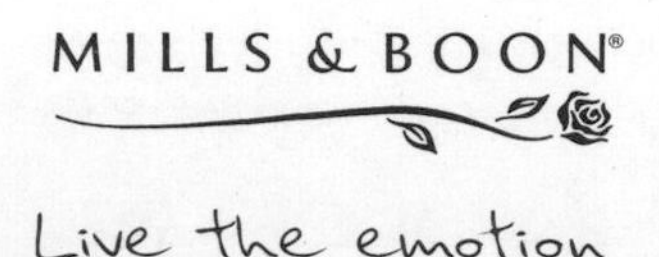

HIST0905 HB WW